HAURON
of the
ELEVEN

HAURON
of the
ELEVEN

2nd Novel in the Shaylae Trilogy

J. Antony Miller

authorHOUSE®

AuthorHouse™ LLC
1663 Liberty Drive
Bloomington, IN 47403
www.authorhouse.com
Phone: 1-800-839-8640

Cover artwork by Jeremy R. Miller.

Published by AuthorHouse   06/17/2014

ISBN: 978-1-4918-6877-5 (sc)
ISBN: 978-1-4918-6876-8 (hc)
ISBN: 978-1-4918-6875-1 (e)

Library of Congress Control Number: 2014903748

PROLOGUE

❧❀❧

Some would call it a stroke of fortune that at the same time Shaylae Gentle Heart was coming into her power on Earth, a young man was ascending to the leadership of the planet Yurob, eleven light years away. Others, this writer among them, believe there are no coincidences in the Universe, and attribute this astounding conjunction of minds to the foresight and planning of the Holy Ones. Whichever position you, the reader, take almost one half-century from those events, you will have to agree that without them the future of the Three Planets would have unfolded in ways that none of us care to speculate upon.

While Hauron and Shaylae were both brilliant, indeed geniuses, it is Hauron's brave heart and Shaylae's gentle heart that we remember most about them. (The Heart of the People, Asdzá Lucero Gentle Heart, DIT Publishing, 2157)

PART ONE

Hauron

CHAPTER 1

Hauron and Dyllen, his father, just managed to squeeze into the elevator that would take them back to ground level. It was more like a metal crate really, hanging from a rusty old cable. The gate slid shut, scraping Hauron's back as he sucked in his breath, desperately trying to avoid being the cause of the gate opening again and the impatience of those waiting to take the two hundred and fifty meter ride to the surface. The car shuddered, squeaked and groaned as it began its long, slow ascent. He wondered if this would be the last ride any of them would take in this antiquated death trap. One day the cable would snap, or the brakes would fail, or the bottom would simply drop out, taking a hundred men to their deaths. It wouldn't be the first time the mine owners had been inconvenienced by such an accident.

He looked over his shoulder at the men who would have to wait until the elevator finished its round trip, returning to pick up another hundred. The bright lights shining toward the shaft made it hard to see their faces. Not that it would have made any difference; all would have the same hopeless, despondent expressions. Many of them were coughing, a dry hacking cough that went on all day and into the night without respite. None of them spoke. Soon they were absorbed into the blackness below as the elevator left them behind.

It was cruel, hard labor in the lithium mines; labor that took its toll on the health of the miners. Most would eventually develop lesions from the acrid dust that constantly filled the poorly ventilated tunnels.

So far Hauron had been able to escape the awful affliction, but then he had only been working there since the beginning of spring-year. His father was not so lucky. After seven-and-a-half sun-cycles Hauron was beginning to think Dyllen might escape the disease, but just in the last few months his breathing had become labored, and his coughing insistent. Hauron knew that the death sentence would likely take its toll before the beginning of fall-year.

The elevator ride took about two minutes, its wheels scraping and grinding their way up the tracks. If he had reached his arm through the open grating he could have touched the featureless wall of the shaft.

Eventually they reached the surface and the gate slid open again. All piled out and headed toward the terminus where the transports would take them to their meager homes. None of them used the inadequate showers; they probably hadn't been used for five sun-cycles, long before Hauron was born. The pipes were rusty, the faucets stuck, and the water, when it did come out, was brown and cold.

They stood with the others waiting for the transport. Many were much further along with the disease than Dyllen, some with only weeks to live, but they were still required to work the mines every day. He watched in disgust as the director of the mine rode by in his sleek hover-car, not even deigning to look at the men whose lives were sacrificed so that he and the others in the ruling classes could live in luxury. There was no middle class on the less populated eastern continent of Yurob, and most of the working class were slaves in the lithium mines. Some of the luckier ones slaved above ground in the plants extracting lithium-6 from the ore, and an even smaller number worked loading the sub-orbitals that made sure the precious cargo found its way to the fusion reactors on the central and western continents.

The transport swished to a halt, and a hundred men crammed into the cabin which had seats for twenty. Of course Hauron and Dyllen had to stand, but it was not a long journey; their housing complex was the second stop the transport would make.

Dyllen leaned against his son, and smiled weakly. "Hope you can support the weight of an old man, Hauron."

"You're not that old, Dad," said Hauron unconvincingly, reflecting on the sad fact that among the working classes most would be dead by their fiftieth birthday, not even seeing out thirteen sun-cycles, whereas the rich could easily live for thirty sun-cycles, and more.

The rest of the journey took place in relative silence. Most of the men had little to say to each other, their lives futile, their eyes empty and their faces expressionless. Dyllen certainly looked a great deal older than his forty-four years. His once luxurious brown hair was now thin and gray. His body was wasted and bent from the grueling work. In complete contrast Hauron was the picture of health, although he knew that it would not last. He stood a hundred-and-eighty-five centimeters and his well-defined muscles looked strong as was usually the case with the young miners; the hard work strengthened them initially, but as the years wore on it ravaged them. His brown hair was short, and the features on his pale white face were well balanced and strong. His blue eyes were piercing and intense and still had fire in them, but that too would fade in time.

He found his mind wandering back to the previous night. He had had another vision. Since he was fourteen he had had many visions and had discovered that he had certain powers of the mind. If he concentrated hard he could hear other people's thoughts. He could even move things with his mind if he really concentrated. He had managed to keep it a secret even from his family. If the ruling classes were to discover that one of their slaves had developed The Power they would certainly kill him, possibly his whole family. They would not risk having the genes that carried The Power in the minds of their slaves.

Last night's vision hadn't lasted long, but it had been particularly vivid and detailed; much more so than previously. It had occurred just as he was going to bed. A beautiful dark-haired girl about one sun-cycle younger than him was in danger. Two men, who looked like members of the ruling class on Yurob, seemed intent on killing a her, but just as it appeared she would succumb she disappeared. A few hours later he watched as the same men killed an old man and woman, and now looked as if they were about to try to kill the girl again. But just at the crucial moment she raised her hands and the men disappeared. Hauron had no idea what this vision meant; he didn't even know if it was in his imagination or if he had witnessed a real event. Either way, he was scared that somehow the rulers would have been able to sense the manifestations of his Power.

The transport stopped and settled to the ground hissing loudly. Hauron and his father climbed down, not even looking back to bid farewell to the others still on board.

"Well, here we are," said Dyllen, looking at the small shantytown that was euphemistically called Forest Glen. Whatever trees had existed here once had all been hewn down to construct the poorly built homes, or had simply been removed to make way for the crowded development. Summer-year had just begun, and the poorly insulated houses would become as hot as ovens. Hauron was not sure which was worse, the brutally hot summer-year, or the bitterly cold winter-year, both of these extremes a result of the four-year orbit of Yurob around Procyon. The only years that were comfortable were spring-year and fall-year.

The lithium mines were right on the northern edge of the northern zone. Not too much further north the land was barren, unlivable. The year-long winter just about precluded all but the hardiest forms of plant and animal life; equally, the year-long summer would suck the life out of the plants before they were able to yield up their crops. To the south, closer to the equator any life that managed to grab a hold during spring-year would be burnt off during summer-year.

As they entered the house Hauron saw his mother, Geoan, at the stove cooking dinner. She looked up and managed a weak smile. It was almost impossible to keep her small family fed on the meager allowance the slaves were given and she was as discouraged and without hope as her husband. It had been quite different when he was young. Both his mother and father had been vibrant and full of hope in a hopeless situation. He missed his mother's happy smiling face.

His sister Kazzy was reading a book. She was nine years old and as sharp as a titanium pick. Very few of the slaves could read; what was the point? But for some reason his mother had always insisted that they all learn how to read. Hauron would be forever grateful for this, although he was not sure when, if ever, he would be able to use the knowledge gleaned from the pages of the few books they had access to. Kazzy was still bright-eyed and happy. It would not last, he observed sadly. Soon she too would realize the hopelessness of their existence and she too would develop the same resigned sadness that characterized the lives of all slaves. Hauron wondered if she would be one of the girls who all too often disappeared from the town, ending up who-knew-where.

Jerrod played on the floor with the same handmade wooden toys his father had made for him when he was a baby. Born halfway through winter-year he was not yet two. What kind of future did he face? What kind of future did any of them face? A life without hope, a life without dreams, a life without freedom. Sometimes Hauron wished he had never been born.

Suddenly there was a loud knock at the door. "Open up. Agents of the Empire. Open up in the name of First Prophet."

An overwhelming sickening feeling suddenly filled his stomach. He had been found out, and now they had come to kill him? His life was over. He knew that, but perhaps he could still save his family. He opened the door and six agents pushed past him, knocking him to the floor as they burst into the home, weapons drawn and ready to fire.

"I'm the one you want. Take me," he said falteringly as he stood up bravely to face them. He jumped as he felt a hand on his shoulder. He whirled around to find himself staring up into the penetrating eyes of a member of the Council of One Hundred. His long white cloak reached to the floor in a sweeping skirt, the collar reached high on his neck, almost enclosing his head and the light behind him left his face in an ominous shadow. Hauron sensed the power emanating from him. He had never imagined he would ever be this close to someone so high in the government.

"Take them all," he said to the agents.

Bravely Hauron spoke up again. "No, leave them alone. They've done nothing wrong."

The cloaked one turned to him and raised his hands. Hauron felt a sudden burst of energy throughout his whole body. As he lost consciousness he looked at his mother. Fear and horror filled her eyes.

CHAPTER 2

Hauron awoke to find himself lying on a hard, narrow bed in a small badly lit room. His head was pounding and his muscles ached. He swung his legs over the side of the bed and buried his head in his hands. Oh how his head hurt. What are they going to do with me, he thought. What will they do to my family, and where are they? And how long had he been unconscious?

Suddenly the room was flooded with brilliant light. "Shower and change into the clothes hanging in the closet," came a voice from the speakers in the room. "You have five minutes." As his eyes adjusted he managed to squint around the room. Sure enough, there was a small shower. Not wanting to get into any further trouble, he did as he was told, as quickly as he could. The clothes were simply a large gray robe that covered him from head to feet, and a pair of gray slippers.

There was the sound of an electronic bolt sliding and the door opened.

"Bring him to the throne room." Hauron could not see the man giving the orders, but two others grabbed him and half-led, half-dragged him along a bleak corridor to an elevator. The door opened and he was forced inside. After a short ride the elevator opened and he was led into a large hallway, well-lighted, carpeted, and well-appointed with lavish decorations.

At the end of the hallway was a huge, carved, gold encrusted double door guarded on either side by well-armed men. As they approached, the guards opened the door and Hauron was dragged inside. The sight that greeted him was beyond belief. The room was huge; probably bigger than a hundred houses. Glass chandeliers hung from the high domed ceiling which was decorated with a huge fresco depicting the destruction of his world seven hundred and fifty sun-cycles earlier. The walls were covered in paintings, murals, and other wall hangings, representing other events from the same awful period of history.

About two hundred lavishly dressed people were milling around the room watching slave girls and boys, most of them younger than him, being forced to do things that were degrading and obscene. His stomach heaved as he looked into the eyes of these poor slaves being forced to do such hideous and vile acts. He was revolted. He was disgusted. But his pity was helpless and impotent; he knew there was nothing he could do to help them. How could anyone do such things to other people, kids? It sickened him to his stomach. He almost did vomit when he thought of Kazzy being used in this way.

But it was what Hauron saw at the far end of the room that both terrified and confused him. Standing on a raised dais were a hundred men in a large semi-circle, all dressed in white cloaks that reached to the floor. In front of them were eleven other men, similarly dressed in white cloaks with purple skirts. Hauron stared in disbelief. This couldn't be the Council of the Hundred, and the Quorum of the Eleven? The whole Assembly of Rulers? Seated in front of them on an ornate throne was First Prophet himself. Why would he, an insignificant slave, be brought in front of the whole government? Somehow, he realized, he had been brought from the Eastern Continent to the Central Continent, some five-thousand kilometers while he was unconscious.

First Prophet stood up, his white, purple and red cloak swished around his feet. The room became silent. "Exquisite isn't it?" The voice was authoritative, loud and clear, and yet Hauron could sense an aging man behind the smiling mask of his face. "Come forward; come stand before me."

He was transfixed, couldn't move. One of the guards pushed him in the middle of his back and he almost fell to the floor.

First Prophet beckoned. "Come, young man. There's no need to be afraid."

The crowd parted as Hauron slowly made his way toward the throne. His heart was pounding and his head felt ready to burst. His feet were hardly able to carry him the fifty meters across the room. As he reached the dais he stole a glance at First Prophet's face. It was the face of an old man with gray hair. His blue eyes penetrated Hauron's very soul. This was the first time been this close to any of the members of the ruling councils, let alone First Prophet. Hauron quickly bowed his head, certain he should not be looking directly into his face.

"Well, young man," he said. "It appears you have been hiding something from us."

Hauron was frozen with fear, not knowing what to say.

"I could have you put to death right now, right here. Do you understand?"

Hauron nodded his head but said nothing.

"Your family too. They deserve to die also."

"Please, Excellency, they never knew. I never told them." Hauron spoke quickly without looking up from the floor.

"Interesting. You will not to speak to defend yourself, but you will to defend your family." Hauron was silent once more. "What would you do to spare your family, young man?"

"Anything, Excellency."

"Anything? Very well. You must choose. A quick, painless death for you and your family, or a slow agonizing death for you, and your family goes free."

Hauron's heart was pounding, his stomach churning. Could he face a slow tortuous death? Could he sentence his family to death?

"Speak now or the Assembly decides."

"Free my family, Excellency." Hauron was not a particularly brave young man, but there was simply no other choice.

"You have chosen well, Hauron." Had his ears deceived him? Had First Prophet called him by name? "Had you chosen the alternative, you all would have died slowly." He turned to the citizens in the throne room. "Leave us."

The hall emptied, as people hastily bowed and backed out of the room. First Prophet was someone who was obeyed very quickly. He turned to the Assembly. "You also; leave us." For a moment the men on the dais did not move, but then bowing, they too left the throne room. Soon they were all alone; not even a bodyguard remained, although Hauron knew well that First Prophet needed no bodyguards; his power was supreme.

First Prophet walked across the dais and down the semi-circular staircase that brought him to the floor of the huge room. He walked over to a large table against the wall and beckoned Hauron. "Come, eat. You must be hungry."

He dared not question First Prophet so he slowly walked to the table.

"These are delicious," he said indicating a bowl of strange fruit. "They're from the western continent." He picked two up, took a bite from one and carelessly tossed the other to Hauron. He bobbled it clumsily, but managed to hold on to it.

Hauron was unsure of what to do. He had no idea what was happening. Why was he still alive? And why was First Prophet acting so intimately with him, a mere slave. It was all too much for him; sobbing, he fell to the floor on his knees, his forehead touching the floor.

"Excellency, please forgive me. I meant no harm, and my family is innocent. My father works hard and is loyal . . ."

"Calm yourself, Hauron. Please, stand up and face me."

He stood up, keeping his eyes firmly fixed on the floor.

"Look at me. Look me in the eye." He put his hand under Hauron's chin and lifted it. "If you cooperate with me, tell me what I ask of you, then I give you my word that your family will be spared. I haven't yet decided what to do with you, but if I decide to kill you, you will die quickly and painlessly. Now, look me in the eye."

The last was clearly a command, so Hauron obeyed. His eyes bore deep into Hauron's soul. They were enigmatic; cruel yet kind, old yet young, sad yet content.

"There, that's better. Now, eat." He handed Hauron the fruit and not daring to refuse he took it and bit into its juicy flesh. The taste was wonderful, cool and sweet, like nothing he had tasted before. The juice filled his mouth and ran down his chin. He could have sworn First Prophet grinned.

"Now, tell me, young Hauron, what is this about your power. Tell me everything."

"There's not much to tell."

"Oh, I'm sure that's not true. When did you first notice that you had The Power?"

"It was about a sun-cycle ago. Not quite four years."

"And you were thirteen then?"

"Yes."

"Was that the same time you were going through puberty?"

"Yes, I suppose it was."

"Let me see; when exactly were you born, Hauron?"

"First of First, in the spring-year of sun-cycle seven hundred and forty eight."

"Hmm. Hauron, did you know that among the ruling classes, the ones with the most Power were born at the beginning of spring-year?"

"No, Excellency, I did not."

"I myself was born on the third of First, in the spring-year of sun-cycle seven hundred and twenty." He smiled. "So you see, young man, we have a lot in common."

"Yes, Excellency." He was a hundred and twenty three years old!

"Now, tell me some of the things you can do."

"I can sometimes hear people's thoughts, if they are particularly happy, sad, or scared."

"Really, can you hear my thoughts?"

"Oh no, Excellency! I would never . . ."

He laughed and waved him off. "Oh don't worry, I doubt very much you could ever read my thoughts. Are there any near us now whose thoughts you can hear."

Hauron concentrated hard. Yes, he could sense the thoughts of at least two people just outside the throne room.

"There are two men close by who are afraid of your anger. They feel they have failed you."

"Very good," he said almost casually. "And what else can you do?"

"Sometimes I can move things with my mind."

"Really? Show me."

Again he concentrated really hard. He looked at the table and tried to move a piece of fruit, but was unsuccessful. He shook his head.

"Never mind, Hauron. Perhaps you are too nervous right now." Hauron nodded. "And now, I want you to tell me everything you saw last night. Everything."

Hauron repeated what he had seen in the visions; the two men, the girl, the old man and woman. Prophet First seemed genuinely surprised.

"Hauron, I may let you live." He walked back toward the dais. "She who you saw was Asdzáán Nádleehé!"

Hauron was horrified. Asdzáán Nádleehé? The witch, the eternal enemy of his people? No, it couldn't have been. She was only a girl, a beautiful, young girl.

"Come with me." Hauron followed as he walked back up the staircase and sat once more on his throne. "Stand beside me."

The two doors at the back of the dais opened and the Council of the Hundred and the Quorum of the Eleven returned and took up their positions behind the throne.

"See how they come at my command, Hauron?" he smiled again. "Now, tell me how much you know of Asdzáán Nádleehé?"

"Not much, Excellency. Only what we have been taught in temple." First Prophet held his hand out, indicating he wanted to hear more. "She was the witch who destroyed our planet seven hundred and fifty sun-cycles ago."

"What else? What can you tell me about Revenge?"

"I know nothing of any revenge."

"Fifteen sun-cycles ago the world on which she was born was discovered by my predecessor. He ordered the construction of a huge interstellar craft that would travel to that world and destroy it. The craft is called Revenge."

"To destroy the planet?"

"Yes. It left on its voyage fifteen sun-cycles ago. It was equipped to remain in the Earth system indefinitely, until the witch returned, and then she was to be captured and killed; slowly. They arrived five sun-cycles ago. We have just learned from the two men whom you sensed, that eight years, two sun-cycles ago they thought they had found her. They captured her and brought her back to the ship, but the Prophet aboard that ship was quick to realize that she was not Asdzáán Nádleehé; it was not her they had sensed, it was her daughter, who at the time was only five years old."

This was all new to Hauron. He was not aware of any of this. "Did they kill her Excellency?"

"No, they did not." First Prophet paused. It seemed he was not pleased with the decision made by the council on the ship.

Hauron felt compelled to ask. "Why not, Excellency?"

"Why don't I let them tell you?" He clapped his hands twice. "Bring in the prisoners."

Four guards came into the room, dragging two men with them. Hauron gasped.

"Recognize them, Hauron?" he whispered.

"Yes, Excellency. These are the two men I saw in my vision." First Prophet looked pleased. The guards brought the men to a point in the middle of the throne room, facing the dais.

"You!" he said, pointing to the one on the left. "You will repeat your report. In full detail; leave nothing out."

He looked quite scared. Hauron was sure he knew his life was forfeit. He retold the story of how the woman captured had been identified as the mother of Asdzáán Nádleehé. "We were about to execute her when the Prophet discovered that she was also the life-partner of the leading authority in Hyperspace. He decided that he would bring back not only the body of Asdzáán Nádleehé, but Hyperspace to your Excellency."

First Prophet turned to Hauron and whispered, "A worthy decision wouldn't you say. Hauron?"

"I don't know, Excellency. What is Hyperspace?"

"In due time, Hauron, in due time." He turned back toward the prisoners. "Continue."

"In addition, the earth scientists know how to fuse two deuterium atoms; they no longer need lithium-6 for their fusion engines. We thought this also would be a worthy gift to bring back to your Excellency."

Hauron was definitely intrigued by this; if they could fuel the reactors without using lithium there would no longer a need for the lithium mines.

"Go on."

"Well, Excellency, by the time she came into her Power, her father had not yet completed his research, so the Prophet decided we should capture them both; hold her as insurance with her father, and hold her father against her using her Power. We first took her father captive, and then we attempted to capture her." He stopped.

"Well, where is her father?"

"On board Revenge, Excellency."

"And the witch?"

He paused again. "We don't know, Excellency."

"You don't know? Well then, perhaps you will tell us how you came to be back here?"

"Yes Excellency. It seems she was able to sense us. Her Power was even greater than the Prophet had anticipated and before we had an opportunity to approach her, she shifted us back here."

First Prophet stood up. "You Lie!" he shouted.

He turned to Hauron and spoke quietly. "This is the story they told. I would have believed them, but your version apparently conflicts. I want you to repeat what you saw. And Hauron, in spite of your fear I want you to speak loudly and with confidence. Do this and not only will I let you and your family live, you will live with us here, in comfort and luxury."

Turning back to the prisoners he repeated, "You Lie. Hauron will now tell us what he saw." He extended his arm toward Hauron.

Hauron cleared his throat and began. "She was asleep in her bed," he began uncertainly,

"More authority, Hauron, and your family will live," reminded First Prophet.

"She was asleep in her bed and you approached her. You made an attempt to subdue her but she disappeared."

"She shifted, moved with her mind," said First Prophet quietly.

"Later, after you had killed the old man and woman she raised her arms and shifted you back here!" Hauron finished with a loud, confident voice. The prisoners looked terrified.

"Nicely done, Hauron," whispered First Prophet. He stepped forward again. "Is this true?"

After a futile pause, the prisoner spoke again. "As I said, we had under-estimated her Power, Excellency."

"And that is a reason to lie to First Prophet?"

They remained silent.

"Second, come forward." Hauron turned. The man in the center of the Quorum of the Eleven stepped forward. Hauron sensed intense evil emanating from him. First Prophet pointed to the prisoner on the left. "Kill him."

Second raised his arm toward the condemned man, who immediately fell to floor clutching his chest in a silent scream.

"Very good, Second." To the condemned man he said, "You will die very slowly, in exquisite pain, unable to scream, fully conscious. So die all traitors." The man continued to writhe on the floor. He turned to Hauron. "Hauron, come forward."

Hauron stepped forward and stood beside Second.

"Kill the other."

"Excellency . . ." he stammered.

"Kill the other, now."

"Excellency, how? I don't know how to."

"You will find a way. You need incentive." He turned to Second and raised his arm. "Second, when my arm reaches my side, you will kill his sister; in the same manner." Second nodded.

Hauron panicked. He had no doubt what he would do if he could; he would do anything to spare Kazzy, but how? He saw out of the corner of his eye First Prophet's hand descending slowly. He looked at the terrified man without pity. He would kill him without a second thought to save his sister. His mind became attuned, he could sense the man's very being, his body, his brain, his lungs, his heart. Without another thought he took the man's heart with his mind and shut it off. The man fell to the floor clutching his chest, quite dead.

"Very good, Hauron. I would have hoped for a long painful death, but so be it." He thought for a moment and then turned and pointed to the other. "If you wish it, you may end his suffering."

Hauron did not need to be asked twice. No matter how evil the man was, surely he didn't deserve to die so slowly, in such agony. He reached inside of his body and stopped his heart. Mercifully the man died instantly.

"Leave us!" commanded First Prophet. The guards dragged the dead bodies out, and the Assembly once again began filing out of the doors at the rear of the dais. "Second remain."

Soon, the throne room was empty.

"Second, what do you think? Can he be trained?"

"I believe he can, Excellency."

Hauron was sure he could detect resentment, perhaps even jealousy coming from Second.

"Very well. Hauron, I make this offer to you once, but you must decide immediately. You and your family will remain here. You will be given the finest teachers, both for your body and mind. Your family will be given a luxurious apartment. Your father will be treated and cured. What say you?"

Hauron was indeed intrigued, interested, but why would First Prophet offer such a reward. With nothing to lose, he decided he would ask. "Why would you offer me such an honor, Excellency?"

"Second and I are sure that the witch will come here, perhaps with the intention of destroying our planet again."

Hauron was horrified. Regardless of how he felt about First Prophet and Second, they at least shared this common enemy, this common danger. "If you think I can help, Excellency, then I would be honored."

"Good. Actually, Hauron, I am counting on you being able to help. You have an extremely powerful mind. There are many in the Council of the Hundred who do not yet have The Power you do. You would be no match for any of the Quorum of the Eleven of course, but with training I feel you could be of vital importance in fighting the witch."

Hauron was flabbergasted. Could this be possible? Could he be trained to be a match for the witch who had destroyed his planet? Of course, he would accept, but he doubted his Power was that great.

"Excellency, I doubt I can live up to your expectations, but I will certainly do anything in my power to help destroy the witch. Live or die, I am yours."

He saw a genuine smile on First Prophet's face as he took hold of Hauron's shoulders. He wasn't so sure about the sincerity of Second's smile.

First Prophet beckoned to one of the guards. "Show Hauron to his new apartments." Turning back to Hauron he said. "Go, rest. We will talk again later."

CHAPTER 3

First Prophet Shunaro sat alone in his bedroom. He had sent all of his servants away, and his family, sensing his desire to be alone, left him undisturbed. Being First Prophet had suddenly become a lot more complicated. The reincarnation of Asdzáán Nádleehé, so long looked forward to by all of his predecessors, was now an unwelcome addition to his reign. Why did she not wait until he was gone and another of his successors would be on the throne? But that was foolish. He and all of his predecessors were all reincarnations of The First Prophet, as would be all of his successors. So, regardless of when she returned, he would have to face her in one of those incarnations. At least that's what he was taught to believe.

The appearance of the boy was an additional complication. While he was sure that he could be trained to help fight the witch, he was unsure of how much of a threat he would be to his own power.

All of his early life Shunaro had blindly accepted the teachings of Temple. He had been born a few months after the previous First Prophet died. He knew that the Quorum of the Eleven would be searching for his reincarnation, but he never for one moment suspected he would be the one. For seventeen years they searched. Throughout that time Shunaro grew in strength, physical, mental, and spiritual. He was always the brightest in his school; his masters even called him genius. While he never took such talk seriously, he was indeed skilled in all forms of learning, from math and physics, to politics and religion. He excelled at everything. His mental Powers too were unequaled among his peers; in fact no one else he had ever come into contact with seemed to have his Power.

And then, shortly after his seventeenth birthday the leader of the Quorum of the Eleven came into his home and knelt before him, announcing to his family that First Prophet had been found again. Of course his family was ecstatic. It would mean a life of luxury and indulgence beyond their wildest dreams. Shunaro was not quite sure. He even had his doubts to this day, although he never confided such thoughts to anyone. Was there even such a thing as reincarnation? If so, why had he never been able to remember anything about his previous lives? 'It is the way The First Prophet ensures that new ideas are always being introduced into their doctrine and teaching, and that old ones are constantly being evaluated,' his mentor had told him. That at least made sense, but it did little to assuage his doubts.

His mind went back to Hauron. Even though he had not been born of the ruling classes, he was sure his Powers were greater than his at the same age, and that was without any training of any kind. If that were so, then could not Hauron be the reincarnation of First Prophet; and if so, how could he himself be his reincarnation? But, these thoughts were getting him nowhere. Besides, he had more pressing needs to worry about.

"Second," he called out with his mind. Within a few minutes Kildane was in his room. He was the strongest man in the Empire, besides him. He had risen quickly through the Council of the Hundred, and by the age of twenty five had taken the first available position in the Quorum of the Eleven. Almost immediately the previous Second had died, quite mysteriously, and Kildane took over without so much as a discussion. He was certain that Kildane had had something to do with it, but he was not going to question. He needed the strongest most powerful man in the Empire by his side. That he could not trust him was irrelevant; he still had more Power than him.

Kildane came and stood before First Prophet and made a perfunctory bow. "Yes, Excellency."

"Don't be so formal here, Kildane. Call me Shunaro. We are quite alone."

Kildane nodded briefly. "Yes, Excellency."

Shunaro gave up. He knew full well Kildane would never be so informal with him. "What did you think of the boy?"

"He seems quite talented, Excellency."

"Yes, doesn't he? And that's with no training." Kildane nodded his head again. "Imagine how powerful he could become with the training." Kildane was adept at hiding his thoughts, even from First Prophet, but he had never thought it as any cause for alarm. It was unlikely he would ever try to usurp him; too many people in the Assembly accepted his divine right to be on the throne, far too many for Kildane to handle on his own.

"I think he will be quite useful."

Shunaro smiled inwardly. He suspected there would be a showdown eventually between the two, and frankly he didn't particularly care who won. If the boy was more powerful than Kildane, so be it. The only question he had was would the boy eventually try to usurp him. Unlikely, for the same reason Kildane would never try it. Still, he would watch him very closely; watch them both very closely.

"See that his training begins tomorrow. I want him trained not only in The Power, but also in science, art, social customs, religion, history and politics."

"Certainly, Excellency."

"I want you to take personal interest in his growth, Kildane. He must be ready. We have half a sun-cycle, maybe a complete cycle, before the witch comes."

CHAPTER 4

——◦◦◦◦◦——

Hauron's head was still spinning as the guard showed him to the apartment First Prophet had given him. All of his life he had hated and despised the ruling classes for their treatment of the slaves and now he was in league with them in defending their planet against Asdzáán Nádleehé. Well, the ruling classes may be his enemy, but the witch was an even greater enemy. Once the witch was destroyed, perhaps he would have an opportunity to change the power machine on his planet.

"Here you are," said the guard as he held open the door. "You will find everything you need in here."

He thanked him and walked into his new home. Nothing could have prepared him for the luxury he saw before him. Three wide steps formed a two-meter perimeter around the huge sunken square living room. From wall-to-wall it must have been at least fifteen meters; the vaulted ceiling, six meters. The floor and the walkway around it were covered with a thick carpet; he had never even seen a carpeted living area before. There were six well-padded chairs, three comfortable couches, side tables, lamps, and even flowers and plants in golden vases, carefully placed around the room. A huge bowl of fruit sat on the marble, glass-topped table in the middle of the room. The wall to his left and the far wall were floor-to-ceiling glass, providing breathtaking views of the city and the mountains beyond. The other two walls were covered in wallpaper with a raised gold pattern. Paintings depicting past and present First Prophets hung on those walls, alongside gold-framed mirrors, and gold-plated wall lamps. In the middle of the wall to his right a large hallway led off, presumably to bedrooms, kitchen, and other rooms.

"Where's my family?" asked Hauron turning to the guard, but he had already closed the door behind him.

"Hauron, is that you?" It was his mother's voice, calling to him from the hallway. "Isn't this wonderful? Hauron come here quickly."

He walked over to the hallway. It was about thirty meters long and had five doors on either side. His mother was standing in one of those open doors beckoning him. He followed her into the bedroom. Lying in a huge bed was his father, propped up against huge fluffy pillows. Wires and tubes ran from various parts of his body to a machine sitting by the bed. Another man he had not seen before was carefully studying the monitors.

"Father," he exclaimed. "Are you OK?" He feared the worst.

The man turned around. "You must be Hauron," he said stepping forward, hand extended. Hauron took his hand somewhat cautiously. "I am Doctor Rosaduin."

"Is he OK? Has he gotten any worse?"

The doctor had a kindly face, reassuring. "He's going to be fine. In fact once this treatment is complete he should be completely healed."

"Completely?"

"We're using a combination of undifferentiated cells, antibiotics, and mild steroids. Within six weeks there'll be no trace of the lesions whatsoever."

Hauron barely suppressed the tears of joy and gratitude that threatened to overpower him. He resisted the urge to ask why such treatment was not available to all of the slaves, realizing he would be asking the wrong person. In the meantime, this was the best news he had heard. And what was even better, his mother was smiling; smiling with excitement, expectation, and enthusiasm, just as she did when he was younger. The combination of his father's prognosis and his mother's joy was enough to push aside any thoughts of unfairness.

Geoan came to him and took him in her arms. Tears filled her eyes as she laid her head on his shoulders. "Oh Hauron, I don't know how you did this, but thank you. Thank you."

I had to kill two men, came the dark unspoken response to his mind. But at the moment, even that sounded worth it. He would have done just about anything to give his family this opportunity.

Kazzy came into the room, positively bouncing with energy. "Oh, Hau, come see my room." She grabbed his hand and pulled him across the hallway into her room. Aside from the huge canopy bed the room was filled with countless toys. On the desk was a computer, something he had never seen before. "I'm going to have teachers come here to teach me stuff, how to use the computer, how to find out all kinds of stuff. Isn't it great?"

"Yes, Kaz," he said smiling, but at the back of his mind he couldn't help wondering if this was all some kind of trick, some kind of cruel hoax to raise all of their hopes and expectations only to dash them. It was all too unreal, too good to be true. Hauron made a silent vow to himself that whatever it took, he would never let his family return to the squalor they had come from. Whatever it took. He picked Kazzy up in his arms and hugged her tightly.

"Hauron, your father wants to speak to you." He put Kazzy down and went back into his parent's room.

"Dad, are you OK? Are you really going to be OK?"

"I guess so, son," he said with a smile. His face became more serious and he asked, "How is this all possible."

Hauron was about to tell the whole story, but decided to hold back; for now at least. "I have The Power, Dyllen."

"Your mother and I had suspected it."

"I'm going to be trained and educated, and perhaps if all goes well, I may get a job in the government."

"But we're slaves."

"First Prophet told me . . ."

"You spoke to First Prophet?" said Dyllen, incredulously.

"Yes. He said that sometimes the genes that carry The Power appear in the slaves. When they discover such a person, they usually bring him to Central and train him up to see if he can be useful, and to keep those genes from getting any further into the slave population." It wasn't a complete lie, but Hauron hoped it would satisfy his father.

"Either that or they kill them," added Dyllen.

Kill them is what they have always done before thought Hauron to himself. Was he just lucky to have seen what he saw? Would he already be dead if it hadn't been for the vision of Asdzáán Nádleehé he had had? How much could he trust First Prophet? He knew he couldn't trust Second. He would have to play things very carefully until he felt more in control of what was happening.

"Oh, Dyllen! Don't worry. Everything will be fine." He turned to Geoan and Kazzy and repeated, "Everything's going to be just fine." He hoped they didn't sense his lack of confidence in his words.

CHAPTER 5

Hauron's training began the next day. He knew how to read, thanks to his mother's insistence, and he had already read many books, from science to history. He particularly enjoyed physics. He already knew that lithium-6 from the mines was used in the fusion reactors but he had no idea why. From his new teachers and his new books, he learned that lithium-6 was used in the production of tritium, which was fused with deuterium to produce the energy that ran the Empire. If the Earth scientists had learned how to fuse deuterium then not only would there no longer be a need for the lithium mines, the supply of fusion power was effectively limitless.

He was also fascinated by history, particularly the story of Asdzáán Nádleehé. How had she been able to all but destroy his planet from so far away? Thank goodness for The First Prophet who had been able to gather the survivors together and reestablish their civilization. Hauron wasn't too happy with the outcome though; why did a civilization so advanced in technology have to treat so many of its citizens so badly, keeping them in bondage and slavery? Surely such a society could take care of its entire population, not just the ruling classes. Perhaps he might be able to do something to help them.

His religious studies bothered him the most; the subject of Rolling Darkness had always confused him. He was a cruel, vindictive god, quick to anger and slow to forgive. In the temple he had attended since childhood not much had been taught, except fear and ritual. But now he was being taught about how Rolling Darkness had created the universe; how he had set the stars in place and fired up their fusion reactions; how he had placed worlds in orbit around those stars and peopled them with his children. It all seemed so unlikely to Hauron. Why would a creator be so cruel? What would be the purpose in that? And by what power had he been able to accomplish such a creation?

He was also taught that Asdzáán Nádleehé represented the antithesis of all that Rolling Darkness and the empire stood for, and that she was determined to see the destruction of him, and all of his followers. She was intrinsically deceptive, without feeling or conscience. He was reminded how when she had destroyed their world seven hundred and fifty sun-cycles ago, she had killed millions of men, women and children, ruling class and slave alike.

On the fifth day a new vision began to form in his mind. He could see a large gathering of people. The same girl was facing a rising sun, singing, and a crowd of people had gathered around her. Something big was about to happen. He decided he should tell First Prophet. He ran all the way to the throne room and found it crowded with courtiers, all of them enjoying the same kind of degrading entertainment he had seen before, involving some slave girls, even younger than those he had seen previously. Hauron shuddered. How absolutely horrific.

"Come with me," said a guard. "First Prophet has been expecting you."

The guard led Hauron down a narrow corridor behind the dais, and then into a small windowless room. First Prophet was sitting on the floor, surrounded by thick cushions. A lone candle burned on a small shelf on the wall.

"Come, sit, boy." Hauron bowed and walked toward First Prophet and began to sit by his side. "No, sit facing me." Hauron did as he was instructed. "You sense it too?" Hauron nodded. "Tell me, what do you see," he said taking both of Hauron's hands in his.

"I see the girl, Asdzáán Nádleehé, surrounded by her people, facing the rising sun, and I think she is singing." First Prophet looked surprised. Perhaps his vision was not so clear.

"Something is about to happen, Hauron," he said quietly. "Tell me everything you see."

"I do not see it very clearly, Excellency. Wait," he said sitting up straighter. "They have been surrounded by vehicles, perhaps fifteen or twenty, and there's some sort of struggle going on. I think some of them are our agents but all of them seem to be frozen, motionless. She's healing another girl and a boy," he said, continuing his running commentary of what he was seeing. "Now she's sending most of them away. She seems to be in a trance of some sort. Two remain. She's . . ." Hauron suddenly got a really strange feeling, a shiver ran down his back, "She's here."

"Here?"

"Yes, here in the throne room."

First Prophet stood up quickly. "Come with me."

Together they hurried back into the throne room. Nothing had changed. People were still laughing raucously at the entertainment.

"I see nothing. Are you sure?"

"Quite sure, Excellency. She's moving unseen among us." He pointed to the center of the throne room.

First prophet was searching around the room frantically but apparently saw nothing. "Yes, I can feel her."

"I feel a build up in her Power. I can sense her anger." First Prophet definitely looked quite scared but Hauron sensed no danger. "She's going to destroy us like she did before."

"I do not think so, Excellency." Hauron was feeling something quite different, something like sadness, pity, and caring. Certainly she had a more powerful mind that any of the ruling council, but he felt compassion coming from her.

"She's gone now, Excellency."

Suddenly two men appeared in the middle of the room. Everyone was immediately silent, but First Prophet still looked . . . scared. "It's fine, Excellency; she's gone, it's over."

First Prophet seemed to regain his composure. "Come forward," he said to the two. To Hauron he whispered, "They are from the Council of One Hundred on Revenge. It seems even they were unprepared for her Power."

"You underestimated her," he spoke loudly.

One of them spoke. "Excellency we . . ."

"Silence. I do not wish to hear your excuses. You failed just as the others did, and just as the others did you will feel my wrath."

"Excellency . . ." he began again.

"Enough! Why did you not take her sooner? Why was her mother allowed to live? Why did you think you needed her to obtain the secrets of Hyperspace?"

"First of Revenge was convinced . . ."

"I do not need to hear your answers. They are irrelevant to me. I will deal with First in due time. You, on the other hand I will deal with now." He motioned toward Hauron. "Come forward, boy." Hauron stepped forward. "Hauron, kill them. Both of them." He turned again toward the condemned. "If you defeat Hauron, you live." Turning once again to Hauron he said, "And if you die, so dies your family."

Hauron needed no further encouragement. As disgusted as he was with himself, he would not let his family suffer in the place of these men. With his heart beating wildly in his chest, he felt only minor resistance from them as they quickly succumbed to his Power. Both fell to the floor, quite dead. A gasp went up from the crowd. Hauron thought he even heard some gasps from behind him.

For a moment there was dead silence, and then First Prophet spoke. "Get them out of here," he said. "And all of you, leave us."

Very quickly the vast room was empty, leaving only Hauron and First Prophet.

"Would you kill me also, Hauron?"

Hauron fell to his knees and touched the floor with his forehead. "Excellency. I could not. I would not."

"Are you sure, Hauron?"

"Even if I could, Excellency, I would not. You are the reincarnated First Prophet. All things depend on you. Without you we would not even be alive. Without you we would never be able to face Asdzáán Nádleehé. You are my First Prophet and I pledge to you my undying loyalty."

"Yes, Hauron. Now leave me."

Hauron quickly got up, left the throne room and made his way back to his apartment, still filled with disgust at what he had done, and concern that First Prophet did not trust him.

A figure stepped silently out from the shadows at the back of the dais.

"No need to hide, Second. Come; tell me what you make of young Hauron."

Second came to stand by First Prophet. "He should be killed, Excellency, immediately."

"Perhaps, and another time I would have been the first to agree with you, but there's the matter of Asdzáán Nádleehé. You think we can handle her when she comes?"

"Yes Excellency. All of us together . . ."

"Are you quite mad? You saw how easily she dealt with those two. And she sent them back here as if they were nothing to her."

"Yes Excellency, but in like manner, you saw how quickly he disposed of them. Surely you were expecting some sort of struggle."

"I was. In fact I was half expecting him to be killed. Yes, I was quite surprised at the ease with which he dispatched them."

"The longer you leave it, the more powerful he will become. He could be a threat to me; even to you, Excellency."

"I realize that, Kildane, but I think he is our only hope against the witch."

"You are sure she will come?"

"Quite sure. Oh yes, she will come."

"Well, it is a difficult decision, Excellency. Leave him alive and he may well kill us all. Have him killed and we may not be able to defeat the witch. But remember, he has had many years of bitterness ground into his soul. Behind his mask of loyalty he certainly hates us all."

"I agree."

"Excellency, he is the immediate danger, we should kill him now while we still can. The witch will not be a threat for at least half a sun-cycle."

"Let me think about it, Kildane. In the meantime, let us watch his progress very carefully."

Hauron walked into his apartment, trying hard to smile, to hide his disgust at what he had done, and what he was becoming. As usual, Kazzy was the first to greet him with a big hug and a wide smile. She was so full of energy and vitality. Only six days ago he had been depressing himself with thoughts of what her future held, and now, if he could only hold on to his precarious position here her future was assured. And yet would she become desensitized to the plight of her own people?

Jerrod was playing with his new toys, quite oblivious of the hopelessness he had escaped from, or the luxury he now found himself in. To him, at half a sun-cycle, things just were. In a year or two all he would know would be this life of luxury. He would never have the bitter memories, and hopefully he would never have to return to the life of a slave.

Dyllen was already looking much better. He hardly coughed, and his breathing was no longer labored. Geoan was looking quite beautiful. It's amazing what a life without hope will do to a young woman, quickly robbing her of her youth. But now she looked ten years younger. Her face too was filled with joy and hope. Once again Hauron vowed to himself that he would do anything and everything in his power to make sure that no harm came to them.

There were no more crises over the next sixty-six days. No more visions, no more encounters between Asdzáán Nádleehé and those sent to capture her. Instead Hauron fell into a rigorous routine of learning and developing his Power. As fast as his mentors gave him new knowledge Hauron absorbed it and craved for more. It was not long before he had exceeded the knowledge of all of his teachers. His Powers also grew, exponentially it seemed. Hauron could now hear the thoughts of all of his teachers, all of whom were members of the Council of the Hundred, although he decided to keep that fact from them. He began to realize how much he was hated and feared. Most wanted him dead.

He was even able to catch glimpses of the thoughts of the members of all but one of the Quorum of the Eleven. Denab was his name and Hauron could not even get the slightest glimpse of his mind, or his feelings. Still, Kildane he recognized as his greatest enemy; the other would remain a mystery, for now. First Prophet's mind was also closed to him, but that did not surprise him. First Prophet had so much more experience than him. And while he knew that First Prophet was suspicious of him, he felt fairly safe for the time being; he needed him too much in the upcoming confrontation with Asdzáán Nádleehé.

So, Hauron was content to wait and watch, and to learn and grow.

CHAPTER 6

On the morning of the seventy-first day since Hauron had come to the palace Shunaro once more began to receive strong feelings that something was happening on Earth. He made his way to his meditation room and found Hauron already there, waiting for him.

"Something is happening again, Excellency."

"Yes, I feel it too." They went inside the small dark room, sat on the cushioned floor facing each other. "Tell me what you see, Hauron."

"The girl and some of her friends, three others, are riding horses. Two of our agents are tracking them via satellite, and are now bearing down on her in a flying vehicle."

Shunaro was amazed at the detail in which Hauron saw things. Never had he been able to see such things, even within his own empire. All he had ever experienced was sensations. Once again doubt began to fill his mind. Once again he questioned how he could be The First Prophet reincarnated who had, after all, seen Asdzáán Nádleehé destroy his world.

Hauron continued. "They have fired some sort of missile at them, and all four have fallen to the ground, including their horses."

Shunaro sensed sadness, or perhaps it was disappointment in Hauron's voice. He however was elated. If his agents on Earth had been able to destroy her then his worries would be over; he could dispose of Hauron and his family and continue with his life of luxury with no worries.

"The agent has shot the pilot of the vessel. Wait. They're not dead. She has overpowered the agents. And she has brought back to life the pilot of the vessel."

Shunaro's heart skipped a beat. Not only can she defeat the most powerful men aboard Revenge, but she can bring people back to life. His fear returned, this time even more powerfully than before. "You think she will send them back here?" he asked falteringly.

"No Excellency. She means to use them to expose the rest of our agents on Earth."

How could he possibly know that? Unless of course he could read her thoughts.

"The vision is fading Excellency."

For a moment neither of them said anything. Shunaro was beginning to wonder if he had underestimated both of them, Hauron and the witch. Now instead of one danger, he faced two. One of them was sure to better him, and to kill him. Even as he approached his final years, the prospect of death still terrified him. Were all the stories of Rolling Darkness true? He had never really given them much thought; his religious practices had been perfunctory at best. Was he ready to face his maker? For the first time in his life Shunaro felt totally out of control of the situation, totally unsure of himself and his future, and totally afraid.

"Leave me now, Hauron."

Hauron stood up, bowed and left without saying another word.

Hauron lay awake in bed, unable to sleep. His mind was a mass of confusion. It was clear that his Powers were far greater than he had ever imagined. Today, while sitting with First Prophet in his meditation chamber he had begun to sense his feelings. He still could not read his thoughts, but he had definitely sensed fear and uncertainty. Was First Prophet beginning to doubt his divine inheritance? Was he beginning to doubt that he was The First Prophet reincarnated?

This girl, Asdzáán Nádleehé, also confused him. He kept getting the distinct impression that she was not in the least bit evil. Why did she not kill the agents she overpowered? Why send them back home? Unless of course she realized that they would be killed anyway once they arrived. Her actions were not those of an evil person. Her friends seemed to be totally loyal and devoted to her, quite unlike in the Empire where loyalty was obtained through fear, and devotion was totally absent.

CHAPTER 7

It was one quarter of the way through summer-year. Dyllen was now fully healed and spent most of his waking hours studying. Hauron had told him that the scientists on Earth could fuse two deuterium atoms, and explained what that meant. Dyllen's interest was piqued; from that day all he wanted to read, or to research on the computer, was nuclear physics. He found he had a natural talent for it.

Geoan also had an opportunity to explore her talent and love for music. She had played the harp as a child; only a handmade one made by her father, but she had really loved it. Now, she had at her disposal the finest instruments and musicians in the Empire, and she took full advantage of them. They didn't seem at all like the other courtiers. They seemed to be more sensitive and kind, and they took an immediate liking to Geoan. She spent a great deal of time in their company, making music.

Kazzy had risen to the challenge of becoming educated in a way that impressed Hauron. She was after all only nine years old but seemed to be insatiable. Two things captured her imagination more than anything else, history and computers. She had already programmed some really fun three-dimensional holographic games for Jerrod.

Jerrod was almost three years old and was already starting to read. Once again Hauron wondered if he would ever fully understand the plight of the slaves. All he would remember as he grew up would be his life of ease and luxury at the palace.

It continued to hurt Hauron thinking about what he had become in order to keep his family secure, and he had to struggle to hide it from them. So, he spent as little time with them as he could, explaining that First Prophet needed him by his side, or that his mentors insisted he study and practice most of his waking hours. There was some truth in this, although he did over-use the excuse.

Exactly ninety days after his arrival at the Palace Hauron discovered the plot to kill him. He knew of Second's hatred and of First Prophet's fear but he did not think they would try to kill him just yet. Oh, he knew it was going to happen one day, but he had expected them to wait until the confrontation with Asdzáán Nádleehé was over. He sensed a sinister satisfaction in Second now that the decision had been made but it was from First Prophet's mind he gleaned the details of the plot which was actually quite simple; it was to be a combination of distraction using The Power, and plain old brute-force weapons. He reflected how drastically his opinion of First Prophet had changed during the last three months. How initially he had looked upon him as a man with unimaginable Power, now he was a pathetic old man who could be so easily swayed to embark on this suicidal plot by Second. But Hauron had doubts that even Second was the most powerful man in the Assembly; Denab was still the bigger mystery. Not only could Hauron not read his thoughts, he could not even get the vaguest of impressions from him.

But now that First Prophet sent for him his hand was forced; he had no choice but to take the offensive. If only Second had realized that he had no intention or desire to usurp anyone, perhaps he would have lived longer.

As he walked the opulent corridor to the throne room, he formed a picture in his mind of everyone in the room. There were a dozen guards; heavily armed, weapons ready to fire. First Prophet stood on the dais, surrounded by the Quorum of Eleven, and behind them stood the Council of One Hundred.

As he neared the throne room, he felt his strength grow within him. It was a new feeling to him. As he breathed, it was as if he was breathing in more power, and as his power grew, so did his confidence. He now had no doubt that he could defeat the whole assembly.

The two men guarding the door averted their eyes and swung wide the huge doors. Even before he stepped over the threshold, the dozen guards in the throne room and the two he had just passed fell to the floor unconscious. He sensed panic coming from the cloaked men in the room; this was not part of their plan. Hauron almost smiled to himself as he rendered all but First Prophet and Second immobile; he wanted the Quorum and the Council to see the outcome of their ridiculous plot. He quickly concentrated all of his energy on Second, knowing that he was the only one who posed a threat.

Before he could mount his attack, he felt a burning sensation deep in his gut which almost caused him to fall. Quickly he countered with a bolt of energy to Second's mind. The burning sensation ceased, but Second was still standing. For tense minutes they engaged in a war of wills, neither of them budging an inch, but Hauron could feel Second gradually weakening. His mind was indeed strong but Hauron knew he would prevail.

And then, just as Hauron thought he had defeated Second a new sensation began creeping into his mind: a wave of fear. It caught him by surprise and caused him to lose his advantage. Unable to defeat him with the strength of his Power, Second had changed his tactics. Feelings of dizziness and nausea now compounded his fear as Second increased the strength of his attack. The room began to swim. Everything seemed to lose proportion. Close objects seemed far, and distant objects were almost on top of him. The floor was no longer level; it undulated sickeningly. He swayed back and forth a few times then fell forward, crashing to the floor with a sickening thud, retching violently.

He felt smug satisfaction coming from Second as he prepared for the kill. Inwardly he cursed himself for his bravado in underestimating Second's Power. It would only be a matter of time before Second totally defeated him. He had let his family down. Now they would surely die. A picture of their happy, healthy faces filled his mind, as he imagined the horror they would be put through as they were killed slowly, in indescribable pain and torment for the amusement of the man who was about to defeat him.

"No!" he shouted from the floor. "No, you will not defeat me." He raised his head, pushing himself up with his hands. The force of his anger grew and as it grew it began to push out the fear. The room lost some of its bizarre appearance. Things began to return to normal, and the feelings of nausea and dizziness abated. He could feel Second stepping up the energy of his attack, but his determination to save his family surged in the very depth of his soul as his anger began to take control. Adrenaline pumped through his mind and body causing his heart to beat wildly in his chest. Fear is the enemy, he thought. Fear is the enemy, not Second.

"The fear is mine, but so is the anger, and it is more powerful than my fear," he shouted. "And it is more powerful than you, Second."

Reaching with his mind he took Second and lifted him into the air. Second frantically clutched his throat as his breathing stopped. "So die all who would challenge me," screamed Hauron at the top of his lungs. He stretched forth his hands. There was a mighty flash as ashes and sparks fell from the air where Second had hung.

Hauron turned to First Prophet and fell at his feet, but spoke to him with his mind, forcefully and deliberately.

"Never try anything like this again or you will die, not as Second died, but over many years as insects and rodents devour your body. Do you understand?" He felt a shudder from First Prophet.

"Your life is forfeit. It belongs to me. You must now make a choice. You may continue as First Prophet, but only as a figurehead. I will become Second, and you will do nothing, make no decisions, carry out no policies without my approval. If you agree to this then you continue to live. If you cannot carry out my will as I have spoken it then you will die. Do you understand?" Hauron sensed only panicked acquiescence from First Prophet who was clearly too terrified to even speak.

"You will never speak of this arrangement to anyone. If you do you will die. Do you understand?" First Prophet again gave his terrified affirmative response.

"I give you my word that if you carry out this charade you will live in peace and prosperity the remainder of your days and your family will protected thereafter. If for one moment you let down your guard, or try to usurp my power you will die. Do you understand?" First Prophet nodded.

Denab stepped forward and smiled at him, a knowing smile. Hauron jumped, startled, almost frightened. Why had he not been immobilized with the others? Still, he looked pleased and not surprised at the outcome of the confrontation; he nodded his head as if to say congratulations. Hauron smiled back at him, then released the remainder of Assembly from their unseen bonds. He would have to think more on this turn of events later.

"First Prophet," he spoke clearly and confidently, still kneeling at his feet, staring at the floor. "I pledge my loyalty to you as your new Second if you will accept me as such. I am honored that I was able to destroy this plot to usurp your power, hatched by my predecessor. You are The First Prophet reincarnated. You are the supreme power in the empire. You are the object of my worship and loyalty."

First Prophet quickly regained his composure, and spoke as the statesman he was trained to be. "Arise, Second. Stand by my side." He turned to the Quorum. "Here is our new Second. Are there any among you who cannot pledge loyalty to him? Speak now."

It was merely a formality. Obviously no one was going to challenge Hauron ever again. One by one they came before him, bowed and kissed his hand, uttering the simple phrase, "To you I pledge my loyalty, Second."

When it was Denab's turn he didn't seem as worried or confused as the others in the Quorum. In fact he looked a little smug. Hauron didn't know quite what to make of it. Should he be worried? Should he try to find out more about Denab? But as quickly as his concern had surfaced, it was replaced by a calm confidence. Denab was surely one his main allies.

And so, Hauron the slave became Hauron of the Eleven.

CHAPTER 8

Hauron sat alone in his meditation chamber. A new, more powerful vision had begun to form in his mind, which he decided he would experience alone. He left strict instructions he was not to be disturbed under any circumstances, by anyone. His personal, handpicked, guard stood watch. Their squad leader was a young captain named Cerid. He too had been born on the Eastern Continent, and although he had risen through the ranks quite quickly, he was nevertheless not happy with the way the ruling classes treated the slaves. There were others too who felt the same way. These Hauron picked to be his personal guards.

Two days had passed since he had taken control of the government of the empire. He had not met with the Quorum or the Council, or even First Prophet since then; let them digest what they had seen and build up their anxiety about what changes he would make. He was almost ready to make a sweeping dictate that all the slaves should be freed immediately, but he realized that any sudden change in the infrastructure of the Empire could have drastic effects throughout the whole economy. No, whatever he did would have to be gradual and purposeful. In the meantime, a few days for him to gather his thoughts would not make a big difference.

The vision was becoming clearer. The girl Asdzáán Nádleehé was on her own, lying on her back, staring up into the sky. Nearby a horse grazed peacefully. Nothing much seemed to be happening, so why was the vision reaching him so powerfully? And then he realized; her Power was increasing dramatically, exponentially, with no apparent stimulus. Perhaps she was drawing Power from her gods.

After five hours she suddenly got up and climbed on to the horse. The sun had set and it was getting dark, but still the vision became stronger. She spurred the horse to a gallop, and then without warning shifted both of them about eighty kilometers. A few more times she shifted, seeming to be wildly delirious. Hauron was impressed, and wondered if he would ever have the ability to shift himself. But in this one matter he did still have the advantage; she was clearly unable to sense his silent observation of her.

She continued to confuse him. She was a mass of contradiction. She was probably three or four years younger than him and she seemed so innocent, almost naïve. Her face was alive, intelligent and vibrant; she reminded him of Kazzy. Still, he must not be swayed by her appearance. Of course she was brilliant, and could portray any image she wanted that would suit her evil purpose.

The vision faded, until there was nothing to see. He remained in his chamber, sure that he had only seen the beginnings of a much more significant confrontation between her and the agents of the Empire.

Eight hours went by before the vision returned. The witch was on board a small spacecraft tending her friends who seemed to be wounded. She was being assisted by what looked like a soldier of the Empire, the captain of the shuttle, but how could that be? Suddenly a man of Quorum stature came into the room. At first it seemed as if the girl would easily defeat him, but then she fell to the floor clutching her neck. Hauron was sickened as he watched him brutally beat her, devastating her body. But he must learn to control such reactions. She was not to be thought of as a normal human being; she deserved no pity.

The vision faded again. Three more hours went by before once again he saw her. The small spacecraft had landed on the mother ship, which was surrounded by a Quorum and a Council, as well as a number of soldiers. He watched as the soldiers brought the prisoners before the ship's First. The witch was not among them! But how? She had been beaten senseless. First took hold of one of her friends, the girl, and held a knife against her chest. He hadn't really paid much attention to her before, but now he saw she was slightly older than the witch, and quite beautiful. No, he mustn't let himself be drawn into such wandering thoughts about people who were his sworn mortal enemies.

First held a knife against her chest, and gradually pushed it into her body. Hauron winced as he saw her mouthing a scream, blood pouring from the wound. Her eyes rolled back into her head and she crumpled in his arms.

Suddenly the witch was there, on the back of her magnificent white horse. She was wielding a huge sword, which was almost as tall as she was, and with one stroke sliced off First's head. The Assembly combined their power against her, and at first it looked as if she might be quickly overpowered, but her whole appearance began to change. The young woman who had been killed by First stood up and joined her, as did a young man. Both mounted horses, which suddenly appeared in the hangar. Horses and riders began to glow until they were blinding white, and they rose into the air until they were two meters off the ground. Gradually the three of them began to overcome the Assembly, as one-by-one all were subdued, and apparently frozen in place. His trepidation mounted, as he realized she was much more formidable than he had originally thought. She had controlled over a hundred extremely powerful minds, and then killed them all.

It was time to meet with his court.

"First Prophet, please could you call the Quorum and the Council to the throne room. It's about time we met to discuss the witch."

"Yes Second, at once."

"Shunaro. You must never defer to me! Never! Not even now. You must continue to act as First Prophet. No one but you and I must know of the arrangement we have."

"As you wish."

"It is more than my wish. Without you as First Prophet we will never defeat Asdzáán Nádleehé. You will treat me in all respects as you did the previous Second. You have nothing to fear from me. I hold you no ill will. Please trust me as I trust you. I have had another vision, and I am even more convinced that having you at the helm is the only way we will survive."

"Very well, Hauron."

"We will be discussing our plans for defeating Asdzáán Nádleehé." He paused for a moment and then continued. "And then I want to discuss my plans for freeing the slaves."

"What? Are you mad?" Hauron was surprised, pleasantly, at the intensity of First Prophet's reaction, compared to his subservience only a moment before.

"We will see. But it is my command."

"Hauron, how do you ever intend to get the Assembly to agree to this?"

"I'm not, you are."

"I am! But that's impossible. I could never . . ."

"Let me make it easy for you. What percentage of the Empire belongs to the ruling classes, and what percentage are slaves?"

"About two percent are ruling class; the rest are slaves."

"Now think about this. If Asdzáán Nádleehé is intent on destroying us then she already has four billion people who hate us, and would be ready to do anything she asked to get rid of us."

"Well, this is true, but they have no weapons, no organization, no leadership . . ."

"Listen to what you are saying, Shunaro! Can she not provide all of those things?"

"Well, yes. But why would she?"

"Because then she doesn't have to do anything to overthrow us. The slaves will do it for her. And then it will be a much easier to task to dispose of them, or perhaps even enslave them for her own purposes. Remember, it is us, the ruling class she hates and wishes to destroy."

"I see your point."

"We have to be united as an Empire to defeat her. Of this I am convinced."

"But, Hauron, does this have anything with you once being a slave?"

"Of course it does. And this is why there will be no compromise on this issue. If I must, I will destroy the entire Assembly, and you if necessary to accomplish this. Which is why the idea must come from you, not from me."

"I see. But I cannot imagine how this can be accomplished."

"I do. Which is why you will assign the project to me. Have no fear though, Shunaro. I understand that these things cannot change overnight. No, these changes will occur gradually, perhaps over a complete sun-cycle, but some things must happen quickly, such that by the end of winter-year, we have them fully behind us."

Hauron could sense Shunaro's deep and disturbed fear of this new policy he was about to propose to the assembly. Hauron prodded him slightly.

"Remember, Shunaro. It is my command," he said with determined finality.

The throne room was soon filled with the Assembly. The Quorum of the Eleven stood in a semicircle on the dais, with Hauron in the center. Behind them stood the Council of the Hundred. First Prophet was seated on his throne facing them.

"Members of the Quorum and Council, I believe Second has something he wishes to tell us. Come stand by me, Hauron."

Hauron bowed low. "Yes, Excellency," he said as he took up his position beside the throne. "I have seen what I believe is the final confrontation between our agents in the Sol system and the witch, Asdzáán Nádleehé." He described in detail all the things he had seen in his vision. "The Quorum and the Council on board Revenge are dead, and we can assume the witch has control of the ship." Hauron paused as he let this sink in. Clearly, they all saw the significance of what she had done, and all, including First Prophet looked concerned.

"What do you recommend, Second?" asked First Prophet finally.

"Excellency, I think we should hear some of the thoughts of the other members of the Assembly first."

"I agree. Does anyone have any comments, questions, or ideas?"

Denab stood forward. "I think Hauron is correct. We can assume she has control of Revenge. And if the agents who she sent back here are correct in their assessment, then they will probably have a Hyperspace drive within a sun-cycle. I believe your Excellency is quite correct in saying we can expect them to return shortly after that."

"I agree, Denab, but please go on."

"I believe I am also correct in saying that in spite of the large number of ships we have in the fleet, none is capable of destroying Revenge, and that Revenge is quite capable of destroying our cities."

"Yes, but do you have any ideas to offer besides your analysis of the situation."

"I do, Excellency. But first I have a question, if you would permit me." First Prophet nodded condescendingly. "It is this. Why do we suppose it is her aim to destroy us?"

A gasp went up from the usually reserved Assembly. First Prophet stood up. "Denab, do you realize you are questioning everything The First Prophet has said, and that every First Prophet since then has reiterated."

"I do, Excellency, but . . ."

"Then I suggest you never again speak such blasphemy."

"With all due respect, Excellency," said Hauron, "Denab is a most revered member of the Quorum, and I am sure it is not his intention to speak blasphemy. Perhaps we should hear what he has to say."

"Very well. Continue, Denab, but watch where you tread."

Denab bowed. "Thank you, Excellency. The reason I ask this question is this: from what Hauron has told us her Power is beyond anything we have seen here on Yurob. It is my belief that even without Revenge she has the ability to destroy us all without leaving her home planet. Why has she not done so?"

There was a stunned silence in the room. Even Hauron had not considered this. Denab continued. "I think we all agree that she has not had a change of heart; that she has not turned from her evil path. Having said that, I think we need to consider what her intention could be, if not our destruction."

For a moment the room was silent. Hauron could almost hear the minds furiously digesting and processing this information.

Finally another stepped forward. "Excellency. I think there is a strong possibility that Denab is correct in his assessment. As to her intention, perhaps it is to conquer and subdue, not to destroy."

How glad Hauron was that he had decided to maintain the Assembly of Rulers. Their experience and intelligence were proving invaluable. Hauron looked over to First Prophet and spoke to him with his mind. "I believe there is a strong possibility they are correct, Excellency."

"Thank you, Wulsa, thank you. Denab, I think you have given us some valuable insight into what she may be planning."

"It is of course only one possible scenario, Excellency."

"Yes, I agree, but a strong possibility nevertheless. Does anyone else have any other possible scenarios?"

This time it was one of the Council of One Hundred who stood forward; a young man who appeared to be about the same age as Hauron. "Excellency, I also agree with Denab and Wulsa. I believe the 'subdue and conquer' scenario seems the most likely given Denab's insight, but that the possibility of destruction, though lesser, is still one we must seriously consider." He paused for a moment, as if gathering courage. "But there is also the possibility of a third . . ." He seemed reluctant to speak.

"Please go on, Sigmun."

"Excellency, I am afraid of your wrath . . ."

"Given the seriousness of our situation, I think we need to hear all ideas. The Assembly must not be afraid to speak, even if they are wrong."

"Sigmun, I appreciate your dutiful respect, but I think given the gravity of our situation that it is important to hear all points of view. From this day forth, let it be decreed that within these walls and in our present company, there shall be no boundaries on what may be spoken. How say you?" he said turning to the Quorum.

"So let it be decreed," they affirmed one by one.

"Sigmun, please continue."

Sigmun bowed deeply. "What I say represents just the smallest of possibilities, and does not even bear the attention of the Assembly, but nevertheless I believe we should consider all." There was still some reluctance in his voice.

"Sigmun, please, tell us your thought."

"Excellency, it is this. What if she comes to us with an offer of peace?"

The gasp that went up from the Assembly was even more pronounced than that which greeted Denab's suggestion. Again, Hauron watched as in silence they pondered this seemingly ridiculous idea.

After a few moments First Prophet asked, "Sigmun, not only is she our sworn enemy, but her god and our god are sworn enemies. How can she possibly offer reconciliation?"

"Of course," he said with a bow. "I apologize, Excellency."

"I agree, Excellency, there is not even the remotest of possibilities that she would want peace, but Sigmun has given me an idea," said Hauron. "What if she is indeed set upon conquest, but she approaches us with an offer of peace, simply to trick us into lowering our guard?" There was a general nodding of agreement around the room. He turned to Sigmun and bowed. "Thank you, Sigmun. This would not have occurred to me had you not spoken up." Turning back to the Quorum he continued. "Her evil mind will stop at nothing to accomplish her goals, and this is perhaps exactly the way she may attempt to trick us."

"We could use this to our advantage," said Denab.

"Please explain, Denab," said First Prophet.

"We could follow along with her masquerade. Let her gain confidence that her plan is working. With her increased confidence her guard may fall. Rather than her taking advantage of our decreased vigilance, we could take advantage of hers, giving us an opportunity to overpower her."

"Use her own tactic against her," said Wulsa. "I like it."

"Excellent, Denab," agreed First Prophet.

The discussion continued as they considering all of the alternative ways she might come, until Hauron decided it was time to bring it to a close.

"Well, brethren. I think we have had a very useful discussion. Now I think it is time for us to start making plans as to how we might counter each of these possible scenarios. Almelic," he said turning to one of the more junior members of the Quorum, "I would like you to consider all of the possible ramifications should she still attempt a direct attack bent on destruction. Consider no other alternatives, no matter how likely you think they are. I want you to assume that this is her plan and come up with every possible angle; every possible way she might carry it out; how we can counter each of these potential attacks. Chose five other members of the Quorum to work with you. Make this your highest priority."

Almelic bowed. "Thank you, Second. This is a good assignment for me since I believe that this is still the more likely of the plans she will follow."

"Denab, you will take the remaining members of the quorum and consider all of the ramifications and counter-measures associated with your suggestion. Again, please assume that this is her intent." Denab bowed. "Sigmun and I alone will work on the possibility that she will use subterfuge and lies to lower our guard." Hauron could tell Sigmun was both surprised and honored to have been chosen. "I think it is safe to assume that we have at least half a sun-cycle, perhaps more. We can begin to expect her no sooner than the beginning of winter-year, and no later than the beginning of summer-year."

"Excellency, I think that is all the business we need to discuss at this time," said Hauron.

"I think there is another issue we should discuss," began First Prophet. Hauron could sense his distaste, but doubted anyone else in the Assembly could. He was doing a fine job of being the statesman. "There are approximately four billion slaves here on Yurob, and I think it is safe to assume that they despise us." There were a number of blank stares around the room. "Hauron, you were once a slave. Do you agree?"

"Well, Excellency, despise may be too strong a word. Hopelessly frustrated and impotent anger may better describe how I felt."

"Regardless, it is my belief that if Asdzáán Nádleehé was to somehow unite them, organize them, even arm them, the devastation this could cause our civilization could be significant. She may simply be able to use our own people against us to accomplish her evil designs."

"Well, I'm not sure how that would be possible," said Hauron, inwardly smiling to himself. First Prophet was doing an excellent job. "How would she even go about such a task?"

"Let me answer that with another question. What is the common mistake all of our agents have made at every confrontation they have had with her?"

"They were overconfident," said Almelic.

"A crucial mistake wouldn't you agree but there is an even bigger, more obvious mistake they made."

"They underestimated her Power," said Denab.

"Exactly," said First Prophet. Hauron almost got the feeling that First Prophet was beginning to convince himself. "Hauron, what do you think?"

"Excellency, I'm not sure what you're proposing."

"Well, I'm not proposing we simply free them overnight; or even over the next few years. No, I think what we have to do is to win them over by somehow making their lives more bearable, let them think that our ultimate goal is an egalitarian society. By the time she arrives there must be no possibility that she finds a world divided."

One of the council stood forward. "Excellency, are you sure this is what you want."

"It is, Zomra."

"But once the crisis is over, we can simply revert to our old system. We can enslave them once again?" asked Zomra, an evil smile on his face. "I'm going to miss those young girls." Hauron was horrified, and wondered how many in the Quorum and the Council felt the same way—many of them perhaps. Nevertheless, it was Zomra who had voiced the opinion, and by so doing had signed his own death warrant.

"Hauron, I am assigning you to work out a plan to accomplish this goal. It's imperative that all of our citizens are one hundred percent behind us by the time Asdzáán Nádleehé comes."

"Certainly, Excellency," said Hauron with a bow.

"And now, I think our business is concluded," said First Prophet with an air of finality. The Assembly filed out.

"Excellency, I think you almost had me convinced."

"Well, the more I thought about it the more it made sense. I think it is the approach I would try if I were in her place."

Hauron smiled to himself. His job would be a lot easier now. He did not for a moment expect her to try to use the slaves, but as long as the rest of the Assembly still had their doubts, it would make his job a lot easier. And now that he had set in motion the planning for her downfall, he was feeling confident for the first time that he might actually defeat her.

"It was your idea wasn't it? Not First Prophet's," said Cerid as they walked back to his apartment.

Hauron raised his eyebrows. "Yes, Cerid. It was."

"You don't really think the witch will try to use them do you? The slaves I mean."

"No I don't. But I intend to have every slave living as a free man within two sun-cycles, being paid a fair wage for the work they do, living in decent homes, having proper medical care." He stopped and turned to Cerid, placing his hands on his shoulders. "I intend to bring the ruling classes down, Cerid."

Cerid fell to his knees, bowed his head and held out his weapon in front of him. "Excellency, my life is yours. I speak also for the rest of your guards. All of us would willingly give our lives for you. You have not only given us something to live for, but also something worth dying for."

"Cerid, I hope it doesn't come to that." Hauron took him by the arms and helped him up. "And Cerid, I want you to think of me as your friend."

"Yes, Excellency."

Hauron knew that he could trust Cerid with his life. Hauron vowed to himself to reciprocate that trust. Cerid was a good man, a worthy man. He had chosen well.

CHAPTER 9

It was quite late when Hauron walked into his apartment, and he was exhausted. He was surprised to find his mother and father still awake.

"Hauron, you have been so busy the last few days, we have hardly seen you," said Geoan.

"The weight of government," said Dyllen proudly. "Now that our son is the second most powerful man in the Empire, I guess we'll be seeing less of him."

"Father, have you so soon forgotten how much we hate the government?"

Dyllen's face turned serious. "No son, I haven't. But since there is nothing we can do about it, I suppose all we can do is thank the gods that at least we are OK."

Hauron brightened. "Ah, but there is something we can do about it."

"There is? What?"

"I am going to make you governor of East Continent, and you are going to develop a plan that has the slaves free within two sun-cycles, and has them loving the ruling classes within half a sun-cycle."

Dyllen was speechless. He simply pointed to the middle of his chest. Hauron nodded, a smile covering his whole face.

"Hauron," exclaimed his mother. "How can this be?"

He told them of the decision made in the Assembly, how he had tricked them to going along with it, and how he had recruited First Prophet to be its greatest champion.

"But, Hauron, why me?"

"Why not?"

"What do I know about government?"

"I will make sure you get the most loyal advisors." He tapped his head. "And I will know if any are disloyal. And who better than you knows what those poor hopeless souls on the Eastern Continent need."

"Well, I suppose that's true."

"You have to move slowly," said Hauron, as he went on to caution Dyllen about the risks and dangers of proceeding too quickly, but of the importance of having the slaves united with the Empire in the defeat of Asdzáán Nádleehé. "You must choose important changes to make first, to have the greatest impact."

"And I think I know exactly where to start. First, we need to provide medical treatment to those with the lung disease, and second, we need to find ways to prevent it."

"Excellent, a perfect place to start. I will also make sure you have the best physicians and scientists at your disposal to help them, and to determine what has to be done to minimize the risk to all of our people."

Sometime during the night Zomra died quite mysteriously. He had shown no signs of any illness, but if anyone suspected his death was not natural they didn't say anything. Sigmun became the youngest member of the Quorum.

Hauron liked Sigmun; his soul did not seem quite as dark as the other members of the Assembly. Perhaps his youth accounted for that, but Hauron doubted that was all there was to it. He seemed particularly intelligent and a much more independent thinker than the rest of the Quorum, and that was exactly what Hauron needed; someone who could visualize possibilities that other members of the Quorum would not even consider.

As part of the ceremony to induct Sigmun, Hauron also announced that all forms of exploitation of slaves were to be strictly forbidden. He made it quite clear that there would never again be entertainment of the kind he had witnessed in the throne room, involving those poor slave girls. Such actions would not be tolerated, and would be subject to termination.

Dyllen found he had a natural talent for leadership. By the end of Summer-year he had many programs in place for the betterment of the slaves who worked in the lithium mines. First of all, he had been surprised to discover that there were huge supplies of lithium, enough to keep the reactors going for at least another twelve years, three sun-cycles, even if the supply were completely cut off. But in spite of that he had taken Hauron's advice and not made any drastic changes to the mining operation. Instead he reduced the work day from ten to seven hours, and the work week from six to four days, giving the workers more time to rest. As for the lung problems most miners developed, there were simply not enough physicians or supplies to treat all of the afflicted right away, but he did allow the men with the more serious cases to retire.

Hauron was pleased with the progress. By all accounts, the slaves were turning their hatred of the government into love of Dyllen and Hauron. Spurred on by this success, Hauron decided it was time to introduce similar changes on the Central and Western continents. Unlike the Eastern continent where there was only one region, the Central continent had ten regions, and the Western continent had five. Fifteen regional governors to deal with, but Hauron made it quite clear that they were to follow Dyllen's example. All of them agreed, although most reluctantly. Hauron decided he would keep a close watch on them, and if necessary, replace them.

Another year went by, and by the end of Autumn-year Hauron's plans were well underway. Within another year he was sure that the slaves would be firmly behind the government and there would be no room for Asdzáán Nádleehé to turn them to her advantage. According to First Prophet she would be here soon, very soon.

He was also quite pleased with the progress the Quorum was making with the plans for the Asdzáán Nádleehé's arrival. Almelic had supervised the development and construction of drone ships, loaded with fusible hydrogen, which could be placed at strategic points around the planet. At the first sign of Revenge they could be deployed quickly and zero in on her. The hope was that they would catch them off guard and be able to destroy, or at least disable her before she could be brought to bear on the planet. The more time passed, the more Hauron was convinced that she was not bent on destruction, but he was not willing to play a waiting game. If they could be destroyed as soon as they materialized, so be it. There was nothing to lose by not giving her a chance to try anything else.

Sigmun still intrigued him. His relationship with Hauron was such that he could now speak his mind freely, and while Hauron disagreed with him on many points, he did nothing to discourage his ideas, although he cautioned him not to share them with other members of the Quorum.

Quite soon after he had been inducted into the Quorum he had confided in Hauron. "You know, Hauron, I wasn't entirely convinced that I was wrong about Asdzáán Nádleehé." When they were alone Hauron had insisted they be less formal. He needed Sigmun's complete trust and confidence, and treating him as an equal seemed the best way to accomplish that.

"What do you mean, Sigmun?"

"I still think it is a possibility that she wants peace."

Hauron was surprised that Sigmun would continue to express this opinion, considering how much it had obviously displeased First Prophet.

"Why do you say that?"

"Well, first off, our whole philosophy, our whole belief system is so fragile."

"Go on." Hauron was interested, although far from convinced.

"I mean, does it make sense to you? This notion of reincarnation?" Hauron said nothing, so Sigmun continued. "I mean, even before you came along, I was never truly convinced that First Prophet, or any of his predecessors for that matter, were actual reincarnations of The First Prophet. I tried not to dwell on it too much; I mean, it's something we had had drilled into us at temple since we could walk. But when you appeared it made me even more unsure of it."

Hauron knew what he was driving at, but he wanted to hear it from Sigmun's own lips. He paused, as if waiting for some sign from Hauron to either continue or desist. When none was forthcoming, he decided to continue.

"I don't know how many others in the Assembly know, but it's quite clear to me who is running the Empire now; and it's not First Prophet."

"Well, even if others suspect, all I ask is that they never voice that opinion, as I have allowed you to Sigmun."

"If you want me to speak no further on this matter, then simply ask."

"No, Sigmun, I want your ideas, as long as we keep them between us."

"Certainly," he said, nodding his head. "So, how can he be First Prophet reincarnated, if you are so much more powerful than him?"

"The question has occurred to me also. But just as when we had questions when we were young, we were always told that we were so much less intelligent than Rolling Darkness, and that we should simply accept that which we didn't understand, or could not explain."

"And that's another thing. Does this whole 'Rolling Darkness' concept make any sense to you? I mean, why would a deity so dark and fearsome create this wondrous universe in the first place? What would be his purpose? Doesn't it make more sense to you that the universe and everything in it is simply the result of natural phenomena? Personally, I'm not sure he even exists, or that there is any creator of this universe."

Sigmun was definitely troubling Hauron. He was giving voice to the same doubts he had had. "As I said, Sigmun, I try not to think about these types of questions too much. They give me a headache; like you're giving me a headache now." They both laughed spontaneously at this comment, the first time Hauron had felt so light since he had arrived at the palace. He truly liked Sigmun, and enjoyed his intelligent conversation, and his pleasant company.

"Enough for now. And be sure to keep this between us. I will give it some thought, but I have to remain practical and pragmatic. There's too much at stake."

"Fair enough," said Sigmun. "But one final thought. If First Prophet is not the reincarnation of The First Prophet, then might this girl not be the reincarnation of Asdzáán Nádleehé?'

That was the final straw. "Enough," said Hauron quite loudly, though clearly good-naturedly. "My head is throbbing."

Sigmun held his hands up in a submissive gesture and smiled. Nevertheless, Hauron did spend a lot of time thinking about it that night. While it made some sense, it was too risky. If Sigmun were wrong, and he had modified all of his plans based on this thinking, the result could be devastating. No, it was much better to be safe than sorry. Things must proceed as planned.

And proceed they did. So successful had been the improvements in the lives of the slaves that they actually started showing loyalty and even love of their rulers. Hauron, it appeared, had become a folk hero.

Winter-year came and went, and no sign of Asdzáán Nádleehé. Spring-year turned into Summer-year, and still she had not come. Hauron was beginning to doubt she ever would, but he forced himself to renew his determination to defeat her. He regularly met with the Assembly to review their plans and to stress the importance of not letting down their guard.

And then, at the end of Summer-year, she did come to him, although not exactly as he had expected.

PART TWO

Sigmun

CHAPTER 10

June 18, 2108—El Huerfano, Dinetah

Micah looked longingly at the holo-image of Shaylae he took with him wherever he went. It was a repeating loop, about thirty seconds, of her laughing and smiling nervously and stood about twenty-five centimeters high. Her sparkling blue eyes were on fire with intelligence, compassion, wisdom and beauty, but at the same time they betrayed a touch of enigmatic innocence and naïveté. Her mouth was full and sensuous. His heart raced as he recalled the moment when she had kissed him, her soft lips gently touching his.

Her face was oval with high cheekbones and her olive skin was perfect, unblemished. Her long black hair hung loosely down her back, thick, shiny and luxurious. She was truly the most breathtakingly beautiful thing he had ever seen. As he watched the image turn he looked in awe at her precious body. Her gentle curves, subdued by her modest traditional Navajo clothing, took his breath away. He forced the encroaching thoughts out of his head. The time would soon come when he would be able to drown in such thoughts but until then, he would honor her virtue, even in the privacy of his own dreams.

It was 6 pm, June 18, 2108—the day before her eighteenth birthday. He and Ayanna were already at El Huerfano for the annual Todich'ii'nii gathering to celebrate the summer solstice. Shaylae would be arriving later that evening. Micah could hardly contain himself. Other than videophone calls two or three times a week he had not seen her for two months, and those calls had been awkward and clumsy. Somehow making small talk with Shaylae Lucero seemed inappropriate after the experiences they had been through together four years earlier.

They had graduated High School two years earlier, all at the same time; Micah on schedule, Ayanna a year ahead, and Shaylae two years ahead. They had been accepted at Dine'h Tech and all had chosen physics as their majors. Two months ago they had finished their junior year and Shaylae had returned to Salt Lake to be with her parents, but tonight, in a few short hours, she would be hugging him tightly. As he had so often before, with the back of his hand he gently caressed the empty space that the holo occupied.

There was a knock at the open door of his cabin.

"What are you doing, as if I need ask?" It was Ayanna, his second cousin and lifelong friend. He smiled as he quickly flipped the switch that turned off the holo.

"Oh, nothing," he sighed.

"I've never heard of it happening, but at the rate you're going, you'll wear that holo out. Anyway, she'll be here soon."

He felt a little embarrassed, but not at all sorry. He noticed Ayanna was in her brown Chulukua-Ryu sparing jacket and pants.

"I thought you might want to get your butt kicked instead of moping over Shay. It'll help to pass the time."

"Kick my butt! That'll be the day." Micah smiled. He could usually beat Ayanna, but only by a point or two even though she was a year younger than him, and quite a few kilos lighter. Both were black belts in the Native American form of Martial Arts. "Give me a second. I'll be right out."

Quickly he changed into his fighting gear and hurried outside. Ayanna was already doing her warm-up katas. She too was a beautiful Navajo girl. She was leaner than Shaylae, and a lot meaner too, he mused. Like Shaylae her face was oval but her nose was smaller, with a cute little up-turn. Her slim body was in perfect condition and in perfect control as she balanced motionless on one foot, the other high in the air. Micah fell into his warm-up routine, quickly stretching and toning his muscular body.

"Are you ready?" she asked. He turned. She was certainly a formidable sight—legs bent at the knees, feet apart, elbows tight at her waist, and fists clenched in front of her menacingly.

He quickly adopted the same pre-fight stance. "Begin," he said.

She came at him quickly, a blow to the stomach with her left hand, followed by a punch to his head with her right. He was easily able to block them. Their sparing usually followed this pattern; Ayanna coming out fast, while he blocked her attack, assessing her strategy.

It was almost four years ago when Shaylae had first watched him practicing his routines. She had so distracted him that he had stumbled; she had smiled, but he was mortified. And it was almost four years ago when he had first felt the touch of her soft skin against his as he taught her how to hold a tomahawk.

He saw it coming too late. Ayanna's kick landed solidly in his gut, bending him forward, almost double as the air was forced from his lungs with a loud "umph". He fell backwards, two meters, and hit the floor clumsily in a cloud of dust. Once again Shaylae Lucero had distracted him.

Quickly Ayanna was at his side. "Oh my gosh, Mike, are you OK?"

Micah was more embarrassed than hurt. It was a simple kick that he should have been able to block easily. He sprang lithely to his feet, trying hard not to betray the pain in his stomach, or the fact that he was still fighting for air.

"Again," he said.

"Ayanna, Micah." It was Luci, Ayanna's mother.

"Yes, Mother," shouted Ayanna in return.

"Can you come over to the Hogan? Shay's mom is on the phone."

A sudden feeling of disquiet filled Micah's mind and body. He turned to Ayanna. She too seemed worried.

"It's probably nothing," she said unconvincingly.

Together they ran over to the Hogan that Matron Lapahie had assigned to Ayanna's family.

"What is it?" said Micah as they rushed over to the phone. On the screen were the concerned faces of Reycita Lucero and Mateo Rodrigo, Shaylae's parents.

"Is Shaylae with you?" asked Reycita.

"No. You don't know where she is?"

"We haven't seen her since breakfast."

"You have no idea where she is?"

"She left this morning on Snow Lion. She said she needed to take a ride into the mountains."

She often went riding on her own, but it was unlikely she would have forgotten about the annual Todich'ii'nii clan gathering. It just wasn't possible that she would miss it willingly.

"Did she say where she was going?"

"Yes, she said she was going up to Little Water. And we dare not call the authorities. She still continues to fear there are Dark Ones still hidden here."

"Is Snow Lion's tracer chip activated?" Mateo shook his head sadly.

Micah turned to Ayanna. "We need to get over there."

Ayanna turned to her mother. "Can we take the car?"

"Anna, I don't know. It's . . ."

"Please mom. It's important, I know it is."

"But it's got to be more than eight hundred kilometers . . ." She paused a moment. "OK, but be careful." She handed the key card to Ayanna.

"Thanks, mom." She kissed her quickly on the cheek.

"Wait, you might want to take warm coats, maybe blankets and a heater." Probably not a bad idea; who knows how long they could be looking for Shaylae in the mountains. They grabbed their coats, blankets and the heater, ran quickly to where the hover car was parked and jumped in.

"Please insert your key and driver's license," said the car.

Ayanna inserted the key that her mother had given her, took her driver's license out of her wallet and inserted it.

"I'm sorry, you are currently in a free-flight zone, and your license does not permit free-flight."

"You'd better drive Micah," she said quickly moving the console to his side of the car and removing her license. She was only nineteen, not yet old enough to take the free-flight test. Micah had passed his seven months ago on his twentieth birthday. He took the wheel and inserted his license.

"Please state your destination."

"Mill Creek Canyon, Salt Lake County, Utah," he replied.

"Please be more specific," complained the car.

Micah flipped down the console and pulled up the map. He selected the Little Water trailhead and hit the send key. The route showed itself on the GPS screen and the car quickly rose vertically to five hundred meters.

"Proceed on the indicated setting until you reach the Farmington traffic control area."

"Redraw route to avoid as many traffic control areas as possible." Said Micah.

"New route computed," said the computer. Micah examined the new route. It took them west northwest, directly over Shiprock Peak for a hundred and ninety kilometers, till just south of Mexican Hat, then shifted north-northwest for about three-hundred kilometers. From that point on it would be impossible to avoid the Salt Lake metropolitan traffic control area which extended all the way from Brigham City in the North down to Nephi over a hundred kilometers south of Salt Lake. But for five hundred and fifty kilometers they would make good time. Micah hit the accelerator and very soon the car was hurtling forward at three hundred and fifty klicks.

"Aren't you going a bit fast?" questioned Ayanna.

Micah just looked at her with a so what? look.

"She's OK Micah," she said. "I'm sure she's OK."

Micah nodded but said nothing.

Shaylae's family had moved to Salt Lake City four months earlier when her father's research had taken him to the University of Utah. Since the end of the semester he had only seen her twice, and each time she had traveled by conventional means. It frustrated him a little, knowing she was less than a heartbeat away by hyperspace shift, but three or more hours by hover car. Still, he wasn't going to question her judgment when it came to using her power. He looked at his watch; it was 6:45. They should arrive at the south end of the metro traffic region by 8:15, and depending on how busy the area was, they should reach Mill Creek no more than an hour after that. The sun would set about 9 pm, so they would be looking for her in the dark.

After forty minutes Micah banked the car gradually to the right. Soon they would be leaving Dinetah and entering the United States. He looked out of the left window to the ground five hundred meters below where he could just make out the town of Medicine Hat. The land was spectacular. The Colorado plateau was one of the most beautiful and fascinating geological formations on the face of the earth and home to his people for three thousand years since Asdzáán Nádleehé had come here from Tal'el'Dine'h. And for those three thousand years the People, the Dine'h, had looked forward to the coming of one of her descendants to save them from the Dark Ones. That person was his precious Shaylae of the Gentle Heart, Yanaba, 'She Who Meets the Enemy'. And he had no idea how they were going to find her.

"We'll find her," said Ayanna, as if reading his thoughts. "I'll be able to sense her when we get close, I'm sure I will."

Micah nodded. Even though his relationship with Shaylae was deeper than any other he had had in his life, he knew that Ayanna and Shaylae had a special bond, much stronger than sisters.

Not much was said between the cousins for the next hour; both lost in their thoughts. Micah felt as if he was on a roller coaster. One minute he would be thinking everything was fine; Shaylae could take care of herself. The next, he would be worrying that the Dark Ones had found a new way to overpower her. They had after all, been able to defeat her aboard the shuttle. Micah shuddered when he recalled how badly Second had beaten her. Ayanna had often said she couldn't even imagine in her wildest dreams that anyone could be so evil that they could do that to a young girl. Micah could. He had no false illusions about the evil contained in the deepest recesses of the Dark Ones' minds. Her leg had been mangled beyond anything that Earth medical knowledge could heal. In fact for a while it had seemed as if Shaylae would lose her leg, but fortunately the scientists of Yurob had developed some remarkable procedures using undifferentiated cells. They had not been able to completely heal it; the doctors had said she would carry a constant reminder of the terrible trauma she had suffered aboard the Dark One's shuttle, in the form of a slight limp, for the rest of her life.

Directly ahead in the northwest Father Sun was setting, almost as far north as he would ever get.

"Entering the Salt Lake traffic control area in five minutes," announced the car. Micah looked at the map. Yes, they were about twenty-five kilometers south east of Nephi, and it was only 8:15. They had made good time. Five minutes later the car banked to the right and slowed as it began to follow the old interstate corridor. Micah grimaced when he saw how slowly. One hundred and fifty kilometers per hour! He had not been expecting the corridor to have been so busy it would result in crawling at 120 kph. And they were at least a hundred kilometers away. It would be after nine o'clock when they arrived.

It wasn't long before the car passed to the west of Provo, and not long after that Mount Timpanogos. One of Micah's favorite hobbies was Indian lore, and he recalled the legend that tells of Utahna, an Indian Princess of one tribe, falling in love with Red Eagle, the son of the Chief of an enemy tribe. She was sacrificed to the great God of Timpanogos and her body was laid on the top of this mountain. To this day the shape of her body in its final repose, arms folded across her chest, could be seen across the seven peaks. Micah's heart leapt when he thought of his own Indian Princess in danger.

He felt his frustration building as the car crawled along a hundred meters above the valley floor west of the Wasatch Mountains. There was certainly a lot of traffic. Where were they all coming from? And where were they all going? If only Anne had been with them. She probably could have gotten them FBI clearance to navigate over and through the National Parks, which was forbidden to regular civilian traffic.

The car banked right and headed northeast toward the mouth of Mill Creek Canyon, and in a few minutes began the fifteen-kilometer run up to the Little Water trailhead. There was an altitude difference of about a thousand meters from the Salt Lake Valley floor to where they would begin their search, and Micah watched in dismay as the outside temperature began to drop. He queried the computer as to what the low overnight temperature would be high in the Canyon in June. The average was about five degrees, but tonight it was forecast to drop to near freezing. The thought of his Shaylae being out in that cold made him shiver.

"Can you feel anything yet? Can you sense her?"

Ayanna cocked her head and squinted slightly. "I think so," she said slowly.

"We headed in the right direction?"

"Oh yes. She's up here all right," she said. And then with a little less certainty she added, "Somewhere."

Very much the pragmatist, Micah felt uneasy not having a concrete plan to rely on, no real idea as to how they would find Shaylae. Even though he had witnessed startling evidence of Shaylae's incredible mental and spiritual power, and to a lesser extent Ayanna's, he still preferred to use logic, the scientific method, and practicality. Now, he had no choice but to rely on Ayanna's ability to find Shaylae through what he characterized as psychic powers. The car finally slowed and came in for a gentle landing in the parking lot next to the trailhead.

"Which way?"

"That way," said Ayanna, pointing east, across the riverbank. Micah pulled up a topographical map on the computer and hit "print".

"There's no way we will be able to take the car, so . . ." They grabbed their backpacks and headed west. To the south the path suddenly became quite steep, it was a popular hiking and biking trail up to Dog Lake.

"She didn't take that trail," said Ayanna. "She continued along the river."

"Well, that's good news," said Micah. "It's going to be really cold up there tonight."

The sun had set almost an hour ago, and the moon, though just past full, had not yet risen. Fortunately their strong lanterns lit their path well, making it easy to avoid roots and rocks that littered the mountainside.

After ten minutes Ayanna stopped and pointed north, away from the river.

"This way," she said.

Micah was glad she sounded so confident. It made him feel a lot better. They crossed the narrow creek and wound their way through the trees, until they saw a small clearing up ahead.

"She's over there," said Ayanna beginning to run. Micah fell in easily behind her.

As they got closer Micah pointed. "Isn't that Snow Lion?"

"Yes, I think it is."

They looked at each other, and without saying a word, they both broke into a sprint to cover the last hundred meters. As they drew closer they saw that Snow Lion was without a saddle, of course, but there was no sign of Shaylae. It wasn't until they were almost on top of her that they saw her lying motionless on the ground. Micah panicked. It looked as if she had fallen, but no, that was impossible. She would never fall from Snow Lion. Still, his heart was racing. He reached her first and knelt down beside her. He touched the side of her face. It was stone cold-freezing.

"Gods! No!" He drew back, hand over his mouth, certain he was going to vomit. "No! Oh Gods. It can't be."

Ayanna knelt down and touched her face. She looked as shocked as he felt, but she didn't draw back. Instead she put her ear to her chest, holding up her hand signaling him to be quiet. "Micah, she's fine. She's alive."

"You sure?" said Micah, still unable to contain his panic.

"Yes, now pull yourself together. We have to get her warmed up. Blankets and heater." She held out her hands toward him.

Glad that Ayanna at least was staying calm, he reached into his backpack and pulled out the thermal blankets and the heater.

"Here. Put it there and roll her on to it. We need to get her off this cold ground." Together they gently wrapped her up in the blanket and connected it to the heater. Micah took out another blanket, folded it up and placed it under her head. He checked the temperature; five degrees, and falling. He looked upward. Not a cloud in the sky; a blessing and a curse. A curse because what little heat there was would escape without a blanket of clouds, but a blessing in that it would not snow. Here in the mountains there could be ten to twenty-five centimeters of snow in an average June.

"You think we should get her to a hospital?"

"No. Something tells me she knows exactly what she is doing. We should just keep a close watch on her and keep her warm."

"You mean she planned this?" he said, indicating the prone Shaylae.

"Don't ask me how I know, Mike. I just do."

Micah shrugged. There was nothing to do now except wait. He drew his parka close around him and sat on the ground. For two hours they sat and watched her, not saying much. Just wishing that she would return.

"Why don't you get some sleep? I'll wake you in an hour."

"OK," she said, as she snuggled into her parker and lay down next to the heater. Within a few minutes she was sleeping peacefully. How could she possible sleep at a time like this?

Throughout the night Micah sat and watched. There was no way he would relinquish this charge of looking after his precious Shaylae. Let Ayanna sleep. His mind wandered back to all the times he had been with her. Her smiles and laughter; her grace and charm; her brilliance and tenderness; all these thoughts made him smile and filled him with warmth.

Silently, under his breath, but deliberately, he spoke these words. "You are mine, and I am yours Shaylae Lucero. And so it always will be." The peaceful aspens silently bore solemn witness to his covenant.

CHAPTER 11

—◦◦❦◦◦—

Shaylae had woken early. This was going to be a great day. Tonight she would be reunited with her friends, Micah and Ayanna. She could hardly wait. It had been hard to be separated from them, especially Micah. What had been even harder was to resist the urge to shift over to them in New Mexico, an urge that had come to her most days since they had been apart. But deep down she knew that her Powers were not to be used gratuitously or for simply personal reasons. So, she had settled in to life in the Salt Lake Valley with no complaints.

Her father's research into hyperspace had reached the point where he was ready to construct a prototype field generator so the government had set up a huge lab at Fort Douglas on the University of Utah campus. He had taken most of his team from the National Lab with him, including of course Reycita, who had quickly caught up the nine years she had missed while held captive on the Dark One's ship. The team of theoretical physicists had been complimented with a team of top engineers from Thiokol whose long history with NASA, and then WWSA, had made them the perfect partners.

The government had also provided a beautiful home one and a half kilometers up Mill Creek Canyon, with plenty of land and plenty of room for Snow Lion. She could ride out of the stable, directly onto the trail that took her up the beautiful canyon, never having to go near a road. It was ideal.

Even before she finished getting dressed her jubilant mood was replaced with foreboding. For a few months now she had been getting fleeting feelings that something was happening on Yurob, something big. She was not sure what it was, but each time the feelings had become stronger. Today the feelings were unmistakable. Something was definitely happening, and she had to find out what it was. She wondered if it was anything to do with the hundred and ten Dark Ones that Elder Nashota had taken back to Tal'el'Dine'h. She hadn't heard anything from her since the day she had defeated them aboard Revenge, and had driven Rolling Darkness from their souls. Nor had she tried to find anything out for herself. Elder Nashota had made it quite clear that she shouldn't.

"Shaylae, dear child," she had said. "You must not come to Tal'el'Dine'h, or even try to contact us until the time is right."

"And how will I know when the right time is?"

Elder Nashota had just smiled. But she had to admit, even though she was troubled, it still didn't feel like the right time.

She looked at the clock. It was just after 6 am. She found her mom already at the computer—it would be an hour before her dad got up, but like Shaylae, Reycita was an early riser.

"Mom, I'm going for a ride up the canyon. Won't be long."

Reycita looked up from the computer. "Don't forget we're leaving at four."

Shaylae smiled. "You think I would miss it?"

*　　*　　*

Snow Lion felt a thrill of anticipation as she bridled him, but of course put no saddle on his back. For almost four years now he and his friend had been inseparable. He had been with her through most of her encounters with the Dark One's and had proved as trustworthy, reliable and brave as any human companion. He had learned to read her every mood, just as she could read his. He was certainly pleased to see her—he always looked forward to his rides with her. They were not so much rider and steed, they were like a single entity as they galloped through the forests. The feel of her legs gripping his muscular body without the impediment of a saddle only heightened the pure joy he felt whenever he was with her.

He sensed mixed feelings coming from her. The exhilarating anticipation of the ride, but also there was a dark, somber side to this mood. Still, he whinnied with wild abandon and shook his magnificent golden main as she leapt onto his back and spurred him on. While he was on the even, first part of the trail he couldn't resist galloping. He would have to walk most of the way up, but for now she left him free to indulge himself. He felt the shock of her sudden excitement as she whooped for joy.

*　　*　　*

"Snow Lion, you're the best," she shouted against the wind in her face.

They soon reached the heavily wooded area and began the fourteen-kilometer climb up to the Little Water trailhead. She had not had much opportunity to explore the canyon since they moved to Salt Lake. In fact at the higher elevations it would be still snow covered. Still, the river valley that ran eastward from the trailhead was absolutely beautiful. Lush green forests boasted their new spring foliage. Perfumed wild flowers grew with opulent abandon along the riverside. Animals filled with the excitement of new life scurried busily about.

It would take her about two hours to get there which should give her a plenty of time on her own to do what she had to do. She passed a young couple. They seemed very much in love as they laughed, clinging to each other far more than the relatively easy hike required. They smiled and waved as Snow Lion carefully made his way around them. A little further ahead was another couple, maybe in their eighties. They were walking a lot slower, but seemed to be just as much in love as their younger counterparts. A yappy dog ran circles around them, clearly devoted to his elderly friends. Shaylae smiled, a warm cozy feeling filling her breathing soul. This is how she saw herself and Micah in sixty years or so. This is what it's all about. This is what makes life worthwhile; love, family, the beauty of nature, the river, sky, and Father Sun, all filled with the Holy Wind, all bringing life to the universe.

She led Snow Lion out of the woods into the parking lot at Little Water. She had not met any other people on her ride. That was fine with her; she didn't want to be disturbed. She rode a little further east, perhaps another kilometer or so. The trail up to Dog Lake took a southward turn up the ridge, but she continued along the creek, not a very large creek by any means, but still flowing fast and furious from the winter runoff. A little further along she turned northward, crossing the creek until she found a secluded spot. She brought Snow Lion to a halt and jumped off his back. There would be no need to tether him; he wouldn't go far from his beloved friend.

She had not been to this particular spot before. It was magnificent. Behind her she could still hear the restful sounds of the creek rushing over its rocky bed. The ridge rose sharply to the south, beautifully covered with pine trees. Ahead of her to the north the slope was gentler, with not a pine tree in sight, only aspens, hundreds of them.

She knelt down, bowed to the east and touched her forehead to the earth. She sang her morning prayer toward Father Sun, asking the Holy Ones to guide her. She stood and went through the age-old ritual motions to greet her ancestors. Even though she was on her own, she knew she would never be alone, the Blessed Ancestors were always with her; White Cloud had promised her he would never leave her.

"I call upon the power of the People," she spoke slowly and gently as she drew her hands to her face. "I call upon the power in all living things," again drawing her hands to her face. "I call upon the power from the Blessed Ancestors, and I call upon the power of the Holy Ones."

She sat down again, cross-legged on the ground, her hands on her knees, palms up. She closed her eyes and raised her head. "Holy Ones, Father and Mother, Creators of the Universe, source of all knowledge, power and goodness. You showed me how to free my spirit from my body without passing over. Once before I have done this. I would do so again that I may visit the home of the Dark Ones."

A strange detached feeling came over her. She could still feel her heart beating in her chest, as it rose and fell with each breath she took, but she felt an incredible lightness. She opened her eyes and looked down on her body. "Watch over me Snow Lion." He looked up from his grazing, seeming to be a little puzzled. She smiled. He would never leave her.

She was about to make the shift when she had another idea. In an instant she was at the foot of El Huerfano. The place where Changing Woman had first come to Earth; the place where she had first met Ayanna and Micah; the place she had celebrated her own Kinaalda. There was Micah performing his daily ritual—katas of the Chulukua-Ryu. Oh how beautiful he was, how handsome, how gentle and kind, yet so strong and brave. Oh, how she loved him. "Tonight my love; tonight we will be together." He stopped suddenly and looked around, but he saw and heard nothing. She saw a smile break out on his handsome face. She came close to him and kissed his cheek. He blinked, and then slowly drew his hand across the spot she had kissed. "Tonight my love," she repeated, and then she was gone.

She turned her mind to Procyon. She faced eastward. Although not visible in the bright sunlight, almost directly below Father Sun, fifteen degrees above the horizon was the star Procyon. She gasped involuntarily as she was suddenly above its sixth planet. How beautiful it looked from space. The huge northern polar icecap, twice as large as Earth's and the much smaller southern icecap gave the planet a jewel-like appearance. She was surprised to see a large moon, about the size of Earth's moon, at about the same distance. Now, that can't be a coincidence she thought.

She knew that what she was looking for was on the large central continent, but she first had to investigate the eastern continent. It was there where she had first witnessed the cruelty of the Dark Ones to their own people. She entered what appeared to be a mining town. It was late afternoon and workers were leaving the mine, preparing to return to their homes. They were smiling and joking one with another. She was totally dumfounded. The last time she had visited all she had seen was poverty, despair, hopelessness, sickness, and deprivation. She followed one of the miners home, a young man perhaps in his early twenties. As he entered his meager home his young wife and little girl greeted him warmly. Inside she saw that it was not lavishly furnished by any means, but it was clean and well-kept by people who were proud of what they had.

How could this be? How could things have changed so much in such a short period of time? Perhaps this was not the place she had first visited. Perhaps it had been an isolated village, and the scene on which she looked now represented life on Yurob, but everywhere she went similar scenes greeted her. How could she have been so wrong? She returned to the first village, and uneasily entered the mind of the young wife. There she found the beginnings of an answer. For almost four years now things had been changing. The people were no longer treated as slaves. Their children were educated, their sick were healed, and their young men and women were no longer at risk of being violated by the ruling classes. Best of all, there were none of the miners who were sick with the awful lung disease. The young wife wasn't sure what had brought this change, but she welcomed it with eager happiness.

As Shaylae peered deeper into the woman's mind she saw the propaganda that had started about the same time as the reforms. The common people were being constantly bombarded with stories of Asdzáán Nádleehé. They were told how she had almost destroyed their world, and how she had been reincarnated and was determined to return and complete the destruction.

In the woman's heart though she felt no hatred, only skepticism. The things that filled her mind were thoughts of her family, her devoted husband, and lovely child. She found it hard to believe all that she was being told; she found it hard to relate to something so far and so distant from her daily life.

Shaylae reached out once more with her mind to the ruling classes here on the eastern continent. She reeled as she found the same terrifyingly dark, soulless minds. This was something she would never get used to, yet now they seemed to lack the strength, confidence, and bravado she had previously found there. They had bitterly acquiesced to the demands of the central government, and now their hatred was focused in two directions; toward the people who they no longer could control as they might, and to the government who had mandated these changes.

She must go now to the central continent, to the palace, to discover who and what had brought about such changes. There she found the First Prophet. He would be a good place to start looking for answers. But as she looked into his mind all she found was a broken old man. He still had a dark soul, but now his every thought was filled with fear. Once he had been ruler of an empire, now he was a puppet, but a puppet to whom? Once he had thought of himself as a reincarnation of The First Prophet, but now she found he had lost that faith. Once he had thought of himself as the most powerful man in the empire, but now he felt impotent, powerless. No, this definitely was not the man she was looking for.

She searched the palace and found other members of the Quorum and the Council and while not as morally defeated as First Prophet, they were nevertheless subdued. They had a new leader, a new Second. Hauron was his name. She was amazed to learn that he had once been a slave. He had to be the cause of all of this upheaval. As she was about to leave, to find this Hauron, one of the older members of the Quorum caught her eye. She could sense the evil in his mind but his thoughts were closed to her. How could this be? He was not First Prophet; he was not even Second. She had not felt this unnerved by a Dark One before. She quickly gathered her composure and searched for the mind of this Hauron. She found him in a small windowless room, guarded by two heavily armed soldiers.

As she entered the room she was surprised to discover he was quite young, perhaps in his early twenties. His hair was not blonde, and his eyes were not blue. He had brown hair, the same lifeless mousy color that many white Americans had, and his eyes were grayish brown. His mind was certainly not dark either. His breathing soul was alive and strong, although she did sense uncertainty and guilt in his thoughts.

Carefully she probed his memories and learned how he had lived back in the small mining town he had come from. She was very confused to learn how he had been discovered. He had tremendous powers of perception and somehow he had seen her, right from the very beginning. How could this be? He had watched her from her first encounter with the Dark Ones to the final battle aboard Revenge. Was his power greater than hers? The ruling councils had sensed this display of power and had brought him to the Palace.

Through his thoughts she relived the terrifying battle he had to come to power, and watched as he began to reconstruct his society. She wondered if his power was enough to counteract the feelings and resentment of the others in the ruling classes. She was particularly concerned about the older man whose thoughts she was not able to read.

But, she had to be optimistic. Maybe this is the way the Holy Ones wanted it. It seemed only right that it should be one of their own people who could right three thousand years of wrongs. And perhaps now that this Hauron was in power her mission would not be needed, she would not be needed. Perhaps by the time Reconciliation arrived, these people would welcome them with open arms. For a moment she was elated. For a moment she saw her life return to normal. She would be able to finish school and college. She would be able to marry Micah and have a family of her own and . . .

"Well, witch, aren't you going to say anything?"

Had her ears deceived her? This could not be! Did he know she was in the room? How? And he had called her "witch"?

"You can't hide from me you know. You might as well reveal yourself."

Not knowing exactly how she did it, she instinctively brought an ethereal form to her spirit. She looked down at her body, or the spiritual manifestation of her body. She was transparent. I'm a ghost, she thought.

"There, now that wasn't hard was it?"

"My name is Shaylae of the Gentle Heart," she said, somewhat nervously.

"You are Asdzáán Nádleehé, the enemy of my people, and of our gods."

Realizing the futility of arguing she moved on. "Hauron, you have done wonderful things for the lives of your people."

"And why would you care, witch?"

"The last time I was here things were quite different."

"Yes, a sun-cycle ago you came. You were in the main hall. I felt your presence. Lie all you want, witch, I will not be swayed. You are Asdzáán Nádleehé and you are determined to destroy us all."

"Hauron, how do you know such things?"

"The First Prophet sensed you when you nearly destroyed our world seven hundred and fifty sun-cycles ago. He prophesied that you would return to complete what you began then. Every First Prophet since then has been his reincarnation, and has reinforced our vow to destroy you and your world."

"So, your First Prophet is a reincarnation of The First Prophet?" Hauron said nothing, so she continued. "You have your doubts I see."

"None," he shot back loudly but without conviction.

"Then, why am I not talking to him?"

"I am his Second. He is too busy to . . ."

"To do what? He is a broken old man. He has no fire in him."

Now Hauron was on the defensive. He spoke unsurely. "He is old, but he is not broken. He . . ."

"He is scared, terrified of you, Hauron." Again Hauron was silent, but she could sense fury behind his eyes. "You may not admit it, even to yourself, but you do not believe he is the reincarnation of The First Prophet." Another pause. "And if he is not the reincarnation of The First Prophet, then you have to accept the possibility that I am not the reincarnation of Asdzáán Nádleehé."

"No!" he thundered at the top of his voice. "No! Everything I have believed since I was a boy has taught me that you are an intelligent, cunning liar. You twist things and sow the seeds of doubt. You speak in half-truths. You are able to disguise the truth as lies, and lies as truth. You are evil, and yet you present this façade of reason. I will not turn my back on my people and let you use this advantage to destroy us."

"Hauron, I have no desire to destroy you. The only reason I would have had to return is now gone."

"And what reason is that?"

"The last time I was here I saw things that were depraved beyond belief. Your young women . . . In this very hall." She gestured behind her to the large hall.

"I know, and now that has all stopped. Within two sun-cycles all of our people will be free. But what has that got to do with you?"

"I felt I had a mission, to help . . ."

"You felt you had a mission! How condescending is that? You had a mission to help us from ourselves did you? And who gave you that mission? You are a liar and a witch! And even if I believed you, as you can see, we do not need your help."

"You think you can control the resentment of the Dark Ones in the Quorum and the Council?"

"What do you mean, 'Dark Ones'?"

"People whose minds have no compassion, no feelings. And not just the Assembly of Rulers, all of the ruling classes have Dark Minds, no soul, they are filled with Rolling Darkness."

"Do not speak of our god that way, blasphemer!"

"He is your god? Hauron, how can that be? He represents all that is evil. That is why your ruling classes are so depraved. That is why they have no soul."

Hauron seemed to stop and think about this. Then he said, "Regardless, I have defeated them all before when I took power. I can defeat them again."

"What about this man?" She put a picture into his mind of the man she had not been able to read.

"What? Denab?" he laughed. "You are mad. Denab is my greatest ally."

"I think not. He is the only man on this planet I cannot read, but I did sense his soul and it is the darkest of all."

"Nonsense. Besides, if he has power then why did he not use it to help the previous Second destroy me?"

"I have no idea, but he must have felt your coming to power was to his advantage. Perhaps he sees himself as First Prophet."

"No, you're doing it again. Your lies will not turn me away from my duty."

"It matters not. You will not see me again Hauron of the Eleven. There is no need for me to return."

"You lie. It has always been your intent to return and destroy us. And now you see we are united as a people. I will not rest, we will not rest until you are destroyed; you and all of your people."

This was not expected. Shaylae was put right back on the offensive. "Do not threaten me, Hauron," she shouted, authority ringing from her voice. "Do not threaten my people or you will answer to the wrath of Yanaba!" She reached out her hand and Hauron fell to the floor, gasping for breath. She felt his weak resistance, but it was nothing she could not handle with ease.

"So, now we see your true form," he gasped, holding his chest. "The reasonable has been replaced by the vengeful."

Shaylae instantly regretted her outburst. She released him. "I will leave you now, Hauron of the Eleven, and wish you success in your worthy endeavors, but once again, I warn you, do not attempt to send your people near my world again."

She prepared to leave. And then added "One final thing you should know Hauron. Earth is not the home world of the People. Asdzáán Nádleehé came to earth to hide from your people three thousand years ago, leaving her own world behind her."

* * *

It took Hauron a few moments before he could breathe normally again. He had not expected her to have the power she had shown. His own power paled in comparison. She could have killed him easily, but why didn't she?

"Sigmun, come to me."

The seeds of doubt that had haunted him lately were growing. In spite of her outburst he had received the distinct impression that she was not evil at all, and that her intentions were just and honorable. But still, the nagging in his mind reminded him of the consequences of underestimating her—the future survival of his people depended on his correct assessment of the danger she represented.

"Hauron, you called?"

"Yes, Sigmun. Come, sit by me."

"Hauron, are you alright. You look like you've seen a ghost."

Hauron laughed at the irony of that statement, then quickly related all that had happened, all that she had said, and the doubts it had raised in his own mind. Sigmun stopped for a moment, deep in thought.

"She called the Quorum and the Council 'Dark Ones'?" he said finally.

"Yes. Interesting. What do you think she meant by that?"

"No soul? It makes sense if you think about it. I mean, could you or I have done the things they used to do, with no sense of remorse or pity?"

"Well, I just put it down to the way they were brought up; that they never knew any better."

Sigmun shrugged. "I don't know. I think her explanation makes more sense. And that's another thing. If she's right, then how is it that you are the exception? Why were you selected for the Council if you are not one of these 'Dark Ones'?"

"I've always wondered about that, and to be honest have never been able to figure it out. Denab told me . . ."

"Denab selected you for the Council?"

"Yes."

"She said he was the darkest of all. Why would he have selected you if what she said is true?"

"What Denab said when he interviewed me was that they needed more balance in the Council. I had supposed that there would be others like me, but I think not."

"So, if what she said about him is true, there must be a motive beyond that. There has to be something else behind his choosing you."

Sigmun shrugged again. "But what?"

"I don't know. But I'm going to find out. If she's right, it may be a clue to what he has in mind."

"Getting back to this . . . Shaylae, is that what she calls herself?" Hauron nodded. "So, do you think she was telling the truth?"

"I don't know. But I don't think I have to decide right now. She will be back."

"Even though she said she would never return?"

"Oh yes; she'll be back."

CHAPTER 12

It took a moment for her to get her bearings. She was disorientated. Someone had covered her in a warm blanket, which was a good thing since she could feel that the air was really cold air as she breathed deeply. Her left leg was aching, throbbing. She should have kept it warmer. It was constantly playing up since her encounter with Second aboard Tregon's shuttle.

Sitting directly facing her was Micah. He had fallen asleep, head bent forward resting on his chest. Lying next to him was Ayanna, also fast asleep. They must have come looking for her when she didn't show up. How long had she been gone? Micah would have been watching over her. She wouldn't wake him just yet. She didn't want him to feel badly that he had fallen asleep during his watch. She lay back down and sent a quick hello to Snow Lion. He whinnied with joy to feel her spirit return.

"What the . . ." said Micah as his head snapped back, suddenly roused to wakefulness. "Oh, it's only you, Snow." He shook his head to clear his mind.

That was Shaylae's cue. She stirred and shifted position, letting out a small sigh.

"Shaylae! Are you awake, Shay?"

"Oh, Micah, it's you. What are you doing here?" she said as she sat up, rubbing her eyes.

He immediately reached for her and held her in a warm embrace. "Shay, what happened? We were so worried."

"What time is it?"

"It's 3 am."

"Oh, I'm so sorry, Micah. I wasn't supposed to be gone that long." She squeezed him really hard.

"Shay!" Ayanna sat up and hugged her. "Oh, Shay, what happened?" And then added angrily, "Don't ever do this again. Don't ever scare us like this again."

"I had no idea I had been gone for so long. It only felt like a few hours."

"Gone? Gone where? You've been right here all the time."

"My spirit traveled to Yurob."

"What?"

"How?"

"Remember when I was in the gel chamber on Tregon's shuttle." They both nodded. "When I stopped screaming, it was because my spirit had left my body."

"You mean you died? You really did die?"

"No," she said with a reassuring shake of her head. "The Holy Ones said I had the power to leave my body without passing over to the land of the dead. That's how I was able to heal myself so I could make the shift back to Sandia Park."

"And you did it again?"

"Yes, I had to go. Something really big has been happening there and I had to find out what it was."

"But Shay, what if something had happened to your body when you were gone? I mean, you could have frozen up here. Then what?"

She was suddenly filled with guilt and remorse. They were right. What she had done had been reckless. Without her friends she night have died. "Oh, I'm so sorry. I shouldn't have done anything without you. You are my eternal companions and I left you out."

"Shay, it's OK. Don't cry," said Micah, kissing away the tears from her cheeks. "Just promise us you'll never do anything like this again."

"OK, so tell us what happened?" said Ayanna.

She brightened a little. "Oh, you're not going to believe it. There's a new leader, a new Second actually, but he's the one with all the power." Shaylae related everything she had seen and heard, every word of her conversation with Hauron. "I think he wants to believe me, but for some reason he's afraid to trust me," she finished.

"From what you said, he dare not trust you," said Micah. "Look at it from his point of view. All his life he's been taught that you, as Asdzáán Nádleehé, are the most evil person in the universe. What reason does he have to trust you? What if he did, and you then destroyed his world once he had let his guard down."

"But I would never do such a thing," said Shaylae superfluously.

"Of course not, but he doesn't know that. What cause have you given him to trust you?"

"What could I do to make him trust me?"

"You told him you were never going back," said Ayanna thoughtfully. Shaylae nodded. "But are you?"

"I have to, Anna."

"Then take us with you."

"Oh, I couldn't. I wouldn't. You would be in terrible danger."

"Exactly," said Micah, understanding what Ayanna was getting at. "You are going to have to give him something Shay. From what you said, he knows that there's no risk to you when you go. You have to do something that he knows would be a risk."

"But if anything happened to you."

"Perhaps, but when he sees that you are willing to put our lives on the line."

"Micah, Ayanna, I couldn't." Shaylae sounded horrified.

"Hear me out, Shay."

"No, I won't do it. I couldn't do it."

"Then the war continues," said Ayanna.

Micah nodded his head. "She's right, Shay. This war could carry on for another three thousand years. And you won't be here to stop it then."

"And Hauron won't be here either. You and he must have come together at the same time for a purpose. Who knows if this chance will ever come again. It has to end here, Shay."

"No! I can't and I won't. That's final."

"But, Shay . . ."

"Please, not another word, Anna."

It was a somber group that made their way back to the hover car.

"Let's go celebrate Father Sun," said Shaylae, sounding somewhat deflated. Ayanna and Micah nodded, but no one felt like celebrating anything at the moment.

CHAPTER 13

June the twentieth. Exactly four years had passed since Shaylae had first come to El Huerfano to celebrate with the Todich'ii'nii the ceremony of long day. Four years later, and once again she and Ayanna were helping to prepare the evening banquet. Their mood had lightened since they had left Mill Creek and not another word had been said about going back to Yurob. This was a time to celebrate. This was a time to renew their connections to Father Sun, Mother Earth and all the wondrous gifts of nature the Holy Ones had provided for them.

The Todich'ii'nii were a remarkable group of people. They represented just about every walk of life, every profession, every trade, and every artistic and creative skill, yet here they were all brothers and sisters. Shaylae loved being here. Until her first celebration with them she had not really given a second thought to her Navajo heritage, but now she was so connected to the People and her ancestors that she could hardly imagine how she had ever existed without it.

The next two days were wonderful. Shaylae felt so happy and carefree, even though she knew that it would not, could not last. But for now, she put all thoughts of the Dark Ones, Yurob, and Hauron of the Eleven behind her.

On the evening of the twenty-first, as the celebrations drew to a close she sat with Micah and Ayanna, looking westward toward the setting sun. It was an amazing sight, but it had been more beautiful four years ago when she had enjoyed it with White Cloud and Nana Lucero, and now they were both gone to join the blessed ancestors. Still, to be here with Micah and Ayanna was a great blessing.

A few minutes after eight thirty the bell rang, signifying the setting of Father Sun, and the fire was lit. For a while no one said anything. For thirty minutes they just reveled in the sight of the sky changing color from pink, to violet, to deep blue.

Micah grabbed Shaylae's hand. "Let's go dance."

"Just a minute," she said as a tear formed in her eye. "Four years ago I wanted to join you but White Cloud held me back." She pointed to a spot just above where Father Sun had set. "There's my star sign, Pollux and Castor,"

"And there's Venus," said Ayanna, pointing up at the brightest object in the sky.

"She was right there when White Cloud told me about Procyon," she said, pointing to the horizon. "And there's Procyon now," she added, pointing to the left, "just above the horizon. Right where he was this time four years ago."

Micah and Ayanna looked at each other but said nothing.

Shaylae continued staring at Procyon. "I've thought about it, and I've decided that you're right. We all need to go there." She turned to look at them. "But I'm going out of my mind with worry. If anything happens to you I'll never forgive myself."

"Shaylae, I'm sure Hauron will come round. From what you've told us I have to believe it."

"It's not him I'm worried about, it's Denab. He's still a closed book to me, a black hole."

"You really think he's a threat to Hauron, and to you?"

"Oh yes. His mind is as dark as any of the Dark Ones I've ever encountered."

"So what can you do?" asked Ayanna.

"You can't do anything until you've got Hauron's trust," said Micah. "And the only way you're going to get it is to take us there with you."

Shaylae leaned over toward Micah and put her arm around him, tears in her eyes. "I know, but I'm so scared."

"Perhaps the fate of three worlds rests on what we do now, at this very moment, Shay. Throughout history people have put their lives on the line for higher causes, and sometimes they have lost them. But remember this, we are willing to risk our lives, and if we die, we still have the rest of eternity to be together."

"I know, but how will I live the rest of my life if you're not in it?"

"I don't know, Shay, but we have to do this. You know that?"

She nodded sadly, and snuggled up closer to him.

CHAPTER 14

June 21, 2108

Sigmun was quite worried. Hauron had asked him a question he probably should have asked himself a long time ago—why had Denab picked him for the Council of One Hundred? He had appointed him four years ago, before Hauron even came to the palace, so it couldn't possibly have had anything to do with Hauron, could it? That would have meant Denab's plans were conceived long ago? But try as he might, he could not come up with an answer.

Growing up he had been a pretty normal kid, or at least he had thought so at the time. Sure, he was always the head of his class in just about every subject, from physical to artistic, from scientific to engineering; every subject but one—the powers of the mind. There were other boys in his classes who had the gift, but never him. So when Denab himself had come to the school to interview him a few eyebrows were raised, especially from the parents of those who had shown aptitude for The Power. He was probably the most surprised of all, but Denab had been so convincing.

"Sigmun, my boy," he had said, "there's room for someone of your talents on the Council. Bright, articulate, sense of humor—we need more humor in the Assembly." He had smiled, and it had seemed odd to him at the time, that smile, it didn't seem quite right. But,

Denab had been quite persuasive. "Not everyone in the Assembly has The Power you know. Besides, there is a lot more to running the government than just being able to control the minds of others. Anyway, it'll probably come to you." He had patted him on the shoulder in a friendly, almost paternal gesture, but it had lacked warmth.

Now, the doubts had resurfaced, stronger than ever before. The more Sigmun thought about it, the more he wondered if Denab had seen the closeness he would have to Hauron. Was he there as a plant to undermine Hauron? The implications of such an idea were frightening. It would mean that Denab had more power than Hauron, and not only that, he had managed to conceal that from him. And, could he really see the future? He must. He had watched as Hauron had come to power, let him defeat Second, let him control and even change the empire, and still he waited. For what?

But was he just being paranoid? No, he had a strong intuitive feeling that this was the truth. After all, this Shaylae who so easily controlled Hauron hadn't been able to penetrate Denab's shell. She was sure that Denab was Hauron's real enemy. Even if she really was the witch Asdzáán Nádleehé, the fact that she had singled Denab out like that had to be significant.

He had to talk this over with Hauron. He made his way to his meditation room, certain he would find him there. But when he got there, the room was empty. He went back to Hauron's apartment, not sure if he should disturb him at home, but he really did think this was important. The door was guarded, Cerid of course. He had become more than dedicated to Hauron, and seemed to take more of the watches than any of the other guards, even though he was their captain. He refused to let him even ring the bell.

"Sorry, Sigmun, he gave strict instructions he was not to be disturbed."

Sigmun held up his hands and smiled. "No problem, Cerid. See you later."

He was about to walk away, when the door opened. Hauron was smiling, and looked more relaxed than he had ever seen him.

"You can let Sigmun in, Cerid, but no one else," said Hauron putting his arm around Sigmun's shoulder and leading him into the huge sunken living room. There were two well-equipped game consoles in the middle of the room. Hauron must have been using one of them, Kazzy sat in the other, and behind her sat Jerrod.

"Hiya, Sig," said Kazzy running up to him and hugging him, followed closely by Jerrod. Sigmun loved Hauron's family; he almost felt they had adopted him.

"C'mon, Hau," said Jerrod. "Do it again. It's fun."

"You want to play, Sig?" said Hauron. Sigmun shrugged, and was about to confess to not being very skilled at vid-games, but Hauron was insistent. "You'll hurt Kazzy's feelings if you don't. She wrote this game."

"Sure. Why not. But I'm sure I'll be pretty hopeless."

"Don't be silly," said Kazzy, grabbing his arm and sitting him at the control console. "This controls yaw, this one pitch," she said indicating two joysticks. "These buttons control your lasers, these your grav fields." She pointed to the pedals at his feet. "These control your thrusters, forward, reverse." She handed him a helmet and placed hers on her head. "Ready?"

"Whoa! What exactly am I doing?"

"Oh, right. I guess you need to know that." Kazzy took off her helmet again; she was smiling uncontrollably, obviously very proud of what she had done. "You're in a small fighter making your way through an asteroid field. You can either avoid them, or vaporize them." Sigmun nodded, that didn't sound too hard. "If you vaporize a space-mine though, you'd better be ten klicks from it, else . . . well, you know." OK, so it was getting more complicated. "The enemy fighters will show up red. You have to use the grav-fields on them, lasers can't touch them," she said, indicating another set of controls. "We will show up blue. Don't shoot me, or crash into me or we're both out of the game." She laughed.

She put her helmet on and Jerrod followed suit. Sigmun noticed that Hauron had a smirk on his face—he wasn't expecting him to do very well against his sister. Sigmun put his helmet on, and was immediately transported into a virtual world, that didn't look at all virtual. He was in the cockpit of a small craft with an almost three hundred and sixty degree view of space. Below him was his home planet. It was a beautiful, marvelous sight. His craft was stationary, and directly ahead he could see the asteroid field. A blue fighter was already making its way toward it. He touched the pedal gently, but the fighter lurched forward. Probably takes some getting used to he thought. The sensation of motion was so real that he felt slightly nauseous. Ahead of him he could see the blasts from Kazzy's fighter and the puffs of debris from the vaporized asteroids.

Now, he was getting close to the asteroid field. He tentatively edged the yaw joystick very gently to the left. His craft banked left. He pulled the pitch joystick back slowly and his craft pulled up. Involuntarily he gasped at the thrill of flying in deep space. He turned toward a large asteroid and when it was directly ahead of him he hit the laser. He saw the beam of light shoot out and narrowly miss the target. He adjusted the yaw and fired again. This time the asteroid disappeared in a huge spherical cloud. He shouted so enthusiastically that he hadn't realized that his fighter had plowed right on through the cloud, dangerously close to another asteroid. He instinctively yanked at the yaw control, and immediately went into an uncontrollable sickening spin, and crashed, full speed into the other asteroid. The view went black, and a red "Game Over" sign flashed before his eyes.

"Holy Darkness," he exclaimed breathlessly. "That was incredible. How do you create the sensation of spinning like that Kazzy?" He took off the helmet.

Directly in front of him were three newcomers. Beautiful, dark skinned newcomers, two young women and a man. There was not a sound in the apartment. "It felt so real . . ." he finished lamely, breaking the silence.

"There's a low-frequency feedback mechanism in the helmet that connects with your inner ear," said Kazzy slowly, sounding quite detached, not paying attention to him, and looking directly into the eyes of the newcomers.

"I am Shaylae of the Gentle Heart," said the one in the middle.

"I am Micah Hale," said the one on the left.

"I am Ayanna Lapahie," said the one on the right. Sigmun felt a stirring within him. She was beautiful.

Hauron walked carefully over to Kazzy and Jerrod, and helped them out from the game console. "You two—you can go watch a vid. Off you go."

"Aw, Hau, can't we stay?" pleaded Kazzy.

"No, now blast."

A somewhat subdued and reluctant Kazzy took her younger brother by the hand and led him back along the wide corridor, and into another room.

"You have a beautiful family, Hauron."

"Sigmun, this is the witch Asdzáán Nádleehé," he said, ignoring Shaylae's comment with a disdainful wave of his hand. "And two of her accomplices, no doubt."

Sigmun stood up, and bravely walked over to her. She was a head shorter than him. He looked into her eyes, beautiful blue eyes. He looked at the girl next to her. She was a little taller, and had fire in her dark brown eyes. A fighter, he noted, and beautiful; more beautiful than any other girl he had ever met. His heart raced. The boy was about his height and he too was a fighter. And though Sigmun had no powers of the mind, he could sense their intrinsic goodness and honesty.

He shook his head. "No she's not," he said turning back to Hauron.

"Sigmun, how dare you . . ."

"Hauron, look at her," he interrupted. He turned back to Shaylae, and couldn't help notice a look of genuine surprise in her eyes. He smiled reassuringly at her.

"Sigmun, you would question me?"

"As you said, Hauron, when we're alone I can say what I feel, what I think. And for what it's worth, I've said my piece. Ignore it if you like, but she's not Asdzáán Nádleehé."

Shaylae spoke up. "Hauron, please forgive this intrusion, but I had to return." She held her hand out to Sigmun. "Perhaps you could introduce us to your friend."

Hauron was clearly quite disoriented by this sudden change of events. "Sigmun. He's my only friend in the Quorum, the whole Assembly for that matter."

"Pleased to meet you, Shaylae. And you, Micah, and Ayanna." He bowed to each as he spoke their names.

"You're in the Quorum?" Shaylae sounded quite surprised.

Sigmun looked at Hauron with an upraised eyebrow. "Yes," he said.

"How can that be? I hate to be the one to break this to you, Sigmun, but you seem to be lacking the two basic requirements."

Sigmun laughed at Shaylae's good-natured sarcasm.

"And those would be?" said Hauron, rotating his hand indicating her to continue.

"Well, first, like you, Hauron, his breathing soul is strong, vibrant, good, and alive. But unlike you he seems to be devoid of . . ."

"Of The Power," finished off Sigmun with a smile.

"Well, yes. Exactly."

Sigmun laughed again. "Hauron and I were just talking about that yesterday. We can't figure out why I would have been invited to join the Council almost two years ago." He turned to Hauron, "In fact, that's why I came to see you, Hauron. The only reason I can figure out why Denab would have called me is to get to you, Hauron."

"Denab called you into the Assembly?" said Shaylae. She sounded a little disturbed by this news.

Sigmun nodded. "Yes."

"Hauron, I agree with Sigmun. Somehow Denab is using him, or will use him, to get to you."

"That's ridiculous. Anyway, you made a huge mistake coming here. And now I will have you all arrested." He raised his wrist to his mouth and spoke into the small console. "I want twenty guards and the full Quorum in my apartment, now," he spoke with authority.

"Shouldn't we just talk first, Hauron?" said Sigmun franticly, but Hauron seemed not to hear him. Instead he was tapping his wrist computer.

"It's dead," he said.

"Not dead, Hauron. We're all in a quantum space-time shift. For the moment there will be no communication with your people."

Sigmun felt a wave of relief; she was quite the resourceful girl this Shaylae. He looked again at Ayanna. His heart just wouldn't stop beating.

"So, now what will you do? Dispose of us?"

"Oh, of course not, Hauron!" she said with compassion. "Don't you know that I could have destroyed your planet without leaving Earth? Why would I come here if my intention was to destroy you?"

"Clearly you have some sort of trick up your sleeve."

"Hauron, why would she?" said Sigmun. It was so obvious to Sigmun that Shaylae was not in the least evil. Why couldn't Hauron see it?

"Last time I came to you I came to you in spirit. This time I have come to you in body, and I have brought with me the two people I love the most. Why would I risk their lives? Why would I have brought them if my intention were to trick you? They have very little power; you could easily overpower them."

Hauron said nothing. Sigmun couldn't tell what he was thinking. Was he was ready to trust Shaylae?

"With your permission Hauron, I would communicate with you directly. Mind to mind. Soul to soul."

"No. You expect me to trust you?"

"Hauron, I give you my word I will not trick you. I give you my word on the lives of my friends."

"On the lives of your friends?" Hauron thought for a moment. "Very well, then return to your home world, but leave your friends here."

"I . . . I . . . couldn't." Shaylae was clearly taken aback by the suggestion.

"Then all three of you, leave," he said with a disdainful wave of his hand. "I will hear no more from you."

"No, Shay. It's OK. I will stay," said Ayanna.

"If that's what it takes, then I too will stay," said Micah.

Oh yes, please stay; let them stay, Shaylae, thought Sigmun.

"No, I couldn't let you." Shaylae was still clearly disturbed.

Ayanna took Shaylae by the hand and looked into her eyes. "Shay, you know that we would do anything for you. Anything to help set right what was done all those years ago. This is our chance, please let us take it."

Micah nodded his head in agreement.

"I give you my word that no harm will come to them, even if you are Asdzáán Nádleehé."

"Hauron, it's not you I am worried about. What will Denab do when he realizes you have two of Asdzáán Nádleehé's friends here?"

"I will protect them."

"I'm not sure you realize what you're up against."

"We've had this conversation before."

"Hauron, you say you saw me defeat every other Dark One I have come up against."

Hauron nodded.

"And each one of them, I was able to sense their feelings and their thoughts. But this Denab, his mind is closed to me."

"It doesn't prove anything. Even if what you say is true, he may just be a lot more powerful than I have supposed, more powerful than you. It doesn't make him my enemy."

"Yes, but if you will just let me show you . . ."

"No! Enough! I cannot let you do that, I told you I'm not yet prepared to trust you. Either leave your friends here, or all three of you leave! Now! These are the only choices I will agree to." He finished up with a wave of his hand, turning his back on her.

Shaylae seemed at a loss. Sigmun felt sorry for her, it was not an easy choice. She obviously cared for her friends, yet at the same time she wanted to do whatever she had to do to gain Hauron's trust.

"You said 'on the lives of your friends'. It was an empty statement. You are unwilling to risk their lives, even though they are quite prepared to do so." He turned to face her once again. "What am I supposed to think of your words?"

"Hauron," she said desperately. "I told you. It's not you, it's Denab. I have no idea what he is capable of. I have no idea how much he knows already. I mean, if Sigmun and I are right about him putting him here as a plant then he is already way ahead of us."

"Is there any way you can protect them from him?"

"I don't think so."

"What if they were on a different continent? My home. What if the four of us went there for a few weeks and you went home?"

"I don't know. He still may be able to reach you there."

"Then we are at an impasse?" It was a question, not a statement.

"Shaylae, you must leave us here," said Ayanna. "Everything Asdzáán Nádleehé has suffered, and worked for the past three thousand years could all be for nothing. This may be our only chance to right the wrongs done on three worlds. I am more than willing to do my part" Sigmun couldn't help but admire her bravery.

"Wait!" said Hauron. "So Asdzáán Nádleehé is involved in all of this? And you said 'three worlds'. And as I recall, the first time we met you said that your home world is not the same as hers."

"Yes. But she has been involved ever since that awful time, three thousand years ago. And yes, the world on which she was born is not Earth."

"Really? Please explain."

"It would be easier to show you. I can take you there. You will be able to see exactly what happened."

"No. And do not ask me again! For now, just tell me."

Shaylae looked at her friends questioningly, and then she said, "OK. But later, after I live up to my side of this bargain, then you must let me take you there."

"Agreed."

"Ayanna, would you please relate the story of Asdzáán Nádleehé to Hauron and Sigmun."

"I would be honored." She turned toward them. "Let us sit in a circle," she said, extending her arms. Hauron looked at Sigmun. Sigmun smiled and nodded. Shaylae and Micah sat next to her, and Hauron and Sigmun followed suit, completing the circle. Sigmun could feel her breath as she breathed deeply, closing her eyes. He too breathed deeply, sharing the same air. He was not sure what to expect next. He had never witnessed such a telling before. The girl sitting opposite him was surely the most wonderful, beautiful creature he had ever seen. Everything about her face spoke of her strength and determination. Her eyes were commanding, regal.

"Three thousand years ago, seven hundred and fifty of your sun-cycles, Asdzáán Nádleehé lived on a planet called Tal'el'Dine'h, orbiting a star many light-years from here." Sigmun was almost hypnotized by her voice. It was rich and sensuous. Her eyes and hands, her face and body, moved beautifully, an expressive dance, as she related the story. "The people of Tal'el'Dine'h lived in complete harmony with their world, in complete harmony one with another. They loved their world, and she cared for them, teaching them much about their place in the universe, and in the plan of the Holy Ones.

"Their world changed catastrophically when an interstellar craft took up orbit around her. Emissaries from that craft came to the planet's surface, and announced that the planet now belonged to them. Our elders were at a loss as to what to do. The concept of ownership of their planet, or any part of it was not in their philosophy, or even their vocabulary. After the negotiations failed, the Dark Ones returned to their ship. Two days later Asdzáán Nádleehé, a fourteen-year-old girl watched in horror from a hundred kilometers away as her city was instantly vaporized. Unlike the doomed citizens of her city she had time to prepare before the shock wave hit her and she was able to shift herself out of harm's way. But her anger and fear combined to give her powers she never suspected she had. She was able to shift that enormous interstellar craft twenty light years back to a sub-orbital position fifty kilometers above your planet, at the same time fusing the complete fuel store of hydrogen in an instant."

"You lie!" interrupted Hauron. "No such thing took place. First Prophet never spoke of such a thing." He was angry, indignant.

"He never knew," said Ayanna. "All he could sense was Asdzáán Nádleehé's awesome power and anger. How would he have known the cause of that anger?"

This all was beginning to make sense to Sigmun. "If what you say is true," he said, "then why did Revenge find your people on Earth?"

"After the devastation most of the knowledge of my people was lost. Asdzáán Nádleehé was the only survivor. Her world could no longer support life due to the destruction so Asdzáán Nádleehé transported herself to Earth. We," she said indicating herself, Micah, and Shaylae, "are her descendants. Shaylae in particular is a direct, matrilineal descendant of her."

He walked over to the computer console and pulled up a star map. "Show me this other star system," demanded Hauron.

"I will, but not now," said Shaylae. "Once you have let me communicate with you, mind to mind, and to have shared with you the experiences Ayanna has just related, I will show you, I will take you there."

Hauron thought for a minute. "Agreed," he said finally. "But there still remains the question—will you leave your friends here?"

Sigmun saw the sadness and fear in her eyes as she spoke. "I see I have no choice."

"I swear I will protect them, Shaylae."

Shaylae smiled, as did Sigmund; she wasn't the only one who had noticed that Hauron had called her by her name for the first time.

"Tomorrow I will go to Tal'el'Dine'h to talk with the elders there. It is time. They will be able to help me. How many days will it take to satisfy you of my sincerity?"

He shrugged. "Two to three weeks would be sufficient."

"Very well, Excellency. I will leave them in your care."

"OK, why don't we get you set up in an apartment and let you rest. We can talk again in the morning." He spoke into his wrist console. "Cerid, could you come in please?"

Cerid walked into the apartment and saluted crisply.

"This is Cerid, one of my most loyal guards. This is Shaylae, Ayanna and Micah." They nodded to each other. "Take them to one of the spare apartments and see that they have everything they need."

"Certainly, Excellency" said Cerid.

"And could you give them believable histories, say, from the Eastern Continent. I don't want anyone wondering where they're from."

"Should be no problem, Excellency."

Micah looked at Hauron with a questioning eye.

"Oh, don't worry, Micah. Cerid is captain of my guard, and as loyal to me as it would seem you are to Shaylae. And he is as trusted a friend as Sigmun," said Hauron, adding with a wry grin, "Even though he still won't call me Hauron."

Cerid smiled, and Micah nodded his head, satisfied.

CHAPTER 15

—◦≫✿≪◦—

The living room of their new apartment was huge. Comfortable luxurious furniture was tastefully placed around the room, a thick carpet covered the floor, and paintings in extravagant gilded frames covered the walls. Shaylae could not imagine who would want such luxury, especially since most of the citizens of Yurob lived in abject poverty. But of course, it was probably built for the decadence and avarice of the ruling classes. The far wall was a huge window overlooking the mountains. The view was spectacular.

Micah and Hauron were standing by the window in an animated conversation about hyperspace. Ayanna looked so comfortable, so relaxed, as she chatted to Sigmun. Shaylae was quite jealous, well, not really, but she often wished she could overcome her shyness as easily as Ayanna.

She looked back at Micah and her heart leapt, as it usually did when she thought about him. The first time she had met him she had become instantly infatuated. By the second time she had met him, when he had been practicing his Chulukua-Ryu the next morning, that infatuation had already become love. She had known then that she would spend the rest of eternity with him, although they never spoke of their love for each other for another three months. She loved everything about him, from his stunning good looks, to his physical strength and fighting prowess, and his gentleness and compassion. Where else could a girl hope to find such a combination in a future husband? And even though she knew he had very strong feelings toward her, as a girl, not once had he ever tried to press those feelings upon her. He honored her virtue in a way that never ceased to amaze her. A huge grin spread itself across her face. Micah must have sensed it because he turned to her and smiled.

"Hey, Shay, don't be sitting there on the sidelines," he said beckoning her over. She shook her head. She was quite content to enjoy watching her friends in silence. He walked over to her and sat on the couch, putting his arm around her shoulders.

"What are you thinking about?"

"Oh, just how lucky I am to have such friends."

"You worried?"

She nodded.

"Shay, there's no point. What will happen, will happen. All we can do is face it when it does, one day at a time"

"I know. And I guess there's no turning back now either."

"So we should enjoy these moments as we can."

"And I am," she said.

She leaned up and kissed his cheek. "I have to leave soon."

"Can't you stay a little longer?"

"I guess a little while wouldn't hurt."

"Can we be alone?" he asked.

Since the first time they had kissed they had only been on their own a dozen or so times.

"Sure," she said standing up, her heart pounding in her chest.

He smiled as he stood up and took her hand. Arms around each other they walked toward his bedroom. Out of the corner of her eye she saw Ayanna about to say something, but she must have changed her mind as she shrugged and smiled.

Like the rest of the apartment, Micah's room was huge, another example of over indulgent opulence. He led her to a couch against the wall. As they sat down he put his arm around her and she snuggled up against his shoulder. He gently stroked her hair with one hand and caressed her cheek with the other, brushing his thumb softly against her lips. His touch was electric. Her lips felt so tingly and sensitive as she kissed his thumb.

He leaned his face closer to hers, she raised her head to meet him and their lips joined in a tender kiss. She closed her eyes and almost fainted with the love she felt for him. She could feel his strong arms encircling her, his hands caressing her back, shoulders, neck and hair.

She broke the kiss and held his face. "Oh, Micah, I love you so much. I want this to go on forever."

"It will go on forever. You believe that don't you?"

"I do, but, what if something happens to one of us?"

"We'll be together for eternity. Even if we are separated by death, it won't be forever."

She shuddered at the thought. "I know that," she said. And then she added shyly, "but I want to get to know you now, as only a man and wife can get to know each other."

Micah leaned toward her, hugged her even more tightly. "Oh, so do I," he said, kissing her eyes, her cheeks, her forehead, her ears, stroking her hair gently. "Shaylae," he said, almost a whisper.

"Yes, my love."

He was silent. She sat up and stared him in the eye. She punched him gently in the chest. "What?"

"Oh, it's nothing. You'll think I'm nuts."

"I already think you're nuts. Now tell me, or I'll be forced to punch you again," she said waving her fist menacingly in front of his face.

"It's just . . . I can't believe that you would love me."

She kneeled up on the couch, and took his head between her hands, laughing. "Micah Hale. How can you say that? You would doubt me?"

"It's not that. It's just that I feel I'm so . . . that you're . . . you know . . . so far above me."

She grabbed his ears in her hands, almost roughly, using them to shake his head. "Listen to me, you dolt," she said. "Do you know how often I've had the same thought about you?"

"But that's not possible."

"Of course it is. You are so strong, and not just physically. I've never once heard you express any doubts about who you are, what you should do, or what you believe."

"I have doubts all the time."

"Yes, but it doesn't stop you from being decisive like it does me. Look at how long it took me to make up my mind to bring you here."

"Yes, but . . ."

"'Yes but' nothing! Was there any other possible decision? Of course not," she said, not waiting for him to answer, "and yet it took me days to make it."

"It wasn't an easy decision . . ."

"Look, I'm not going to argue with you. But think back to the first time we soul-shared."

"Back in Sandia Park?"

"Yes. When you saw us all together, you, Ayanna and me, what was the one thing that impressed you the most?"

"Your strength, and power . . ."

"I'll smack you!" she said, interrupting him playfully. "What about Anna?"

"Well, yes, her strength, loyalty, determination. And one thing that surprised me, at first at least, was the compassion she felt for all things. Before that I'd always thought of her as a little bit cynical."

Shaylae laughed. "I know exactly what you mean. What else did you sense though?"

"I felt her honesty and strength, the brilliance and sharpness of her mind of course, her unique sense of humor. And her fighting spirit, she's a warrior princess. But most of all I sensed her dedicated and fierce loyalty to you."

She leaned over and kissed him gently. "You want to know what I saw in you?"

He shrugged and nodded.

"I sensed the incredible strength and courage of an ancient warrior. You have the fiery blood of war chiefs flowing through your veins; I felt it, Micah." She lowered her eyes and her face flushed. "I also saw myself through your eyes and shared the strength of your love and passion for me." She blushed. "I was a little embarrassed at first."

Now it was Micah's turn to be embarrassed. "You saw my desire for you?"

"Remember," she said, poking him in the chest, "that when you're soul-sharing, you can't hide what you feel, or cover it up. Besides, I was more flattered than embarrassed."

"You were?"

"Oh yes. If there had been any doubt in my mind before that, it was gone, forever. I knew than that if I didn't marry you, I would simply die."

She leaned forward and kissed him again.

"Let me ask you another thing? Didn't you feel that when we joined we complimented each other?"

"Yes. It was like three pieces of a puzzle."

"Exactly!" she said triumphantly. "And without all three pieces the puzzle could not be complete? Do you think I could have defeated the Dark Ones on board Revenge on my own?"

"Well . . ."

"I couldn't," she said quickly. "If I hadn't had you and Ayanna by my side, I would be dead now. And who knows what would have happened to Earth? No, Micah, it all happened as it was meant to be, planned by the Holy Ones, who knows how many thousands, millions, of years ago. And that's exactly what it's like between us now. Our love unites us, makes us whole."

"I hear what you are saying," he said, "but I still feel . . ."

She placed her hand over his lips. "Not another word about this. Not one more word, ever. Promise me you will never doubt our love again."

"OK."

"Promise it. Say it."

"I promise you, Shaylae."

They kissed again.

"What was it you said before?" he asked, breaking the kiss.

"Before what? I said a lot."

"Did I hear you say that if you didn't marry me, you would die?"

"I did."

"When," he asked. "How soon can we get married?"

"Oh, I don't know," she said, shrugging her shoulders. "I guess we should wait 'till this is all over. Probably after we finish college. A few years at least, maybe longer."

"I suppose." He sounded a little disappointed. "OK, I guess we should go back and join the others," he said.

"Not just yet. I want you to kiss me some more."

Micah didn't need to be asked twice.

Micah's heart was soaring as they walked back into the living room. He noticed Ayanna mouthing the words 'what happened' to Shaylae. He turned to see Shaylae mouth back 'nothing happened'. The heck it didn't thought Micah, smiling all over his face.

"Well, glad to see you made it back," said Hauron. "We were just about to send a rescue party, weren't we Anna?"

"You look so very happy," said Sigmun. "I have never seen a couple so in love as you two."

Shaylae's eyes misted over. "Well, my dear friends, I really need to get going."

They somberly said their good-byes. Micah reflected sadly that it would be a few weeks before they would be together again.

Shaylae gave a teary-eyed wave as she shifted.

CHAPTER 16

Jun 22-July 12, 2108

An overwhelming feeling of peace filled Shaylae's whole being. She had expected to materialize on the planet Tal'el'Dine'h, but instead found herself in a very unusual place, like nothing else she had experienced. It was void and without form, bright and misty, with a distinct dreamlike quality. Nothing seemed real, not even the ground on which she stood. She walked around, exploring this strange place, not in the least concerned, just enjoying the tranquility. She took a deep breath and was immediately filled with the Holy Wind.

Her clothes were not what she had been wearing when she had shifted. A long flowing robe of the finest silk, green and gold, covered her from her neck to her feet. Around her waist was a purple waistband and on her feet she wore white slippers. The thought entered her mind that perhaps she had died, and this was heaven. Everything seemed so perfect, so right.

She continued walking, not sure where she was going, but feeling drawn to something good. There, just ahead of her was a pleasant garden, filled with brightly colored flowers. Underneath a beautiful vine-covered latticework arbor was a white bench on which sat a young woman. She smiled at Shaylae and beckoned her over. As she got closer she recognized the Matriarch of Tal'el'Dine'h.

Shaylae knelt at her feet and kissed her hand. "Elder Nashota, I am honored."

She was wearing a robe similar to Shaylae's. "The honor is mine, Yanaba. Now, please sit next to me, and let's talk a while," she said, patting the bench beside her. Her voice sang, a beautifully precise contralto filled with authority and experience, as if she was speaking to her with the voices of all of her blessed ancestors.

"It's so good to see you again, Matriarch."

"You too, my young friend." She took Shaylae's hand in hers.

"Am I dead, Matriarch?"

"Far from it, child."

"Then where am I?"

"That I cannot tell you, only that Tal'el'Dine'h is sealed, so I decided to meet you here," she said, extending her arms around her.

"Why is it sealed?"

"Again, I cannot yet tell you."

"Then is this why we haven't heard anything from you for four years?"

She squeezed Shaylae's hand tightly. "You have done a very brave thing leaving your friends in danger."

"Was it the right thing to do?"

"Only you know the answer to that. Didn't the Holy Ones tell you that there is no right or wrong in the decisions you make, Yanaba? Even we do not know what will happen, or what decisions you will make, or should make."

"We?"

"Yes, all of the Elders of Tal'el'Dine'h."

"You say it was brave; but I think it may have been foolish."

"Sometimes bravery does appear to be folly."

"Are they going to be alright?"

"Yanaba, we cannot see the future. But tell me, do you feel worried? Scared?"

The feelings that filled her and surrounded her were definitely not worry or fear. Nothing could be wrong in a place like this. "Not at the moment. No, Matron, oddly enough I don't." And then after a moment she said, "This is a very holy place."

"It is, Yanaba. No evil thing can enter here. Now, tell me, why have you come here, child?"

"I came to ask you the nature of Denab?"

"That too, you will have to find out on your own." She smiled. "I'm afraid I'm not being very helpful am I?"

Shaylae smiled. "Well, perhaps your reluctance to answer tells me that Denab is no ordinary foe. And the fact that your world is sealed is somehow comforting."

"Quite so," she said with a smile. "Not even holy people such as you can enter until it is time."

"You call me holy?" asked Shaylae with surprise.

"We all have holiness within us, or the potential for holiness. When we call the Holy Ones our parents, it is not just a figurative expression. We have their divine nature with in us, Yanaba. You especially, child."

"Then, we will prevail?"

"I'm sorry, but even that is uncertain."

"You mean I could fail? I and all of my friends, we might fail?"

"Oh, Yanaba, don't you see, you and your friends can never fail; you have already won. Your eternal life with the Holy Ones does not depend on whether or not you win this struggle against the Dark Ones, only how you fight the fight."

"Then what will become of the Dark Ones if we lose this war?"

"Just as you have already won, they have already lost. The final outcome of this struggle is known. The Holy Ones will have the victory. But how it will come about, or who will bring it about, or what will happen along the way is not known."

"Then why do I have to risk my friends, if we know the Holy Ones will win no matter what happens?"

"Now you're asking me questions to which you already know the answer," chided Nashota. "But I'm curious; why do you worry about risking the lives of your friends, and not worry about your own?"

"Because it is a choice I have made for myself. I have no right to make it for them."

"But you didn't. They made this choice to follow you, to the death if necessary. It is their choice, not yours."

"I came here hoping to get some reassurance that we would be OK, but now you're telling me that we could all die."

"What is death, little one? It is no more to be feared than passing from girl to woman, from woman to wife, or from wife to mother."

"I'm not afraid of death, but I want to pass through those steps. I want to be a wife to Micah, and a mother to my children."

"Let me remind you of something you already know." She took Shaylae's hands in both of hers. "Your life did not begin with your mortal birth, any more than it will end with your death."

"Yes, I've always believed that."

"And that this mortal life represents only an infinitesimal fraction of your eternal life?"

"Yes, of course."

"Then, if you know that, have you ever wondered why we had to have a mortal life at all?"

"No, I never did." Shaylae was surprised by this question.

"And why so much depends on it?"

She shook her head.

"Think on these things Yanaba. The answer is found in three questions. What is the true nature of the Holy Ones? What is the true nature of our relationship to them? And what is our destiny?"

"And you can't tell me the answers, can you?" Shaylae smiled.

"That is right, because these are not truths that can be taught, they can only be learned. Deep in your heart you already know the answer to the first two questions, but there is one major misconception you have that you must overcome before the full impact of that knowledge will hit you."

"I would ask you what it is, but you're not going to tell me, are you."

She smiled. "Actually I can. At least I can lead you to the answer as I tell you a very important piece of history. At the beginning of our space and time, when the Holy Ones first breathed the Holy Wind and created our spirits, and organized the universe in which we could live, some of their children rebelled. One in particular."

"You mean Rolling Darkness don't you? But why would anyone want to rebel against the Holy Ones?"

"Ah, it is a mystery to me also. But it seems he wanted to take their glory, to rule their creation. I can only conclude that he believed he could win, in fact, I think he still does. He has never given up. The Holy Ones allowed him to rebel; they even allow him to come amongst their children to cause some of them to fall. But, they withheld from him and his followers a very important blessing that you and I, and all of their faithful children received."

"What blessing, Elder?"

"Think back to the question I asked you earlier: why do we have a body?"

"I don't know. But obviously you're implying it is very important." A spark of understanding filled Shaylae's eyes. "And is that the blessing that Rolling Darkness is deprived of?"

"Exactly!" She touched her shoulder. "Your body is the source of much pleasure, or perhaps I should have said joy. You experience things through your physical senses that would be impossible to experience if you were only spirit." She opened her eyes wide and nodded at Shaylae. Shaylae nodded her agreement. "And your spirit experiences those sensations also, yes?"

"Yes, I suppose that's true."

"You have heard that there are two parts to us humans; body and spirit."

"Yes, and it's true isn't it."

"Partially. But a living soul is both of those parts living in harmony, no real boundaries, perfectly and seamlessly integrated." She placed her hands together, interlocking her fingers. "Anything less, and that person is not complete."

"Interesting. I've never heard of the word 'soul' being described that way."

"Well, think of your own term, 'breathing soul'. It is not used on any of the other planets by the way; it is unique to Earth, beautiful. What does it mean?"

"Well, our breathing soul is the Holy Wind within us. It is what makes our bodies alive."

"And your eternal soul?"

"It is our spirits. The part of us that is a child of the Holy Ones."

"And together they make a complete person. Just as the world must be in balance, so must a person, their breathing soul in perfect harmony with their eternal soul. One is not complete without the other."

"But our breathing soul dies when our body dies; only our eternal soul goes on to the land of the dead."

"Really?" said Nashota with a knowing smile.

"What?" said Shaylae. "Everyone knows that."

"Do they? In one of the most sacred records on Earth there is a scripture that says 'And the Lord God formed man of the dust of the ground, and breathed into his nostrils the breath of life; and man became a living soul.'"

A look of sudden understanding filled Shaylae's face.

"The imagery of that scripture is perfect, wouldn't you say?"

"Well, yes, I suppose. But I'm interested that you would say that the Bible is a sacred record."

Shaylae expected Nashota to elaborate, but instead she took up her earlier thought.

"Our body is one of the greatest gifts they gave us," she said with a smile, stroking Shaylae's hair. Shaylae at once understood the significance of the intimate and loving caress—it was not something her spirit could have appreciated without her body. "And having a body gives you power over Rolling Darkness. I'm not entirely sure why this is so, but think on it; if he has no body, then he has no breathing soul."

"But once we die and return to the Holy Ones we will no longer have a body or a breathing soul, so do we lose our advantage over him?"

"Are you sure?"

"Sure about what?"

Nashota raised her eyebrows, but said nothing.

"Sure that we won't have a body after we die; that only our spirit, our eternal soul, returns to the Holy Ones? Yes, I'm sure. Everyone knows that."

"You mean the Navajo believe it, and many of the religions of Earth believe it, but not all. There are some who believe in a physical as well as a spiritual resurrection."

"Wait a minute, are you saying that our bodies stay with us throughout eternity?"

"Why would the Holy Ones send us to live out a mortal life, an infinitesimal fraction of our eternal life, to gain a body, only to give it up again?"

"But that's impossible. Our bodies are corruptible, weak, destined to die. We have to give them up."

"That is only true of a mortal body."

"There's no such a thing as an immortal body," she said. Nashota smiled. "Is there?"

Once more Nashota raised her hand and touched Shaylae's cheek. Shaylae once more felt a thrill of intimacy, a feeling she would not have been able to experience without her body.

"Why would the Holy One's give us experiences like this, only to take them away?" she asked, continuing to stroke Shaylae's face and hair. "These are experiences that can only be enjoyed by a complete living soul; experiences denied to Rolling Darkness and his followers."

"This is all so new. I cannot imagine an eternal life with a body."

"And I cannot imagine eternal life without a body. You've seen our Holy Parents. You are truly blessed. You are one of only a handful of people in the history of the three planets who have. I myself will have to wait until I pass over to see them."

"Yes, but . . ."

"Did they look like us?"

"Yes, but couldn't their spirits look like us?"

"Why? Why would a spirit look like a body?"

Shaylae shrugged.

"When Asdzáán Nádleehé came to Earth she only brought with her a fraction of the knowledge her elders had learned. Much of the old knowledge was lost. When we came back to Tal'el'Dine'h we found that knowledge again. There is something very special about Tal'el'Dine'h, something I can't tell you just yet. But there is knowledge there. The thoughts are already in your mind, they just need to crystallize; then you will know the answer to that final question: what is your destiny? Once you do you will never again worry about the things you will miss should you die young."

Shaylae was quiet for a moment as she tried to absorb what Nashota had told her. And then another thought struck her. "There's an implication in what you say that this struggle extends way beyond the battle between the children of Asdzáán Nádleehé and the Dark Ones."

"Ah, you are very astute, Yanaba."

"Then why is Asdzáán Nádleehé so important, and the Dark Ones for that matter?"

"Another very important question . . ."

". . . that you're not going to answer are you?"

She smiled again. "Think on these things. Let these thoughts loose in your mind. Let them take root and grow. What is happening will make so much more sense once you begin to understand."

"Well, I'll have a couple of weeks to think on it before I go back."

"Before you go I have one more piece of advice, a suggestion really."

"What is that?"

"That you get married."

Shaylae was taken totally by surprise; she had not been expecting such an outlandish suggestion. "But Matriarch, I'm only eighteen."

She shrugged. "So what? Many of your ancestors were married younger than that. One of your heroines, the one you call Sonora of the Long Walk, was married at fifteen."

"Yes, But that was two hundred-and-fifty years ago. Things have changed since then."

"They have, have they? Would it surprise you to know that I was married on my fifteenth birthday?"

Shaylae's eyes widened.

"Do marriages on your planet today last any longer as a result of this change? As a result of people marrying when they are older?"

Shaylae shrugged. "Well, no."

"Are married couples any happier than they were then?"

Again Shaylae shrugged. "I don't know. I suppose not."

"Sonora was married for fifty-three years. Almost half of marriages on Earth end in tragedy. So, was it a change for the better?"

"I guess not."

"Do you love him?"

"Micah? Of course. With all my heart."

"And he loves you?"

"Yes. I'm certain of it."

"Is there any doubt in your mind, or your spirit that you will one day marry?"

"None whatsoever."

"Does he share the same certainty of your marriage?"

"I'm sure of it."

"Then there is no reason to wait? Think on it, child. There is much at stake. Not just the outcome of this battle, but your own eternal happiness as well."

"I will consider it, Elder, I will." Shaylae was smiling now. "But, I 'm curious why you would suggest such a thing."

"Well, partly because it is abundantly obvious you are both madly in love. But there is yet another reason, perhaps even more important, why you should consider getting married."

"There is? What is that?"

"What happened to you at your Kinaalda?"

"I became a woman . . ."

"Yes, of course. But what happened to your power."

"I guess it took a huge leap forward."

"As it will when you and Micah become man and wife. There is great power in the love that exists between a man and a woman."

Another flush came to Shaylae's face. "Well, I'll think about it." She couldn't stop the tingling feeling flowing through her body at the thought of Micah becoming her husband.

Nashota continued. "And later, as you become a mother, your power will take another leap forward; in fact the power of motherhood is the greatest of all."

"At least I have a couple of weeks to think about it before I go back to Yurob."

"Fifteen days have already passed on Yurob, Yanaba."

"How can that be? I've been here less than an hour."

Nashota just waved her hand, and then with a serious tone said, "You need to get back there. Your friends are in danger."

"Are they OK?"

Nashota didn't answer but she hugged her again. "It has been such an honor to be with you."

"Oh, Matriarch, please, the honor has been mine." She stood up and bowed her head, but Nashota took her by the shoulders and looked directly into her eyes.

"Dearest Yanaba, Shaylae of the Gentle Heart," she said shaking her head, "you may not believe it yet, but win or lose, you are the greatest woman who has ever graced the face of the three planets."

"Oh, no. That can't be. There has to be other people . . ."

"I didn't say 'person', I said 'woman'."

Shaylae was about to ask her to explain, but before she could say anything Nashota had gone. She realized it would be a while before she would be able to absorb everything she had said, but in the meantime, she had to get back to Yurob. Suddenly with full force it hit her. Nashota had said her friends were in danger. Her breathing became more rapid and shallow, her heart rate doubled, and a cold empty feeling filled her body. "Micah!" she said.

CHAPTER 17

June 23, 2108

Micah woke the next morning feeling better than he had in months. He still wondered if he was in a dream. Last night Shaylae had driven him almost insane with desire with her kisses. Oh, how he wanted her. But he could wait. It wouldn't be hard for him because he loved her so much.

He looked at the clock. It read 8:05. Dang it! Ayanna would definitely give him a hard time about sleeping in—she was quite the early riser.

As if on cue, she knocked at the door. "Are you ever getting out of your bed, you lazy butthead?"

"I'll be right there my mentally challenged cousin," he shouted. They sparred verbally just like they did when they were fighting, although she usually ruled the repartee ring, so he was surprised when she didn't respond. He showered as quickly as he could and carelessly threw on a pair of comfortable shorts and a T-shirt; there would be time to shave and to dress properly after breakfast.

"Hope you kept my breakfast warm," he shouted as he opened the door. Again, not a sound from Ayanna. "Anna, where are you? You OK?"

His voice trailed off as he saw her. Elbows resting on the kitchen table, hands supporting her chin, and an almost dreamy look in her eyes. Sitting opposite her was Sigmun, chatting animatedly, not even looking up to acknowledge Micah's presence. Her hair hung loosely down her back, a large lock of it pulled forward over her left shoulder. He had to admit, in her own way she was just as beautiful as his Shaylae. No wonder Sigmun was captivated.

"Ah. Comfortable bed Mike?" she said.

"Yes," he said, still catching his breath.

"You didn't have to sprint. We saved you breakfast," she said, pointing to the stove. "'Course it's all cold."

"Oh, thanks," he said sheepishly.

Ayanna turned to him, the sarcastic glint gone from her eyes. "Everything OK, Mike?"

"Oh, sure. It's just . . ."

"I know. You miss Shay already don't you?"

"Yes. Dunno how I'm gonna last two weeks."

"You mean you didn't get two week's worth of each other last night?"

"OK, knock it off cousin!"

"Micah, Ayanna tells me you are an accomplished hand-to-hand fighter," said Sigmun, trying to change the subject.

"So is she. Didn't she tell you?"

"Well, yes, but . . ."

Micah chuckled. "Girls don't figure too highly on your planet do they?"

Now it was Sigmun's turn to be embarrassed. "Did I make it that obvious? I'm sorry, Ayanna, I didn't mean . . ."

"It's OK," said Ayanna graciously. "Amongst the Dine'h our society is matriarchal. Many other cultures on Earth are also."

"And you'd better not underestimate Anna. She'd rip you a new one in ten milliseconds flat."

"Micah!"

"Could you show me?" he said. "Give me a demonstration?"

"You want to watch me humiliate Mike?"

"OK, that does it! Get your stuff," he said, heading back to his room.

"Is there somewhere we can fight, Sigmun?"

"Sure." He spoke into his wrist computer. "Cerid," he said.

"Yes, sir," came the crisp reply.

"Is there anywhere close by we can work out?"

"Certainly, sir. There's a gymnasium very close to their apartment. I'll come and take you there."

"Great." He turned back to Ayanna. "OK, get ready."

Ten minutes later Sigmun watched as the two cousins stood facing each other. He wasn't sure if she looked even more beautiful in her sparing gear, although she certainly looked menacing. She had tied her hair into a bun at the back of her head, but rather than tighten up her face, it actually emphasized its lapidary perfection—and her beautifully turned-up nose. She looked more like an exquisite bronze statue rather than a flesh-and-blood girl. She had looked so graceful warming up; it was more like a ballet than preparation for a fight.

"Begin," said Micah, bowing to her.

Slowly they circled each other, like two predators. Then suddenly she was on him. Raining blows at his face and upper body. Some landed, but most did not. He grabbed the lapel of her shirt and rolled over backwards, pulling her down with him, and then with a quick flip of his feet, sent her flying through the air. Sigmun's heart leapt to his mouth. Surely Micah had not intended to do that? She's going to injure herself when she lands. But somehow, miraculously, she turned in midair, and as she hit the floor she rolled and sprang to her feet like a tiger. Now it was Micah's turn. Taking advantage of her recovery, he leaped into the air and aimed a kick at her head, but she was too fast. She grabbed his legs flipping him over on his back. In an instant she was on him—one knee in his stomach, the other pinning his right arm and her upper body over his left arm. They held that position for a moment, and then stood up, bowed to each other, and then to Sigmun.

Sigmun clapped enthusiastically. "Fantastic," he exclaimed.

"Would you like to see more?" asked Ayanna.

"No, I like to learn," he replied enthusiastically.

"Sure, why not? Let me go get you a sparing jacket and pants," said Micah as he started back to the apartment. "Be right back."

"So, you liked it then?" asked Ayanna as soon as they were alone.

"Yeah. It looked more like a dance than fighting. Does it really work though, in a close combat situation for example?"

"Oh, sure. Especially if you're dealing with brawlers."

Her face and forehead were glowing, covered in an almost imperceptible sheen of sweat. She was still breathing heavily from the exertion; Sigmun could taste her breath as she exhaled.

"Ayanna," he began as he put his left hand on her right shoulder.

"Yes," she said, making no attempt to remove his hand.

"You're so beautiful," he said. "You're perfect." His heart was pounding, and his breathing was rapid.

"Thank you," she said with a little mock curtsey. "You're pretty cute yourself," she replied, putting her hand on his.

He put his right arm around her waist and pulled her closer, not sure how she would react. She made no attempt to pull away or to resist him, quite the opposite; she leaned up to him and looked into his eyes. He moved closer until only centimeters separated their lips. She leaned her head to one side as his lips touched hers in a gentle kiss. He felt drunk with the passion and desire welling up inside of him. She smelled so fresh and clean filling him with an intoxicating rush. He pulled her even closer as the kiss became more urgent. She pressed her body into his, a body seemingly made to mold into his.

"What's going on here?"

The kiss abruptly ended, as Sigmun whirled around to see a red-faced, angry Micah striding toward them.

"Micah, I . . ." began Sigmun.

"I don't recall you asking me if you could court my cousin," he said.

Sigmun was at a loss. Had he broken some important cultural taboo by kissing Ayanna? She had certainly not given him any cause to think so.

She laughed. Like a rushing river she laughed. "Oh, Sigmun, he's only teasing you."

Micah's face mellowed a little but he still looked serious as he held out the sparing clothes to Sigmun. "Here, try these on for size," he said.

To say that Sigmun was relieved would have been the understatement of the sun-cycle. He certainly did not relish the idea of crossing Micah's path.

Together, he and Micah headed for the changing rooms. Once he closed the door behind them Micah turned to him, a deathly serious look on his face.

"She is an incredible person," said Micah. "She seems tough, but deep down she's sensitive and vulnerable."

Sigmun nodded. "She certainly is . . ." he began, but Micah interrupted him.

"If you ever," he paused dramatically as he slowly emphasized the word 'ever', "hurt her . . ." and that was all he said. It was all he needed to say; the message was loud and clear.

CHAPTER 18

⸺❦⸺

Ayanna could hardly believe what had just happened. Sigmun had caught her eye the moment she had first seen him in Hauron's apartment. She had been kissed a few times before, and it had always been fun. She loved dating, but she had never felt really attracted to anyone—until now. Now her skin was still tingling all over from the beautiful kiss they had shared.

Micah and Sigmun walked out of the changing rooms both dressed alike, aside from the white belt Sigmun was wearing, but that was where the similarity ended. The most obvious difference was of course Micah's dark complexion and long black hair, compared to Sigmun's fair skin, pale would be a better description, and short blonde hair. But, oh, he was so handsome. Their bearings were also quite different. Micah walked with fluidity—Sigmun walked awkwardly, almost out of place dressed in the sparing gear.

"How do I look?" he asked, holding out his arms.

She couldn't repress a giggle as she shrugged her shoulders.

"That bad, huh?" he said sounding quite deflated.

"No, no," she said quickly, grabbing him by the arm. "You look great." She took him to the center of the mat. "Sit down," she said. "Legs straight out in front of you, back straight, arms by your side."

Quickly he complied.

"Now, let yourself down slowly, until you are lying flat."

Sigmun let his body lean backwards.

"No, no," she said. "You're bending your back. You have to keep it straight." She pulled him back upright.

Once more he tried, a little better this time but she was still not satisfied. "Straighter," she said. A few more tries and she said, "OK, that'll do. We can work on that again later."

"What moves are these?" he asked.

Again she giggled nervously. "Warm-ups" she said.

"Oh."

"OK, now, from a prone position, raise your feet as slowly as you can, up as high as you can, and don't bend your legs."

This seemed to be a little easier for him, as he got it right the first time.

"Now, alternate; back, legs, back, legs." As he began she once again chided him. "No, breathe deeply, from your diaphragm. Long and deep through your nose, slowly out through your mouth."

He repeated the movements about five times, and then let out a huge breath, lying flat on the mat. "Wow. That's getting to my stomach."

"It will at first. You do any sort of work-out?"

He shook his head.

"Well, you'll get used to it. Micah can do two hundred of these without even breaking a sweat."

"OK," said Micah. "Let's try a few fall techniques."

"Fall techniques?"

"Yes. So you don't get hurt when she throws you through the air." Micah shot a smile in Ayanna's direction.

For an hour Sigmun practiced. Simple falls at first; learning to slap the mat with his whole arm just as he hit the floor. Then he moved on to various rolls; forward rolls, side rolls, and neck rolls. He was a quick study and mastered them fairly easily. Ayanna was quite impressed, and even Micah seemed pleased with his progress.

"OK, now for some simple blocks," he said.

Sigmun learned simple forearm blocks, knee blocks, leg blocks, two-handed blocks. After an hour Micah said that it was enough. Sigmun wanted to continue, but Micah insisted.

"We've already done more than we should have done for one day. You'll be regretting this tomorrow."

"Oh, I don't think so. I've never had this much fun."

"We'll see," said Micah with a smile.

"Can we do some more tomorrow?"

"Sure. We can move on to your yellow belt katas."

"Katas?"

"Yes. A kata is a choreographed sequence of movements and positions, designed to give you coordination and balance. You have to master two katas before you can be awarded your yellow belt."

"And you can award that to me?"

"Yes, as an eighth Dan black belt I am an official Master Instructor and can award all but the black belt."

"Will you teach me some attacking moves tomorrow?"

"No, Sigmun, katas."

And maybe you'll kiss me again tomorrow, thought Ayanna wistfully.

CHAPTER 19

⸙

"Sigmun, you've done well," said Denab. "I'm pleased."

"Thank you, Excellency." His eyes stared into the middle distance, glazed over, as if half asleep.

The wind was howling, making eerie noises as it blew its way between the buildings of the great city. The black midnight sky was a psychotic mantle, ever changing, as the wind ripped the angry clouds apart, reformed them, only to tear them asunder once more. Lightning flashed, followed quickly by the bellowing thunder that shook the balcony on which they stood, facing each other.

Denab smiled inwardly. It had been tricky securing Sigmun's place in the Council of One Hundred, persuading the others in the Quorum of Eleven to appoint such a young man without The Power. But he had prevailed. His respect among his fellow Quorum members was such that even without cashing any favors First Prophet and Kildane had acquiesced. When Hauron had disposed of Zomra and appointed Sigmun in his place, it was more than Denab could have hoped for. His planning and foresight had finally paid off, and now he was only months away from recruiting the one person who could help him defeat the Holy Ones, the witch Shaylae.

Last week Sigmun had told him of Shaylae's first visit to Hauron, and how Hauron had almost believed her story. That was not good. It was important that Hauron continue to accept the myths surrounding Asdzáán Nádleehé. Sigmun had also told him that when she returned, Shaylae would share everything with Hauron.

"Do you think she will share it with you also?" he had asked.

"I think so. I think I made it obvious to her that I already believed her and that I could win Hauron over."

"Sigmun, that's good that they both trust you so much."

But now she had made a fatal mistake. She had brought with her two of her vulnerable friends. They would be quite useful. He looked at Sigmun. He stood, not moving, unaffected by the biting wind.

"Tell me more about these two people the witch has brought with her from Earth."

"Micah is Shaylae's lover; at least that is how it appears. He is strong, a skilled fighter, but very practical and logical. I think he has trouble accepting all of the mythology that surrounds the story of Asdzáán Nádleehé."

"You think he is a threat?"

"Physically I would imagine he could handle three or four guards at once, his fighting prowess is superb, but as to The Power, he has none whatsoever."

"And the girl?"

Even in his hypnotic state Sigmun smiled. "She is the most beautiful person I have ever seen."

"Hmm, interesting," said Denab. If she could be compromised into a relationship with Sigmun . . . "You are attracted to her? Physically?"

"Yes. And emotionally too."

"Have you had any sort of relationship with her yet?"

"Not really. We have become good friends, and we did kiss."

"Very good, Sigmun. I want you to pursue this relationship. See if you can get her to sleep with you, to have sex with you. This is very important for them. If you can get her to go against her moral values it could be quite useful."

"It would be my pleasure, Excellency."

He reached forward and patted Sigmun on the arm.

"Now, back to the girl Shaylae; do you think she is the witch Asdzáán Nádleehé?"

"No, Excellency. I don't believe in reincarnation."

This was interesting news for Denab. During these conversations Sigmun was totally honest, his programming ensured it. "Then do you not believe that our current First Prophet is a reincarnation of The First Prophet?"

"No, Excellency, I don't."

Sigmun was certainly a bright young man, a free thinker. He had recruited well.

"Is there anything else you can tell me, anything at all?"

"Yes, Excellency. The girl Ayanna related the story of Asdzáán Nádleehé as they have been taught it."

"Tell it to me."

Sigmun repeated word for word the story as Ayanna had told it to him. Denab was startled by some of the revelations it contained. So, Earth is not the original home of Asdzáán Nádleehé. "Did they say where this star they call Tal'el'Dine'h is?"

"No, she wouldn't point it out on a star chart."

Denab was not surprised, but it shouldn't be hard to find. How many stars could there be within twenty light years that would be suitable for human life? "Is there anything else you can tell me? Anything at all?"

"No, Excellency."

"Very good. We will talk again soon."

Once he was alone, he leaned his hands against the railing of his balcony and stared out into the dark night sky. He wondered if this Tal'el'Dine'h posed any kind of threat. It must. Why had he not been able to sense it? Of course it was possible it was still uninhabited, but somehow he doubted it—how would the witch know of it if it was? Why would they have mentioned it? And, how did Asdzáán Nádleehé make the journey from there to Earth? He had a thousand questions, and he needed answers. But he would not make any overt moves until after she returned.

PART THREE

Denab

CHAPTER 20

June 24, 2108

Sigmun woke, as Micah had predicted, aching all over. His muscles were not used to any sort of strenuous exercise. He kicked off his blankets and slid his legs over the end of the bed and buried his head in his hands. Another headache! And it was much worse than last time. It was the third time in less than a month. Odd, because before he had joined the Council of One Hundred he had rarely been troubled by headaches.

"Sigmun, come to me." It was Hauron.

He threw his clothes on as quickly as he could and made his way over to the throne room; he didn't want to keep him waiting.

"Tell me how it has been progressing with Shaylae's friends," said Hauron, once they had settled themselves into Hauron's meditation room.

Sigmun's smile filled his face. "Great," was all he said.

"Sigmun, I think I deserve a little more than just 'great'," said Hauron amiably.

"Either they are both extremely clever in covering up their evil, or they are the most decent people I have ever met."

"Oh, tell me more."

"They are totally without guile. I don't think there's a mean bone in either of their bodies, but don't get me wrong, I think they would defend each other or Shaylae to the death. In fact I wouldn't put it past them to defend someone they didn't even know the same way."

"Would you describe them as loyal?"

"And then some."

"So, if Asdzáán Nádleehé were evil then they as her friends would do anything to defend her secrets and further her agenda?"

"Well, yes, but . . ."

"Sigmun, I have to consider every possibility here," he continued. "If I make the wrong decision then our whole planet, all of our people, could be in danger."

"I understand, but as I said they'd have to be really good actors."

Hauron shrugged. "OK. For the moment I haven't done anything that commits me one way or the other, so I guess I shouldn't worry too much."

"There is one other thing I have to tell you, and which I have to admit colors my opinion." Sigmun paused, still smiling.

"Yes, go on."

"I've fallen in love with Ayanna."

"I thought I noticed something between you the first time we met her," said Hauron, shaking his head. "But I wish you hadn't. It makes you practically useless in being an objective observer, doesn't it?"

Sigmun nodded. "I suppose. But another way of looking at it is that it would be even harder for her to pretend."

"She has returned your love? She feels the same way toward you?"

"I think so. Yes, I'm sure of it."

Hauron was still shaking his head. "Well, I truly hope that everything works out, but I don't think you should count on anything definite just yet."

Sigmun pursed his lips and nodded his head.

"Sigmun, you're extremely bright, and you're my friend. You have to promise me that your first loyalty will be to me and to the people of Yurob."

Sigmun thought about this a moment. Hauron was right. Regardless of how he felt about Ayanna his most important goal was the safety of his people.

"Hauron, I swear it."

CHAPTER 21

July 8, 2108.

"Sigmun, I'm so proud of you. You've learned really quickly," said Ayanna as she kissed him on the cheek and threw her arms around his neck.

Micah had just completed the ceremony presenting to Sigmun his lower yellow belt and like a child he found he couldn't stop smiling.

"Hey, I'm still here," said Micah, but if Sigmun and Ayanna heard him they showed no sign of it. Micah shrugged, turned, and left the room.

For the first time in fifteen days Sigmun did not want to spend any time in the gym. The beginning of summer-year was always unpredictable. The monsoon season that began at the end of spring-year was at its height, bringing with it torrential rains, floods, and mudslides. But today was glorious. The sun shone brilliantly in a clear blue sky, and there was barely a breeze. It was the first beautiful day since Ayanna and Micah had arrived.

"Ayanna, why don't I show you some more of my world? It's quite beautiful you know."

She took hold of him, one hand grasping his upper arm, the other on his chest. It was a simple gesture but it was unique to her and as a result always seemed so intimate to Sigmun. "Sigmun, that sounds like a great idea." She leaned up and kissed him again.

Sigmun shivered at the touch of her lips on his skin. His feelings for her were so intense that he wondered how long it would be before he exploded. He just had to get closer to her. His passion for her was like fire in the sun.

"OK, let's grab some food and drink, and head on out to the mountains."

"And let me change into something more comfortable. Don't move. I'll be right back."

She wasn't gone long. As she ran back to join him he couldn't help but stare. She had changed into a pair of light blue shorts and a white tank top. On her feet she wore white socks and white sneakers. She had tied her hair into two braids, and then had pulled them back into a loose bun. Her shorts emphasized her long athletic legs. Her tank top left an enticing gap revealing a perfect navel and the dark tantalizing skin of her midriff. He marveled at the gentle curves of her beautiful body.

She looked coyly at him through downcast eyes and long eyelashes. "Sigmun, stop staring at me. You're embarrassing me."

"I'm sorry, I can't help it. You're the most beautiful girl I've ever seen."

"Actually, Sigmun, I'm a woman, not a girl," she said with a grin. "I'm nineteen years old."

"I'm sorry," he said. "You're the most beautiful woman I have ever seen."

"No, I'm just kidding. I like it when you call me a girl," she said and squeezed his arm again. "Anyway, you're very handsome yourself, but you don't see me staring at you."

"OK, I'll try to stop staring."

Again she laughed. Like a spring shower her laugh washed over him. She playfully punched him in the arm. "It's OK, You can stare at me all you want. I like it."

A few minutes later they were on their way, Sigmun flying the car, and Ayanna hanging on to his arm. The weather was certainly cooperating with him today in his determination to win Ayanna over. The scenery was as spectacular as he had ever seen it. Green grass, trees, and shrubs covered the hillsides, wildflowers covered the ground with reckless abandon; animals played as if it was the first time they had ever seen such a glorious day.

"Where are you taking me anyway?"

"To one of my favorite spots." He pointed straight ahead. "Just over that ridge is a valley with the most beautiful rivers, and a perfect lake. We'll be there in a couple of minutes."

"Is it where you take all of your girlfriends?"

"You're the first girlfriend I have ever had," he said. And then added hastily, "That is if you don't mind me calling you my girlfriend."

She smiled and nodded her head. "Yes," she said.

"You do mind?"

"Oh, no. Yes, you can call me your girlfriend." She grabbed his arm and leaned against him. "I am your girlfriend.

Sigmun's heart soared as it rose with the car over the top of the ridge, and then gently descended toward the valley floor. The lake looked perfect, like a blue mirror. The trees and bushes that surrounded it were in full bloom, a blazing fire of blues, reds, yellows pinks, and violets.

"Oh, Sigmun, it's beautiful," she said breathlessly.

He looked at her then smiled. Let's see if I can scare her, he thought wickedly. Swinging the car around, he dived for the ground, then at the last minute raised the nose and pulled back on the power so that it almost stalled, just as it touched down, feather soft. He turned to her. Her eyes and mouth were open wide, but then she smiled through her clenched teeth, wagging her index finger in his face.

"One day I'll repay you for that maneuver, then you'll wish you'd never tried it!"

Before he had a chance to respond she had jumped out, kicked off her sneakers and socks, and was dipping her toes into the water.

"Ouch, that's cold."

"So would you be after a year-long winter, and a slow-to-warm-up spring. The water won't be warm until halfway through summer-year. In fact, its warmest the first half of fall-year."

She extended her toes into the water again, stretching out her leg in a perfect line from her thighs to her toes. He gasped as he marveled at her beauty.

"How big around is this lake?"

"Oh, about ten klicks."

"Then we could walk around it before lunch? Let's do it!" she said, as she put her socks and sneakers back on.

She reached toward him and took his hand as they began their hike around the lake. "These flowers are beautiful, Sig. I swear we don't have anything to compare."

"They are, Ayanna, but they pale in comparison to your beauty." He turned to her and gently put his hand under her chin and kissed her.

"Oh, Sig, you know all the right things to say to a girl."

About half way around the lake the shoreline turned into a muddy quagmire. Sigmun pointed up the mountains. "This is where most of the runoff enters the lake. There's a river just ahead, but for the last few months of spring-year it overflows its banks and gives us marsh."

"But my shoes," she said, stretching out her white sneaker.

In one swift movement Sigmun gathered her easily into his arms. She smiled as she put her arm around his neck and laid her head on his shoulders. His right hand was on the skin of her midriff, and his left on her thighs. He was about to kiss her when she covered his mouth with hers in a passionate kiss. He lost his footing and stumbled on a wet rock dropping her unceremoniously in the mud. She landed with a sort of 'sploosh', mud splattering all over her legs and arms, her head and face, and her clothes. Her lovely white shoes were now a dirty brown. Sigmun was waiting for her angry outburst, but instead she began laughing hysterically.

"Now look what you've done," she squealed through her laughter. She picked up a handful of wet sloppy mud and threw it at him. He stepped back and tried to dodge but it hit him square in the face. He wiped the mud from his eyes, bent down, grabbed a handful and threw it back. It landed on her head, oozing down her lovely hair.

"That does it," she screeched as she grabbed his legs and pulled him down in the mud with her. He tried to wrestle her down, hoping to rub her face in the mud, but she was too quick and much more skilled in close combat. In a flash she had him lying on his back, straddling him. The hysterical laughter stopped, her chest rose and fell with her rapid breathing. She bent down, grabbed his face and kissed him. It was the most exciting and passionate kiss they had yet shared. It was as if her lips were trying to devour him, nibbling at his lips, her tongue darting in and out of his mouth. Even the mud that covered their faces tasted like the sweetest fruit.

"Oh, Sigmun, I love you so much," she said as she kissed his cheeks, his chin, his eyes, his ears.

"Gods, how I love you too."

Ayanna pressed herself against him and he raised his hips to meet her. He reached round her back and slid his hand up underneath her tank top, luxuriating in the sensual feel of her soft, silky skin.

"Sigmun . . ." she began. "I'm sorry, Sigmun, but I can't."

"Oh, Ayanna, I want you so badly. Please don't stop me. I've never felt this close to a girl before, and now I know that I never want to be, except with you."

"Oh, and so do I. I really do. I've never wanted to give myself so completely to a boy before, but I just can't."

"What's wrong? You don't feel right about this?"

"Oh, I do," she said shaking her head. "And I don't. Sigmun, you have to understand that virtue is so important in our culture, and to me." She climbed off him, and flopped down, sitting beside him in the mud.

"You mean you can never make love to anyone unless you are married."

"Once a couple is betrothed it's OK, but many still wait until they are married."

"Ayanna, I know with all my heart I want to marry you. Don't you feel the same way?"

"Yes, I do."

"Then let's swear to each other our undying love and loyalty. Let's get betrothed."

"It's not that simple. To be considered betrothed, and released from our vow of chastity, both families must approve. My father would have to get to know you very well before he would consent to an official betrothal."

"Oh, Anna, I don't know if I can wait . . ."

"And that's another thing. I wouldn't consider becoming betrothed until I'd known you for at least . . . I dunno . . . six months."

"But, Anna . . ."

"If you truly love me you can wait."

"Anna, these aren't normal circumstances. We could die . . ."

"And because of that I should surrender my virtue?" There was the beginning of anger in her voice.

"I'm sorry, I didn't mean that," he said sincerely.

"But you said it, Sig! You said it." She sounded hurt.

He took her head in his hand and gently turned her face toward him. "Anna, I am so sorry. I didn't realize it was so important to you. I love you more than I've ever loved another person. I would never hurt you."

She laid her head on his shoulder. A solitary tear rolled down her cheek, leaving a little trail in the mud. "Oh, Sigmun, I can't surrender my virtue, regardless of how much I love you."

They stayed locked in that embrace for a few minutes, and then Ayanna giggled.

"What?" said Sigmun.

"Well, look at us," she said, holding her mud-covered arms out, palms up.

Sigmun laughed. "What should we do?"

"Well, I don't know about you, but I'm going in that lake to wash off." And she headed toward the water.

For a moment Sigmun's heart pounded, wondering if she would take off her clothes before jumping in. But instead she simply waded out, fully clothed, shoes and all, squealing. "AH! It's cold."

Sigmun followed her into the freezing water, quickly caught up to her, and jumped on her, causing them both to fall, totally submerged in the freezing water.

"Oh! Oh! Oh!" was all she could manage as she surfaced. Quickly she rubbed herself down, washing off the mud, rubbing her clothes, trying to get the mud off them. Her wet tank top enticingly clung to her. He tried to look away, but he couldn't; she was so beautiful. She looked down and blushed. She came closer to him, pressing her body against his and through her kisses said, "Sigmun, I told you, I don't mind you staring at me. You can look all you want."

As the afternoon worked its way into evening the young couple made the return journey. Ayanna looked up at Sigmun who was concentrating on his flying. She had not expected to fall in love so easily. Now she understood how Shaylae had felt about Micah. Her head rested on his shoulder, her arm snaked around his waist. She felt complete for the first time in her life.

"Ayanna," said Sigmun as the car landed at the palace. "Why don't you come on over to my place, we could have dinner together."

Her heart leaped in her chest. "I don't know. You think that would be a good idea?" She was not sure if she would be to resist him if they were alone together in his room. It didn't take her long to come to a decision. "OK, but let me shower and change into some decent clothes."

She ran all the way to her apartment and burst in the door. Micah was there, pouring over something on the computer with Hauron.

"Where have you been?" asked Micah.

"Sigmun and I went for a picnic." She replied. "Up into the mountains. A beautiful lake."

"Looks like you went swimming too," observed Hauron.

"And mud wrestling," added Micah.

She laughed. "Oh yeah. We had lotsa fun."

She ran to her room, threw off her clothes and jumped into the shower.

When she was finished and dried off, she picked out one of her favorite dresses. It was plain black, sleeveless, silky and slinky. The neckline, while certainly not plunging, was the lowest of all the dresses she owned. She double-checked to make sure she wasn't showing any cleavage, well, maybe a little when she leaned forward. She put on a pair of shiny black pumps. As she brushed her hair she decided she would leave it loose, hanging down her back. She looked at herself in the full-length mirror, and was surprised at what she saw. "Ayanna Hale, you're quite cute," she said, twirling around, admiring herself. "I guess that's what love will do to you,"

She hurried out of her room. Hauron and Micah were still hard at work. "See you later. I'm off to have dinner with Sigmun. Don't wait up."

"Bye," they both said, but she had already slammed the door behind her.

CHAPTER 22

※

Ayanna knocked on Sigmun's door, and almost immediately he opened it. Gods, he looks so handsome. She had expected him to be wearing his formal red and white cloak, but instead he was wearing a simple yellow shirt with wide sleeves. His pants were white, and for a moment reminded her of the loose fitting linen pants she had seen White Cloud wearing the first time she had met him. His blonde hair was short, though not as short as was usually worn on his planet. There was no part in his hair, it just sort of radiated out from his crown. His blue eyes shone like diamonds as they looked at her, drinking her up. He took her arm and walked her into his apartment, sitting her on a luxurious couch.

"Would you like some wine?" he asked.

"Thanks, but no. I don't drink any alcohol."

"OK, some juice then?"

"Actually, water would be fine."

"Water for me too then," he said walking over to his 'fridge and pouring two glasses. He came back and sat next to her on the couch, handing her one of the glasses. "To us," he said, clinking her glass, and taking a sip.

"To us," she said, raising the glass to her lips.

The lighting in Sigmun's apartment was subtle and subdued. Romantic music was playing over the sound system. She slipped off her shoes and pulled her feet up underneath her body.

"You ready to eat?" he asked.

"Sure. What we having?"

"Fish; found in the lake we were at today."

"I love fish."

As they ate, sitting opposite each other, she saw herself reflected in his eyes, and knew then that this was where she belonged. His eyes were alive, intelligent, caring. His conversation was easy, honest and genuine.

After dinner they talked, they danced to the music, and they kissed. She admired the art he had hanging on his walls and they kissed. She looked through the books he had in his cabinets, and they kissed. But all too soon the evening hours slipped away and it was time for her to leave.

"I have to go," she said reluctantly. "Micah might come looking for me, and I'm sure you don't want . . ."

"Stay with me tonight," he said, interrupting her, kissing her ear, holding his breath. "Ayanna, I promise I won't try to make love to you." She almost melted in his arms as he spoke those words, half wishing he would try, so afraid that she would surrender.

"OK," she said breathlessly.

They walked arm in arm into his bedroom. The bed was huge. "I'll sleep on the couch," he said, anticipating her unspoken question. "The bathroom is there," he said, pointing to a door off to the side. He slid open a drawer and pulled out a nightshirt. "Here, you can use this—it's clean."

She gulped, trying to moisten her dry throat, but it didn't help. "OK," she said, almost croaking the words. "I'll be out in a minute."

"You'll find a new toothbrush in the cabinet."

She went into the bathroom and after getting ready for bed, looked at herself in the mirror. The baggy nightshirt came to about mid-thigh and felt smooth against her bare skin. She leaned against the sink and put her face right up to the mirror. "You shouldn't be doing this. If you had any sense at all you'd leave," but she couldn't be persuaded.

She took a deep breath, straightened her hair, and walked back into the bedroom. She neatly placed her underwear and dress on the chair by the bed.

Sigmun had arranged a blanket and pillow on the couch, and had already changed into pajama pants, his chest bare. Gods, he looked so gorgeous, she wanted to eat him up. They kissed passionately for a few minutes, pressing her body up against him, before she realized she had to stop now or she never would.

"I need to get some sleep," she said.

"OK," he replied breathlessly. "Sounds like a good idea."

She climbed into bed, pulled the covers over her and lay back on the pillow. Sigmun lay down on the couch and hit the remote, turning off the lights.

Clouds had begun to fill the sky, bringing to an end the beautiful day she and Sigmun had enjoyed. A few stars shone through the window giving very little light, but Sister Moon was new, not visible tonight. She sighed; tonight would have been a perfect night for her to have shone on her and her lover. After five minutes she knew she wasn't getting any sleep. Her heart had shown no sign of slowing down, keeping up its insistent beating, telling her it was not going to stop until it had received its due. Oh how she wished that they were betrothed. She would not be one of those who waited.

Another minute passed, and then another, and with each passing minute her resolve faded.

"Sigmun," she said finally.

"Yes," he replied, even before she had finished speaking his name.

"Could you get me a drink of water please? I'm thirsty."

"Of course," he said, hitting the remote and bringing up a soft, gentle light. He walked into the kitchen.

With an almost painful tingle at the back of her throat she slipped off her nightshirt and tossed it onto the floor. Sigmun returned holding out the glass. She made no attempt to take it from him. Instead she pulled back the covers and patted the mattress beside her.

"Are you sure?" he said, stammering the words and staring at her.

"I'm sure," she said, a hoarse whisper.

Afterwards, as she lay nestled against him, she smiled. She felt so cozy, so safe. He was asleep and the gentle rise and fall of his chest soothed her. The guilt she had felt earlier had left her as they had forged bonds of love that she knew would last through their lives, and beyond. The Elders didn't actually approve of young people making love before they were betrothed, although they did turn somewhat of a blind eye, knowing there was little they could do to stop it. She wondered if Shaylae and Micah would understand, but she pushed that thought away from her mind; this is not about Shaylae and Micah, it's about me and Sigmun. She squeezed Sigmun tightly. She could hardly contain the joy that filled her whole body. She was still tingling all over. Eventually she drifted off into a peaceful sleep, still smiling.

She wasn't sure how long she had been asleep, but they were no longer locked together. Suddenly, Sigmun sat up in bed, apparently still asleep. It made her jump, startled at first, but then she almost giggled. He's having a waking dream she thought. And then, with strong determined movements he climbed out of bed strode over to his closet, and took out his Quorum robe. He pulled it over his head, and walked toward the door.

"Sigmun?" she said, not sure if he was still asleep. An uneasy feeling began to creep up her spine. The clock read 4:10 am. Quickly she jumped out of bed and slipped on her dress. He was already out of the bedroom, heading for the front door. She followed him, not even taking time to put on her underwear or shoes. Before the door slammed behind him she ran after him and followed him down the huge corridor.

He's having a waking dream, she kept telling herself, trying to smile, trying to see the amusing side of the situation. In a moment he would awake, and she would be able to taunt him mercilessly; they would go back to his room, arm in arm, and get back into bed.

But still her uneasiness grew.

He reached an apartment she didn't recognize, and knocked on the door. She drew back into the shadows. Her heart almost stopped as Denab opened the door.

"Come, walk with me, Sigmun," he said.

"Yes, Excellency."

Denab put his arm around him. "I am extremely pleased with you," he said, as they walked out onto a balcony.

Ayanna could not believe what she was seeing and hearing. There had to be some explanation. There had to be. From the shadows she watched, sure they could not see her.

"So, you spent the day with her. How was it?"

"It went well, Excellency."

"And have you managed to persuade her to have sex with you yet?"

"Yes, Excellency."

The shock hit her like a brutal kick in the gut. Her will drained from her body. Pierced by this meteoric revelation, the life-giving air exploded from her body. She stopped breathing. Her stomach heaved; she wanted to vomit, but could not. The tears that welled up inside her would not come out. Even the terrifying scream that filled her very being could not find its way out of her body.

"Excellent. And where is she now?"

"In my bed asleep, naked." She thought she heard a sneer punctuate the word 'naked'. Her life had ended. Betrayal was a meaningless word, not even beginning to scratch the surface of the emptiness and utter horror she felt. She had descended from the highest reaches of heaven to the lowest depths of hell in but a few short seconds. Her hands automatically balled into fists, her elbows unconsciously drawn into her body as she adopted her attack position. After killing them she would jump from the balcony to her death.

"She's where?" There was a tinge of panic in Denab's voice. "Did she awaken when you left?"

"I don't think . . ."

"Yes, she awoke," she said, stepping from the shadows.

Surprise and shock filled Denab's face. And was that also fear? Sigmun did not even turn toward her.

"All that remains now is to decide which of you dies first."

The decision made, she launched herself at Sigmun.

CHAPTER 23

Denab cursed himself. Why had he not sensed her presence? Was she also a witch? Her face was red, on fire. Her eyes blazed, and her stance was both terrifying and beautiful. For a fleeting second, for the first time in his long life, he experienced fear. She launched herself at Sigmun, kicking him squarely in his stomach. He collapsed on the floor. She leaped on him, raised her fist high above his neck ready to deliver a deathblow, but she faltered. Bitter tears flooded from her eyes and her whole body shook. She threw back her head and screamed; it was more like the howl of a wild animal.

Sigmun shook his head, as if clearing it, and looked frantically into her eyes. "Ayanna, what's happening? What are we doing here?"

Denab had now recovered from the shock, and taking advantage of her hesitation he reached out his arms toward her and held her fast in a field of Power. He raised her off the ground, off of Sigmun. Sigmun turned his head toward him.

"Denab, what . . ."

But Denab silenced him also. What was he to do? He had not intended to move just yet, but now the situation had forced his hand. "Sigmun, you fool," he said with utter disdain and contempt. Quickly a new plan formed in his head. He pointed at Sigmun, who fell back unconscious, comatose. "And you, you slut. You will regret the day you were born."

She spat. "I already do. I'm already dead. There is nothing further you can do to me."

"Oh, but I think there is. Because of your foolishness and weakness I can now get to your beloved friend Shaylae." He laughed, an evil, bitter cackle.

"No!" she screamed, but Denab silenced even that as she too fell to the floor unconscious.

He spoke into his computer. "Come to me, guards."

Within seconds eight of his guard arrived, weapons at the ready.

"Take Sigmun to the infirmary, he is seriously ill, thanks to her!" He pointed disdainfully at Ayanna. "She is one of Asdzáán Nádleehé's accomplices, sent here to spy and to prepare for her coming. Take her to the level three dungeon and post two guards outside her door at all times. I want no harm to come to her, either by your hands or hers. If anything happens to her you will suffer endless pain. Now, go!"

Suddenly other guards appeared. Damn, it was Cerid and his platoon.

"What's going on here?" demanded Cerid. "Hauron sent me to look for Sigmun and Ayanna."

Yet another complication, but he knew Cerid would not dare to challenge him. He was surely fully aware of the situation, being so close to Hauron. Perhaps this was an opportunity to discredit him also. Frantically he was improvising new plans.

He spoke quietly into his wrist computer. "I want two more platoons here immediately." He turned to Cerid. "Cerid, you were aware that the girl and her friends are from Earth, yet you did nothing to warn us?"

"Second . . ."

". . . does not know anything. Am I correct? This deception was all part of a plot you had conceived, yes?"

Cerid's mind presented no challenge. "Yes, Excellency, that is correct."

The other platoons came, running. "Arrest Cerid and his platoon. I want all other guards loyal to Cerid arrested and confined."

Cerid and his platoon put up no resistance as they were taken into custody.

Denab turned to the captain standing nearest to him and quietly said, "Kill all of them except Cerid. All of them."

"And the girl?"

"For now she lives. I need her to overcome the witch." Denab turned away. "But once this is over, and if you serve me well, you may have her."

The captain leered, and beckoning a few other guards to follow him, made his way toward the dungeons.

Now, would Hauron challenge him in front of the whole Assembly? "Call the Quorum and the Council to the throne room. We have a crisis."

*   *   *

"Hauron!"

The anguished cry from Sigmun woke Hauron. "Sigmun, where are you? Are you OK?" Nothing. He looked at his clock; it read 4:15 am. "Sigmun, where are you?" he sent out his thought once more but there was still no response.

"Cerid, meet me at Sigmun's apartment. Bring a platoon."

"At once, Excellency."

Quickly he dressed and hurried to Sigmun's apartment. The door was open. He walked in and went straight to the bedroom. The bed had been slept in but there was no sign of Sigmun or Ayanna anywhere. He saw girl's underwear on the chair by the bed, and a nightshirt and pajama pants carelessly thrown on the floor.

"What is it, Excellency?" Cerid and eight of Hauron's guard were at the doorway.

"I can't find Sigmun anywhere. I want you to search everywhere. He may simply be out walking with Ayanna for all I know." He doubted it though; it looked like they had left in a hurry.

He hit a button on the videophone. "Micah, are you awake?"

The screen came to life with Micah propped up on one elbow looking very sleepy.

"Who is it?" When he saw it was Hauron he sat up straight. "I am now," he said. "What is it, Excellency?"

"Do you know where Sigmun is?"

"No. Ayanna was with him last night, and she must have stayed there late. I was already asleep before she came home."

"Could you wake her and ask her?" Hauron doubted Micah would find her, but he wanted to be sure.

"Sure." Micah jumped out of bed and pulled on his robe.

The scene on the videophone changed, presumably to Ayanna's bedroom.

"She's not here," said Micah, the level of concern on his voice rising. "And her bed's not been slept in."

"I think she spent the night with Sigmun."

"No, that's not possible," he said indignantly. "She wouldn't . . ."

"Micah, they're both missing."

"Denab?" said Micah.

"That was my thought also. I've sent Cerid out to look for them, but somehow I doubt he'll find them. I'm going to call the Assembly to the throne room. I'm sure one of them has an answer."

"I'm coming too."

"No, Micah, wait. That's not a good idea . . ." but he had already disconnected the call.

"Cerid, did you find them?" No answer. "Cerid?" Still nothing. Denab must have taken them. He made his way to the throne room as quickly as he could. Micah came running up behind him.

"Go back to your apartment," he said before they were in sight of the guards. "No, better still, go to mine."

"Excellency, please . . ."

"Micah, I insist. This is too dangerous. Cerid is not responding to my calls. He could be captured already. You need to stay low until we can formulate some kind of plan. You'll be no use to anyone if you're captured too."

Reluctantly Micah nodded his agreement. "Yes, Excellency."

Hauron spoke into his phone. "Geoan, I'm sending someone to you. Hide him as best you can. If he is discovered you must disavow all knowledge, do you understand?"

"But, Hauron . . ."

"Please, mother. This is important."

"OK, but what is happening?"

"I'll explain later. Now please, do as I say."

CHAPTER 24

⟶⦿⟵

In the throne room, waiting for the Assembly to arrive, Denab realized he was still shaking. With all his power, with all of his evil, he was still a coward. What would have happened had she gone for him first? He would have been unprepared. She could have easily killed him, and then he would have been forced to start all over again, to look for another host. But fate had smiled on him that day; although he still had to develop a new plan from the ashes of his failure.

"Brethren of the Quorum and of the Council," he said once they were gathered. "We are facing a grave danger, a crisis."

"Where's Second?" asked one.

"And Sigmun?" asked another.

"I'm afraid that's why we're here. First of all I have to tell you that Hauron has been deceived. His guards, led by Cerid, have somehow managed to smuggle Asdzáán Nádleehé and two of her friends into the palace. Hauron has somehow been convinced that they are from his own continent and has welcomed them."

"That's not possible . . ." began one.

Denab held up his hands. "Brethren, please. Let me finish. I know you're all thinking the same thing. How could Hauron have been fooled? I would remind you of his inexperience. Certainly he has great power, but he has not been brought up, surrounded by the fear of Asdzáán Nádleehé, as have we. And let us not forget, she has a cunning, brilliant mind. It is no reflection upon Hauron that he has been thus deceived. That is why, in his wisdom, our First Prophet set up the Assembly, to protect against the cunningness of the witch."

"What information have you been able to get from Cerid and his guards?"

"I'm afraid they're all dead. I can only assume the witch did not want them revealing her plans and so she killed them."

For the moment he had silenced them; at least to the point they would dare not challenge him.

"Now, before Hauron joins us I must tell you of our poor brother, Sigmun, he also has been duped by one of the witch's accomplices, a girl by the name of Ayanna. A new danger that we had not foreseen has come upon us. It seems that the girl Ayanna has brought with her viruses from Earth, viruses not known on Yurob. Because of her seduction of Sigmun he has contracted an Earth disease and is deathly ill. He may even die."

"Where is this girl, Ayanna?"

"She has been safely quarantined. We are in no danger."

"What of the other accomplice?"

"A young man by the name of Micah. We are not sure where he is, but it is likely he will seek out Hauron once he discovers that the girl is missing. He will not expect us to know the depth of their deception, and that should work to our advantage."

"So, what is our next move?"

"The next move belongs to the witch and her friends, and should occur soon. We will wait and maintain our advantage."

*　　*　　*

As confidently as he could Hauron stormed into the throne room to find First Prophet and the Assembly already gathered.

"First Prophet," he said as he bowed. "I wasn't aware you had called an Assembly. I apologize if I am late"

First Prophet looked almost paralyzed with fear. Hauron almost felt pity for him. He looked anxiously between him and Denab, not knowing anymore where his greatest danger lay. Denab must have finally showed his power to him, but there was no way he could have known who was the more powerful. No wonder First Prophet looked so confused. Not that Hauron cared anymore; First Prophet was clearly out of the game, and the rest of the Assembly knew it too.

Denab stepped forward. "Actually, I called the assembly, Second," he said calmly

Everything Shaylae had warned him about was coming to pass. His trust of her, though not yet perfect, was strengthening. He sensed a malignant Power emanating from Denab; something he had not felt before.

"By what authority?" thundered Hauron, hoping his will would not fail him.

Denab held up his hand submissively. "If you'll give me a moment to explain I'm sure you will understand."

"Proceed."

"Second, it appears you have been the victim of an extremely clever and well-conceived plot."

Hauron felt waves of fear and doubt working their way into his mind, trying to take hold of him. Denab! With all of his willpower he fought, managing to keep Denab's attack on his mind at bay. "Oh, how so?"

"It appears that the witch, Asdzáán Nádleehé, has somehow managed to infiltrate your guard. She and two of her accomplices have been given safe haven by you, under the guise of being visitors from the Eastern Continent."

Very clever. He knows I won't challenge this in open Assembly, thought Hauron.

"I'm afraid I also have some bad news about Sigmun," he continued, pressing his advantage.

"What?" said Hauron, feeling more and more helpless.

"The witch and her friends have introduced viruses not found on Yurob, and Sigmun has been infected. He may not survive . . ."

"Take me to him at once."

"I'm afraid we cannot risk that. Until we have formulated the antibodies there is great danger to our whole planet. He is in quarantine."

He probably could have forced this issue, but wanted to find out more first.

"And the girl?"

"Under arrest, and of course quarantined."

"What about the boy, Micah?"

"We have yet to find him?"

"Cerid will know where he is," he said, hoping to buy some time. He spoke into his phone, knowing of course there would be no response. "Cerid." There was no response. "Cerid," he repeated.

"Cerid has been arrested. And since we couldn't take any chances I have had all of your guards also taken into custody . . ."

"How dare you!" Hauron was speaking with confidence he did not feel, although the anger was real. Yes, anger was his friend, just as it had been fighting Kildane.

"Second, please understand, we have no idea how far this plot extends . . ."

"Take me to Cerid at once," he said, turning to a guard.

"He also is in quarantine."

Hauron was backed into a corner. All he had left now was his bravado. How far would Denab challenge him in open Assembly.

"Leave me. All of you. Leave." No one moved. He raised his arms in anger, ready to use his Power. "Leave me I said. Now!"

Finally Denab spoke. "We will leave. But I advise you not to do anything rash. Let us make sure we understand the danger before we take any action which may harm our beloved Yurob."

He felt the attack on his mind strengthen as Denab tried to take control of him, but somehow he still managed to keep it at bay. It must have been his anger. He breathed a silent sigh of relief. For the moment he knew he had forced Denab to back off. But for how long?

"I understand, Denab. Now, please. I need to be alone."

Slowly, the Assembly began to file out of the throne room and he was alone. First things first, he thought. I have to find Cerid, that is if he's still alive.

CHAPTER 25

July 10, 2108

It was totally dark. Ayanna could not even see her hand in front of her face no matter how much she strained. She was lying on a narrow, uncomfortable bed that was up against a cold metal wall to her left. The only sound was the sound of her labored breathing. The smell was sickening and the air was damp.

She lay still, not wanting to move, not wanting to even explore. She wanted nothing more than to be dead. But why was she still alive? Oh yes, she remembered; Denab had said he would use her to get to Shaylae. How could she have been so stupid? She began to cry again. Her own life was meaningless now, but because of her foolishness she had put Shaylae in grave danger. She slammed her fist against the wall and didn't even notice the pain.

It was cold. She shivered. Her dress had ridden halfway up her thighs. She pulled it back down to her knees. It was the only thing she was wearing. She didn't even have any shoes on her feet. Her state of undress once more pounded her fall from grace into her mind.

How could Sigmun have been so cruel, so uncaring? He had seemed so decent, so kind and gentle. They had been so natural together, so perfect. The memory of that wonderful day, and the incredible evening that followed, flooded into her mind, making her humiliation even more devastating. He had used her! Why hadn't she killed him when she had the chance? Because she still loved him that's why, even though she hated him with all her being.

She turned over on the cot, burying her face in the thin mattress, sobbing almost hysterically. "Sigmun," she cried bitterly. "I hate you. I wish you were dead. I wish I was dead." She repeated it again and again, a tragic mantra.

Suddenly the cell was filled with light so blinding she had to close her eyes and cover them with her hands. The door opened and something, or someone, was pushed inside the cell. Whatever it was hit the floor with a dull thud. The door slammed and the darkness returned. She sat up. She heard breathing, almost gargling, coming from the person on the floor. Gods, could it be Shaylae? No, it sounded more like a man. Oh no! Micah!

She carefully slid off her cot, not wanting to tread on him. She felt his body at her feet and reached out with her hands to find his head. It was definitely Micah. His long hair and strong features were unmistakable. His face was wet. She touched her fingers to her lips; blood. He groaned.

"Micah, are you OK? It's me, Anna."

"Anna," he said weakly.

Just the other side of him was another cot. "Micah, there's a cot right here. See if you can climb on to it."

He struggled up, she half lifting him until she had him on the cot.

"Micah, are you OK?" she repeated.

The only response she got was another groan. She felt his face. The blood was seeping steadily from a nasty gash on his face. She had to stop the bleeding, but with what? She grabbed at the sheet on her cot and ripped off a strip. She put it to her nose, and almost gagged. Blessed Ancestors! She couldn't use that—it would do more harm than good. She reached for the hem of her dress and with both hands tore off a big strip. She carefully dabbed it on Micah's cheek, trying to soak up the blood, but it didn't make a very good bandage, it had no absorbency. She folded it into a compress, put her left hand behind his head and with her right hand held it against his cheek.

After about ten minutes she pulled it back. The bleeding still hadn't stopped, so she quickly re-applied it. Her arm began to ache, and the muscles in her back were knotting up. She slid Micah over as far as she could against the wall, and climbed onto the cot with him. It was easier for her to hold the compress against his face. She drifted into a shallow, fitful sleep.

Later, she was not sure how much later, Micah stirred.

"Micah, are you OK?"

"Anna, is that you?"

"Yes. Are you OK?"

"I think so. My head is pounding and my face is on fire, but I don't think I have any other injuries."

"What happened?"

"Hauron called me in the middle of the night. He couldn't find you or Sigmun. He suspected Denab was involved and headed over to the throne room. I wanted to go with him but he insisted I hide at his place. I never made it. The next thing I remember is waking up in here."

It was strange being so close to Micah like this, hearing his voice, feeling his breath on her face, but not being able to see him.

"I'm assuming we're in some kind of prison. What else is in here, beside the beds? How big is it?"

"I've no idea?"

"Anna, how long have you been here, and you haven't even reconnoitered?"

"Micah, all I've done is cry and curse myself. I'm sorry. I did a terrible thing. I . . ." She couldn't finish. She began to sob again.

"Hauron told me," said Micah.

"Told you what?" she asked when he didn't continue.

"You and Sigmun—he said you . . . spent the night at his place."

"It's true," she said.

He didn't say anything. She stood up and lay down on her cot again. The shame of what she had done filled her breathing soul with anguish once more, and she sobbed bitterly. Micah's silence was more crushing than if he had gotten angry at her.

"Did you . . . ?" he said finally, leaving the rest of the question unspoken.

"Yes."

"Do you love him? Does he love you?" He got up and sat next to her, stroking her hair. "Ayanna, please don't cry."

"You don't know what happened do you?"

"No. What?"

"Sigmun's in league with Denab."

"What?"

"We were asleep in his bed. He woke up in the middle of the night. I thought he was sleepwalking so I followed him. He went to Denab's apartment."

"Do you think he was hypnotized or something?"

"I don't know. I don't think so. Mike, you should have heard him bragging to Denab about what we had done."

Micah drew a long breath through his teeth. "Anna, if I thought for one moment that he had betrayed you I would kill him."

"You don't think he did? Mike, you weren't there."

"Well, maybe. But remember what Shay said? She's convinced that Denab recruited Sigmun to . . ."

"But how would Denab possibly have known what was going to happen? That was ages before Hauron showed up at the palace. He wouldn't have even known anything about him."

"I know, but you should wait until you find out what happened."

"Micah, he bragged about having made love to me." She was crying now. "Even if he was under some kind of compulsion, I heard him say those things. I don't think I could ever forgive him."

"Well, we can worry about that later. Now we should see what we can do to get out of here."

Ayanna sobbed again. "Micah, I don't want to get out. I want to stay her, die here."

"Anna, how can you say such things?"

"I can never face anyone again. Especially Shay. And Denab said he was going to use me to get to her. I'd rather be dead."

Micah put a strong comforting arm around her shoulder. "Anna, please . . ."

But she shook herself free of him and lay face down on her cot, sobbing bitterly.

CHAPTER 26

―•❀•―

Shaylae sat on the bench thinking on what Elder Nashota had said. It was a lot to think about, particularly what she had said about getting married to Micah. But then, as she thought of returning to Yurob, she realized she would have to be cautious. Nashota hadn't been very helpful, only telling her that things were heating up. She straightened up suddenly, wondering if that meant that Micah and Ayanna were in trouble. Should she leave her body here and travel in spirit back to Yurob? Not even sure where 'here' was, she decided she would have to shift directly to Yurob. But where?

She closed her eyes and peered across space until she found Procyon and then Yurob. She couldn't find Micah or Ayanna anywhere. For a moment she panicked, but then relaxed. If anything had happened to them she would have been sure to sense it. No, they were still alive. There had to be another explanation. She couldn't find Sigmun either, but again was able to convince herself not to worry. Hauron she found; he was on his way to a confrontation with Denab. She had to hurry. She directed her mind to Hauron's apartment in the palace. Kazzy was there, in the living room on the computer. She had to take a chance—she shifted.

Kazzy jumped as Shaylae appeared in the room. She turned and looked at her, then smiled. She had an incredibly bright and intelligent face.

"Oh hi, Shaylae," she said.

"You know who I am?"

"Oh yes. I saw you here the first time you came."

"But how did you know my name?"

"Oh, I know all about you. Sigmun told me. 'Course he spoke mostly about Ayanna—I think he likes her."

"Do you know where Sigmun is?"

"No. I haven't seen him since yesterday morning"

"Your parents?"

"They're not here. Nanny is though. You want to talk to her?"

"No, I think I'd better go looking for your brother and Sigmun?"

"OK."

"Kazzy, I'm going to need somewhere safe where I can . . . . I need to be in a sort of trance so I can travel about the palace unnoticed."

"Cool! How do you do that?"

Shaylae smiled. "One day I'll show you."

"You could hide in my closet. It's huge. I could work on the computer in there and we could lock the door."

"Sounds great. Thanks, Kazzy. You're a good friend."

Kazzy beamed all over her face and led Shaylae to her bedroom. Once she was hidden and settled her spirit left her body and she was free to follow Hauron to his meeting.

*   *   *

"OK, Hauron. Let's cut the pretense. I think you know by now I could destroy you, but I'm prepared to leave you in power if you keep your head down, stay out of this situation."

Hauron's mind was racing. How far was he prepared to go to stand up to Denab. Any illusion he had held about being the most powerful man on Yurob had long since departed. But Denab still wanted him around; the question was, how badly did he need him and for how long?

Suddenly he sensed Shaylae's unmistakable presence. She was here. Did Denab realize it also?

"Fine. But let me have my guards back. And Sigmun. I want Sigmun back."

"Out of the question. How could we explain freeing Cerid and his platoon now that the Assembly thinks he is the source of this plot?"

"You sure that is what they believe?"

"Doesn't matter. None will question my assessment."

Hauron felt hopeless. Now he understood how First Prophet must have felt when he had usurped him and kept him as a figurehead only. It was exactly what Denab was doing to him.

"Then you must guarantee their safety."

"That I cannot do."

Hauron was not getting anywhere. They may already be dead, he feared.

"What about Sigmun?"

"No. He's deathly sick."

"Is he?"

Denab snorted. "Regardless, he will not be harmed. He has been very useful to me, and will probably be useful again."

How was Sigmun going to be useful to him in the future? Obviously Shaylae had been right; Denab had used Sigmun to get to him. At least Denab had guaranteed his life, but could he be trusted? Probably. What possible reason would he have to lie?

"And Micah and Ayanna?"

"Again, I won't release them but no harm will come to them. They will be vital in trapping the witch."

"She's not Asdzáán Nádleehé. But you already know that don't you?"

Again Denab snorted. "You finally figured that out?"

By now it was apparent to Hauron that Denab had not sensed Shaylae's presence. But why?

"What makes you think she will return?" Hauron took a chance and glanced around the room, letting his eyes rest briefly at the place where she stood. He wanted her to know that he knew she was here.

"Hauron, don't press me. Don't ask me these things again. I had not intended to show my hand until much later, but Sigmun and the brat, Ayanna, forced me to change my plans. If necessary I will destroy you and modify my plans again. I'd prefer not to, but do not overestimate your usefulness to me. And then of course there's your family. I could cause them intense suffering. And I like little Kazzy; she's a little cutie . . ."

Hauron lost control and lashed out at Denab, but he moved too quickly and Hauron's fist passed through empty air! Denab laughed. "You can't hurt me you fool. You can't even touch me. But try that again and the little brat dies in great pain."

Hauron fell to his knees, his face buried in his hands. "Denab, don't touch her. Leave my sister, my family out of this. I'll do anything."

"Fine. Just see that you do."

Denab turned on his heels and strode briskly out of the room. He turned back as he opened the door to leave. "Just let me know the minute the witch returns."

Shaylae was stunned! Would Hauron betray her to save his family? He was still on his knees, hands covering his face. Finally he spoke.

"Shaylae, I'm frightened. What can I do?"

"Come back to your apartment. I'm in Kazzy's room."

Shaylae reentered her body and waited until he arrived.

"Hauron, we need to get you away from here. You and all your family."

"Where will you take me where he cannot reach? And why not just take my family? I'm not afraid of what he can do to me."

"I'm fairly certain he couldn't reach you if you were off the planet. And I think it's vital that you are here to resume leadership of the planet once we defeat him. You are far more important to your people than you realize, and as soon as he found out your family had left and you remained, I'm sure he would kill you."

He shook his head hopelessly. "You think he can be defeated? There's nothing we can do. Not you, not me . . ."

"Perhaps not individually. And perhaps not even together. But with our friends, and all the people of Yurob who have come to love you . . ."

"They have?"

"Hauron, I saw them. Before the first time we met I saw them, and trust me, they love you."

"But even with all that help, can he be defeated?"

She tenderly put her hand on his arm. "Hauron, I have always believed in the triumph of good over evil; perhaps not always at an individual level, but when the fate of an entire planet rests on victory, yes, I believe we will win."

"And what if I do go with you? What then? You think he will kill Sigmun and your friends."

Shaylae's eyes saddened. "Perhaps. And I cannot imagine life without Micah and Ayanna, but there are more important issues at stake here. And I know they would willingly give their lives to see us triumph. But I don't think he will harm them. He sees them as his leverage to get me. I'm not sure why he wants Sigmun alive, but again, I don't think he will kill him."

"Then I will come with you. My father is governor of the Eastern continent. I'll call him back; it will take a few hours for him to get here. Mother is with her music group, she should be home soon."

"No, that will raise Denab's suspicions. We need to all go within the same fraction of a second before Denab has time to react. I can pick him up."

"What about Cerid? I am sure he is already dead."

"No, Cerid is alive. I'm afraid Denab has killed all of your other guards, but has left him alive."

"Gods. Those were good men. Family men some of them." Hauron was visibly upset by the news of the loss.

"I'm sorry, Hauron. But we have to hurry. I don't know how long it will be before he figures out I'm back. Let me locate your father and Cerid and then we'll go."

She closed her eyes for a few moments and then said. "This is going to feel really weird to you; and worse for your family, because they won't even be expecting it. You, Jerrod, Kazzy and I will instantly transport to Cerid's cell, then to your mother's music group, then to your father, and then to Reconciliation. All in less then a second."

"Reconciliation?"

"Yes, it's what General Shasck renamed Revenge."

"Is he in charge now?"

"Well, initially he was, but only until he could organize elections. He's one of those rare military men who think government should be in the hands of the people, not soldiers."

"I wonder how I will be received."

"Ah, there's another thing. You're arriving as Second of Yurob. You're going to have to act like it. Forget your defeat at the hands of Denab; put yourself mentally back where you were when you first put me in my place." She smiled, and then briefly, so did he.

"Then I should put on my robes?"

"Yes, the most opulent and finest you have. While you're getting ready I'm going to shift aboard Reconciliation to let them know to expect us, and to bring out the red carpet."

Thirty minutes later they had all gathered in Kazzy's room. Hauron's mother had returned. She was holding Jerrod and looking quite scared. Shaylae held Kazzy's hand.

"We're going on a trip," Hauron had told Kazzy.

"Why?"

"Oh, just for fun," he replied.

"Hauron, don't lie. We're in danger aren't we?" said his mother.

"It's only for a while," said Shaylae. "And we're going to pick up your father and Cerid so they'll be safe too."

"What about Nanny? They'll kill her," said Kazzy.

Shaylae was astounded by the incredible insight of Hauron's young sister. She looked at Hauron, who nodded his agreement.

"I don't know how to find her."

"Let me call her back," said Geoan.

"That should be safe enough," said Shaylae, hoping it would not make Denab suspicious.

Finally, they were all ready. Nanny's name was Francis, and she was no more than two years older than Shaylae. She looked terrified.

"Don't worry, Fran. We're in good hands," said Hauron, holding her hand.

"OK, here we go. When we arrive, Hauron, you're in charge."

Blessed Ancestors, Holy Ones, she thought quietly to herself. Be with me on this perilous journey.

It happened exactly as Shaylae had said. Like a changing scene flashing before their eyes, they were in Cerid's cell, then in their father's office, then aboard Reconciliation.

CHAPTER 27

July 11, 2108

All Hauron wanted to do was vomit. His stomach was churning and his head was reeling. He felt Shaylae's hand behind him, out of sight, steadying him. Standing in front of him was an impressive reception committee.

"I am Hauron of the Eleven, Second of Yurob." He held his arm out to his family. "My father and mother, my sister and brother, and our good friend, Francis." and then turning to Cerid, "And this is Cerid, captain of my guard. I believe you already know Shaylae of the Gentle Heart."

The welcoming committee bowed in deference to their leader. The woman in the center spoke.

"I am Seri, Governor of Reconciliation. Welcome aboard, Excellency."

He gave the barest of bows with his head. Shaylae smiled to herself. He was behaving perfectly.

"They put a woman in charge?"

"Yes, but not exactly put in charge, she was democratically elected," thought Shaylae, hiding her smile with as little success as Hauron had hidden his surprise. "A move in the right direction wouldn't you say," she added, driving home the point.

Seri continued. "This is General Shasck, Military Chief of Staff, Lieutenant Colonel Tregon, his second in command. Special Agent Anne Lawrence and Colonel Harley Davidson from the Defense Intelligence Agency of the United States, Earth."

Shaylae bowed her head. "Governor Seri, if it pleases you, I would like to help Hauron and his family settle, and then I believe we should meet to discuss the latest developments on Yurob."

"By all means. At Second's convenience." She turned to Anne and Harley. "Could you please show Second and his entourage to their accommodations?"

"Of course," said Anne. She smiled at Shaylae, and it was obvious to Hauron that they wanted to hug each other, but the dignity of the moment precluded that.

As soon as they were settled, Shaylae, Anne and Harley indulged in their hug. Hauron was moved by their deep and enduring affection. How he wished for the day when all of his citizens could enjoy such unaffected relationships, unafraid of the terrors of their leaders.

"How's little Shay-Anne?"

"Not so little anymore," said Anne. She pulled a miniature holo from her pocket and activated it. A cute little girl, about two years old smiled out at them, a face radiating with the ease and calm of a child who is adored. "She'll be two this month."

Harley patted Anne's belly. "And little Harley will be here in about four months."

"Oh, Anne, congratulations. Harley, that's great."

They hugged again.

Hauron cleared his throat.

"Oh, sorry, Excellency," said Anne. "It's just we haven't seen Shaylae for over a year now."

He waved her off. "Oh, please, it's wonderful to see how much you love each other. And when we're alone I want you to call me Hauron."

"Anne, Harley," said Shaylae. "Can you leave us now. Hauron and I have some catching up to do."

Shaylae took his hand. "Hauron, you promised you would soul-share with me once I returned."

He nodded. "Yes, and I'm ready, more than ready."

"Give me a few moments to freshen up. I'll be right back."

Shaylae went into her bedroom. Standing before her was a young woman; a beautiful woman, about her age.

"Who are you?" And then she gasped as she recognized the woman who came to her Kinaalda in vision. "Asdzáán Nádleehé?"

"Yanaba, it is so good to meet you?"

"How . . ."

"Yanaba, for me it has been four years; four long painful years since those terrible events on Tal'el'Dine'h. For the citizens of Yurob it has been three-thousand years. I had to come here to meet Hauron in person and beg his forgiveness."

"But how did you get here?"

"It is a gift of the Holy Wind; a gift that you will soon need. Just as all points in space can be considered contiguous in the various planes of the universe, so it is with all points in time."

"I don't understand . . ."

"You will. Now, Yanaba let me hold you."

She reached for Shaylae and held her in her arms. Shaylae felt the warmth of this great woman, the mother of The People, fill her breathing soul.

"I'm not yet the mother of the people," she said, reading Shaylae's mind. "I'm not even wed. In truth, I have not yet found my husband."

Asdzáán Nádleehé broke the embrace, took Shaylae by the hand, and led her to the mirror. "See, we could be twins, you and I."

It was true. This goddess looked just like her.

"Now, Yanaba, Shaylae, may we soul-share?"

Shaylae nodded. She opened her mind, and felt Asdzáán Nádleehé join her. How alike they were. They shared the same faith, the same virtue, and the same love of the Holy Ones and awe of their wonder. Asdzáán Nádleehé shared with her all that had happened to her since she had left Tal'el'Dine'h. She felt her sadness at the loss of her parents and all those she loved; she shared her fear as she journeyed to her new home; she felt her joy as her new father, Long Life Man, found her on Ch'óol'í'í, and took her to her new mother, Happiness Woman. She relived the excitement of her own Kinaalda as Asdzáán Nádleehé showed her how she introduced the ceremony to her people.

Shaylae reached for her and held her close. "We are sisters, you and I."

"Indeed we are, Yanaba, Shaylae of the Gentle Heart. Now, let us go and join Hauron of the Eleven."

Hauron was startled to see two young women leave Shaylae's room.

"There is another I would like to join us, with your permission," said Shaylae.

Hauron nodded. "Of course," he said somewhat dazed; she could have been Shaylae's twin.

"The eyes give it away," said the newcomer.

"What?"

"The eyes. Mine are brown, hers are that beautiful shade of blue," she said, with a half-smile-half-frown.

"Hauron, I would like you to meet Asdzáán Nádleehé."

That took him by surprise; to be standing face to face with the girl who had been his enemy all his life was, to say the least, a shock.

"Forgive me, Hauron, but I wanted you to see and hear first-hand what happened on Tal'el'Dine'h three thousand years ago. I have traveled through time and space to be with you."

Hauron managed to stammer a "Hello."

Shaylae sat on the floor, cross-legged. Asdzáán Nádleehé followed. They joined hands, and extended their other hands to him. He sat down, not quite sure what to expect, and completed the circle.

"Hauron, you're familiar with mind speak but I would like us to soul-share. You'll find it quite different, even a shock at first, but it is necessary to take you to Tal'el'Dine'h, rather than just tell you what happened," said Shaylae.

He nodded. "I'm ready."

"You must join with us willingly. To soul-share all must be willing," said Asdzáán Nádleehé. "Open your mind."

He closed his eyes, opened his mind, and immediately was filled with an incredible feeling of power as the souls of these two sisters joined with him.

"Don't resist it, Hauron."

Why would he have done? How could he have done? It was if he had just been born. All of his life he had wandered lost and alone,

160

and now he was joined in a way, so intimately, so deeply, with two incredible minds. Both were strong, both had seemingly infinite kindness and gentleness. Both were brilliant, although that word hardly did justice to the depth and breadth of the intelligence he found there.

Their chests rose and fell slowly, perfectly synchronized, as they breathed. He found himself falling into the same rhythm. Not only were they sharing minds and souls, they shared the same air.

"It's called the Holy Wind, Hauron."

"Holy Wind?"

"The Spirit of the Holy Ones that permeates everything in the Universe. As we become one with that Wind, we become one with each other, and with Them."

For a long time nothing was said. And for Hauron that was just as it should be. He basked in the souls of these two wonderful people. He gloried in their presence. He immediately loved Shaylae as his sister, but Asdzáán Nádleehé—for Asdzáán Nádleehé he felt a lot more. He felt an immediate and powerful connection with her, a connection deeper than he had ever shared with another soul.

"Hauron, the Holy Ones smiled on Yurob when they gave birth to your spirit," said Asdzáán Nádleehé.

"But I am nothing. You are . . ."

"Hauron, you cannot hide your strength, goodness, and wisdom from us. Not when we are soul-sharing."

"But I have done terrible things."

"Those things we see also, but do not punish yourself. You acted out of the most unselfish of motives, and the Holy Ones love you. There is nothing you need forgiveness for. The timing of the Holy Ones is perfect. You were reserved to come forward at this time, just as Yanaba was."

For hours, or was it days, nothing more was said as Hauron, Shaylae, and Asdzáán Nádleehé became friends, came to know each other, came to understand each other as only humans who have been privileged to soul-share can.

Finally Asdzáán Nádleehé spoke again. "Hauron, please come with me, back to Tal'el'Dine'h, three thousand years ago" In an instant he was with Asdzáán Nádleehé on her home world. It was beautiful, peaceful and holy. Everything was in perfect harmony.

Everyone loved and was loved. All animals, plants, and the land itself were held in the highest regard by all of these wonderful people. If there was such a thing as heaven in the universe he had found it.

And then he was standing with Asdzáán Nádleehé, high on a hill, watching as a cataclysmic explosion shook her planet and a devastating shock wave crashed its way toward them. It was so real that he flinched. But just as it arrived she shifted them from harm's way. He shared her sorrow, her anguish, her loss, and then her anger as if it was his own. It was so intense and so powerful it frightened him; it was unrestrained, unfettered. He felt the almost infinite power that emanated from her as she shifted the huge vessel back to Yurob and then fused the hydrogen fuel. Almost at once he felt the remorse and pain at the realization of what she had done, but it was too late; she could not take back what so impulsively she had done. Her guilt was intense, it was devastating, and she was unforgiving.

"You had no idea did you?"

"That I had that kind of power? No, none whatsoever."

"Oh, Asdzáán Nádleehé, I am so desperately sorry for what my ancestors did to your planet. How can you ever forgive us?"

"Hauron, my crime was worse."

"How could it have been? You had no way of knowing . . ."

"But, I had to be thinking those thoughts. I had to have wanted to bring that kind of destruction to your planet, else how could it have happened."

"You were fourteen years old."

"Hauron," interrupted Shaylae with kindness and warmth. "She won't be consoled. She will never forgive herself. The only thing that will redeem her is to set right what she started all these years ago. And that requires both you and me."

"Asdzáán Nádleehé, I love you for who you are, and will you accept not only my forgiveness, but also accept my love. Whatever I can do to help you cleanse yourself from this guilt, give my life if necessary, I will do it."

"Hauron, the citizens of Yurob are blessed to have you as their leader."

Hauron thought for a moment, digesting what he had seen, and more importantly, what he had felt.

"Shaylae of the Gentle Heart, could you now show me those final moments aboard Revenge, when you defeated the Assembly." He had to know how she had felt, destroying those men; what it had done to her, even though it had been for the greater good.

"Certainly. Come with me."

In an instant he was aboard Revenge. Shaylae, Micah, and Ayanna were on horseback, shining brilliant white, suspended above the floor; a terrifying and awesome sight. He watched as one-by-one the members of the Assembly succumbed to that awful power and fell dead to the floor, until only one of them stood. He heard the conversation clearly:

"So, after three thousand years you have the victory Asdzáán Nádleehé?" said Second, resignation in his voice, but no fear. "And now, kill me as you have killed the others."

"What is your name, Second?"

Hauron could hear the pride and arrogance in his voice as he answered, "I am Lanai of the Eleven."

He watched as Shaylae slid from her horse and tentatively stood on her right leg. He winced as he recalled the brutal beating he had seen the previous Second give her. Micah and Ayanna joined her, supporting her weight as they walked toward him. Shaylae reached out and took his hands in hers as Micah and Ayanna placed their hands on his shoulders. Is this where she kills him, he wondered? He watched as Shaylae leaned forward and whispered something into his ear. He tried to pull back, but Micah and Ayanna continued to hold him firm. She released his hands and put her hands on his head. He watched as Lanai's eyes widened, first in horror, then in anguish. This is it, he thought, this must be where she kills him.

But then, a sudden gust of wind surrounded the four of them. It was so real Hauron could feel it. It was cold, hollow, threatening.

Shaylae threw her head back in agony and with what sounded like fear shouted, "Lanai, my brother, command the evil wind to leave. It has no power over you, only that which you choose to give it. You must command it to leave you."

Lanai closed his wide-eyed stare, took a deep breath and tensed his face muscles. Immediately the wind dispersed. He sank to his knees, sitting back on his heels, and buried his head in his hands sobbing bitterly. Shaylae reached out once more and took his hands in hers and helped him to his feet. Hauron gasped as he felt the love flowing from her into Lanai.

"Shaylae of the Gentle Heart, why?" said Lanai, tears in his eyes.

"Lanai, you are free. Now, free your brothers."

He did not move. The tears continued to fall from his eyes as he held onto Shaylae's arms, not wanting to let go. "But why would you help us?"

"Lanai, you are my brother." She gently stretched out her arm to the fallen Council and Quorum and said, "And now your brothers await you."

"Shaylae . . ." began Hauron. He was almost lost for words, even in the midst of their soul-sharing. "You are a goddess, you are divine. I thought you had killed them all. No one would have blamed you."

"Hauron, as much as I agree with your assessment of her, I have to tell you she is not a goddess, but she is divine; we all are," said Asdzáán Nádleehé.

"We all are?"

"Yes. All of us have inherited divine nature from our Holy Parents. And none more so than Shaylae of the Gentle Heart. There is no doubt in my mind that she is the greatest woman to have ever lived."

Hauron sensed Shaylae's discomfort with Asdzáán Nádleehé's words, but after what he had witnessed how could there have been any doubt?

Gradually Hauron felt himself coming down from the incredible spiritual high of having being united with these two beautiful souls. He could hardly breathe. He had been one with Shaylae of the Gentle Heart and Asdzáán Nádleehé.

"The others will be wondering where we are. How many hours have we been gone?"

Shaylae pointed to the clock. "Less than three minutes, Hauron."

"How?" he asked, mouth wide open.

Shaylae and Asdzáán Nádleehé looked at each other, huge smiles on their beautiful faces.

"And now, dear sister, dear brother Hauron, I must leave and return to my people."

"Wait!" said Hauron almost in a panic. He could not bear the thought of letting her leave, he wanted her to stay forever. "Don't go."

"Hauron, I have to. I don't belong here . . ."

"Then take me with you."

She looked surprised, but nevertheless she smiled shyly. "Hauron, this is not possible. We come from different times and places. Besides, you are needed here; you have a divine purpose, and you must fulfill it."

"And then?"

"I don't know." She paused, looking at Shaylae. And then she smiled again. "We will see."

In those three words Hauron found hope. He had a new incentive to prevail against Denab and all that he stood for.

CHAPTER 28

⊸⊶⊶⊷⊷⊸

July 18, 2108

Micah had no idea how long they had been held prisoner. It may have been a week, or maybe even two. There was no way to determine accurately. Even the food and water that had been pushed through the small slot in the base of the door didn't occur at regular intervals. Not that Micah could rely on his own sense of time in this awful place.

The food wasn't much. It tasted foul, but it was nourishment, and he had to keep his strength up. Shaylae must still be alive and she must still be free, else why would he still be alive? He was worried about Ayanna though. She had not eaten, and had barely drunk any of the water. Each day when the food arrived he would try to persuade her. "Anna, you have to eat. Sooner or later we may have to fight alongside Shaylae. She's going to need us."

"She doesn't need me. I'm nothing but a liability to her." Anna's voice sounded weak, not only physically, but spiritually. "While I'm alive Denab can use me against her."

She didn't extend the idea to include Micah as a liability, but it was clearly implied. Most of the time she simply lay on her cot, not moving, not talking, totally ignoring Micah's attempts to console her. And then she'd usually add, "I'll never be able to face her again after what I've done."

Micah didn't really know what to say in response to that. He could understand how she felt after Sigmun had betrayed her.

The lights came on, blinding Micah. He heard the slot in door open and the metal tray being slid in the cell. The slot closed and the lights went out. It was the same every day—there was never a chance to jump down and look through the slot, or try to grab the hand of the person delivering. He climbed off his cot and took one of the canisters of water. As usual, he put his hand behind Ayanna's head and tried to coax some water down her throat. Instead of choking and gagging, trying to refuse, this time she didn't even move.

"Dear Gods, Ayanna. Please drink. Please take some water. Say something." But she was totally motionless. Other than her slow shallow breathing he would have sworn she was dead. He fell to his knees on the floor and raised his hands heavenward. "Holy Ones, Blessed Ancestors, please help me." He was not usually taken to praying, but this time with all his energy, with all the sincerity of his heart, he pleaded with the Gods. "Please, take me, not her; not dear Ayanna. Hear me oh Holy Ones."

He didn't touch his own food or water. He stayed on his knees, begging for Ayanna's life. All night he prayed, but to no avail. Nothing. She was still breathing, but it seemed to have become even shallower, more strained. He put his ear to her chest. Her lungs sounded as if they were filled with fluids.

"Oh Gods! Shaylae! Please help us!" He cried out in the deepest anguish of his soul. "Oh, Shaylae. Please."

"Micah!"

"Shaylae!" The relief that filled Micah's mind almost overwhelmed him.

* * *

For a week Shaylae had been trying to find Ayanna and Micah. After nine days she was beginning to wonder if they were still alive. No, drive that thought out; they had to be. But search as she could, she could not find any trace of the spirits of her friends. Something had to be stopping her, there had to be some kind of barrier that her mind could not penetrate.

Night after night she would try again. She would begin by going through the sacred motions to greet the Blessed Ancestors. She would prostrate herself before the Holy Ones, begging them to guide her. But there was nothing, no response. She would then sit in lotus, concentrating, calming her mind, driving out her fears. Time and time again she would almost reach Karma, but then fear would enter her mind and she would have to begin again. Each night it was the same. Each night would end with the same bitter disappointment.

By day she would try to occupy herself with things of no consequence. Hauron, Cerid, Anne and Harley spent all of their time discussing strategy for whatever may come about. Cerid had drawn detailed plans of the palace, including all of the secret passages into the dungeons, but they knew not to bother Shaylae with such things. When she came to them they would put away their plans and strategies and try to keep her calm and relaxed.

So, tonight she would try again. She had felt a special urgency. Something had tried to come into the remotest corner of her mind. It was almost like a begging plea. She wondered if it was Micah and Ayanna trying to reach out to her. She cleansed her mind of all extraneous thoughts and concentrated. Somehow it came easier tonight. She felt her mind going blank, fought back the tendrils of thought that kept on trying to insinuate themselves upon her, and with each success, those tendrils weakened.

Her mind wandered the palace, down corridors, through doors, across courtyards, down stairs, but suddenly she came upon a door through which she could not penetrate. That's it, she thought triumphantly. Somehow there's barrier to my mind here. Micah and Ayanna have to be behind this door somewhere. And then, there was the unmistakable spirit of her lover.

"Micah," she said out loud.

"Shaylae!" came the response.

"Oh Micah, I'm coming for you." But there was no response. She tried again, but could no longer feel his spirit. But she had felt it. She knew where he was, and she was going to rescue him.

Slowly and carefully she brought her body back to its normal state of consciousness and readiness. As soon as she was able she sent out a frantic thought to Anne. "Anne, I've found them. Bring everyone here. And bring Cerid's plans of the palace."

Five minutes later they were pouring over the plans of the Palace, laid out on Shaylae's desk. Harley looked at her face. For the first time in a week she had a look of hope in her eyes. He smiled warmly at her and she shrugged nervously.

"Here," she said, her finger on the plans. "They're here, somewhere behind this door. There's a barrier of some kind I can't penetrate. But they're there, I know it."

"What's behind this door, Cerid?" asked Harley. The plans were noticeably lacking behind that door. Details of rooms, doors, and corridors covered the whole map, with the exception of behind the door where it was just blank paper. Harley felt a little worried about that. They would be going in blind.

"Sir, I believe it's dungeons. I've never been there and I'd always assumed they were unused."

"Well, now we know different. We have to get behind there."

Cerid looked around at the small band. "With all due respect, sir, how. We're going to need trained close-combat troops."

"There's a hundred US Marines on board."

"Sir, that would be too many. We would need a small strike force of ten, no more than fifteen."

"I know exactly who can do this job." Harley went to the videophone and hit a few numbers. "Captain Martin, could you please come to Shaylae Lucero's cabin."

"At once, Colonel," he said briskly, adding with a smile, "And it's major now, sir."

"My apologies, Major."

"Who's he?" said Anne, once the connection had been broken.

"He was the captain of the company of marines aboard the shuttle when we followed Shaylae here four years ago."

"Oh, I remember. I didn't know he was here."

"He's a good man. A better marine doesn't exist. If anyone can plan an assault it will be him."

"An assault?" said Shaylae, clearly disturbed.

"I'm afraid so, ma'am," said Cerid. "Since you cannot get us in there, we're going to have to fight our way in."

"I can put us right here," she said, tapping the map with her forefinger.

"Yes, but we have no idea who or what will be the other side of that door. I'm afraid there will be fighting."

The door announced Major Martin's arrival. He walked in, looking as if he had stepped off a parade ground. He marched up to Harley and clicked his heels and crisply saluted.

"At ease, Major."

Harley turned to the others. "Please excuse us a moment. I need to have a word with the major alone." Turning to Major Martin he said, "Follow me please."

"What do you know about Shaylae Lucero, Major," said Harley as soon as they were alone.

"Not much, sir," he replied. "She somehow managed to get herself mixed up with this situation four years ago."

"Hmm. I'm going to tell you some things now that are top secret, need to know, and may sound unbelievable, but I want you to hear me out."

"Of course, Colonel."

"First, she wasn't 'mixed up' with the situation four years ago— she was the center of it."

"How is that possible, sir? She's only a kid."

"The Matriarch of Tal'el'Dine'h has characterized Shaylae Lucero as the most important person alive."

Major Martin almost snorted. "Really? And what is Tal'el'Dine'h?"

"Tal'el'Dine'h is the third planet in this crisis."

"Third planet? I thought there were only two planets involved in this mess."

"Very little is known about it, but it is the home of Shaylae's ancestors."

"Really?"

"Yes. This war has been going on for three thousand years. The mission from Yurob was sent here to kill Shaylae and to destroy Earth."

"Kill Shaylae? Why her? And destroy Earth?"

"Yes. They thought Earth was Tal'el'Dine'h. And if it hadn't been for what Shaylae did four years ago they may have accomplished their goal."

"How can that be?" Major Martin's face was not conveying acceptance of what Harley was telling him. "She's only a kid," he said, repeating himself.

How was he going to convince him without telling him the whole story? Which he wasn't prepared to do.

"Suffice it to say that she has incredible power."

"Power? What kind of power?"

"You're going to witness some of it. She's going to take you to Yurob."

"What? How?"

"With her incredible mind, major." Major Martin raised his eyebrows, skepticism all over his face. "Are you aware of the principle of Hyperspace? Well, she has the ability to see, and to move through other dimensions."

"I've never heard of such a thing before."

"That's because it's not a very common talent. You know of course Dr. Rodrigo is her father."

"Yes. He and his wife were kidnapped by our visitors from Yurob."

"Those 'visitors' knew of his research, and also knew of Shaylae's powers. They guessed that her power held the key to her father's final insight into hyperspace. And they were right. That's exactly what happened. When he found about her power it was the catalyst to his solution."

Major Martin was a good marine. Harley could tell he wasn't fully accepting everything he had been told, but was still willing to do what was required of him.

"Very well. And why are we going to Yurob?"

"Four years ago Shaylae defeated—won over would be a better way to describe it—the citizens of this vessel. The rulers back on Yurob are not yet 'won over' except for his Excellency Hauron, whose life is now in danger because of it. They are holding hostage two of Shaylae's friends, two people who were also crucial in our success four years ago. They are using them to get to Shaylae, and to kill her. If that happens, major, I'm afraid we will be in terrible danger. We will never be able to defeat them."

"And our mission is to rescue them."

"Exactly."

"I want you to know, sir, that I find it hard to believe what you have told me. But I do understand how to conduct a rescue mission. You can count on me."

"Thank you, major. I knew I could. Now, let's get back to the others so you can go over the tactical situation."

"Cerid, could you please explain the situation to Major Martin."

"Certainly, sir. Major, this is a map of the palace. Behind this door are the people we need to rescue."

It took about half an hour, Cerid explaining what each door and passage represented

"How do we get this far?" he had asked early on.

"Shaylae can put us right here," Harley had replied, pointing to the door on the map.

"And this corridor," he said, outlining with his finger, "is about ten meters."

"Yes, sir."

"And how far from here to this doorway over here?

"About twenty meters."

"What troops can we be expected to be posted here, here, and here," he said, pointing out three strategic spots on the map.

"It's unlikely there will be any permanent postings. Instead they will patrol in groups of three."

"Hmm," said Major Martin, deep in thought, rubbing his chin.

"And you have no idea what's behind this door."

"None whatsoever, sir."

"What is it made of?"

"It's the same titanium alloy as all of the other doors, ten centimeters thick."

"That should be no problem." For a few more minutes he poured over the map. And then looked up confidently.

"Can it be done, major?" asked Harley.

"Yes, colonel. It'll be risky, but I think we can do it."

"How many men will you need?"

"Fifteen," he said without hesitation. "Including me. And they won't all be men."

"Fifteen? You sure that will be enough?"

"Actually, I was initially thinking twelve. But we will probably need two to carry our hostages, and another to baby-sit the kid."

Harley smiled to himself. He wouldn't be calling Shaylae 'the kid' much longer.

"I'm in," said Cerid.

"I was counting on it, Cerid."

"Me too," said Harley.

"No, sir."

"No? But these are my friends."

"No, sir. You're not trained for this kind of mission."

"I insist, Major . . ." he began, using his best colonel voice.

"You're a pilot, correct?" Harley nodded. "No planes to fly here, sir. Sorry, I must insist."

Harley smiled, "Very well. You're the boss."

"How long do we have to prepare and brief my troops?"

Harley looked at Shaylae. She seemed at a loss, surrounded by all of this military planning. She shrugged.

"How long do you need, minimum?" asked Harley.

"Absolute minimum," he said, sucking air through his teeth, "one hour."

"Do it."

"Cerid, with me." Major Martin quickly left the room, barking the names of thirteen of his company into his radio. "Combat ready in twenty minutes, indoor low-light 'flage, thirty wafers of C-12, ten magazines each marine, flack and armor vests, oh, and extra set of non-com gear for a skinny sixteen year-old girl . . ." his voice trailed off as he hurried away.

"I'm eighteen," shouted Shaylae after him but he was already out of earshot.

CHAPTER 29

—⁂—

"OK, here's how it's going down." Major Martin was squatting on the floor of a gymnasium surrounded by thirteen battle-ready marines and a battle ready Cerid. Shaylae noticed he had taped out a full-size plan of the corridors on the floor. "This is Cerid. He's our guide. He's walked these corridors countless times, but unfortunately not behind this door," he said, pointing behind him. "Ah, and here's our transportation, Shaylae Lucero." They barely acknowledged her. "Sarah, get her dressed."

One of the marines, a young woman in her early twenties stepped forward and handed her a flack suit. "Here, Sweetie, this should fit," she said a little patronizingly, but Shaylae didn't mind. She knew how well trained and skilled this young marine was.

She helped Shaylae climb into it. It was heavy and hot.

Martin went back to the layout. "OK, deploy as soon as we arrive. Wally, Ice, Stretch: I want you to take up position there," he said pointing to the end of the corridor, to the left, where it T'd into another corridor. "Alice, Mac, Stu: there," he said pointing to the other side. "Jonesy, Wilf, Bogs: you're babysitting," he said pointing to Shaylae. "Bangs, Sword, Hops: I want that door down less than ten seconds after we arrive. Sarah, Cerid, and me are first through the door. Bring the kid in behind us. Once we're through you six fall back here, hold your position at the door. Got it? Questions?"

"Yeah, after the door is down . . ."

"The kid's the bloodhound. We follow her. We have no way of knowing what's behind there, but it's not a very big area, maybe thirty by thirty based on the blanks here," he said indicating the map. "Cerid, how many guards can we expect outside their cell?"

"Two, sir. Four if they're close to change over."

"OK, once we're through the door shoot at anything that moves. Shoot to kill."

"To kill?" said Shaylae.

Major Martin nodded. "To kill. Sorry, kid, but sixteen going in, eighteen coming out." He turned back to his troops. "Got it?"

"Got it," the marines all shouted in unison. "Sir!"

He removed his helmet and bowed his head. The rest of the marines followed suit, as did Shaylae and Cerid. "Dear God: As we go into battle be with us. Spare our lives and the lives of those we are sent to rescue. Bless our enemies that they may die with honor. Amen."

"Amen," came the chorus.

"We're ready, miss," said Martin.

She was not only surprised by the curtness of the prayer, but that they had said it at all. She wasn't expecting to see Marines pray.

"There will be a three to five second feeling of disorientation when we arrive," she warned them. "Ten seconds for me to reconnoiter." She closed her eyes and looked across the void. Opening her eyes again she pointed. "Three men stand talking down that corridor," she said. "Otherwise deserted. Here we go."

Even before she had recovered from her disorientation the marines were already deployed. She had to admire that; she had been shifting for years.

Bangs, Sword, and Hops were already inserting the wafers, three either side of the door, two underneath, and two above.

"Fire in the hole," yelled Bangs.

The explosion occurred just as the marines at the head of the corridor opened fire. Cerid, Martin and Sarah were through the door as it hit the ground. Shaylae felt herself being hustled through quickly.

She almost fainted with relief when she felt Micah's strong spirit. Ayanna's spirit was weak, hardly even detectable. "This way she shouted," pointing down a staircase. "And one of them is injured." They ran down the stairs in two steps, in perfect unison. "Around there," shouted Shaylae indicating another corridor. Sarah was the first to round the corner and took a shot to the stomach, knocking her back three meters. Blood poured from the wound. Major Martin and Cerid instinctively and in unison turned the corner, weapons blazing.

"Go," he shouted into his radio. Cerid reached the door first. There was a control panel. He hit the button and the door slid open. "Wilf, Boggs, the hostages. The rest of you to me. Ready for transport."

"Wait, there's another hostage," said Shaylae, almost in panic. "Sigmun! That way." She pointed down the corridor the way they had come, "And to the left."

For a microsecond Major Martin looked as if he would refuse, but then quickly barked, "Three o'clock, to my position, Sword, Hops, another hostage. On the double."

More shots rang out. Quickly they followed around the corner. Hops was lying on the floor, blood pouring from his stomach. The two guards lay dead. Sword had the door open and Sigmun was in his arms. "To me, now."

Within seconds all of the marines, except Sarah and Hops had gathered around Shaylae. Shots rang out as two more soldiers rounded the corner. She held out her hands and the shells hit the floor harmlessly in front of them, just as she shifted.

They were back in the gym. "Medics," shouted Martin. And then more somberly said, "We lost Sarah and Hops."

Shaylae immediately transported back to the spot where Sarah had fallen, and holding her as best she could, transported to where Hops lay. Holding him, she shifted, just as two bullets slammed into her body.

The Marines ran to help her as soon as she reappeared.

"No man or woman left behind, sir," she said falteringly. Her head swooned backward and she breathed the words, "I've been shot." She felt herself spin around, and then . . . darkness.

CHAPTER 30

—◦⊱⊰◦—

"Colonel, you have a moment?"

"Certainly, Major."

"I owe you an apology."

"No, not at all. You performed brilliantly. Better. You are a credit to the men and woman who have gone before you wearing the Green Beret."

"Thank you, sir, but we lost two of our finest."

"Yes, and I'm sorry. But the mission was a great success."

"Sir, about Shaylae . . ."

"Yes, what would you like to know? I'm afraid I can't tell you everything, but try me."

"Actually sir, I already know everything I need to know about her. She not only has an incredible mind, she has great courage. That she would go back to get our fallen comrades . . ." Major Martin was a Marine's Marine, but that was a tear he was trying to hide. "I would willingly give my life in her defense, as would all those who witnessed what she did."

"Major, there's no shame in being moved by her. I myself have shed a tear or two thinking about her courage and I too would willingly give my life for her."

"There's one thing I don't understand though. How come she wasn't killed by those shots? The physical shock to the body being hit at such close range should have been enough to kill her, even if the wound itself wasn't immediately life-threatening."

"Let's just say she's special; incredibly special."

"I guess I saw that firsthand. But she'll never recover from those wounds though, and that's a terrible shame."

"Oh, I think she will, major."

"That's not possible. Her leg was shattered."

"Four years ago I was shot in the chest, at close range, with a 9 mil' soft-nosed bullet. She removed all the pieces of that shattered bullet and totally healed me just before I expired."

At first Major Martin looked at him with disbelief, but then said, "She has that much Power?"

Harley nodded. "And it's not just her power over physical things that's amazing. One day, when I'm given the clearance, I'll show you the video of those few hours aboard what was then called 'Revenge' . . ." He laughed as he wiped his eye. "Now I'm going to lose it. Major, when she had defeated all of the ruling council of this vessel, over a hundred men, she could have killed them all. No one would have blamed her. But instead she redeemed them."

"Redeemed them? Sir, that's a strong word."

"I understand, Major. But when you see it, you'll understand why I use that word. I truly believe that she was put here, at this time and place in our history, by the Holy Ones."

"You mean God, Sir?"

"Yes, Major. That's exactly what I mean."

CHAPTER 31

―――

"Brethren of the Quorum and of the Council; I'm afraid I underestimated the extent of the plot against us. I had thought it only involved Cerid and I could not bring myself to accept the fact that Hauron was involved. It's now clear to me that he was the mastermind; he and the witch." Denab spoke quietly and without passion. "We have lost the first battle in this war against our eternal enemy because we trusted Hauron—we will not lose any more, and Hauron and all of his accomplices will die."

"We should have suspected it," said Wulsa. "We should have stopped him a long time ago, a sun-cycle ago, when he made all of the changes to our way of life."

"Well, it's too late for that now. But from today, a new regime takes over. From today a new order has begun. And to mark this new beginning I want the guards who were on duty when our prisoners were rescued brought to the parade ground. They will be executed, slowly and painfully, in front of the whole company of palace guards. Let no man be in any doubt of the fate of all who would dare to fail in their duty to this Assembly. Record the proceedings and have them broadcast to the entire planet. Let the slaves know that the old ways have returned with vengeance.

"As to the future, our lack of vigilance has placed our whole planet in serious danger. With Hauron by her side she will know of our plans to defeat her."

"Do you think she will still try to destroy our planet?"

"I did, but not anymore. Why did she come here under cover? The answer is clear. She wants to take over, and she is using Hauron like a puppet. She means to overthrow us and take the planet for herself. I think she will take the fight to the streets of our cities; try to find supporters still loyal to Hauron. That is the only reason she would have taken him with her."

"Excellency, already pockets of resistance loyal to Hauron have sprung up all over the planet. I think unless we stamp them out immediately she will find may such supporters."

"We will double the size of our armies; triple them. Have every man older than four sun-cycles report to recruitment stations for duty. From them chose the best, the most able, the strongest. From them, chose the ones who will willingly carry out our will. Subject them to every physical and psychological test to determine their willingness to give their lives in our service, and their ability to carry out our every order." And then with what looked like a smirk he added, "Find those who will enjoy the cruelty that will be required of them. Wherever they find any resistance, have them eradicate it with malice and viciousness. We were fools to believe that we could win the slaves over to our side. We don't need their love," he said with a sneer, "we need their fear."

"What about our entertainment here at the palace?"

"Resume it at once."

A murmur of approval went up from the Assembly.

"Now leave me. I need to be alone."

"Subdue," said Denab once the throne room was empty. The lights dimmed until the whole room was in darkness. All that remained was the eerie glow of a red lamp, shining weakly from the center of the high ceiling. Denab gathered his cloak around him and strode to the middle of the room until he stood directly beneath the pale light. He raised his hands high above his head and spoke with thunder in his voice.

"I underestimated you once, witch. A mistake all of my predecessors have made, but one I will not make again. You will be mine, you and your pitiful people. I will not be stopped this close to my goal. When you come to me again I will be ready. Even though your friends escaped me they will be no help to you. They are not as strong as you think.

"And now, I call upon the powers of hell to assist me. Let the evil wind fill me, encompass me, surround me." He threw his head back and laughed raucously, an evil hateful laugh.

A diabolic turbulence began around his feet, encircling him. It gathered momentum as it rose, a small tornado whipping his cloak until it billowed around him. The whole room was soon filled with the swirling maelstrom. An unearthly howling emanated from the wind, as if from millions of disembodied spirits. Small bolts of lightning born in the evil wind crackled into Denab's outstretched fingers.

"The universe will be mine," he screamed, almost drowned out by the awful noise within the wind. "And no one will stand in my way."

CHAPTER 32

Micah had not left Shaylae's bedside since they had gotten back. She was still unconscious, hooked up to machines, tubes coming out from all over her body. She had taken two bullets; one in her right shoulder, one in her left leg, just above the knee. He winced as he recalled it was the same leg Second had broken.

Her hands felt warm, and she was breathing regularly. The monitors by the side of her bed showed all her vital signs within safe limits. He wasn't really worried about her, just so desperately upset that she had been hurt again on his behalf.

He was still worried about Ayanna, however. She lay in the next room and had not yet regained consciousness. She had been severely dehydrated and half starved. They were introducing fluids and nourishment back into her body as quickly as they dared, which wasn't very fast. They said it could be days before she would regain consciousness. He wasn't sure if he sensed an 'if ever' addendum to their diagnosis.

Sigmun's situation was different. There seemed to be nothing physically wrong with him; he just could not be woken. His brain activity showed none of the typical patterns of someone in a coma, so even the physicians could not explain why he was unconscious. It has to have something to do with the brainwashing, or whatever it was that Denab had done, which was causing his problem, he thought.

He looked at his darling Shaylae again. How brave she had been to have taken those marines on the rescue mission. And how much braver it had been to have gone back on her own. He smiled affectionately. Without fail, just when he thought he had this incredible person figured out she would go do something crazy, like return to a war zone just to bring back two dead bodies. But, she had paid the price. The doctors had been amazed she had survived. It was a miracle they said. He had long since given up his pragmatic notion that miracles didn't happen. He was looking at one right now.

Suddenly one of the machines by her bed started beeping frantically. He jumped as his heart rate instantly doubled. He ran to call the nurse and almost bowled her over as she walked unhurriedly into the room. Her crisp white uniform rustled as she walked over to her bed. She was about as tall as Ayanna, but with a slighter build. Her short blonde hair and blue eyes gave her away immediately as a citizen of Yurob.

"Nothing to worry about, Mike," she said. Micah had gotten to know the nurses well over the last couple of days. They had tried to persuade him to go rest; they would call him if there were any change. But of course, he could not be moved from his vigil. "It just means she's coming around." She put her hand on Shaylae's forehead. "She still has a slightly elevated temperature, and when she wakes she will be in considerable pain."

"Micah," she said weakly. "What happened? Where am I?"

"Oh, Shaylae, you were shot. You went back to get those two marines, and they shot you."

Her face scrunched up in pain. But then she closed her eyes. Peace filled Micah's mind as she soul-shared briefly with him.

"I can fix this." She said.

"Shaylae, welcome back to the land of the living. I'm nurse Jansher. You've suffered quite a traumatic injury and you need to rest. You're going to be here a while."

"I don't think so, nurse," said Micah with an almost triumphant smile.

Nurse Jansher turned to look at him curiously. But then turning back to Shaylae said, "I have to change your dressings. It will be painful, so please try to be brave." Carefully she removed the dressing that covered her right shoulder, wrapped diagonally around her body from waist to shoulder. Micah was not surprised to see that her shoulder was totally unblemished, but Jansher's brow furrowed in utter confusion. "What the . . ." was all she could manage. "Let me look at your leg." She pulled down the blankets and began removing the bandage that covered her from her shin to the top of her thigh.

"I don't understand . . . It's perfect."

Oh it's perfect all right, he thought. "I told you she was a miracle worker, nurse."

"Let me get the doctor."

Dr. Wyckoff wasn't as amazed as Jansher. It was he who had fixed her leg four years ago. He still wanted to keep Shaylae under surveillance for a few days more, but of course Micah told him that would never happen. Oh, she would stay in the hospital all right, but only as long as it took to heal Ayanna and Sigmun.

"I have to tell you something first before you try to reach her," said Micah as they stood by Ayanna's bed. "She and Sigmun . . ." he paused, trying to find the right words.

"What?" prompted Shaylae, breaking the awkward silence.

"They spent the night together."

"And?" she again prompted, after another brief silence.

Micah was surprised that she wasn't shocked. She put her hand on his arm. "Micah, it doesn't matter what they did. I will love Ayanna with all my heart throughout eternity. And so do the Holy Ones, more than we love her. I will not be her judge."

It was not what he was expecting her reaction to be. "There's more." He went on to explain what Ayanna had seen when Sigmun had met with Denab. "It wasn't so much that he betrayed her that devastated her, it was the way he did it."

"What do you mean?"

"She said he bragged to Denab about what they had done."

Shaylae's brow furrowed. "Oh."

"I tried to tell her that he was not in control of his actions . . ."

"Yes, I figured right from the start that Denab was using him."

". . . but she wouldn't be consoled. Even if he was under compulsion she says she'll never be able to forgive him for that. She loves him— loved him—as much as we love each other I think."

"OK, let's tackle that problem when we get there. But first, I want to find out from Sigmun what happened; what Denab did to him."

Sigmun looked peaceful enough. He was hooked up to a single I.V.; nothing like the tubes and machines that Ayanna had protruding from her body; he simply looked as if he was in a deep sleep.

"Hello Shaylae."

Shaylae turned around to see Dr. Wyckoff.

"Oh, hi, doctor," she said. "What's wrong with him?"

"Nothing. At least nothing we can discover. Physically he's in great shape. No injuries, illnesses. Everything's working as it should."

"What about his brain, his mind."

"Well, to look at him it would appear he is in a coma. Same lack of movement, same lack of reaction to external stimuli, but his brain patterns don't show any of the signs we would expect to see in a coma patient."

"So you're saying there's nothing wrong with him?"

"No, clearly there's something seriously wrong, but it's nothing we can find a reason for."

"Could you leave us please, doctor. I'm going to try to reach him."

"Certainly."

Micah sat next to Shaylae by Sigmun's bed. She took Micah's hand in hers and smiled warmly at him. She didn't say anything; she didn't have to. He could feel her love for him in every fiber of his being. She leaned up to him and kissed him gently on his lips.

"Micah, come with me," she said. At once they were soul-joined. He smiled inwardly as he felt the power of her love, and her relief at having him safely back with her. "I'm not sure what I'm going to do, or even what I'm looking for."

Together they searched for his breathing soul, but it was if he was dead. There was no sign of his spirit anywhere.

"We have to go deeper," she said.

Micah felt nauseous, as if on a fairground ride that wouldn't stop spinning. Round and round it went, making him dizzier and dizzier. Suddenly as well as spinning he was falling. The feeling in his stomach was so real as he reacted to the sensation of zero gee.

"Shaylae, what's happening?"

"I'm not sure, but we have to keep going. I think we're reaching him."

Micah felt himself falling faster and faster. He would have been worried, except for Shaylae's reassuring presence. And then, suddenly, they hit the ground. For a moment he was stunned, but when he looked up they were sitting in the middle of a barren desert.

"Are you seeing what I'm seeing?" said Shaylae.

"If you're in the middle of a desert, then yes."

"Where do you think we are?"

"No idea," he said, standing up and dusting himself off. They were wearing the same clothes they had been wearing in Sigmun's room. "You think this is some sort of trick of Denab's?"

"I don't think so. I don't have any bad feelings about this place. It's just strange is all."

"Look, over there," he said, pointing off into the distance. It was some kind of hut, a stone hut.

"Let's head on over there," she said, as Micah held out his hand and helped her up Hand-in-hand they walked toward the lone building.

Micah couldn't help but turn to Shaylae and give her a little peck on the cheek, but then he stopped. "Shaylae!" he said.

"What?"

"You notice anything?"

She stopped and looked around for a moment. "No, not really."

"You're not limping."

She looked down at her left leg and shook it a few times. "I'm not, am I? And it doesn't hurt either."

"And we're talking. I mean with our voices, not with our minds."

"You're right! So we are. But I think we're still soul-sharing."

Micah thought about that. Yes, it still felt that way. He still felt incredibly close to her. "You think we're not in the real world?"

"That's it!" she exclaimed. "We're in Sigmun's mind."

"We're where?"

"Think about it. Perhaps this is the only way our minds can perceive the intricacies of his mind."

"OK, but if that's true, why are we both having the same illusion."

"'Cos we're soul-sharing, silly."

Micah looked toward the building once more. "Look, we're almost there."

Sure enough, even though the building had seemed to be at least a kilometer away they were already almost on top of it. As they got closer they noticed it had no windows or doors, at least on the side nearest them. A quick walk around the building confirmed that there were indeed none anywhere.

"What do you make of this?" asked Micah.

"I'm pretty sure Sig is in there."

"So, how do we get to him?"

"Well, if this is just our own mind's interpretation of . . . well, I'm not sure what, maybe all we need to do is to concentrate more to take us further."

"OK."

Micah could sense the intensity of her concentration. It reminded him of when they had joined to overcome the Dark Ones aboard Revenge. Their spirits and minds had joined synergistically, giving them more power than the sum of their individual capabilities.

"If only we had Ayanna with us again."

"Concentrate Micah. I think I can sense a weakness in the wall."

He too could feel it. As if there was a small depression in the wall, not completely through yet, but a small chink, something to work on. He willed himself to open and widen that chink. Gradually it gave way, until suddenly it became a hole completely through the wall. A fetid smell escaped, almost sickening, but there, he could sense the unmistakable spirit of Sigmun.

"Sigmun," said Shaylae. "Sigmun, can you hear us." There was no response. "He's in there. We have to break down the wall completely so we can get to him."

Once again their souls united. Micah could feel the awesome power of Shaylae's mind, and wondered how much his feeble attempts were adding to the effort.

"Your mind may be different from mine, but I assure you it's anything but feeble. I couldn't be doing this without you."

"Will you stop reading my thoughts."

She chuckled. "I can't help it. Now, concentrate. Let's get this wall down."

He closed his eyes and imagined punching that wall, flying kicking it. Over and over again he pummeled that wall.

"Micah, I don't think it will come down by force. Think about Sigmun and Ayanna. Think about how they're suffering and how you would do anything to end that suffering. Think about how much you love them."

It wasn't hard to think about how much he loved Ayanna. They had grown up together; they had always been close, like sister and brother. Thoughts of the fun they had had together as kids flooded into his mind. Thoughts of the fights they had had, of her sometimes irreverent and biting humor, of her laughing heart, of her joy in her life, filled his soul. Yes, he truly loved Ayanna.

"Micah, we did it."

He opened his eyes again. The building had completely disappeared. There, lying on the ground was Sigmun. He was bound in chains. From shoulders to feet he was bound.

"Sigmun," said Shaylae, but there was no response. He looked just as he did, lying on the hospital bed. "We have to free him."

"You think these represent Denab's hold over him?"

"I think it all does; this desert, the building, these bindings. I think if we can get him out of here . . ."

"Leave me." Sigmun's anguished words suddenly filled their minds

"Sigmun, we can't do that. We're your friends," said Shaylae.

"Do you know what I've done?"

"Yes," said Shaylae somberly.

"I'll never forget the look in her eyes as she was about to kill me."

"But she didn't," said Micah. Sigmun did not respond.

"Let's get the rest of these bonds off him," said Shaylae, frantically picking at the chains.

Sigmun wept bitterly. "No, please leave me."

Shaylae ignored him and kept struggling. Micah joined her. But they were getting nowhere. The chains were tight, not showing any signs of loosening.

After a fruitless few minutes, Shaylae said, "We're going about this the wrong way. These aren't physical bonds; they represent Denab's evil and hatred and control over Sig, so we have to fight them with our love and goodness."

"Then we should appeal to the good and love that is in him then," said Micah.

"Micah, that's right. That's exactly what we should do." Turning back to Sigmun she stroked his forehead and cheeks. She knelt down and kissed his cheek. Micah knew the power of that touch and kiss; if anything could reach Sigmun it would be those precious expressions of her love.

"Sigmun," she spoke softly. "Ayanna is dying."

"Yes, and it's my fault."

"Oh, Sigmun. It's not your fault. It was Denab who used you, controlled you."

"But I let him control me. I let him use me. I should have been stronger—my love for Ayanna should have been stronger."

"You didn't let him use you. There was nothing you could have done. Denab is powerful, more powerful than me."

Micah was shocked and worried by that. He had not even given a second thought to the idea that Shaylae may be up against someone who has more power than her. A pang of ice-cold fear filled his heart.

"But my love for Anna should have been stronger," he repeated.

"And maybe it is, Sig. Maybe the one thing that Denab can't understand is love. Maybe that's how we defeat him."

"Then you defeat him. No one has love like you two. You don't need me."

Micah sensed an opening. "But we do need Anna. Without her we would never have defeated the Dark Ones aboard Revenge."

"That's right. We're a triumvirate Sigmun. Anna is vital to our success."

Sigmun said nothing, but Micah could tell his will to destroy himself was weakening. "Only you can bring her back." Still he said nothing. "She doesn't know you were under Denab's control. She thinks you betrayed her."

"But I did!"

"No, Sigmun, no," insisted Shaylae. "These chains represent Denab's hold over you. Unless you break free then he has defeated you; he has won. And Ayanna, Micah, and I will die. Probably Hauron and his family too. Yurob will once again be ruled by desperately cruel leaders. Ayanna is the key, Sigmun."

Sigmun tried to move, but his bonds held him firmly.

"Fight them, Sig. Fight these bonds that Denab has put around you," insisted Shaylae. "Only you can break free of them."

"What should I do?"

"Think of Ayanna. You have to be the one to show her how you were compelled to do what you did."

"Will she believe me?"

"She will."

"Will she forgive me? Will she ever trust me again?" Shaylae was silent. "She won't will she?" he said quietly. Micah could feel Sigmun's will drain away again.

"I think she will, but perhaps not right away. You hurt her at the most vulnerable moment a man could hurt a woman."

"Yes, and that makes me . . . what? An animal. Worse. I forced myself on her."

"You didn't force yourself, Sigmun," said Micah. "It was her choice." And then he almost smiled. "Do you think anyone could force Ayanna to do anything against her will?"

"But it is so important to her, to you."

"Sigmun, you're right. It is. But believe me, it's not the end of the world. The love and compassion of our Holy Ones extends well beyond our weaknesses."

He was silent for a moment. "So you think I can help her?"

"I'm sure you can. And unless we do something soon she'll surely die. Even if she never forgives you, do you want her to . . ."

"No, please don't say that. She can't die. I would give my own life for her." Micah could see him struggling against his bonds again. "How do I get out of here?"

"With love, Sigmun. With the love you feel for Ayanna; with the love you feel for us; with the love you feel for Hauron and your people. Close your eyes. Close your eyes and feel that love. Drive out Denab's hate."

Sigmun's eyes closed; his face became calm; his breathing deep and regular. Shaylae reached out her hand and placed it on his head. Micah followed suit. Once again Micah felt the synergy rising. Together they were strong. The desert became a lush garden. Sigmun sat up, the bonds completely gone. He took Shaylae and Micah's hands in his and said, "Thank you."

And they were back in Sigmun's room, sitting by his bed and holding hands.

"Now, let's go get Ayanna," said Shaylae triumphantly. She looked at Sigmun sadly shaking his head. "Perhaps Micah and I should go on our own initially."

Sigmun nodded.

CHAPTER 33

Dr. Wyckoff had insisted he be allowed to check Sigmun out. "Not that I expect to find anything at all wrong with him," he said shaking his head, "but indulge me if you will."

"Of course," said Shaylae, laughing like a fresh spring breeze. "Take your time." Then she whispered in Micah's ear. "There's something I have to ask you."

She shifted them back to Micah's room, and began gently kissing him. "Oh, Micah Hale, I love you so much."

"As I love you, Shaylae Lucero."

"Micah Hale," she said between her kisses, "Will you marry me? Will you take the seven steps with me? Will you eat from my wedding basket? Will you drink from the wedding jar with me? Will you share my Hogan and my Clan?"

"You know I will, my love. I've already promised . . ."

"I don't mean in a few years. I mean next Monday, July 23rd to be exact." And she kissed him again.

*   *   *

Sadness filled Ayanna's soul. So deep it was that she would not allow herself to return to consciousness. So profound that she truly believed she could will herself to die. Hovering on the edge of wakefulness, she knew she was in some kind of hospital, being force-fed. It didn't matter. Without her own will to live there was nothing medical science could do for her. And that was just fine. How could she face the world again? How could she face Shaylae and Micah again? And how could she face the Holy Ones ever again? Her soul was in utter torment and torture.

"Ayanna." Shaylae's kindness and gentleness filled her, cruelly reminding her of a life she had left far behind.

"Shaylae, no, please leave me alone."

"Anna, we're getting married," said Shaylae.

That was not what Ayanna was expecting to hear, yet it took her away from her own plight for a second. "I know that."

"This Monday; at least that's what we're planning. Micah is going to talk to my parents today. We hope they won't object to a short betrothal."

"That's great news, Shaylae, Micah. I know you'll be very happy." Ayanna didn't sound too happy.

"I want you to be my maid of honor."

"Shaylae, I couldn't. It's just not . . ."

"I want to show you how we found Sigmun," interrupted Shaylae, again catching Ayanna off guard with the sudden change of subject. She was silent.

"It was not his fault. Denab . . ."

"I know that. But if he had truly loved me he would have been able to fight it, wouldn't he?"

"No, Anna, No. We're beginning to find out that Denab is much more powerful than we had ever imagined. More powerful than me."

"How can that be?"

"But not more powerful than all three of us, together," said Micah. There was another long silence.

"Anna, we need you. Those poor citizens of Yurob need you. Things are now much worse than before Hauron took over, even worse than when I first traveled there."

"I don't know; I have offended the Holy Ones."

"The Holy Ones are not offended, dear sister. They love you more than you can possibly imagine. And we certainly love you, but you know that. Nothing you could do would ever diminish that love."

"Shay, Mike, I don't know what to say."

"Then please, just let me show you how we found Sigmun."

The cold, drab loneliness of the place pierced Ayanna's heart. This is where Shaylae and Micah had found Sigmun? She knew it was somehow a symbolic representation of his mind, but it was frighteningly real. The solitary building made of soulless bricks called out to her for pity. She knew that Denab had kidnapped Sigmun's will and kept it prisoner in this desolate cell. How long had he been kept there? She watched as Shaylae and Micah tore down the walls with their love, and wept as she saw Sigmun bound like a wild animal. She heard Shaylae and Micah plead with him and then watched as with his will, and his love for her, he burst from those bonds. The words he had spoken tore at her heart.

"Will she believe me?"

"Oh, yes, Sigmun, I believe you," she spoke out loud.

"Can we bring Sigmun in with us?"

"Yes."

Ayanna felt Sigmun join them as Shaylae reached out to him and brought him into their soul-sharing. For a moment nothing was said and then breaking down in tears Sigmun spoke.

"Ayanna, if I could undo what happened I would gladly give my life." No one spoke, so he continued. "I love you more than my own life. All I want is for you to be well, and to have a happy life. I can bear not being part of that life, but I could not bear the thought of you in misery and anguish because of my weakness."

Ayanna felt her heart melting, but still she could not speak.

"Can you forgive me? Can you ever trust me again?"

Finally she spoke out loud, tears streaming from her eyes. "Oh, I will forgive you, my heart; I will trust you again, my soul. Just give me some time. Please."

Ayanna opened her eyes. Shaylae was crying, and that started her off too. Together they hugged and cried, and cried and hugged. Sigmun's eyes were also filled with tears, but he did not reach out for Ayanna. Even Micah's eyes looked a little misted over.

"You're going to put me out of business, young lady." It was Dr. Wyckoff.

"I'm sorry Doctor, but these are my best friends."

He waved her off with a smile. "I just wish you could cure all my patients."

"So do I, Doctor, but I can't do that," she said sadly.

He patted her arm. "I know. And I know why too."

He began examining Ayanna, checking her vital signs, her blood analysis, her muscle tone. "But this one," he said waving his index finger in Ayanna's direction, "you're going to have to leave her a little longer under my care, yes?"

"No," said Ayanna. "I need to be with Shaylae."

"Sorry, young lady. You're seriously dehydrated and badly undernourished. It's going to take a few days."

"But Shaylae can heal me . . ." she began, but Shaylae was shaking her head.

"I'm not a miracle worker, Anna."

Ayanna's mouth dropped open. "Yes you are," she protested, but still Shaylae was still shaking her head. "Shay, you're going to leave me here?"

"It'll just be a few days. And then we're all taking a long vacation to Earth."

Ayanna lay back on the pillows, resigned to her fate. "OK," she said. "But only a few days."

Arms around each other they walked from the hospital into a huge, beautiful park. White clouds scudded across a brilliant blue sky. Micah pointed up. "How do they do that?" he said.

"Do what?"

"Well, look at it! It looks so real."

Shaylae raised her head from its home on Micah's shoulder. "It does, my love."

"Hard to believe we're in the center of an asteroid."

"Yep."

"But what's harder to believe is that back there you asked me to marry you?" Micah stopped, and pulling Shaylae close he whispered to her. "Are you sure? I mean, we're still so young."

"I'm more sure than I've ever been in my whole life. Micah Hale, I love you with all my heart, with all my mind, and with all my soul. And now I want to be your wife, and you to be my husband."

"You said July 23rd. Anything special about that day?"

"Well, for one thing at El Huerfano, at sunset, just as we begin our wedding ceremony, Sister Moon will rise, full, in the east."

"And for another thing . . ."

"Well, for another thing, I'm not sure I can wait much longer."

He hugged her. "Oh Shay, you've just made me the happiest man in the whole universe."

She poked him in the ribs. "Not half as happy as I'm going to make you on our wedding night," she said mischievously.

Micah's blood almost came to boiling point as she said those words. Just a few days ago he had asked himself how on earth he was going to wait another four or five years to be with Shaylae as her husband, now he was desperately afraid he would hardly be able to wait a few days. He took her almost roughly into his arms and kissed her.

"Stop it," she said with a coy smile. "People are staring at us."

"I don't care." And then turning to the few passersby who were smiling at them, he said in a loud voice. "We're getting married. I love her, and she loves me."

CHAPTER 34

⟿⟡⟾

"Hi, Dad. How's it going?" Mateo Rodrigo's image on the video screen looked concerned. He was scratching his disheveled dark hair.

"Um, we've got a problem."

Shaylae felt the wind spill from her sails. "What's up?" In the background she could see Hauron, Tregon, and Harley pouring over something.

"Well, you know we've just about got the hyper drive ready to fire up."

"No, I didn't know that. I thought you had only just completed the tests on drones."

"No, Shay. We're way beyond that. I guess you've been busy, huh?"

She smiled. "I guess I have."

"Well, all I can say is it's a good job you brought Hauron here."

"Oh. How come?"

He gestured behind him. "Apparently they've got tens, maybe hundreds of thousands of drones positioned strategically around Yurob, programmed to home in and detonate near any foreign object larger than a thousand tons."

"Fusion bombs?

"Hauron estimates a megaton each."

"Wow."

"Wow is right. Looking at the three-dimensional map," he pointed behind him again, "our estimate is that anywhere from five to ten drones would be in range of us if we were to materialize in their system. Reconciliation couldn't withstand even one of those blasts; it's not built for it."

"Couldn't you create a reverse hyperspace field around them automatically?"

"A what?"

"Instead of contracting space around a fusible source, couldn't you do the opposite? Expand space so that all the protons were outside the limits of the strong nuclear force?"

His brow furrowed. His eyes rolled a few times, and then he slapped his forehead. "That's it. Shaylae, you're a genius."

"I know," she said, but he had already broken the connection. She laughed and sighed, shaking her head, and redialed him.

"Dad!" she said when he answered.

"Yes," he said, rather abruptly.

"Dad, that's not what I wanted to talk to you about."

"Oh, sorry, Shaylae," he said. "What's up?"

"Micah would like to come and talk to you and Mom."

"He would, what about?" Sometimes her dad could be so dense. "Oh. Really? You mean he wants to . . . you two want to . . . ?"

"Yes, Dad. We want to get married and want your blessing."

"But you're so young."

"I know, Dad, but please trust me on this. Emotionally we're both ready." A wide grin filled her face. "And we already know we're going to spend the rest of eternity together, but there's another important reason that we need to get married."

"Shay, you're not . . . ?"

She blushed a little. "Pregnant?" she said, almost indignantly. "No, Dad. It's nothing like that."

"What then?"

"It's about our mission, the next stage of our mission. It's important we get married before it begins. I can't explain any more than that. You're just gonna have to trust me."

"OK, I guess you know what you're doing."

"Thanks, Dad. Micah would like to come and see you two tonight. I just wanted you to know what it was about, so you wouldn't be too surprised."

"OK. When should we expect you?"

"Oh, I don't know. About eight o'clock."

"Sounds good. See you then." She hung up. She just couldn't stop smiling.

Eight o'clock, on the dot, Shaylae was standing with Micah at the door of her parents' apartment.

"How do I look?" he said, smoothing down his long black hair.

How does he look, she thought? He looked fantastic! He had left his hair loose, down over his shoulders, but pushed back behind his ears. He had on a loose fitting blue and yellow shirt, open at the neck, tucked neatly into a pair of beige khakis. On his feet he wore brown deerskin boots. His broad shoulders, emphasized by his narrow waist and hips reinforced her belief that he would father fine children. She shuddered with the pleasure that being in his presence always gave her.

"Oh, you look so fine, my love," she said, raising her eyebrows and shaking her head. She leaned up and kissed him, just as the door opened.

"Micah, Shay," said Reycita. "How nice to see you. Come on in." She ushered them in to the cozy living room. "Have you eaten?"

"Oh, yes. We're fine," said Shaylae, frantically searching around the room. "Where's Dad?"

"Haven't seen him all day."

"Have you spoken to him?"

"Yes, briefly. He said you'd called him and had a great idea."

"Yeah," she said absently. "He didn't tell you we were coming, did he?" Reycita shook her head and smiled. "Can you call him and tell him we're here."

"Sure," said Reycita. "Matt," she said, once they were connected, "Your daughter and her young man are here."

He slapped his forehead.

"He does that a lot," said Shaylae with a smile.

"Dang it! I'm sorry. I'll be right there. Five minutes I'll be there."

Reycita broke off the call. "Shaylae, how's Ayanna, and your other friend, Sigmun is it?"

"Yes, Sigmun. They're both fine. Ayanna will have to stay in hospital another day or so, but Sigmun is up and about already."

Well within his five-minute estimate Matt burst into the living room. "I'm so sorry you kids," he said, smoothing down his hair and sitting next to his wife, kissing her tenderly on the cheek. "What brings you two over here?"

Micah looked at Shaylae nervously. She smiled and nodded eagerly.

"Sir, ma'am," he began. "As you know Shaylae and I are very much in love. We have been since the day we met over four years ago."

"And wonderful it is too," said Reycita. "You were made for each other."

Micah cleared his throat. "And so, I would like to ask for your permission and blessing to marry your daughter."

Reycita's face lit up. "Oh, how wonderful, how romantic, how soon?"

Shaylae looked at her Dad. Her expression said 'you didn't tell her, did you?' His scrunched up face and shrugging shoulders said 'Sorry, Shay. I didn't get around to it.'

"We were hoping that we could marry this Monday."

Reycita looked to Matt, waiting for his assent. He nodded his head happily.

"Oh, you kids! It's so soon, but yes, yes." She wagged her finger in Shaylae's direction. "But you have to weave your wedding basket, and you only have three days."

"You can help me."

"I can teach you, but it has to be completely made by your own hands." She took Shaylae's hands in hers. "It's important, Shay."

Shaylae nodded. "I know."

Reycita jumped up from her chair and took Shaylae in her arms and hugged her. Then turning to Micah she said, "Micah, come here. Give me a hug."

If Micah's smile had been any wider Shaylae was sure his face would have split in two.

PART FOUR

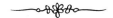

Micah and Shaylae

CHAPTER 35

⸻⁂⸻

July 23rd, 2108

The sun sank majestically in the west behind El Huerfano Mesa. Ayanna would have said 'Father Sun', but Sigmun still had difficulty thinking of stars as anything but huge nuclear furnaces. Toward the east the moon, 'Sister Moon' he had to remind himself, was rising, beautiful and full. Even in the fading sunlight, she shone with brilliance low on the horizon. Shaylae and Micah had chosen their wedding day well, and their Holy Ones had blessed them.

There was still so much for him to get used to. The notion that all people on the three planets, and presumably on countless other planets, were all related, all children of the same Holy Ones, was an incredible idea. But the more he thought about it the more obvious it became. How else could you explain the same race of human beings on the three known planets?

"What you thinking about, Sigmun?" said Hauron. Hauron was dressed in his finest robes, robes of Second of Yurob. Sigmun was relieved that Hauron now fully accepted Shaylae for who she was. He had said that he had been almost convinced the moment she had agreed to leave Micah and Ayanna alone, but watching her free the Assembly on Revenge from Rolling Darkness was the clincher. "She looked like a goddess," Hauron had said. "If only you could have seen her."

A picture of Ayanna came into his mind. She too was a goddess who for a fleeting moment had been within his reach, and now she may be lost to him forever.

"Sigmun?" said Hauron, breaking into his thoughts.

"Oh, sorry, I was light years away," replied Sigmun.

"She'll forgive you," he said. Hauron always seemed to know what he was thinking. Was it his Power, or just his incredible insight? Probably both.

Sigmun nodded his head. "Look at all these people," he said, changing the all-too-painful subject. "They all look so . . . happy."

"Well, it's certainly a happy occasion, but I hardly know anyone here."

"Well let's see. I don't know too many either, but those two over there, are Colonel Davidson and his wife Anne Lawrence; friends of Shaylae who helped her win over Revenge. In fact she introduced them." Harley had his left arm around Anne's waist, and in his right arm he held their daughter, Shay-Anne.

"What a great looking family," said Hauron.

Indeed. One day Sigmun hoped he and Ayanna would share the joy of their own family but so far things had shown not the slightest sign of returning to where they had been. She was always kind to him—kind like she would be to her brother—but it was obvious she still needed time. The words he had spoken to Denab, the words she had heard him say, caused him to cringe in shame. Even though he couldn't remember having spoken them, he still could not forgive himself.

"Standing next to Captain Cerid is Lieutenant-Colonel Tregon and General Shasck." They were dressed in their finest uniforms, looking almost regal.

"Yes, I met them when we first came aboard Reconciliation," said Hauron. "And we've been working together on the plans to return to Yurob."

"Did you hear what Tregon did to save Shaylae's life?"

"Oh yes, but not from him of course. It was one of the first things Shasck told me about him. I will see he is rewarded and recognized when we retake Yurob."

Sigmun smiled. "If he's anything like every other person who has ever met her, her gratitude and smile are all the reward he will ever want."

"I hear you."

Sigmun pointed over to Major Martin and the other eleven marines. They were dressed in smart navy blue jackets, decorated with medals, sky-blue pants with a red stripe, and sharp white caps. They had swords hanging from their belts, and while Sigmun knew they would never actually use them in combat, he had no doubt they could. "That's the team that Shaylae brought to Yurob to rescue Ayanna, Micah and me."

"Brave men and women."

"They lost two of their comrades."

"Yes, and Shaylae went back to get the bodies? I can't figure out why would she risk her life to do that?"

Sigmun shrugged. It didn't make much sense to him either. "I don't know. But apparently those marines value the dignity of their fallen comrades very highly."

Hauron laughed. "You should have seen the way they treated Shaylae before they went on that mission."

"How do you mean?"

"Treated her like a kid. Condescending. Major Martin even called her skinny." He chuckled again. "It was quite a different story when they got back."

Sigmun looked around but couldn't see anyone else he recognized. "Well, now you know about as many people here as I do."

Heads began to turn in the crowd. Micah had arrived. With him were his mother, Toni, and Alex Lapahie, who had agreed to represent Micah's father in the ceremony. Micah's long black hair was drawn back behind his ears and down over his shoulders. Around his head he wore a simple green velvet headband. His shirt was green and his pants beige. Across his left shoulder was his wedding robe, yellow, green, pink and orange horizontal stripes. On his feet he wore brown leather moccasins.

Matron Lapahie, who would officiate at the ceremony, walked behind them. They all walked into the Hogan, followed by Micah's family. Sigmun, Hauron, Cerid, Tregon and Shasck followed Micah as his guests. They entered in a sun-wise direction; the guests sat on the north wall, while Micah and Alex continued to the west wall, facing the door. Micah placed a tomahawk bound with intricately woven white deerskin and decorated with eagle feathers in front of them. Alex placed a jewel encrusted belt and other jewelry next to the tomahawk, and then they sat awaiting Shaylae's arrival.

"Ayanna told me that in her culture it was the groom's family who honored the mother of the bride with a dowry," whispered Sigmun.

Heads turned again, this time accompanied by sighs as Shaylae arrived. His breath was taken away. She smiled, and it was if Father Sun had changed his mind and had decided to stay and see the wedding. It was the smile of a grown woman, but also that of a child, full of innocence, trust, excitement, and expectation; totally unaffected and pure.

Around her shoulders she had a shawl, the same colors as Micah's, except the stripes were vertical, emphasizing her slender figure. Around the border it had yellow and green tassels. She was wearing a simple tiered white satin skirt, a light green crushed velvet blouse with gathered sleeves and white lace trimmings on the cuffs and collar. Her hair had been drawn back into a loose bun, tied with pure white wool. Around her waist was an orange sash, covered in turquoise and white-shell jewelry and around her neck was a silver necklace, heavy with similar jewels. On her wrists and fingers she also wore white and turquoise jewelry. On her feet she wore white knee-length deerskin moccasins, emphasizing her dainty feet. She was carrying the wedding basket she had so carefully woven over the last four days, filled with taa'niil, blue cornmeal mixed with water.

She looked so fragile and slight; her hands and fingers so perfect, so neat and small. Oh, Micah take good care of her precious person, always. Never, never betray her, Micah. The cold feeling that would not leave his heart grew even colder as thoughts of his betrayal of Ayanna again filled him with remorse so deep it almost drowned him.

Fighting back her unrestrained joy, Shaylae walked solemnly into the Hogan, accompanied by Ayanna, her father and mother. Major Martin and his marines joined her as her as her guests, eyes full of respect and admiration. They also made their way sun-wise around the Hogan. Shaylae stopped at the west wall and sat next to Micah. Ayanna and her parents sat next to, and slightly behind her. The remainder of her guests continued around and sat against the south wall. Shaylae carefully placed the wedding basket on a little mound of earth, making sure it was secure.

"Shaylae made that wedding basket. The most important part of the weave is the gap that is left in the pattern. Apparently it represents the passage between their ancestral world and this world. See how carefully she placed it so that the gap faces east toward the door of the Hogan, which also always faces east."

"Sigmun, how come you know so much about these traditions and customs?"

"I'm going to find out everything I can. One day, if Ayanna ever comes to trust me again, I hope to be married to her in such a ceremony."

Hauron put his hand on Sigmun's arm. "Sigmun, she will see the sincerity in your sorrow. I'm sure of it. And when she does she will come to trust you again."

"Yes, but the more I learn of their culture, the more I realize what a terrible thing I did." He looked at Micah and Shaylae. "Look at them, Hauron. Look how happy they are."

Shaylae's face positively shone with happiness as she looked into Micah's eyes, and he looked like a little boy who had just discovered the miracle and the gift of life in the eyes of his beloved.

"And it's because they were true to their traditions that they can be so . . . I don't know . . . bold in their belief that they are pure before their Holy Ones and their Elders as they enter their marriage."

"You know, Sigmun, I think there's a touch of that same boldness in all the Navajo I've met. So mature, so intelligent and wise, and yet they all seem to share that same child-like trust in the world around them."

"Yeah, I've noticed that too. You can see it in their appreciation of simple things, things that are truly important. How they seem to be so unspoiled, so totally unaffected by things that really don't matter, things that some of us put so much value on. I wish I could find so much joy in the things around me as they do."

"Sigmun, I think you're already there. Just listen to what you just said."

Sigmun was about to say something, but the whole company became silent, even the little children. Matron Lapahie kneeled beside the couple and pointed to the wedding jar in front of them.

Shaylae picked it up and poured some water into her own hands and sprinkled it on Micah's hands. She took his hands in hers and with smiling, laughing eyes she tenderly washed them. Micah then did the same to Shaylae. Sigmun couldn't help but notice how tiny her hands were, held so lovingly in his.

"In washing each other's hands, you have washed away your past," said Matron Lapahie. "From this moment you will be starting life anew together."

Matron then took some corn pollen and began sprinkling it on the taa'niil, from East to West to East, and then from South to North to South. She then sprinkled it in a circle, beginning at the east, and stopping just before the circle was complete, leaving a gap, just as in the pattern of the basket, facing east.

Matron pointed to the east part of the basket and Micah took a small portion of the taa'niil between his thumb and two fingers and ate it. Shaylae did the same. They repeated this for the West, and the North, and the South, and then the center, each time Micah eating first and then Shaylae. Alex and Micah's mother then took of the taa'niil and ate, and then Ayanna and her mother, and her two sisters and brother ate.

When all of Micah's family had eaten, and the basket was empty, Reycita picked it up carefully, and smiling sat down again next to Matt.

Matron Lapahie stood once more, holding out the black wedding jar. "Drink now of the wedding jar, symbolizing that all of your nourishment, all of your happiness, and all of your joy will have but one source: each other."

She held the jar out to Micah, who took it and drank from one of the necks. He handed it to Shaylae who drank from the other.

"Micah and Shaylae have decided that as part of their wedding they will walk the seven steps together." Matron Lapahie held her hand out to Micah and Shaylae inviting them to stand.

They walked, hand-in-hand to the center of the Hogan, just to the east of the four supporting timbers. They hugged each other, and then Micah let go of her, took one step sun-wise and spoke. "Oh, my beloved, our love becomes firm as you take one step with me. Together we will share the responsibilities of the Hogan, the food, and our children. May the Holy Ones bless us with noble children, and may they live long in happiness and harmony with the Holy Wind."

He extended his hand to Shaylae and she took a step to stand once more beside him, taking his hand in hers. "Oh, my husband, this is my commitment as I take one step with you. Together we will share the responsibilities of the Hogan, the food and our children. The welfare of our noble children will be the highest duty I will have, that they may live long in happiness and harmony with the Holy Wind."

Micah let go of her hand and took a second step, not taking his eyes off her radiant face. "Oh, my beloved, walk now with me a second step. May the Holy Ones forever bless you. I will love you and you alone as my wife. All other women I will love as sisters. I will fill your heart with strength and courage always. This is my promise to you."

Shaylae took her second step, and once more took his hand. "Oh, my husband, may the Holy Ones forever bless you. I will love you with single-minded devotion. All other men I will love as brothers. I will love you and you alone as my husband. This I promise as I take a second step with you."

"Oh, my beloved wife, as we walk together the third step I promise you that I will provide both material and spiritual blessings for our noble children. I promise you that I will teach them wisely that they may live long in prosperity and joy."

"Oh, my beloved husband. As I take a third step with you I promise that at all times I will fill your heart with courage and strength as you provide for our Hogan and our noble children, that they may live long in prosperity and joy."

"Oh, my beloved wife, walk with me again, a fourth step. I thank you and bless your sacred name that you have brought me such joy and happiness. You have brought me favor in the eyes of the Holy Ones and taught me sacredness in our love."

"Oh, my beloved husband, in all acts of righteousness I will love you. Every form of enjoyment as husband and wife will be sacred between us. Happily and willingly I follow you in the fourth step."

"Oh, my beloved wife, I promise you I will share your sorrows and your pain with as much love and devotion as I share your happiness and joy. Take a fifth step with me to seal this promise."

"Oh, my beloved husband, willingly I also will share your sorrow and pain, as lovingly as I will share your happiness and joy. Taking this fifth step with you is witness of my promise."

"Oh, my beloved wife, as we walk through life together, inseparable, I promise you that I will not keep to myself the blessings of the joy your love has brought me. I will share our love and our bounty with those who are in need, those who suffer, and those who mourn. Take a sixth step with me to seal our commitment to serve our brothers and sisters."

"Oh my beloved husband, how happy it makes me to hear you express your love for all of the children of the Holy Ones. How gratefully and willingly I will share with you your promise to serve them. See, I take a sixth step with you in solemn testimony of this, my vow."

The beautiful couple had almost completed the circle around the sacred timbers. Micah turned now toward his wife and held both of his arms out to her. "Oh, Shaylae, my beloved wife, like a goddess in sacred beauty you stand before me. You honor your Blessed Mother, Asdzáán Nádleehé, as you walk in beauty. By taking these steps together we have sealed our love for this life and to the ends of eternity. Upon my life I will always be true and faithful to you. With all my heart, my mind, and my strength I will love you. With my body I will worship your sacred body. My love for you will be as pure as the water with which you washed my hands. All the spirits are witnesses to this fact. I shall never deceive you, nor will I let you down. I shall love you forever. The Holy Ones have blessed us with each other, and forever I will bless their sacred names in worship and thankfulness. Take now this final step and let me hold you in my arms as my wife."

"Oh, Micah, my beloved husband, my life, my very being. Like a god you wear your honesty, your strength, your courage, your kindness, your purity and your virtue. Willingly I have walked these seven steps with you to seal my love and devotion to you for time and all eternity. Upon my life I will always be true and faithful to you. With all my heart, with all my mind, and with all my strength I will love you. With my body I will worship your sacred body. My love for you will be as pure as the water with which you washed my hands. The Holy Ones have blessed us with each other, and forever in thanks I will bless their sacred names. We have experienced spiritual union in the Holy Ones. Now you have become completely mine. I offer my total self to you. Our marriage will last forever. As I take the final step, and open my arms, I give myself willingly and completely to you as your wife."

Shaylae opened both her arms wide toward Micah. For a moment they simply looked into each other's eyes, and then Shaylae moved into his embrace. Slowly Micah folded his arms around her, and she around him. He leaned his face toward her, and standing on her tiptoes she brought her lips to his in a kiss that would not have disturbed a gossamer wing between them. Shaylae gently pulled back and smiled and cried as she stroked his cheeks, his eyes, and his hair. Tears were also glistening in Micah's eyes as he lovingly caressed her face.

Micah reached into his pocket, as Shaylae reached in to hers, and together they brought out gold rings. Shaylae held out her left hand as Micah placed the ring on her finger.

"My love, freely given to you, has no beginning and no end, like this ring which I place upon your finger."

Shaylae placed her ring on Micah's finger. "No one is the giver, and no one the receiver, for we are both the giver and each the receiver. Accept this ring and wear it as a symbol of the unbroken circle of my love."

Once again they embraced and once again they kissed.

Sigmun couldn't move, as if the power of what he had just witnessed had caused time itself to come to a complete standstill. He knew that he had been a part of something sacred and divine. He was unable to hold back a tear. Looking around the Hogan there was not a dry eye, even among the hardened marines.

Finally, Matron Lapahie stood, and signaled all to join her. She raised her hands high above her head, closed her eyes, and prayed.

"Oh Holy Ones, bless Micah and Shaylae as they stand before you, now husband and wife. Please protect the ones we love. We honor all that you have created. As this couple has pledged to live together in love and harmony, so may we live with all our brothers and sisters. We honor Mother Earth, and ask that their union be abundant and grow stronger through each passing season. We honor fire, and ask that their union be forever warm and alive in their hearts. We honor the wind, and ask that they may sail through life, safe and calm. We honor water to clean and soothe their marriage, that it may never thirst for love. Oh Holy Ones, all the forces of Nature you created for us your children. We thank you and we pray for the harmony and true happiness of this blessed couple, as they grow forever young together. As the Ancestors wish."

"As the Ancestors wish," rang out the chorus.

Micah and Shaylae walked from the Hogan as husband and wife.

CHAPTER 36

———◦⊱✿⊰◦———

Sigmun couldn't sleep. The wedding ceremony had moved him deeply. The words that Shaylae and Micah had spoken to each other still rang in his ears. It had been like a revelation, seeing them give themselves so totally to each other, spiritually, intellectually and physically. No wonder Ayanna and her people valued their virtue so highly—to them the love they shared was not just physical as he had always believed, it was holy. And he had not only forced Ayanna against that conviction, he had insulted and hurt her at the deepest and most vulnerable part of her soul.

He couldn't stop thinking about the last thing he had said to Hauron, just before the ceremony had begun. "I wish I could find so much joy in the things around me as they do," he had said. If he had, he would have realized these things a lot sooner and would never have hurt Ayanna.

It was useless trying to sleep, tossing and turning. It was 1:30 am. If he was going to be awake, he may as well go outside and get some fresh air. The sky was so beautiful. Thousands of stars sparkled in the black cloudless blanket of night. He picked out the North Star, just as Micah had shown him. Turning around, due south he marveled at the moon. When he had first arrived on earth nine days earlier it had been just a thin crescent. Each night he had marveled as it became more and more full. No wonder Ayanna's people called her Sister Moon. Why had he never thought this way about the moon that circled his home planet?

The air was fresh and clean. He took a deep breath. How wonderful it felt. He drew the air deeply into his lungs and held it, eyes closed. He could almost feel the life giving oxygen on its journey to his heart where it received power and energy until it filled his whole body. It was something he had taken so much for granted: breathing. It was something he had done fifteen times a minute since the day he was born, and each and every time it was a new miracle.

Once more he filled his lungs, slowly this time, savoring the pure pleasure as it filled him. Then, like a revelation it hit him. No wonder Ayanna's people find so much joy in simple things; it is because each one of these simple things is a miracle. Each breath he took, each second of his life, each star in the sky, every blade of grass in the earth, every drop of water in a river—all these things are miracles. Every morning he awoke to a new miracle, a new day given to him by the Holy Ones. How frail and empty were the things he had grown up valuing. How petty they seemed now as he considered the miracle of life, the miracle of creation, the miracle of taking breath into his lungs.

He fell to his knees and looking upward, held his arms high in the air. "Oh, Holy Ones. Forgive me. Forgive me for taking for granted these miracles that you have so abundantly given to me. Forgive me for not seeing the beauty of each day you created for me." He lowered his head, his face sank into his hands, and he wept bitterly. "And please, please forgive me for not realizing what a miracle the angel named Ayanna is, and for hurting her. Oh, Holy Ones, even if she never forgives me, then at least let her forgive herself; let her know that you forgive her and love her."

"Sigmun."

He whirled around. "Ayanna!"

"Oh, Sigmun, I do forgive you. I forgive you freely."

He jumped to his feet. "Ayanna," he said again. He stood still, just staring at her beautiful face so stunningly illuminated by the silver moonlight, tears rolling down her cheeks like diamonds. She walked slowly toward him and held out her arms.

He wasn't sure what to do. To take her in his arms would have felt like polluting her heavenly spirit with his material nature, but the decision was not his. She took him in her arms and laid her head on his chest. Slowly, his arms found their own way around her shoulders.

The strength of her love and forgiveness filled him so powerfully he was afraid he would not be able to contain it; afraid he would burst.

"Oh, Ayanna, I'm so sorry. I would die if it would take back what I said, what I did . . ."

"Shh," she said, putting two fingers gently against his lips. "I found the beginnings of healing in your prayer, Sigmun."

"Then is there hope that one day you will love me as Shaylae loves Micah?"

"In time. My soul is healing, Sigmun, but I do need more time. Can you wait?"

"A hundred years if I have to."

She leaned up and gently kissed him. It was a kiss of sisterly affection, not a lover's kiss but it was enough, more than enough. It held a promise of hope in its sweetness.

CHAPTER 37

Eight o'clock in the morning and Shaylae and Micah still lay in bed, nestled in each other's arms. The sweetness of Shaylae's love for him had overwhelmingly surpassed his wildest dreams. Discovering himself as a husband was almost as wonderful as discovering Shaylae as a wife.

"I could stay like this forever," she said, a contented smile on her face.

"Oh, so could I," said Micah. "So, could I."

Through their window they could see a beautiful blue sky, another beautiful day. "But we should get up and join the others," said Shaylae. "They'll be wondering what we're doing."

"Oh, I think they know exactly what we're doing."

She punched him playfully on his bare chest. "I'm serious," she said.

"I know. We need to get everyone back to Reconciliation so we can start making plans for our next step."

She kissed his cheek. "Yes, but we don't need to be there."

"What do you mean?"

"I think what needs to be done now is to plan out a strategy. It's not going to be as simple as us defeating the Assembly like we did four years ago."

"Why not?"

"There's an entire planet to deal with, not just an Assembly of rulers like there was on Revenge. There's going to be millions of troops who may remain loyal to Denab even after we defeat him."

"You think we can defeat him?"

"I'm not sure. He's not like the other Dark Ones."

"How do you mean?"

"Well, for one thing he can hide his feelings and his thoughts from me. For another thing he seems to be far more in control of his own life, his own destiny. The others act like robots, or puppets or something. I think he is an extremely intelligent man."

"And you're not sure if we can defeat him."

She shrugged. "I dare not become too confident. That's their mistake." She turned to him and took his face in her hands. "But live or die I have to try."

"Now you're scaring me."

She let out a huge contented sigh. "Oh don't worry. I'm sure everything will work out. Anyway after last night I feel I could take on the whole Universe."

He kissed her again, a smile returning to his face. "Why would that have made any difference?"

"After my Kinaalda, when I became a young woman, my Power took a leap forward. Now that I have become your wife, and we have made love to each other, it's taken another huge step."

"That good, was it?"

She punched him again, a little flush coming to her cheeks. "Yes, it was." She leaned down and kissed his lips again.

A sad expression replaced her smile. "Things have gotten really bad on Yurob. Denab has reintroduced all the old ways. But he's underestimated the people. Now that they have tasted freedom they're not going back to being the scared, inferior slaves they once were."

"Which I imagine has merely increased his cruelty."

"Yes. Terribly. The sooner we defeat him the better."

"Then let's get started."

"That's what I'm saying. I don't think it needs involve you or me just yet."

"How come?"

"Like I said, once we defeat Denab it's going to be a military operation."

"You mean a traditional military operation?"

"Exactly. And I think the best people to make plans are the trained soldiers, like Captain Cerid and Major Martin."

"You think many will die?"

Shaylae's sad expression deepened. "Some will, perhaps many, but their reward will be assured with the Holy Ones."

"So, what are you suggesting?"

"Developing a plan is going to take two to three weeks. Plus, Tregon, Harley and my dad need to do more tests on the hyper drive and the defense systems against the nuclear drones."

"So, what do we do in the meantime?"

"You and I are going on our honeymoon."

"A honeymoon?" he said, his eyes widening with interest. "You have anywhere in mind?"

"I was thinking of Hawaii, the big island."

"OK," he said eagerly. "I've always wanted to go there."

"Me too! We need to get away, get to know each other better. Ten days to be together as husband and wife."

"That I can relate to," he said, kissing her.

"Let them wait a little longer," she said. The kiss became more passionate as they melted once more into each other's loving embrace.

CHAPTER 38

—◦⊱❦⊰◦—

Micah figured their honeymoon was going to be the calm before the storm, but for now, the storm he would put out of his mind; he was going to enjoy the calm while he could. One hour and a few phone calls later they had booked a hotel, reserved a rental car and were ready, well, he was ready.

"So," said Micah with a big grin. "You're going to shift us over there? I thought you didn't use your Powers for convenience. Only for something truly important."

Shaylae smiled. "My honeymoon with my new husband is important. It's the most important thing in my life right now. Of course, if you don't agree . . ."

Dang it! He wasn't going to answer that one, so he simply said, "Well, let's go then."

"Hold on! I'm going to need new clothes. And I have to get myself a new bikini or two."

He was about to suggest that she looked great, and the clothes she had would be fine but thought better of it. He wisely realized that there are lots of things a new husband has to learn about tact.

"Sure. I guess I could do with some new clothes too."

A quick shift later and they were in a large shopping center in Farmington. Patiently he endured five hours of shopping, not his favorite activity, but once she was done, especially when he saw her excitedly carrying her shopping bags full of her new stuff, it all seemed worth it. Her sparkling eyes, her laughing smile, her whole body language, just melted him. He had to give her another hug.

"Shaylae Lucero, I love you so much." He picked her up, shopping bags and all, and gently swung her around.

"Put me down," she said, squealing. But as soon as he did, she kissed him. "Not as much as I love you," she said with a mischievous challenge.

"I saw you first. I fell in love with you first," he said.

"Ah ha!" she said triumphantly. "But who kissed who first?" She emphasized her crushing coup-de-grace with a swing of one of her bags against his butt.

Micah opened his mouth, kind of uselessly, because he knew there was no winning repartee going to emerge from it. "I still love you more," was all he could manage, and to shut her up he kissed her again.

Shaylae looked around. Micah's eyes followed her gaze. People were staring at them, big grins on their faces. He shrugged, cocked his head to one side, and raised his eyebrows. "We just got married. Yesterday," he said.

There were a few smiles, nodding heads, and even a knowing wink from one of the onlookers.

"How rude," said Shaylae.

A few hours later they were all unpacked, settled into their hotel room in Kailua-Kona, sitting on their fifth floor balcony, looking westward to a perfect sunset. Micah had his arm around his lovely bride, and she rested her head on his shoulder.

"What you want to do?" she asked. "Want to go explore?"

He stretched his arms and yawned. "I dunno. It's late. I think we should go to bed."

"Micah Hale! It's not even eight o'clock. In fact back home it's not even five." She turned to look at the huge king-sized bed and smiled. "OK."

The next morning they awoke early. Today was going to be a relaxing day on a nearby beach where they could snorkel. Micah was amazed. The variety of beautiful fish was seemingly endless; and they didn't seem to be a bit scared. If he reached out his hand to touch one it would dart away, but otherwise they seemed content to share the clear water with as many people as the reef-enclosed bay would hold. What a perfect day it was. It even provided its moments of excitement, like when Shaylae screamed and almost choked as water found its way down her snorkel. It was all he could do to stop laughing—after all, it was only a sea turtle slowly making its way toward her.

As the afternoon wore lazily on Micah decided it was time to just lie out and take in the sun, but he couldn't have dragged Shaylae from the water if he had tried. She just couldn't get enough of it. Later, as he watched her make her way back up the beach, he almost cried she was so beautiful. As she walked her gorgeous body moved in a graceful dance, every movement a choreographed ballet. It was something she seemed to be totally oblivious of. She probably wasn't even aware of the stares she was getting from just about every other male on the beach. But she's mine, he thought with a selfish smile, all mine. He couldn't help but shake his head, his grin widening all over his face. Did the Holy Ones really mean to create her so adorable, so pretty, so cute, and so sexy? She caught his eye and smiled. Oh yes, they surely did.

The days flew by, each one a jewel in the crown of his love for Shaylae. Each day he would learn something new about her, something so utterly charming and loveable.

But if the days were perfect, the nights were divine. He never ceased to marvel or to wonder how he had been so blessed to be the one she had chosen to fall in love with. She was beyond perfection. Not only was she the most intelligent person in the universe, not only was she the most beautiful, she was also the kindest and the gentlest. And yet in spite of her towering intellect there were times she was childlike, totally unsophisticated, totally pure and totally without guile.

"Shaylae, you bring out the best in me," he said one night, just before they fell asleep.

"And you me, my love."

"No, really. I am so much the better person for knowing you."

She raised herself up on one elbow, and looked into his eyes. "Micah Hale, haven't we had this discussion before? Don't you even dare to suggest that you are getting more out of our marriage than I am. You have no idea what you do to me, how you enlarge my breathing soul and my eternal soul." She kissed him. "Oh, how I adore you," she whispered, her soft lips brushing his ear.

He took a deep breath. The thought that kept going through his mind was, 'Thank you, dear Holy Ones, thank you'.

She breathed with him. "Together we share the same Holy Wind, Micah."

On the day before they were scheduled to leave Micah lay back on the bed, exhausted, while Shaylae sifted through the tourist information on her computer. She had said that she wanted to make sure they hadn't missed anything. How could that be possible, thought Micah? Talk about a full vacation. They had snorkeled in Kealakekua Bay where Captain Cook had died, sun-bathed on Hapuna beach, hiked Mauna Loa, been to the observatory on Mauna Kea, seen the lava flows of Kilauea, attended a Luau in Kona, seen the black sand of Punalu'u and the green sand of Papakolea, enjoyed the lush green of the Waipio valley . . . the list was endless. Just thinking about how much they had done made Micah tired. Shaylae on the other hand was totally tireless. Each new sight filled her with joy as she totally immersed herself in its beauty and drank it down to the last drop.

"Oh, look! How could I have missed this," she said, almost shouting the word 'this'.

Micah groaned. It was a stupid thing to have done, but it was involuntary.

"Micah Hale! Are you bored?" she demanded.

"No, no. Not bored. Worn out!"

"Blessed Ancestors, I married a wuss!" she said with a wicked grin.

He grabbed her and pulled her back on to the bed, tickling her mercilessly.

"No," she squealed. "Stop." She struggled, trying to escape, laughing so hard she could hardly breathe.

"Ah ha! You're at my mercy," he said, planting a firm kiss on her lips. She certainly didn't try to resist his kiss; instead she returned it to him a hundred fold.

"Seriously, Micah," she said, not even breaking the kiss. "Just listen to this."

"OK," he said in his best resigned-to-his-fate voice. "What did we miss?"

She wasn't letting him get away with that. She dug the second knuckle of her middle finger just below his ribs and bored in.

"Ouch," he said jumping up. "That hurts."

"Ah ha! Gotta remember that one," she chuckled. She picked up her computer again and then a lot more seriously said, "OK, listen to this. It's a place called Pu`uhonua O Honaunau."

"Pooh what?" he said with a snort.

"I'll be forced to hurt you again," she said, her eyes crossed, brandishing her knuckle like a dagger. "It's about forty klicks south of here. It means City of Refuge and it's a sacred site."

"OK," he shrugged resignedly. "Let's go."

"Hold on a sec," she said, waving her hands in the air. "Let me tell you what it says here. It's a place where someone fleeing for their life could go and receive absolution from whatever crime they had committed. Mostly breaking a kapu."

"Kapu?"

"A religious taboo. Some of them quite silly really; like letting your shadow fall on a chief's palace, or walking in his footsteps."

"You could be put to death for that?"

"I know. Sounds a bit extreme huh? But they believed that such acts could call down the anger of the god of the volcano, goddess actually, Pele. But it could also be used as a place of refuge for defeated warriors, women and children, and the sick.

"Oh, here's a cute story. Queen Kaahumanu, who was King Kahmehameha's favorite wife, would run to Pu`uhonua O Honaunau whenever she had been making trouble for her husband. She would hide under this huge stone which is raised up on pedestals until he calmed down." She giggled, looking at him again waving her knuckle in his direction. "So, you'd better start running, bucko!"

CHAPTER 39

Once they arrived Micah immediately realized that the City of Refuge was going to be Shaylae's favorite place on all of Hawaii. Her eyes said it all.

"Oh, Micah, I'm so glad we came here."

So was he, if for no other reason than to see her so full of excitement.

"I just love it," she whispered reverently as they listened to their Hawaiian guide at the visitor's center.

"We don't provide guided tours through the Pu'uhonua, instead we invite you to enjoy these sacred grounds at your own leisure. The statues and carvings you will see are not the originals that were made here hundreds of years ago. They are replicas built by Hawaiian artists with the same care and respect as the originals, but we still consider them sacred. The same is true of the temples and other buildings. We would please ask you to treat them with reverence and dignity."

As they walked neither of them said much. No one did really. She wondered if everyone else could sense the sanctity of the place.

"This certainly does have a different atmosphere about it," said Micah.

"You can say 'holy', Micah. You're not going to explode if you do. And yes, it does have a very holy feel," said Shaylae.

"It's strange though, don't you think?"

"What's strange?"

"Well, they have a totally different religion from us, so why would it feel so . . ." he paused, looking for but not finding the right word.

"Sacred? It's another safe word Micah."

He smiled. He still couldn't bring himself to admit that he was becoming more religious.

She continued. "I'm not sure that religions are that different. I think they have more in common that they have differences."

"I suppose that's true. I mean most religions teach kindness, honesty, loyalty, all of the virtues."

"Yeah. Sometimes I don't think it's that important what you believe. Much more important is how you treat your brothers and sisters; of any race or religion."

"Well, not being a very religious person myself I would have to agree with that."

"But the most important reason I think is that once any people treat a place as sacred, I think it actually becomes sacred."

"How?"

"I don't know," she said with a shrug and a smile.

Oh how he loved her smile.

"Look over there," she said, pointing to the south end of the bay where lava rocks reached out into the Pacific Ocean. "That man's been sitting staring out to sea ever since we got here."

"Really? I hadn't noticed."

"Let's go find out what it is he's looking at."

"You sure? He may want to be alone." But his words fell on deaf ears. She was already a few meters ahead of him, walking quite quickly. He had to run to catch up to her. As they got closer they saw he was old. His long gray hair hung down over the blanket that was draped across his shoulders. The blanket was an American Indian weave. "You think we should disturb him?" whispered Micah, as they got closer, but still Shaylae kept walking.

Without turning his head the man spoke. "Raccoon, She Who Meets the Enemy, come closer."

Micah jumped.

"I've been waiting for you."

*   *   *

Shaylae was taken totally by surprise. How could this man possibly know who they were, let alone know their Navajo names. He turned toward them. His face was lined and worn. His skin was gray and hung in loose folds around his jaw. He had a full head of hair which hung loosely and disheveled about his face. Though his face looked serious his dark eyes smiled at them.

"Oh, don't be so shocked. Holy people all over the world know who you are Yanaba, Shaylae of the Gentle Heart, your husband Micah, and your friend Ayanna."

"Who are you?" asked Shaylae. He reminded her so much of White Cloud. Not so much the way he looked, but the way he looked at her. His eyes held the same kindness, wisdom, and knowledge.

"My Sioux name is Akecheta, the Fighter, but your great-grandfather gave me my Navajo name, Ata'halne', meaning 'He Who Interrupts'."

"You knew White Cloud?"

He chuckled. "Show me an Indian who doesn't."

"Yes, but you knew him personally?"

"I worked with him at the National Lab."

"You're a nuclear physicist?" asked Micah.

"Was. Retired now." He pointed out to sea to the offshore fusion plant. "I was the chief engineer."

"You said that holy people all over the world know us. Does that mean . . ."

"Does that mean I'm a shaman, a holy man? Not really. Although as I get older I have gotten much closer to the Holy Ones." He pointed at Micah. "I was a lot like you at your age, Raccoon; practical, scientific, not religious at all." He looked out to the sea and sighed. "But when you get older and wiser you'll see that the universe is ruled by the Eternal Spirits, those the People call the Holy Ones, who breathe the Holy Wind."

"Do you come here . . ." began Shaylae.

"Do I come out here often? Yes I do." He took a deep breath and spread his arms out. "You can feel the holiness here can't you?"

"Yes."

"People come from all over the world to this very spot. Last week there was a group of Tibetan Monks who came here to worship. I joined them."

"So, you find holiness in all . . ."

"All people? All religions?" He shrugged. "Not all. No, young lady, there are some religions that preach intolerance, exclusivity, self-righteousness." He shook his head with obvious distaste. "I don't find holiness in them, not in the least. But whenever a people gather together and share feelings of reverence, patience, tolerance, and kindness, yes, I find holiness in them."

"Could you tell me more about . . ."

"About White Cloud? Certainly."

Micah laughed. "What name did you say White Cloud gave you?"

He chuckled. "Ah, I see you noticed that I . . ."

"Finish everyone's sentences for them," said Shaylae with a smile.

He shook his head. "Been doing it all my life. Got me in trouble at school all the time. So yes, White Cloud gave me the name Ata'halne', He Who . . ."

"He Who Interrupts. Yes, I get it," said Micah.

They all laughed.

"Anyway, I didn't know my great-grandfather for very long, so any insights you could share . . ."

He shook his head, sighing. "Ah, what a man. There hasn't been another like him."

"What was he like as a young man though?"

"The same. As I said, some of us develop reverence for Holy things as we get older. Not him. He always had that gift. In fact it was he who taught me."

"How so?"

"After I graduated MIT with my bachelors in 2049, I joined his research team at the Lab as an intern while studying for my Ph.D. I was twenty at the time, he was thirty and was just about ready to bring the first fusion power station online." He nodded his head. "It was a very exciting time."

"You graduated MIT at twenty?"

"Why does that surprise you? You'll graduate DIT at nineteen!"

Shaylae felt a little awkward. She shrugged. "And he taught you about the Holy Wind?"

"Yes. He must have sensed something in me; we would spend a lot of time together. I felt drawn to him, and I think him to me. He helped me see the Holy Wind in all things, even in the fusion reactions we were harnessing. 'Ata'halne',' he would say. 'Tell me this isn't by design, some grand architectural scheme.' It took me a while, but eventually I started to get it. That was when he told me about you," he said, poking his finger in the air toward Shaylae.

"Me?" she said, sounding quite surprised, pointing at the middle of her chest with her index finger. "Forty years before I was born? Even before my mother was born?"

"He told me everything: the three planets, Asdzáán Nádleehé, the three-thousand year old war. He told me I was also a descendent of Asdzáán Nádleehé. It didn't surprise me really; I've always believed that all Indians were brothers." He pointed at Shaylae again. "And he told me how you were going to save the Earth from destruction. Just before he died he told me this day would come, and that I should be here waiting for you"

"And you believed him?" said Micah.

"I know, it all sounded so crazy, but yes, I did believe him."

"Did you meet his wife?"

"Yes, a more virtuous and lovely woman has never been born, until you, Yanaba."

"Oh, no . . ."

He waved her off. "Don't be modest with me, young lady. But you remind me of her: your bearing, your eyes . . ."

Micah nodded his head in agreement.

"She had blue eyes, like me?"

"That she did. Sadly, she was killed about four years later. He was never the same again. He never talked about her again, and he didn't keep photographs of her on his desk, nothing."

"They're together again now."

"Yes."

"What else? Tell me more about him."

Hours slipped away as Ata'halne' shared many precious memories of White Cloud with them. Afternoon turned to evening as Shaylae and Micah laughed at some of the antics White Cloud had gotten up to as a young man. One thing that surprised Shaylae, at first at least, was that White Cloud never had any other love in his life. But when she thought about it she realized that if anything happened to Micah she would never try to replace him in her life either. She had to shake that thought away; it was not one she wanted to dwell on.

As Father Sun wended his way toward the horizon Ata'halne' became more serious. "Enough reminiscing, Gentle Heart. Now we have more pressing things to talk about."

"That's right, you said you were waiting for us? Do you have . . ." said Shaylae.

"Something to tell you? Not you Yanaba, but I have something to tell young Raccoon here, and also She Walks in Clouds."

"You don't have anything to tell me?" said Shaylae, a little put out.

"And just what could I tell you?" he said. "Now, go and get Ayanna, while I talk with your husband."

Once Shaylae had returned to Dinetah to pick up Ayanna, Micah sat with Ata'halne' on the lava rocks. For a while nothing was said. Together they stared out to the west as Father Sun sank gracefully into the ocean. Micah patiently waited, wondering what this old Sioux would have to say to him. Finally he spoke.

"Young warrior," he said quietly, 'How well do you know Yanaba?"

It was an odd question. He wasn't sure how to answer. "I have shared her soul," he replied.

"Then you know her to the very depths of her soul?"

Micah thought about this, and then replied, "I'm not sure I could ever know her that well. Sometimes I believe she is as far above me as Father Sun is above the Earth."

He shook his head. "Not at all! I don't think I've ever met a faithful husband who hasn't placed his wife on a pedestal far above him. But you are her match, Micah, trust me. You know her better than any other person living. I believe only the Holy Ones know her better."

Micah warmed inwardly. He wondered how the man who married Asdzáán Nádleehé would have felt—probably much like him.

"The battle you face will test you."

"Shaylae believes together we can defeat him."

"Ah, but can you defeat him on your own?"

It was not a question Micah had been expecting. He had never even considered the possibility that he would have to face Denab alone.

"Are you strong enough?"

"I . . . think so."

"You are not," he said with finality. "And your defeat could be the defeat of Yanaba."

Micah's heart turned as cold as steel. That he could be the cause of Shaylae's defeat almost crushed him. "What must I do?"

"I will ask you a question, and you will find the answer."

Micah suddenly felt small, inadequate. Like a little lost child, frightened. "What is the question?" he asked.

"It is this. What is the one thing that your beloved would never ask you to do?"

Now that was a really odd question. He could think of a million things Shaylae would never ask him to do. How could he possibly come up with only one thing? And why was it so important?

"I don't know."

"You must search until you find the answer. In that answer you will learn more about her, and yourself. Your courage will be tested, not to overcome your fear because you have already done that, but to overcome hers."

This was becoming more and more confusing.

"Now, young warrior. You may want to be alone." He pointed southward, further down the bay. "This place is holy. Have faith in yourself, Raccoon. Have faith in your love for Yanaba and her love for you. Most of all, have faith in the Holy Ones."

Micah stood up, slowly.

"Here, take this." He picked up a neatly folded blanket from by his side and handed it to him. "Wrap it around your shoulders. By morning you'll be cold."

Micah took the blanket. "Thank you, it's beautiful."

"My grandmother wove this blanket for me many, many years ago. She told me she wove her soul into it." He caressed it lovingly, reverently. "'One day, Akecheta,' she said, 'you will feel of its holiness And when you do, you must share it.' It is very precious to me. May the spirit of my blessed ancestor and yours be with you as you face your fears," he paused, and then, almost darkly, added, "And your wife's."

Chapter 40

It was just after five a.m. Ayanna and Sigmun had been awake all night. It had been one of those fun days that stubbornly would not come to an end. She loved being with him, although her guilt still stood in the way of being totally open with him. It was obvious that he loved being with her too; she probably couldn't have gotten rid of him if she'd tried. But he also trod very carefully. She wondered that even if they did forgive themselves, and each other, would this wedge always be between them? Blessed Ancestors, she hoped not. Physically she was as attracted to him as much as she had been that evening she had shared his bed; perhaps more so. As she learned more of his love for nature, art, music, and science she realized they had so much in common. There was never a shortage of fascinating subjects they could share.

Shaylae had taken most everyone else back to Reconciliation before she and Micah had gone to Hawaii, but Sigmun and Ayanna had wanted to stay at El Huerfano. Matron Lapahie was more than happy to have their company and Ayanna was happy to be able to spend more time with Sigmun.

Oh how she wished she could return to that fateful evening. She would not have followed him; she would not have heard him talking to Denab; she would not have heard him betray her so cruelly; she would still have loved him as trustingly as she did that night. She sighed, it was not meant to be.

"What are you thinking about?" he said.

She smiled and shook her head. Desperately driving that particular subject out of her mind, she pointed eastward to the moon in a sky already beginning to show the signs of Father Sun's awakening. Birds were already eagerly chirping in anticipation. "OK, let's see how much you have remembered the last couple of weeks."

"Try me!"

"OK. Just to the left and down a little from Sister Moon's tiny crescent, what is that really bright star?" she asked.

"Well, that bright star has to be the planet Venus. Closest to the sun, right?"

"'Father Sun', not 'the sun'!" she chided with a grin. "And yes, it's Venus, but she's the second closest planet. Only half a point."

"Pass the binoculars," he said. "I want to see her up close."

She passed him the binoculars, and he quickly adjusted them to their highest setting. "Oh wow! She's in half phase."

"Let me see," she said, eagerly grabbing the binoculars from him. "Cool," she said, once she had Venus sighted. "OK, down and to the left, the other bright star."

"Another planet I think," he said, focusing the binoculars on it. "Oh yeah! Jupiter. I can see the bands, and that great red spot, and three of his moons." He handed the binoculars to Ayanna. "Here, take a look."

"Sweet!" She handed the binoculars back to him. "OK, there's a constellation you haven't seen before," she said pointing below the moon and to the right. "It's not even above the horizon in the northern hemisphere until about August, and even then only in the early hours of the morning. See those three stars in a row, almost vertical, that's the belt of Orion the hunter."

"I recognize those stars."

"Really? OK, Orion is sort of on his side, his head to the left. His left shoulder is called Betelgeuse." She giggled as she pronounced it 'beetle juice.'

"What's funny?" he asked.

"Well, a beetle is a bug, and . . ." He obviously wasn't getting the joke, so she shrugged and gave up. "Never mind." She pointed to Orion's right foot. "That one's called Rigel."

"That constellation looks almost exactly the same from Yurob."

"Cool. I'm not sure what the other stars in Orion are called, but he's one of the most spectacular constellations in the winter."

"What about Tal'el'Dine'h? Where is he?"

"See, there you go again," she chided with a smile. "Tal'el'Dine'h is the planet so she's a she. The star, Chara, he's still below the horizon. Not sure when he is visible."

"You ever been there?"

"Nope. No one has. It's kind of mysterious. Even Shay can't go there."

"Can't go there?"

"Nope. Don't ask me why." Another, broader smile came to her face. "Wait another cotton-pickin' minute!" She punched him in the chest, her eyes even wider. "We might be able to see Procyon!"

"We can?"

"I think so." She searched the night sky but couldn't find him. "I think he must be below the horizon still."

"He should rise soon then?"

"Hmm, maybe. But it's going to be a race between him and Father Sun." She checked the read out on the binoculars. "He's ten degrees below the horizon, so that's another forty minutes or so." She shrugged. "We might just get to see him." She turned to face him. His eyes were sparkling in the pre-dawn light, and they were staring at her. Oh Blessed Ancestors, he was so handsome, and his eyes looked so kind and gentle. She couldn't hold back any longer. She pushed him back on the grass, leaned over him and kissed him. His response was subdued at first—he probably wasn't sure what to think, but she made it clear this was no sisterly kiss.

It didn't last long, just long enough to reassure Ayanna that regardless of what had happened she still loved Sigmun with all her heart, her reservations diminishing every day. She nestled into his arms, resting her head on his shoulders, saying nothing. He squeezed her tightly, not saying anything either. For a long time she lay there like that, comfortable, cozy, and very much in love.

After about forty-five minutes she sat up again. "Oops, I almost forgot. We might be too late." She grabbed the binoculars again. To the northeast the first rays of Father Sun could clearly be seen. "No, there he is. Right on the horizon." She handed the binoculars back to Sigmun.

He didn't even look at his home star; instead he gently touched her cheek, turned her face toward his and said nervously, "Ayanna! Are you sure you can love me again?"

"Yes, I'm sure." She stroked his hair lovingly. "Sig, I never stopped loving you. Procyon is more than eleven light years away. What happened there that awful night is even farther!"

She leaned over him and kissed him again. Yes, she was sure!

CHAPTER 41

August 3rd, 2108

"Ayanna, I need to come pick you up."

"Shay! How come? And how's the honeymoon?"

"Hold on, I'm gonna shift over there."

Suddenly Shaylae was standing right in front of her. "Anna, it's so good to see you again," she said. "You look . . . well, you look absolutely great."

"Yeah." She smiled. "Things are back to normal with Sig. I still feel so bad though about . . . you know . . ."

"Anna! You have to forgive yourself. Pick up and move on. No one else thinks any the worse of you."

"That's easy for you to say. You and Mike are married, and you were true to your virtue. I can never go back to the way I was."

"No one wants you to!"

Ayanna shook her head. "I do! It's no use, Shay. I am who I am, and I can't change the way I feel. Anyway, enough of me; how's the honeymoon?"

"Honeymoon is fantastic. I'll tell you all about it later. In the meantime, Micah and I met a Sioux Elder who knew White Cloud."

"Cool! How did he know him?"

"He was an intern with him at the Lab; worked with him setting up fusion plants. He's retired now but he used to be the chief engineer at the Kailua-Kona plant."

"So, how come you need to pick me up?"

"He wants to talk to you. You and Micah."

"And you?"

"Nope. He said there was nothing he could tell me."

"How did he know you? And how did you find him?"

"He says that holy people all over the world know us."

"Know you, you mean."

"No, all three of us. We're apparently well known. Anyway, we found him at the City of Refuge. He was meditating and worshipping here. Said he was waiting for us."

"And he wants to talk to me?"

"Yes. He's talking to Micah right now."

"Can I bring Sig?"

"Uh, I don't think so. Anyway, you said it's going OK for you two?"

"Well, yeah. He feels really bad. We both do. He didn't understand our feelings about our virtue, and if he had he said he never would have pressured me."

"Did he? Pressure you, I mean?"

Ayanna giggled nervously and shrugged her shoulders. "No. It was all me Shay! I just couldn't resist him. That's why I feel so bad."

"OK, don't start that again," said Shaylae, giving her a little push. "You ready?"

"Yes, just give me a few minutes to change."

"OK."

When they shifted to Hawaii the sun had already set.

"Oh, this is beautiful," said Ayanna. "What's the name of this place?"

"Pu'uhonua O Honaunau. It means City of Refuge. You feel the holiness here?"

"Oh, yeah."

"Look, there's Ata'halne'."

He beckoned them over. Ayanna thought he looked about seventy, but Shaylae had told her he was ten years younger than White Cloud. That would make him about eighty.

"Come, let me look at you." He took Ayanna by the arm smiled. "Indeed, you are a beautiful flower." He turned to Shaylae and said, "You may as well go and get some sleep. You're going to need it; and we'll be a while."

Shay stood for a moment, legs apart, hands on hips, not used to being dismissed so capriciously.

"There's your cousin over there," he said, pointing to a lone figure a hundred meters or so down the bay.

"What did you tell him?"

He looked at her through a sort of smiling frown. "You need to think about what I'm going to tell you."

"OK, sorry."

He sat down on a well-worn blanket, which he patted. "Come, sit by me."

She sat cross-legged next to him, staring out across the dark ocean.

"You love She Who Meets The Enemy?"

"More than my own life."

"More than your lover?"

"You know him? You know what happened?"

"Answer the question, young one."

"I'm not sure. I love them both—differently."

"But, do you think there will be a day when you love someone more than them?"

What is he talking about, thought Ayanna. Others I will love more than Shay, more than Sig? That was not possible!

"You think you can triumph over Denab?"

"With Shay and Mike, yes, I do."

"Then let me ask you a question I also asked Raccoon. Can you defeat him on your own?"

"I . . . I've never given it much thought," she said, shaking her head. "I doubt it very much."

"Hmm, so do I. But you do have the ability. You have great Power that lies untapped. One day . . ." He paused.

"Anyway, why would I meet him alone."

He shrugged. "You do have a terrible weakness though . . ."

She bowed her head and blushed. "I know."

"It's not what you think." He waved his arm in the air toward Micah. "Have your friends deserted you?"

"No, I'm sure they haven't."

"Have the Holy Ones?"

"I . . ."

"You're still not sure are you? You think that what you have done puts you beyond their reach?"

"I . . ."

"There is not a place in this universe, an ocean deep enough, a corner dark enough, or a mountain high enough that their love could not reach you and fill you. There's only one thing that can stop it."

She looked up. "What?"

"You. Only you can stop their love and their Power, from filling you."

"I don't understand."

"You will, in time. You said that you love Yanaba more than yourself, but there is still something between you and her."

"What? Tell me!"

"Your pain."

"My pain?"

"Yes, and it's quite self-centered, quite selfish."

She was taken aback. She had never thought of herself as being selfish.

"Yes, it hurts to face the truth doesn't it? But face it you must. You need to find something to take away your self-pity, your self-doubt, your self-indulgent punishing of yourself, because, young lady, it really is quite self-serving."

"But . . ."

"What? You think you have come to terms with what you have done? You have not. But don't be dismayed." He patted her arm in a grandfatherly sort of way. "It is inside you."

"What is?"

"Inside you is that which will take away your self-centeredness once and for all. When it is time you will find it."

Ayanna watched silently as he casually picked up a rock and threw it into the ocean. "See the ripples?" he asked.

Now that was a puzzling question. "No, of course not. The waves . . ."

"They're still there you know, the ripples. Even though you can't see them, they're still there." He turned back to her. "We may think that the things we do in our lives have very little influence on the grand scheme of creation, but the Holy Ones see all the ripples. An earthquake may bring with it destruction, but after all has settled something beautiful may have been created. So it is with you, Beautiful Flower Girl. What you have done the Holy Ones will turn to your advantage, the enormity of which you could never even begin to imagine."

The sky before them was still black, but behind them Mauna Lea was already beautifully silhouetted in the pale light of Father Sun's awakening. Ayanna was confused. She had no idea what Ata'halne' had told her meant.

"This will be the second night you have not slept. You need to get back to the Mesa of Changing Woman and rest."

She heard noises behind her. She turned around; it was Micah.

"Well, Raccoon, did you figure anything out yet?"

He shook his head. "But I did feel the spirit of your blessed grandmother, and it comforted me," he said, as he handed him back the blanket.

Ata'halne' waved him off. "No, young warrior. I want you to have it."

"Oh, I couldn't . . ."

"It is a gift freely given, from me and my grandmother. She said to share it, and I can think of no better person to take care of it after I'm gone."

The phrase 'a gift freely given' meant that it would be an insult for Micah to not take it, but Ayanna could tell it was still difficult for him.

"Elder, I don't know what to say," he stammered. And then a lot more confidently he added, "But I will treat it with the utmost reverence."

"I know you will."

He turned to Ayanna. "I have something for you also." He reached into his pocket and pulled out a tiny pair of moccasins. "Here. I've carried these with me as a charm since the day my first child outgrew them. He grew very quickly, wore them for a few months only, but his spirit is strong here. Feel them."

He held them out to her and she touched them. There was indeed something very special about them. This was as precious and personal a gift as the blanket he had given to Micah, perhaps more so.

"Freely given," he said with a wave of his arm, cutting off her objections. "He too is a great physicist, but he is also a very holy man, a Tribal Elder of the Great Sioux nation."

"Thank you, Elder." She carefully put the moccasins in her pocket.

He held his arms up, high in the air. "She Who Meets The Enemy, your friends are ready."

Suddenly, standing by his side was Shaylae.

"I have a gift for you, Gentle Heart." He reached into his pocket again and took out a beautiful silver bracelet artistically covered with beautiful turquoise stones. "Naat'áá Leeth, Peace Chanter made it for his granddaughter, Sonora."

"Sonora of the Long Walk?" said Shaylae.

"The same. It was handed down through the generations until Shona wore it at her wedding to White Cloud. When she died he didn't have the heart to part with it. Ten years ago he gave it to me and told me to give it to you."

"Elder, it's beautiful. Thank you so much." She slipped it on her wrist. At once she felt the spirit of this great ancestor, someone whose life had so much in common with her own.

"And, I've decided I do have something to tell you."

"You do?"

"Yes. It is this: there are some places that even you cannot go, where even you cannot be."

Shaylae waited for a moment, clearly expecting him to add something to make what he had said a little less cryptic. But he said nothing.

"That's it?" she said finally.

"That's it. And now, brave warriors, it is time for you to go. And may the spirit of your Blessed Ancestors, and mine, go with you."

They had been dismissed.

CHAPTER 42

August 4, 2108

"OK, first let's hear from Dr. Rodrigo on the hyper-drive readiness," said Hauron of the Eleven, Second of Yurob.

Anne Lawrence, FBI agent on loan to the Pentagon, sat next to her husband, Colonel Harley Davidson. Hauron sat at the head of the table. To his right sat Governor Seri of Reconciliation, and General Shasck, her military Chief of Staff, was sitting on his left. Also seated around the table were Mateo Rodrigo, Reycita Lucero, Lieutenant Colonel Tregon, Captain Cerid, and Major Martin. In front of each person, recessed into the table, was a digital screen illuminating their faces with an eerie blue light.

"Certainly, Excellency," said Don, standing up. He clicked the remote he held in his hand and a large screen on the wall sprang to life. "This is the hyperspace viewer, currently focused at Procyon 15's L3 point."

"I'm curious. How are you getting images back from the Procyon system?"

"The hyperspace viewer is able to send and receive signals through the same path as the hyperspace drive."

"Are these signals regular radio waves?"

"Yes."

"And this 'path', just how far is it?"

"We don't know. In fact the question may be a non sequitur."

"How so?"

"When we talk of distance we are usually referring to a measurable difference between two points in three-dimensional space which for sake of measurement we assume exist in simultaneous space-time. With hyperspace, we are not dealing with three dimensional space, and we certainly can't assume simultaneity . . ."

"I'm sorry, Doctor, you're losing me."

"The problem was first raised by Einstein when he proposed the problems with simultaneity in relativistic space-time which . . ."

"OK, I'll take your word for it," interrupted Hauron. "Back to the issue at hand. You were talking about the hyperspace viewer in the Procyon system."

"Yes, of course, Excellency," said Matt. He pointed back to the view screen. "As I said, this is the image coming from the hyperspace viewer, currently focused at Procyon 15's L3 point, which is the third Lagrange point, a point of stability in the orbit of the planet relative to Procyon and . . ."

Reycita nudged him.

"While we can be accurate within a few centimeters for one coordinate, the best we can do for the other two coordinates is an accuracy of plus-or-minus a hundred meters. Which should not be a problem if we match the 'z' coordinate of the surface of the planet, or the surface of any solid object, like an asteroid, or say another space ship or . . ."

"Yes Doctor," interrupted Hauron.

Anne smiled. In some ways Dr. Rodrigo reminded her of Shaylae. There was the same naiveté, the same basic deep-down goodness. But in other ways he was quite different. For one thing he always seemed so uncomfortable speaking to a group of people, and often belabored points, long after everyone else had either been lost in the science or had gotten the message.

"You sound disappointed, Doctor," said General Shasck. "Wasn't it only six weeks ago you were able to do no better than a thousand kilometers in all three coordinates?"

"Well, yes, but . . ."

"I'm afraid he's always been a perfectionist, General," said Reycita. "But I think your point is that it's more than accurate enough."

"Precisely. Wouldn't you agree, Doctor?"

"Well, yes, but . . ."

"And the drive is fully functional?" asked Governor Seri.

"Yes, we've been able to send many objects with no problems," he indicated some large asteroids with his laser pointer. "The last one we sent through the field was this one." He pointed to a large asteroid. "It's about the size of Reconciliation."

"And there's no danger of it being detected by Yurob?" asked Hauron.

"Unlikely, Excellency. Fortunately Yurob and Procyon 15 are currently in conjunction, so Procyon 15's L3 point is also undetectable by Yurob." He clicked his remote again and another big screen on the opposite wall lit up with a sixty-four-way split display. "In addition, these screens are constantly cycling through and monitoring all commercial, political, and military channels. So far there is nothing to indicate our activities have been discovered."

"I wasn't aware you had established monitoring capabilities."

"Yes, I'm sorry, Excellency, I should have told you. We've had small satellites camouflaged at various points in Procyon's asteroid belt for a few weeks now."

"Then you are satisfied we are ready to make the shift to Yurob?"

"Yes, Excellency."

"Excellent. Now, how about our defense against the fusion drones?"

"I think I'll let Colonel Davidson address that issue." Matt sat down, and wiped his brow, looking quite relieved.

Harley stood up and clicked his remote. The sixty-four way split changed to sixty-four views of space. "Excellency, here we see some of the drones we have detected and mapped. So far we have mapped about four thousand. According to the information you provided there are approximately forty thousand placed primarily within the orbit of Procyon 8, and mostly within fifteen degrees of the plane of the elliptic."

"Yes, that's right."

"By the time we make the shift, we expect to be have all drones mapped within one million klicks of our intended destination. We could initiate the defenses even before we shift."

"How confident are you of the success of these defenses?"

"Colonel Tregon, perhaps you could answer this question."

"Certainly." Tregon stood up. "Excellency, we have constructed about one hundred drones, we believe with the same specifications as the ones you have described and shifted them to positions around Alpha Centauri . . ."

"Is there life on any of Alpha Centauri's planets?"

"Only one of the planets provides a habitable environment and the only life forms we suspect have taken hold there are microscopic. Complex life is probably one billion years in the planet's future."

Hauron nodded, satisfied.

"We shifted these drones to a general predefined area of space close to Alpha Centauri three, with delayed activation. We then sent an unmanned shuttle, armed with the hyperspace defensive capability to the center of that group. The drones immediately homed in on the shuttle. All one hundred drones were neutralized prior to ignition."

"Very well. It seems we are well prepared in that phase of our operation. Now, how are our plans for the surface coming along?"

"Major Martin," said Harley. "Could you please take over?"

"Certainly." He stood and bowed to Hauron. The scene on the large screen changed. "I'm afraid some of these scenes are rather graphic," he apologized. "These are images we have captured of Denab's increased subjugation of the citizens of Yurob." The screen showed thirty-five men and women and children being herded to the center of a small village by at least a hundred soldiers of the empire. "This occurred yesterday in a small town on the Eastern Continent."

Anne watched in horror as the soldiers first lined up the children against a wall as their parents watched in horror. The soldiers raised their weapons. Anne turned her head, afraid she would vomit, but Major Martin had already cut the video feed.

"I'm afraid they were all killed, and not quickly either. They were mortally wounded and left to die, some took hours . . ." He spoke with obvious distaste. "The same with their parents. Scenes like this have been taking place all over Yurob. Hundreds of pockets of badly organized resistance have sprung up all over the planet.

Unfortunately they are no match for the trained soldiers, but there are many yet undetected, who have been forced further underground. They are fine people, brave people, Excellency, people we must help—as soon as we can."

"What is your plan?"

"We have fifty marines ready to transport to the Yurob, all volunteers I may add."

"You think that will be necessary? I was under the impression that Shaylae and her two friends will be able to defeat Denab and the Assembly, much as they did on Revenge."

Anne saw Matt and Reycita shifted uneasily in their chairs, looking at each other anxiously. She too shared their fear for Shaylae. Denab was an unknown quantity. No one seemed to be able to quantify his power.

"Actually, Excellency, we're counting on it," said Cerid, speaking up for the first time. "Unless they can, I'm afraid all of our other plans will be for naught."

"Then, why do you need to send these marines to the surface? And are these all your marines, Major, or are some of my own people going?"

Cerid spoke again. "To answer your first question, we're expecting that the military momentum may take a few weeks to overcome. There'll be communication problems, and certainly some of the local commanders will remain loyal to Denab and the Assembly even after they have been defeated. That's what I would have done in their position if it was you, Excellency, who had been defeated."

"I understand, Cerid. Thank you."

"And to answer your second question, Excellency," said Major Martin, "I'm afraid not. All of my marines are the finest, most highly trained soldiers, the best that Earth has to offer. There are some excellent men and women here, in fact many of them volunteered, all trained for the close-contact encounters we expect."

"You're sure you can't use my own people? Some of them would surely want to be a part of the liberation of their home world."

"I understand, as I would in their position. But their own lives would be at great risk not having the kind of training my marines have had, and frankly, I believe may jeopardize our mission. I'm sorry, Excellency, but if I'm going to be responsible for this mission, and for its success, I would ask that you trust my judgment."

"Very well, Major," said Hauron. He didn't look completely satisfied. He was probably uncomfortable with having to rely on people who were not his own citizens.

"Cerid will be accompanying us, of course. His knowledge of your planet, its military and political structure will be of great value to us."

Hauron waved his arm. "Tell me, how will these fifty marines make an impact. They are so few."

Major Martin pulled up a large map on the view screen. Three cities were highlighted in red, one on each continent. "These are the locations where we find the largest concentrations of resistance."

"There," said Hauron pointing to the eastern continent. "That's my home town."

"Yes, Excellency," said Cerid. "The resistance is particularly strong on the Eastern Continent, and especially in your home town. To say that you are a hero there would be the understatement of the three-thousand years since this conflict began."

Hauron managed a smile. Here at least was some good news for his people's part in this struggle. "Back to the question though. How will fifty marines be able to make a difference?"

"There are two main purposes to our mission. The first is supplies: weapons, communications equipment, computers, medical supplies, food and so on. The second: we are hoping to be able to help organize the resistance, particularly the solidarity between the various groups. Ideally we will not be needed at all, other than the equipment we provide. Worst case, if things get down and dirty, we will fight alongside of your people with all of our hearts." He gestured back to the map. "We intend to place ten marines on the eastern continent, ten here on the western continent, and thirty here, near the palace. Cerid and I will be with that group."

"How do you think you'll be received?"

"We've been able to tap into their secure communications web, and have informed them of our plans," said Cerid. "Prior to our contacting them they didn't have any hope of success. Most were resigned to death, but willingly chose that over returning to the old ways. But now, they're full of hope and determination."

"How long will you need to complete your preparations?"

"We're ready now, Excellency," said Cerid.

Major Martin nodded his agreement. "We're ready. All we are waiting for now is the return of Shaylae Lucero to transport us there."

"Anne." It was Shaylae, right on cue. "We're back on board. Can we join your meeting?"

"Excellency, if you would excuse the interruption," said Anne, "but Shaylae, Micah and Ayanna are back on board Reconciliation."

"Excellent. Could you have them come to the war room?"

Suddenly Shaylae, Micah, and Ayanna were standing in front of them. They reminded Anne of the way they had stood together as they faced Lanai, Second of Revenge, prior to freeing his soul. Shaylae stood in the middle, slightly ahead of the other two, and though she looked younger than her eighteen years she was dignified, commanding, and serene; regal was probably a better word. Marriage obviously agreed with her.

Micah stood on her right. He was an imposing young man. He wore his bravery the way others might wear a uniform. His body was that of a fighter, lean, taut and muscular. He was more than a head taller than Shaylae; in fact he dwarfed her.

Ayanna stood on her left. She was a hand taller than Shaylae, and had more of the appearance of a warrior than Shaylae did. She stood poised and confident, like a tiger, and Anne knew she was just as dangerous.

But in spite of the imposing physical presence of her two companions, Shaylae was clearly the leader of this triumvirate. Their loyalty and devotion to her was obvious in the way they stood, in their mannerisms, and even the looks of awe in their eyes. As a group they seemed invincible. What chance would Denab have against the strength of these three? The thought that came into Anne mind was the same one she had aboard Revenge—they were god-like.

Major Martin stood and saluted them. Less than a heartbeat later, all around the table stood, and those in uniform also saluted. Even Shaylae's parents stood, seemingly in awe of their daughter and her companions.

"Shaylae of the Gentle Heart, Ayanna and Micah, welcome," said Hauron with open arms. "Please, come and join us. We have just finished going over the plans for our return to Yurob."

He proceeded to explain the progress they had made and Shaylae nodded approvingly and confidently.

There was a brief silence. The planning was over and now was the time to move into action. It was a sobering moment.

Major Martin stood up and saluted crisply. "Shaylae of the Gentle Heart, we are ready when you are."

She nodded. "Then let's not waste any more time."

"The marines and our equipment are in shuttle hangar three."

"Micah, Ayanna and I will transport to Denab and the assembly as soon as you are in place."

"With all due respects, once we get there it will take us a few weeks to organize . . ."

"Major, our confrontation with Denab will last at least that long."

Micah and Ayanna looked at her curiously. Anne was startled too. How could it possibly take that long, and how would Shaylae know that?

Shaylae shuddered as she looked out at the marines, strong young men and women, gathered together with their equipment in the hangar. She knew their mission was primarily one of defense but their appearance made them look anything but peaceful. Highly trained soldiers all of them. Skilled at their trade, they could and would kill without a second thought, yet in their breathing souls she found strength and goodness, a commitment to the truth and to the right. In all of them she found faith, not all of the same religion, but a steady and unshakeable trust in their creator. It was the strongest in Major Martin and she wondered if faith had been a criterion in choosing this team.

As she glanced from face-to-face, she recognized those who had come with her to rescue Micah and Ayanna. They smiled and nodded at her.

"My brothers and sisters," she said, speaking to them with her mind. For most it was the first time they had experienced this, and the surprised looks on their faces showed it. "Today you embark on a mission that has been in preparation for three-thousand years.

Today you fight not only for the freedom of Yurob, not only for the defense of Earth, you fight for the cause of honor, justice, and sanctity of humans everywhere. The leaders of those you fight against will not stop should they prevail today. They will conquer other worlds, subjugate other people. Unless we stop it, their evil will roll forward until it has conquered the whole universe. You fight against an evil that is strong and determined. You fight against an evil that would destroy all that we call holy. They have no compassion, no pity, and no mercy. Their depravity knows no bounds. They represent your antithesis.

"But as you fight, please remember that it is their leaders who are the source of this evil. Once freed of their influence the soldiers of Yurob are no different than you. For this reason I ask you to show compassion to those soldiers. As you fight them, treat them as an honored enemy. Let them die with honor if it must come to that.

"You bravely stand here, willing to risk your lives for friends you have never met, friends who are totally unaware of your danger, but friends nevertheless. There is no greater sacrifice, no nobler cause than to face danger for your friends and I salute you. May the Holy Ones be with you."

"God be with us," shouted Major Martin, holding his cap high in the air.

"God be with us," shouted the fifty marines, as if with one voice.

Shaylae closed her eyes and looked toward Yurob. She concentrated on the Eastern continent, and found the small city, Hauron's hometown, where the resistance had organized. She opened her eyes and focused on the ten marines and their equipment.

"Shaulin is ready for you." And then they were gone.

It was the same with the second and third groups.

She turned to her friends. "Are you ready?" she asked them.

"As ready as I'll ever be," said Micah.

Ayanna nodded.

"Then let's not delay anymore." She closed her eyes again. She peered across the void and found the palace. She found Denab in the throne room with the assembly.

"Should we wait until he is on his own?" said Micah.

Shaylae shook her head and made the transport.

CHAPTER 43

—◦◦◦——

Ayanna was disoriented. One minute she had been in the hangar aboard Reconciliation with Shaylae and Micah, and the next she was in some sort of living room, alone, not in front of the Assembly of Yurob, as she had expected. It was large and comfortable, ten meters square, with a five-meter ceiling. The carpet was thick and luxurious, and the furniture was opulent. High-backed armchairs and couches sat in a large semi-circle in front of a blazing log fire. Around the room, against the walls were beautifully carved wooden tables, chairs, armoires, and dressers. In the center of the room was an oval, glass-topped table on which was a huge vase with hundreds of brightly colored flowers. Beautiful, tasteful paintings adorned the walls, framed in carved gold. Hanging from the ceiling was a huge chandelier with thousands of delicately cut crystals that shone with every color of the rainbow. A large window looked out over a beautiful lake and to the mountains beyond. The sky was blue, not a cloud in sight.

Yet in spite of this peaceful scene before her, Ayanna felt a deep uneasy feeling inside of her. The room appeared to be deserted.

"Where am I?" she said quietly. And then a little louder she said, "Is anyone here?"

"Only the two of us."

She jumped, and grew cold with fear as she immediately recognized the voice of Denab. How could she ever forget it?

"Come," he said, sounding almost fatherly. "Come sit beside me." She still could not see him.

"Where's Shaylae? Where's Micah?"

"Oh, now don't you worry yourself about those two. It's just you and me." He stood up and turned to her. The sickly smile on his face turned her stomach. "They're not really your friends anyway."

"Of course they are . . ."

"I'm sorry, but it's the truth." He shook his head. "Now," he said, indicating the chair next to him. "Come and sit with me. We have a lot to talk about."

She took a step, and stopped suddenly. The cold feeling grew as she realized was wearing the same dress she had been wearing the night she and Sigmun had spent together. She was not wearing any shoes or underwear; she was dressed exactly as she had been when she had first seen Sigmun and Denab together. How? Her stomach churned as the painful memories of that night returned. Denab looked at her; up and down he looked at her. She felt naked under his prying eyes. He leered.

"Please, come sit with me," he repeated.

With her heart beating wildly, and her breath short and rapid, she walked over to the chair next to him and sat down.

"There," he said patting her shoulder. "That wasn't so hard was it?" He reached for a bottle on the table before him and poured a long drink of clear liquid into the empty glass. He handed it to her, and almost in a trance she took it from him. He filled his own half-full glass and raised it. "To us," he said, and took a drink.

It shook her momentarily out of her stupor. Resolutely she set the glass on the table. "No. I'll not drink with you, and certainly not 'to us'. There is no 'us'."

"Come, come. It's only water. And besides, I'm all you have left."

"What do you mean? And where are Shaylae and Micah?"

He glanced idly around the room. "I have them. They're mine." He took his seat.

"That's impossible. We only just . . ."

"Only just what? Only just transported here?" he said, gesturing with his arm around the room. "How do you know that? It may have been days ago, weeks ago. Time has no meaning here. And believe me," he repeated ominously, "I have them."

Ayanna's mind raced. It couldn't be possible. Not Shay; not Mike. Yet, in spite of her insistence her courage began to fail her. Perhaps he was telling the truth. Perhaps he had already defeated them. But if so what did he want with her?

"What do I want with you?" he asked, repeating her thought. He shrugged. "It's very simple. I want you to join me."

"Join you. I would never . . ."

"Now don't be too hasty," he said holding up his hand. "You're their only hope."

"Whose only hope? Shay and Mike's?"

"Exactly. Right now they're in limbo, where they'll remain for eternity unless you can win them over."

"Win them over to what?"

"Why, to my cause, of course."

"I would never do that."

"I'll give you time to think it over while I explain their predicament."

Ayanna's heart was pounding so loudly in her ears it almost deafened her. The hollow, sickening sensation in her stomach grew, as she feared the worst for Shay and Mike. Had Shaylae underestimated Denab? Surely not. Shaylae was invincible—wasn't she?

"It was easy actually. They betrayed themselves."

"That's ridiculous!"

"Is it? Think about it. You know of course that I could never have won them over individually. I have to give them credit; they're both very brave when it comes to their own pain, their own lives. But when it comes to watching each other suffer, they were quite easy."

Ayanna's mouth hung open.

"I simply had to give them the choice of watching the other die in great pain . . ." he shrugged, leaving Ayanna to draw the obvious conclusion. "And now they are my prisoners, caught in a timeless place in-between realities."

Her throat was dry. Tears could not even form in her eyes. She had never felt so alone, so helpless, or so hopeless in her life. Her two best friends, defeated by this evil man.

"Then why do you need me?"

He stroked his chin thoughtfully. "You, my dear, are a different story. You have already turned away from your 'Holy Ones'." He spoke their sacred names with a sneer. "Oh, I know, your friends tried to convince you that they still loved you, had forgiven you, but think about it, how could they possibly know their minds?"

"But . . ."

"Don't you understand? Once you turned away from them, once you had sex with Sigmun, you were lost to them. They will never forgive you." He shook his head and paused, taking a drink of water. "You see, not everything you have been told about your 'Holy Ones' is true. Yes, they created the universe; yes, they created your spirits and set in motion the conditions whereby you could be born. They are the masters of this whole universe, and so I ask you, how could a human mind possibly understand the mind and will of such beings?"

She shook her head, unable to speak, unable to answer him.

"All the things you have been told about them were conjured up in the minds of foolish men. Sometimes to scare you into following their rules; other times to lull you into a false sense of security when you broke those rules." He gestured toward her, dipping his head. "As you have." He let that sink in.

It was true, she had betrayed her covenant with them.

"But believe me, my dear, they have not and will not forgive you. In fact, they would be breaking one of their own rules if they did. Some strange notion they have about justice."

Denab stood up and walked to the window. Ayanna was speechless. Somehow, deep inside her, she had a nagging suspicion that what he was saying was true. She had felt it herself when she had first faced the magnitude of what she had done. Only the pleadings of Shaylae had brought her back. But it was true, and she had known it all along. She was a lost soul, a soul without hope. Her whole world had collapsed.

"So you see, Ayanna." It was the first time he had used her name. "Your only hope, their only hope, is for you to join me, and persuade them to join me."

"To join you? To join you in what?"

"In defeating these Holy Ones."

Ayanna let out a bitter, hollow laugh. "Are you quite mad? Defeat them. You said it yourself; they are the creators of the universe, of everything. Even you. How can you possibly beat them?"

"There you go again, believing your assumptions about them. You think they are all powerful." He turned and stared out of the window into the fading light. "They are not."

"How? They created everything," she repeated.

"Ah, but they are bound by rules they cannot break. We can. We can break those rules. Believe me, they can be beaten. And that is where you come in."

"Me? What can I do?"

He shrugged and cocked his head to one side. "I confess I need her, the witch, Shaylae. I can't defeat them on my own. I need her power to combine with mine. What I need you for is to convince her, to win her over."

"I will never do that. Never."

"Ah, but you're wrong. You will. You see, if you don't they will be lost forever in limbo with no hope of escape. And you will die in horrible, indescribable pain."

"She would never turn against her Holy Parents."

"When she sees that you have turned she will. She will see it as her only hope for the future. And believe me, she will see that future. She will see us all, together, ruling the whole universe." He threw his hands up, a wild gleam in his eyes.

"You're mad. Quite mad."

He stood up and walked away from her, toward the window and stared out of it. "I will give you until morning. Think about it. Think hard about, it my dear." His voice had taken a distinctly nasty and evil turn. Turning back to her he said, "Tomorrow you will do as I ask, else your future holds only pain and death."

He reached out his hand toward her. She fell from the chair to the floor, writhing in pain. Every pore on her skin screamed out in burning stabbing pain. Every muscle and organ inside her body cramped violently. Every bone, every joint, felt as if it was being ripped apart. Endlessly the pain consumed her. Her screaming filled her ears, her mind, her soul, and yet it sounded distant, disembodied. She writhed on the floor, contorted by the agony of her torture.

And then, as suddenly as it had begun, it was over. There were no residual effects of the ordeal she had experienced, no lingering pain. Only her own vomit that covered her bore witness to the awful pain she had felt.

"You see," he said, coldly, heartlessly. "I can inflict pain like that upon you endlessly if I wish it. And you will suffer no physical damage. The pain will not kill you. After a hundred years, or perhaps a thousand I may kill you—or I may not."

She raised herself to her hands and knees, her hair hanging limply over her face, staring at the floor, mouth open, saliva dripping uncontrollably from her lips, sweat dripping from her brow. "Never. I will never turn against Shaylae. Better she should remain in limbo and I remain forever in pain than you have even the slightest of false hopes that you can defeat the Holy Ones. Never, I tell you, never."

"You have until morning," he said, ignoring her comment, as he strode from the room. Suddenly she was alone on the cold stone slab of a dark, damp cell. She fell to the floor sobbing.

How long she lay there she would never know. The passage of time seemed meaningless, but eventually, exhausted by her awful ordeal, she fell into a fitful sleep. In her dream Ata'halne' stood before her, his lips moving but she could not hear him. He stopped and looked at her for a moment, his face full of concern. He spoke again, but again she heard nothing. What was it he had said to her in Hawaii? He had said she had the ability inside her to defeat Denab. Was that what he had said? No, think girl, think. He didn't say 'ability' he merely said that inside her she would find the strength to defeat him? No that couldn't be it. There was nothing left inside of her, nothing, only emptiness, betrayal, sin and wickedness. She had let down her Holy Parents and they had abandoned her.

She awoke, and the dream was gone. Dream, or had it been a vision? It didn't matter, it was gone. She sat up and leaned her back against the cold wall. But what was it he had said? She banged the back of her head against the wall. He had said she was selfish, consumed by her own guilt, and it was self-centered. She had to find something to take away her self-pity and self-doubt. And then he had touched her arm. She almost smiled as she recalled the warmth of his touch. 'It is inside you,' he had said. Inside me? What could he possibly have meant? What else had he said? Think, girl, think, she admonished herself. 'Inside you is that which will take away your self-centeredness once and for all. When it is time you will find it.'

It all seemed so hopeless. There was nothing inside her, nothing left but an empty shell. A cruel reminder of what she could have become had she kept her chastity. Once more she fell asleep. But this time no dreams came to her. No visions.

When she awoke she was lying on her back. The smell was awful. Stale vomit, sweat, and fear. Yes, she could smell her own fear. How much longer did she have? Surely it would not be long now before Denab would come for her. Soon he would inflict upon her again that awful pain. These would be her last few lucid moments. She should savor them, make the most of them. She cast her mind back to the first time she had met Shaylae. What a young naive girl she had been then. Shaylae had known nothing about her Navajo heritage, and certainly nothing about her power. She relived those moments over that glorious summer as she came to know Shaylae as the most incredible person in the whole universe. She watched her as she became a person so perfect, so totally without guile, so totally without sin, and so completely full of the power of the Holy Ones. The happy recollections faded as she thought that now that was all ended. Her life was over, and Shaylae was held in some awful timeless prison.

Sigmun, think of Sigmun. Think of that day she had spent with him, and that incredible night as they became one, became lovers. Yes, Denab could not take that away from her. If the Holy Ones had deserted her because of it then she had nothing further to lose as she reveled in the recollection of it. She managed a smile as she recalled the perfection of that night. How right it had seemed, how wonderful it had been. It had been so sudden she had been unprepared, taken no precautions. Why would she have done? She had been sure she would never . . .

She suddenly sat up. She had not taken any precautions! Of course she hadn't. It had never even occurred to her that she could have gotten pregnant. It had never even entered her mind as she had given herself to Sigmun. She flopped back down again. No, that was ridiculous. It had only been three weeks ago, and she had finished her period two weeks earlier.

Suddenly she was back in that living room, back in front of Denab, back in bright sunlight.

"Well. Have you made up your mind? Are you ready to join me?"

Ayanna's mind was racing. Had it been three weeks or four? She tried to work it out, took herself through the weeks after she and Sigmun had made love. She had been held in prison on Yurob for a week, or was it longer? Shaylae and Micah had been married five days after that.

"I need an answer."

Something inside me! Something inside me! He had never said it was a part of me, only that it was inside if me.

"Very well, you have sealed your own fate." Immediately she was filled with agony as she fell to the floor again, writhing in pain. "And this time, there will be no end to your torment unless you speak the words I want to hear."

The pain filled her body, her mind, and soul. It was hard to think, but she had to. Shay and Mike had been almost two weeks in Hawaii, and then they had returned to Reconciliation. It couldn't have been three weeks, it must have been four. And she had not had another period. And she was always regular, like clockwork, she should have started almost three weeks ago.

What else had Ata'halne' said? He had said that the time would come when she would love another more than Shay, more than Sig. Did that mean a child, her child? Yes, if she had a child she would love it more than anything else in the universe, even more than Shaylae or Sigmun. And then she remembered the final thing he had said to her: 'What you have done the Holy Ones will turn to your advantage, the enormity of which you could never even begin to imagine.'

It's inside me. The pain subsided, just a little. That's why Ata'halne' gave me his son's first moccasins! I have Sigmun's son, my son, inside of me. She put her hands on her womb. It no longer mattered what happened to her, she had to protect her son. She would not endanger her son. The Holy Ones may have given her up as lost, but her son would not be lost. And then once more she heard Ata'halne''s voice, clearly she heard him say, 'Inside you is that which will take away your self-centeredness once and for all. When it is time you will find it.'

"I have found it," she said out loud as she stood up. "And whatever happens to me, whatever you do to me, Denab, you will not do to my son."

Now it was Denab's turn to look shocked, disoriented. "What son?" he asked.

"My son. Mine and Sigmun's." The pain had almost left her and she felt the confidence inside of her grow. The kind of confidence she had had when she fought Micah, the kind of confidence she had had as she had stood next to Shaylae and Micah as they faced the Dark One's aboard Revenge. Only it was much more powerful. Now it was not for her, it was for her unborn child. She pointed to Denab, even took a step toward him. "You will not harm my son! I will kill you first. I will kill you for what you have done to Shaylae and Micah."

He fell back on his knees, fear in his eyes. "No," he said, as he raised his hands in front of his face. Ayanna felt no pity, no mercy for this man who was beyond evil. She drew back her arm, her fist solid as a hammer, ready to deliver a killing blow to the bridge of the nose of this sniveling wretch before her.

Everything faded. Denab was gone. The living room was gone. She was in a void of some kind, and she felt peace. The black dress she had been wearing had been replaced by a silk robe, green and gold, which covered her from her neck to her feet. Around her waist was a purple waistband and on her feet she wore white slippers. And she was clean; not just her body, but her soul. She felt cleaner than she had ever felt in her life.

"Ayanna, our beloved daughter, how proud you have made us. How happy we are to call you our own." The voice was unmistakable, a real, tangible voice.

"Holy Ones?" she said, amazed. She had almost come to believe Denab when he had told her they had deserted her.

"We have never deserted you, oh precious daughter. We loved you before you were born, and will love you for eternity."

"You have . . . forgiven me?"

"Of course we have, child. Another already paid for your sins. Your sorrow was the only price you had to pay."

"And my son?"

"Carry him with pride. He will be a fine boy, a worthy young man, and he will make you and his father proud."

Tears began to fill her eyes.

"No time for tears, Shaylae needs you. Now, go with our blessing."

And suddenly she was standing before Denab and the whole Assembly in the throne room, next to Shaylae and Micah, both dressed as she was.

CHAPTER 44

"What the . . ." said Micah. He took a deep breath. "Shaylae! Where are you? Can you hear me? Ayanna? Anyone?" He was totally alone in what looked like a large medieval courtyard. Cobblestones covered the ground and huge stone walls surrounded him. Something had gone wrong with the transport. He figured Shaylae would find him any minute and everything would be fine. But then why did he feel so uneasy? "Shaylae, can you hear me?" he repeated. "Can anyone hear me?"

"I hear you. What is it you want?"

He spun around, and found himself face to face with Denab.

"What have you done? And where are Shaylae and Ayanna?"

"You think your precious Shaylae is the only one who can step out of time?" He chuckled evilly.

"What have you done to my friends?"

"Your friends are already mine. You are the only one left to defeat. Now, let's you and I have a little chat."

"That's ridiculous. You can't possibly have defeated Shaylae. And anyway, I have nothing to say to you, and there's nothing I want to hear from you, so you may as well end this charade now."

"Oh, this is no charade." And then with a much more sinister tone added, "And I intend to have you, young man." Micah's blood ran cold.

Not expecting any success, he nevertheless tried to bring Denab down with a punch and kick combination. Denab was not there to take it.

He laughed derisively. "You really didn't expect that to work did you?"

Micah shrugged, trying to look nonchalant, but sure he was not fooling Denab.

"You have no idea what you're up against, do you?" He snapped his fingers. "I could destroy you like that, but instead I wish you to acquiesce willingly, you will be more useful to me that way." He shrugged complacently. "However, if I have to destroy you I will."

He's lying; he's got to be. Nevertheless his heart was beating wildly.

"You've never really known fear before have you, my young friend," he said, poking Micah in the chest. "How does it feel?"

"I can handle it," he responded with bravado he didn't really have.

"Oh, you can, can you? Well, we will see. I have quite a day planned for you, a few days actually. Maybe weeks, depending on how long you take to crack. But something tells me I should have you by the end of the day. It took me a few days to defeat Shaylae, and you're not as strong as her—but you already know that don't you?"

"You'll never win me over. You can be sure of that."

He laughed again, that cold, heartless laugh. "You know, I really think that you're going to be easy."

Micah said nothing. The cold empty feeling in his gut was almost overpowering.

"Come, let's go somewhere quiet."

Micah immediately found himself in a huge room. It was like an art gallery, or a museum. But instead of tasteful pictures on the wall, there were scenes of unbelievable depravity and violence. He grimaced.

"I see you're impressed with my art collection."

"It's disgusting!"

"How about this one?" he said pointing to the largest, hung in the center of the opposite wall. "It's my favorite."

Micah couldn't stop himself from turning to look at it. His stomach churned. It was a animated three-dimensional collage of various scenes, all involving Shaylae. In one of those disgusting scenes a huge ferocious reptilian animal was attacking her, had her in his jaws devouring her. In another she was high on a scaffold, her head on a block, and an axe-man ready to execute her. In yet another she was on an auction block, a half-naked slave girl, to the obvious delight of the lustful buyers.

Micah's blood ran cold. "I'll kill you for this, Denab. How dare you depict the purest of souls this way? I will kill you."

"But these aren't depictions young man. Now that I have her I can do anything I wish with her." He shrugged casually. "Any of these things." he said, gesturing at the awful picture. "All of them."

Micah's anger reached boiling point and he struck out at Denab again. This time his punch did connect with Denab's face. Micah wasn't sure who was more surprised, but pursuing this advantage he aimed a flying kick at his head, but Denab had recovered and his kick connected with empty air.

Denab reached his hand out to Micah and his body was racked with indescribable pain in every muscle, every joint. "I should kill you now, you worthless peon!" he said, wiping blood from the corner of his mouth.

Micah fell to the floor, rolling around, doubled over with pain.

"Now, tell me I have no power over you!"

Flesh began to fall from his bones. He screamed in agony. "You have no power over me you demon from hell! You can kill me, disembowel me, skin me alive, but you will never have power over me."

The pain abated slightly as Denab looked at him thoughtfully. "Perhaps you're right. But what if I do those things to your precious slut? Will that give me power over you?"

In spite of the intense pain still coursing around his body he shouted defiantly through. "You cannot touch her! She has more power than you will ever have."

"You see, there you go again. Believing everything your 'Holy Ones' tell you. She's not as powerful as you think, and neither are your Holy Ones. You foolishly think that this war has a foregone conclusion, but it does not. You think I am destined to lose, but I am not."

As suddenly as the pain began it was over. There were no marks on his body, no sign of the burning devastation he had felt.

"Enough. Now, you will do as I ask." Micah was about to protest, but Denab held up his hand. "Before you make a foolish decision that will leave you in eternal torment, you should listen to what I have to say."

Micah said nothing, simply stared into the dark, evil eyes of Denab.

"As I said, Shaylae is already mine. I have already defeated her power, her will, but what I need from her will require your cooperation, your help."

"I will never help you."

"Let me finish. Shaylae is helpless, but still quite stubborn. What I offered her, what I offer you, is greater than you can possibly imagine, greater than anything your 'Holy Ones' can offer you."

"What could you possibly offer her?"

"The universe."

Micah let out a sneering laugh. "The universe?"

"Precisely. Together she and I can defeat the Holy Ones. Take from them their power."

"That's ridiculous."

"Not ridiculous at all. You are still bound by the myths and legends you have been taught about your 'Holy Ones'. But they do not have infinite power, infinite knowledge, infinite goodness—they don't possess infinite anything. How could they? They are as much a part of this finite universe as you and I."

"No! They're not a part of the universe—they're outside of it."

"Really? Explain the physics of that statement. Haven't you been taught that there's nothing 'outside' of the universe. Certainly there are multiple planes, or dimensions, in this universe, but there is no hierarchy of universes, no multiverse. That's foolishness and you know it."

Denab was trying to appeal to Micah's rational side, playing on his weakened spiritual convictions, and he was doing a good job of it.

"What I'm offering is far greater than anything the Holy Ones can offer you—complete control of the universe."

Micah felt his will failing him. If what Denab was saying was true, then how could the Holy Ones help them? If he had already defeated Shaylae and Ayanna, what could he possibly do?

"Well, have you decided? Will you help me to convince Shaylae?"

"Never," Micah shouted, making up his mind. Even if he were to lose heart, he would never be a part of Shaylae's downfall. And even if everything she believed in was wrong, and everything Denab had said was true, he would still die before betraying her. "Do what you will to me, I will never betray her."

"Very well," he said with a huge sigh. "You have felt a small fraction of the pain I can cause. Now that you know what it feels like, for the rest of eternity you can watch your precious Shaylae suffer ten times that pain."

Once again the scene shifted and he was in a small cell perhaps four meters square. Gradually his eyes grew accustomed to the darkness. Against the wall was a small cot. Micah involuntarily took a gasping breath as he saw his precious Shaylae lying on that cot, motionless. She appeared to be asleep. Her chest rose and fell rhythmically as she breathed. She looked so beautiful, so peaceful.

"See, she is mine. Shall we disturb her slumber?"

"No, leave her be," said Micah frantically.

"But surely you're curious to see how well she withstands the pain." He reached forth his hand and Shaylae immediately let out a blood-curdling scream, her back arched, her eyes suddenly wide with horror.

Micah tried to move toward her, but he was held fast as if chained to the opposite wall. He watched in horror as the muscles in her legs, arms, and stomach went rigid.

"It hurts! Oh gods help me! I can't bear it!" She screamed at the top of her lungs. Micah felt his will draining from him. Watching his precious wife suffer this pain, knowing how intense that pain was, it was more than he could bear. He cried out in tortured agony far worse than he had experienced just a few moments before.

"Micah, is that you?" Somehow, in the depth of her agony she was able to speak but the sound was almost inhuman.

"Yes, my love, it is I." Tears streamed down his face as he turned to Denab once more, ready to do what he asked. Yes, he would do anything, whatever the cost. He would not watch her in such agony. Denab was smiling, an evil, horrifying smile. Micah was about to voice his acquiescence, when she spoke again.

"Micah, please help me," she screamed through her labored breath. "Do what he asks. Please don't let him hurt me anymore."

He whirled around. What did she say? "Shaylae . . ."

"Micah, please, I can't bear this pain," she croaked.

"No," was all his incredulous mind could manage. Something didn't ring true in what Shaylae was saying.

"Micah, please, you have to do what he asks. Help me."

And then, like a bolt of lightning, the words of Ata'halne' came back to him. 'What is the one thing that your beloved would never ask you to do?' That's it! She would never ask me to turn against the Holy Ones. Not for anything. She would die first. He knew her well enough to know that regardless of what pain she was in, she would never ask such a thing of him. That he would weaken rather than see her in pain was one thing, but she would die a horrible death before she would ask him to turn against the Holy Ones.

"You're not Shaylae," he said tentatively.

"Micah, please . . ."

"No, leave me," he said much more resolutely.

"Micah . . ."

"Leave me before I kill you. You do not know the first thing about the holy person you so poorly imitate."

Suddenly Shaylae, or the imposter, was gone. Before him stood Denab, and he was cowering. "You have failed Denab. You think you understand Shaylae, and me? You do not know the first thing about her. You fool; you should have had your puppet remain quiet one more second and I would have given in to you. But because of your ignorance I now know that you don't have her. You never have, and you never could."

"Micah, listen to me . . ."

"No! I will not hear another word from your lying evil mouth." He steadied himself in a fighting stance. "You are a dead man."

Suddenly everything faded. Denab was gone. Micah's clothes had been replaced by a silk robe, green and gold, which covered him from his neck to his feet.

"Well done, Micah, our beloved son, how proud you have made us. How happy we are to call you our own." The voice was unmistakable, a real, tangible voice. He knew at once he was listening to the Holy Ones.

Tears filled his eyes. Denab had been lying. Shaylae was not his captive, and neither was Ayanna. Best of all, he knew now with a certainty, for the first time in his life, that the Holy Ones were real, were his parents, and were the Gods of the whole universe, and beyond.

"No time for tears, Shaylae needs you. Now, go with our blessing."

And suddenly he was standing next to Shaylae and Ayanna, before Denab and the whole Assembly in the throne room.

CHAPTER 45

Shaylae had expected to find herself in the throne room with Micah and Ayanna; she had seen it before she shifted, but instead of standing before Denab and the Assembly she was alone, in complete darkness, a damp fetid void. It was cold, and horrific. She held her hand in front of her face; she couldn't see it, couldn't see anything. She tried to breathe deeply but her breath froze in her nose. With a stab of fear she realized she was in a place where there was no Holy Wind; not the smallest trace of the Spirit of the Holy Ones was in this awful place. There was nothing beneath her feet—she was not standing on anything, she was somehow suspended in space.

"Blessed ancestors," she breathed.

"They can't help you here Shaylae of the 'Gentle Heart'." It was a heartless disembodied voice that spoke her title with arrogant sarcasm.

"Denab!" she exclaimed, her voice wavering.

"Yes, at least that is what they call my corporal self."

"Your corporal self?"

"Yes, Denab ceased to exist a long time ago. His worthless spirit is here—somewhere—I think. In the meantime, his body has served me well."

"Who are you then if you're not Denab?"

"You mean you still haven't figured it out? I really did give you more credit for your intelligence than you deserved. You are stupid and ignorant, just like fools who worship me."

Her stomach churned, her heart pounded in her chest, her breathing came fast and shallow. And then an even deeper fear filled her breathing soul as she came to a terrifying realization.

"You are . . . Rolling Darkness? No, you can't be." her voice was small and weak. Her will was failing her. She had never for a moment thought of Denab as anything other than a mortal enemy; a powerful one, yes, but not Rolling Darkness himself. Surely she was about to die. Would he torture her before he killed her? And then what? Where would he take her?

"Finally, you have it figured out. But in reality, I am not a lot different than you."

"You are the complete opposite of me," she said.

"Really? We both have the same parents," he said with awful, evil sincerity.

And now she also realized where she was. "Am I in hell?"

"Exactly. And I intend to keep you here until you agree to become my ally. Together we can defeat your 'Holy Ones'." He spoke their name with such contempt it shocked Shaylae. Why did they not strike him down?

As terrified as she was, she spoke in anger to him. "You're mad! I would never turn against my Holy Parents."

"Oh, but you can, and you will. Else you will spend eternity in hell with me."

Grey light began to seep into the void so that she could see her breath condensing in the bitter cold. It was then that she realized she was completely naked; no clothing, no jewelry, not even her wedding ring. She felt desperately uncomfortable, vulnerable, and alone.

A quiet but insistent wailing began, low, almost at the limit of her perception. Vague shadows insinuated themselves at the edge of her awareness, slithering by her at the periphery of her vision. Disembodied spirits, lost and without hope, their sadness was without measure. But as soon as she would turn toward one of these horrors it was gone, and another took its place at the other edge of her vision.

She held her hands up to her eyes, trying to block out the obscene sight, but even with her eyes closed she could still see them. The wailing increased, as more voices joined the mournful and hopeless choir. And now, a smell began to creep into her nostrils, evil, putrid, decaying. A ghost flew directly in front of her and she caught a glimpse of flesh falling, flaking from its bones. And then another! They were without hope, forever doomed to haunt this awful place, and yet they laughed at her. Their fetid faces grinned at her.

"Please, stop them. I can't bear it, please."

"Not until you agree to join me!"

"Never!" she said resolutely. She knew she would never turn against her Holy Parents, even if it did mean spending an eternity in hell.

The ghosts began to crowd more closely into her. All around her they came; beneath her feet and above her head. She could feel their gnarled hands, touching her all over her body, mauling her, leaving behind their rotting flesh on her skin. Their faces brushed against her, their mouths, their lips, covering her body in slimy hellish drool. The wailing grew louder and louder until it filled her ears, her mind, her spirit.

Denab's voice reached a scream. "Join me, Shaylae of the Gentle Heart. Join me or your fate shall be as theirs, for eternity."

"No! No! Nda Yee'! Never!"

She felt herself falling, slowly sinking through the void.

"So be it. Farewell," he said, laughing hideously.

Someone screamed. Down, down, down she fell. It was cold, bitterly cold. All around her hundreds, thousands of wailing dead, all trying to reach her as hands held her fast, dragging her down. Her terrified breath had become so short and rapid it sounded like a flag torn asunder in a hurricane.

"Help us Shaylae. Help us," they cried over and over again, not quite in unison, a bizarre, ever-repeating echo. "Help us Gentle Heart."

The screaming was getting louder. It was the worst sound she had ever heard.

"No, Denab, have pity," screamed the voice.

"Have pity," the hideous choir echoed.

"I can't bear it!" it screamed again.

"Can't bear it."

Below her the air was getting even colder. She felt ice forming on her face, hands and legs. She managed to look down, past the gruesome spirits that haunted her to see an ocean torn by huge angry waves. Down she fell through the dark and ominous sky, tumbling, falling faster and faster toward that ocean. Wildly and helplessly she flayed her arms, trying in vain to slow her falling. "Blessed Ancestors," she screamed, shaking the ghoulish slime from her face and hair. "Blessed Ancestors, hear me. Blessed Ancestors help me." Even though she had willingly chosen this fate, rather than submit to his will, the horror was no less eternally unbearable.

Miraculously, the bracelet that Ata'halne' had given her was suddenly around her wrist. She touched the sacred stones, feeling in them the strength of Sonora. She began sobbing bitterly. "Oh, Sonora, my Blessed Ancestor, help me."

But there was no comfort for her. There was no one to help her here, not here in a place devoid of all holiness. "Oh, Blessed Ancestors, please help me," her voice trailed off as she sobbed, her plea resigned and helpless, as she finally accepted the inevitable; she wasn't going to receive any help.

Her hands touched those turquoise stones again; turquoise, the stone of strength and health, of good fortune and prosperity. Should she give up? But if she died what would become of her? She looked down to her bracelet, and a tear dropped onto one of the stones. It glistened in the awful gloom, a brief respite from the horror of her situation. Wait, what was it Ata'halne' had said to her as he had given her this bracelet? 'There are some places that even you cannot go, where even you cannot be.' Had he foreseen this awful ordeal? But what did he mean? Where can't I go, she thought? I can't go to Tal'el'Dine'h. It's too holy. And then it hit her—how can I be in hell if I'm not dead she wondered curiously, almost apathetically. There are some places even I cannot go. And then, finally, the realization struck her with full force. "I cannot be in hell! It's a trick. I'm not dead! There are some places even I cannot go. This is all a trick, an illusion," she screamed at the top of her lungs.

Immediately she was released from the awful ocean.

"Precious daughter, how proud you have made us." It was the unmistakable voice of her Holy Father, filled with love and compassion. "Since the beginnings of time it has been our decree that Rolling Darkness shall have no power over our children, except that which they allow. He has no body. Your physical body gives you power over him. Dear one, you have proved yourself strong and courageous beyond any other mortal, save one, in spite of your desperate fear. We are proud to call you daughter."

"But those poor souls that Denab has? Are they really there?"

"Only the wickedest of our children are there, and even those will not be there for eternity. As we promised all of our children a long time ago, we will not leave their souls in hell. Let not your heart be troubled for them, Shaylae."

Suddenly she was standing between Ayanna and Micah in the throne room. She was dressed as they were, in silken robes of green and gold. Her whole body felt clean and pure as she breathed the fresh air, filling her with the Holy Wind. She felt Holy.

CHAPTER 46

As soon as they touched hands, they soul-shared and each learned of the others' encounters with Denab.

"Oh, my beloved friends, you are brave and courageous. Thank you for standing beside me."

"Denab is . . ." said Micah.

". . . Rolling Darkness?" completed Ayanna with disbelief, as they shared Shaylae's thoughts.

"He is. But we have already defeated him. Each of us has defeated him on our own, and now we will drive him back to hell."

"You haven't won yet," shouted Denab, as he made his way around behind the Quorum of Eleven and the Council of One Hundred. His voice was strong, but Shaylae could sense his failing will. "The Assembly will prove more difficult than those fools on Revenge."

The three friends felt nothing more than a twinge as the Assembly mounted its attack. For a moment they savored and analyzed it, wondering if they were holding back, but as they probed their minds they realized that this was it; this was the full force of their power. Lanai had been right; it was much more powerful, more devastating than the attack aboard Revenge, but now, with their enlarged power, it was no more than a trivial itch as they rebuffed it easily. They stretched forth their hands, and spoke as if they were one being.

"You must drive Rolling Darkness from your minds. Free yourselves."

The thought went out with such power that as a body the Assembly reeled. Most staggered backward a step or two, some fell to the floor.

"Rolling Darkness has no power over you, only that which you allow. If you wish to be free of him you must command him to leave."

One by one they fell to the floor. One by one the most powerful men on Yurob succumbed to the unimaginable power of the triumvirate until only Denab stood. Alone and frightened before them he stood.

"What are you going to do now?" he asked, his voice faltering.

"We're sending you back to hell, back where you can no longer exert your evil influence over the citizens of Yurob," they thundered with one voice.

"Shaylae of the Gentle Heart," he said, falling to his knees. This time there was no sarcasm, only reverence in his voice. "Have mercy. Have mercy on me as you had on the Assembly."

"Mercy can only be shown to those who have not denied the Holy Ones, those who have not knowingly fought against them. But you, Denab, Rolling Darkness, Satan, with full knowledge of the plan of the Holy Ones imagined you could defeat and even replace them."

"I cannot go back there, back to that awful, dark perdition. Pity me, I beg you."

"There can be no pity. Justice demands your eternal damnation, and even the love and mercy of the Holy Ones cannot reach you there, cannot rob that justice."

Shaylae raised her right arm, the fingers of her hand splayed wide, stretched out toward Denab. Ayanna and Micah followed in complete unison.

"Denab, we cast you out. Be gone!" They spoke as one. There was a terribly finality in the command, an irresistible force. Denab's body became limp, fell to the floor, his eyes clouded over, empty, devoid of life like a doll's eyes. He opened his mouth to scream but no sound escaped his lips as his lifeless head crashed to the floor.

"Hold on, my friends," said Shaylae. "He's not gone yet."

An evil wind filled the room. The stench of hell was everywhere. Their hair billowed out as the wind whipped around them like a tornado. It grew cold, bitterly cold.

Shaylae raised her hands high above her head and threw her head back. She opened her mouth wide, her breath turning to white vapor as it left her body. Ayanna and Micah looked on in awe as she breathed out, a seemingly endless breath of pure white fighting the evil wind. She was acting alone; in this they could not help her. She was breathing out the purity of the wind from deep within her to counteract the evil wind of Denab's spirit. It wrapped itself around the evil, encompassed it, overwhelmed it, absorbed it.

Gradually the cold withdrew, the stench faded, and the evil was replaced by the divine goodness that was Shaylae's eternal soul.

"He's gone, gone forever," she said.

"Shaylae, you did it," shouted Ayanna with exuberant relief and joy.

"Oh, Shaylae . . ." began Micah, as Shaylae's head flopped backward, her mouth hung open and her eyes stared wide. Her legs folded beneath her, her body twisted, and she crumpled to the floor.

Micah looked at her for a moment, horrified, frozen. She looked lifeless, lying on the floor like an old rag doll.

Ayanna fell to her side first. "Micah, she's not breathing."

With his heart beating madly, and without saying a word he took her head in his hand, raised it slightly and bent it backward. With his thumb and forefinger he opened her mouth and placed his lips over hers. He breathed gently, counting to five, his breath filling her lungs. Her chest rose. He pulled back as the wind escaped and her chest fell. Again he brought his mouth to hers and breathed his life into her. Five more times he repeated the life-giving breath. And then, finally, her arms moved and slowly wrapped themselves around him as she turned the resuscitation into the loving kiss of a young wife.

"Don't scare me like that," he said with breathless relief.

She smiled up at him and kissed him again.

"I thought you were dead."

"Oh Micah, don't you know that some things are worse than death. Leaving Denab's spirit loose here on Yurob would have been one of those things, and willingly I would have given my life to drive him out."

Micah could hardly believe what she was saying.

"You gave of your own Holy Wind to defeat him?" asked Ayanna incredulously.

"Your breathing soul?"

"But you, my love, were here to bring me back," she said, giving his arm a quick tug.

Tears filled his eyes as he laid his head on her breast. He wasn't sure if they were tears of joy or fear.

CHAPTER 47

—⸙—

"Fellow citizens of Yurob, my brothers and sisters, I am Hauron, Second of the Eleven. You know who I am, and what I have been trying to accomplish for the last sun-cycle." Hauron spoke from the throne room in the palace. His words and his image were being broadcast across the planet on every available communications channel. He was being heard in homes, in stadiums, in concert halls, city squares. Everyone on Yurob could see and hear him. "For those of you who remain loyal to the Assembly, be advised that they have been deposed. Only Sigmun of the Eleven and I remain. Their evil plans and designs on the citizenry of this great planet are exposed and are ended. You can no longer count on any support from them. Surrender your weapons and join with your fellow citizens in a new era of freedom."

As he spoke, almost shouted that last word, hundreds of millions all over the planet cheered.

"Today we stand on the threshold of new chapter in our history. No more will there be slaves, no more will there be classes who consider it their right to use others for their own pleasure, or gain, or any other unholy purpose."

It had been hard to decide what to tell them, and what to omit. He had decided that no mention would be made of Shaylae's role, nor of Asdzáán Nádleehé, nor of First Prophet. There would be time for that in the future.

"Soon we will embrace a new constitution which guarantees rights to every citizen. Soon elections will be held in every region of this planet so that everyone's voice will be heard. Until then, I propose that Governor Seri of the interstellar starship Reconciliation be appointed interim President. If there are any opposed to this plan let them appoint representatives to come here to the capital and their objections and suggestions will be heard.

"We have brought with us representatives from the United States of America, the country which has the oldest constitution on Earth. They will act as advisors to the interim government in drawing up our new constitution. I quote from one of their most revered political documents: 'We hold these truths to be self-evident that all people are created equal, that they are endowed by their Creator with certain unalienable Rights, that among these are Life, Liberty, and the pursuit of Happiness. That to secure these rights, Governments are instituted among the people, deriving their just powers from the consent of the governed.' It is in this spirit that our new government will move forward.

"Years from now our children, and our children's children for thousands of sun cycles to come will revere this day; they will revere us as the mothers and fathers of their planet. Let us make sure that we are worthy of this reverence as we move forward with this great undertaking."

All over the planet the cheering and applause was thunderous. People were dancing in the streets, hugging one another, laughing with joy.

The mood in the war room on board Reconciliation was jubilant. Things had gone far better than anyone had dared hope. Six days had passed with very few problems. The armies on all three continents had accepted Hauron as their leader. There had been some reluctance at first, but once they heard him speak they realized they could trust him and immediately responded to the call to help organize the citizens. Such a drastic shift in social structure was bound to cause some serious problems. Distribution and control of food, medical supplies, general issues of law and order needed immediate attention. Fortunately many of the army officers were able to use their military training to get things organized.

They also arrested every single member of the ruling classes, whom everyone was now referring to as 'Dark Ones' and confined them in their own prisons, more than two million of them.

"That's a lot of prisoners," said Anne. "What will you do with them?"

"I've given it much thought," said Hauron. "Their sheer numbers make it impossible to try to reclaim them right away, as Shaylae helped the Dark Ones aboard Revenge, not that I would even know how she did it, so in the meantime we're just going to hold them."

"But you're going to try?"

"Yes. But to be honest, I don't hold out much hope for many of them."

"What do you mean?"

"The Dark Ones aboard Revenge were evil in their desire to dominate and destroy, but their evil was more political than moral. The Assembly here on Yurob was the same."

"I'm not sure I know what you mean?"

"Having worked with the Council and the Quorum I found that most of them were not interested in the depraved perversions that seemed to dominate the lives of so many of their underlings. As I said, their interests were more to do with politics and power. Don't get me wrong, they still sickened me, but as Shaylae showed us, many were under the influence of Rolling Darkness, and had allowed themselves to be taken over by him. But the level immediately below them, and others in the hierarchy of rule, they were just opportunists, taking advantage of the regime for their own perverted desires."

"And their leaders allowed this because it made their task of controlling the population that much easier you think?"

"I don't know, but . . ."

"Excellency," said Tregon. He was sitting at one of the control consoles.

"Yes, Colonel Tregon."

"Excuse the interruption, it's probably nothing, but we seem to have lost contact with Major Martin's company."

Immediately the room fell silent, and heads all over the war room turned toward Tregon.

"What do you mean?" asked Hauron. "How long ago?"

"Just a few seconds," said Tregon. "One minute we were receiving video and audio, next minute, nothing."

Hauron had joined Tregon next to his console, as had General Shasck.

"What were they doing? Where were they going?"

Tregon brought up a map of the palace environs on one of his viewers. He pointed to an unmarked building. "They were going into this compound to check it out. Major Martin was suspicious. It was too quiet."

"I don't recognize this building. What is it?"

"All twenty of them went in?" asked General Shasck.

"They had sent in a couple of scouts, but when they didn't return they all went in after them."

"And that was the last you heard of them?"

"Yes."

"Call up some of the other units of the palace guard and get them over there right away," said Shasck. "Four units."

"Yes, do it," agreed Hauron.

Shaylae and Micah, Ayanna and Sigmun were enjoying some of the beautiful countryside of Yurob.

"This is where we fell in love, huh Sigmun?" said Ayanna.

"No it wasn't!" said Micah, almost laughing. "You fell for him the first time you saw him in Hauron's apartment."

"Micah, allow me some dignity will you," she said, joining Micah in his laughter.

"It was when I fell in love with you," said Sigmun quite seriously.

Ayanna turned to him and smiled. "People don't fall in love at first sight, silly."

Micah grabbed Shaylae's hand. "Oh yes they do," he said.

Shaylae was staring off into the distance westward toward the palace a hundred and fifty kilometers away.

Micah shook her shoulder gently. "Don't they?"

"Don't they what?" she asked absently. "Oh, sorry, I was light years away."

"You're still worried aren't you?" asked Ayanna.

Shaylae shrugged. "I don't know. It all went too smoothly."

"Anyway, as I was saying, we fell in love at first sight, didn't we?"

Shaylae's hand flew to her mouth. "Something's wrong."

Immediately Micah's mood became somber. "What is it, Shay?" he asked. "What are you sensing?"

She was silent for a moment. "It's Major Martin. He's in trouble."

"Where is he?" asked Sigmun.

"He's in this compound," said Shaylae, bringing a picture of it to their minds.

Sigmun gasped. "That's Denab's private army's headquarters."

"They're holed up inside. There're about two hundred of Denab's soldiers surrounding them."

"We have to get over there," said Ayanna.

They shifted there just as sixty soldiers arrived.

"Who are you, and what are you doing here?" asked their commander, none too politely. He didn't know Shaylae, how could he; her role in the overthrow of the Assembly had not yet been revealed; it probably never would.

Sigmun stepped forward. "You know me," he said. "I am Sigmun of the Eleven."

"Excellency," said the Commander backing off, and bowing. "I apologize; I didn't recognize you. We've been sent by General Shasck to investigate. There's some soldiers in there we've lost contact with."

"You need to stay here while my friends and I go inside," said Shaylae.

The commander looked at Sigmun who nodded. "But, Excellency . . ."

"That is my command."

He bowed again, and then jumped as Shaylae, Micah, and Ayanna simply vanished.

Micah was stunned. It was the same courtyard he had seen when he had faced Denab. He wondered if there was a museum inside with pictures . . . He couldn't even contemplate the thought.

Major Martin's situation was desperate. They were in the center of the courtyard in a square formation, crouched down, weapons at the ready. The three friends remained hidden, listening to the leader of Denab's army shouting his demands.

"You will all lay down your weapons."

"We will never surrender," came Major Martin's sure reply.

"Then you will all die."

"Not without a fight, we won't."

"It is useless to fight. We can destroy you with a few simple high explosive mortars."

"Then we die, we will never surrender."

"Your cause is useless. You are just pawns in this struggle. We have an unlimited supply of planetary fusion and biochemical weapons. We intend to take back this planet and return it to its rightful owners. We will use these weapons indiscriminately on the citizens of the planet until our demands are met."

"Then you don't need us."

"If you cooperate we will spare your lives. We will show you our arsenal and then you will report back to the traitor Hauron with our demands."

There was silence for a moment. "They will never accede to your demands. They will destroy you, and us if necessary."

"And just how will they accomplish that? Denab anticipated this moment and fitted these barracks with defensive equipment that is beyond anything your puny technology can throw at us. We can withstand any attack you can possibly launch against us. We, on the other hand, can mount an attack anywhere on this planet. We give you one minute to consider your answer. Then we will kill you all."

"They'll never surrender," said Micah quietly, wondering what Shaylae was going to do.

"Come with me," she said, as she began to walk out into the open. Micah was about to protest. "Come," she repeated. It was not a request. The three of them walked toward the center of the compound.

"You there. Hold or we fire," the voice sounded almost surprised.

They continued walking, almost casually.

"Breathe with me," said Shaylae.

Micah took a deep breath and exhaling slowly, joining Ayanna and Shaylae in their rhythm. A feeling of comfort and wellbeing filled him. He recognized it; it was The Holy Wind. He had never felt it quite this powerfully before. It was a real presence. Something, someone more than human, surrounded them, protecting them. He had watched Shaylae many times as she had breathed the Holy Wind. The first time was at the end of her Kinaalda, and the last time was when she banished Denab and now he was getting an inkling of how she felt when she breathed the sacred spirit of the Holy Ones.

"This is your last warning. Hold fast."

He felt invincible as they continued walking.

The sound of automatic weapons firing broke the silence. A hail of bullets came to a crawl and then a stop as they encountered the unseen barrier surrounding the friends and then dropped to the floor with a clatter. Another burst of gunfire, and another volley of bullets joined their predecessors on the floor.

"Hand to hand," came the barked order. "Get the witch first." A hundred desperate men ran toward them. Shaylae looked startled, as if she wasn't expecting this, but before she had time to react, they were on them. Three of them launched themselves at her, knocking her skidding across the ground.

Micah was astounded. How could this be? She could stop bullets dead in their tracks, she could defuse a fusion bomb with her mind, she could transport herself across the galaxy, and yet she could not repel this attack. But he was too preoccupied to think about it; he and Ayanna were fighting for their lives. Their close-combat skills were keeping their attackers at bay; only a few could get within striking distance making it easy for the two Chulukua-Ryu masters to fight off, but it wouldn't last. Soon their attackers would modify their attack and surely overpower them, but before they were able to regroup the marines joined them. Micah and Ayanna both let out a gut-wrenching war-whoop as they renewed their fighting, punching, kicking, making impossible turns midair. Micah marveled at the skill of the marines as disciplined marital arts fighters and, together with Ayanna and him, they easily and skillfully took control of the hundred soldiers who fought as undisciplined brawlers.

He kneeled down next to Shaylae. He breathed a sigh of relief as she propped herself up on one elbow. There was a cut over her left eye, and blood trickled from the corner of her mouth.

"I guess I underestimated them," she said, raising her eyebrows and shaking her head.

"Cut them down, all of them," came another order from where the remainder of Denab's soldiers were entrenched. Three ranks of fifteen men marched out holding heavy machine guns. At a hundred meters, there was nothing they could do to stop them.

Major Martin looked at Micah and Ayanna and shrugged. "I guess we rush them."

They nodded. "Let's go out fighting," said Micah.

They turned, to see Shaylae standing between them and the machine guns.

"No," said Martin. "Get back, Shaylae."

"It's OK," said Micah. "She won't underestimate them again."

Once again, just as on Reconciliation, she was surrounded by a white, almost blinding light, and a tornado of wind. Her hair blew furiously and her dress billowed all around her. What a fearsome sight she was. The machine guns barked, but hundreds of shells fell uselessly at her feet. She stretched forth her arms and it was as if a huge hand had gathered those soldiers up like dolls and thrown them against the wall, thirty meters away.

"Surrender at once," she said. She spoke almost quietly, but the sound of it filled the whole barracks. One by one, as they picked themselves up, the soldiers stood and raised their hands.

A huge explosion shattered the outer gates of the compound. The reinforcements whom Shaylae had left outside had finally broken through. They came running to the center of the compound, weapons at the ready.

"It appears you have things under control, sir," said their captain, as he looked with awe at Shaylae, still glowing bright white, still surrounded by the vortex of wind, Denab's soldiers cowering before her.

"Indeed," said Major Martin. "Captain, we need to secure this compound, Make sure there are no stragglers, and then we need to get a complete inventory of the weapons here—apparently they have enough of an arsenal to wipe out half the planet."

Quickly Denab's soldiers were gathered together and mag-cuffs were placed on their wrists and ankles.

"Headquarters, this is Captain Jural, we need transport for two hundred prisoners."

Major Martin walked over to Shaylae. "Who are you?" he asked, clearly in awe of her.

"Oh, no one special," she replied with a wide grin. "Just a skinny sixteen year-old girl."

Major Martin laughed as he put his arms around her and hugged her.

Epilogue

August 24, 2108

"You think it's over? I mean, is he gone forever?"

They were standing looking over the canyon of the great Rio Grande, a few miles from Shaylae's childhood home in White Rock.

"I don't know about forever, Ayanna, but yes, for now he is defeated. He'll still be able to influence people to do evil things; the Holy Ones will not take that away from him, but as far as being able to exert the influence he did as Denab, yes, he's gone. He may find a way to come back years from now." She turned to Ayanna and smiled. "Hopefully thousands of years from now."

"Hauron hasn't been seen since he gave his speech to the people of Yurob. You think he's resting up before taking up the reins of power again?" asked Micah.

Shaylae smiled.

"Come on, Shay. Where is he? What do you know?" asked a frustrated Ayanna.

"I don't think he will be taking up the reins of power again. I'm sure he wants Seri, the Governor of Reconciliation, to take control until proper elections can take place. But I think she'll be elected easily."

"So has he gone back to his home?"

"Nope, much further away." Shaylae was smiling almost wickedly now.

"Shaylae!"

"But depending on your point of view, he's really close."

Ayanna set her teeth and glared at her.

"OK, OK. But I'll not tell you, I'll show you."

She sat down on the ground and held out her hands. Micah and Ayanna joined her, holding hands in a circle. They closed their eyes, sharing their souls. Suddenly they were standing by a river, a cool rushing river, surrounded by lush trees and generous vegetation.

"Oh, how beautiful," said Ayanna. "Where are we?"

"Look over there," said Shaylae, pointing to the west.

Ten kilometers away stood an impressive mesa.

"Wow, that looks like . . ."

"It couldn't be . . ."

"Dzil Na'oodilii; El Huerfano Mesa; the Mesa of Changing Woman," said Shaylae, extending her arm toward it.

"But where did all this vegetation come from? And what river is this?" asked Micah.

"This is Blanco Canyon. In fact this is Blanco Wash."

"It can't be. Blanco Wash is only a trickle this time of year, almost dry. And there certainly isn't this lush vegetation."

"Not in the twenty-second century there isn't."

"What do you mean?"

"We've gone back in time. About three thousand years."

Ayanna and Micah looked at each other, mouths wide open.

"But that's just about when Asdzáán Nádleehé arrived here from Tal'el'Dine'h." said Ayanna.

"She's been here four years."

"I don't get it," said Micah. "Are you saying that this is where Hauron is?"

"Shh," said Shaylae. "Look."

They heard a rustling through the vegetation. It was a beautiful young woman, about Shaylae's age making her way to the river, singing happily.

"It's Asdzáán Nádleehé, isn't it?" said Micah. "Can she see us?"

"No. We're just looking across time, the way we look across space just before I shift."

"But it feels so real. It's as if we're really here."

"Micah, close your eyes," said Shaylae suddenly.

Asdzáán Nádleehé had started to undress, hanging her clothes on a branch. Quickly he turned away. After a while Shaylae said, "It's OK. You can look now."

He turned back to see Asdzáán Nádleehé swimming lethargically in the water. Suddenly there was more movement behind them. They turned. A young man was walking toward the spot Asdzáán Nádleehé had chosen to bathe.

"No way," said Micah, startled.

"It's Hauron," said Ayanna, not quite as surprised, and almost with a chuckle. "What's he doing here?"

"He has met her before."

"He did? When?"

"Before we came to rescue you. He wanted me to tell him all that happened on Tal'el'Dine'h, but Asdzáán Nádleehé decided it would be better to take him there, much as I have brought us here today."

"Yes, but what's he doing here now?" asked Ayanna again. "And how did he get here?"

"He has The Power. Not as much as me or Asdzáán Nádleehé, but nevertheless it is quite strong in him."

"I don't get it. His Power is not as strong as yours, but he was able to actually transport here?"

"There's a different Power at work here also: love."

"He fell in love with her?"

"Almost immediately. She did too, but I don't think she ever expected to see him again. I think she's in for a surprise. Let's listen."

Hauron had reached the bank of the river where Asdzáán Nádleehé was bathing.

"Asdzáán Nádleehé," he called out.

She jumped, almost out of the water, but quickly submerged herself again.

"Who are you?" she asked, surprise in her voice. "What are you doing here?"

"Don't you know me? Haven't you ever seen me before?"

"Hauron. Is that you?" She looked incredulous, but a huge smile began to spread across her face. "Is it really you? How did you get here?"

"Yes," he said. "My love for you brought me here."

"Every waking moment I see your face. Every dream is filled with you. But I never expected to see you again even though I wished it every day; it was more than I dared hope for."

"Can I join you?"

"No, you certainly cannot. Not today at least. I think you should meet my parents: Happiness Woman, and Long Life Man."

"I would like that."

"Now, please turn around as I get dressed."

"OK, I think we've seen enough," said Shaylae. "They need to be alone."

"So, does he . . . ? do they . . . ?" asked Ayanna.

"Get married? Have kids," said Shaylae, smiling and nodding her head.

"Then . . . he is the father of the People," said Micah.

"I guess that is what he is." She chuckled.

"Unbelievable," he said.

"No one else must know of this," said Shaylae solemnly. "No one."

Twenty-eight light years away, a young woman with blue eyes and golden-hair, about the same age as Shaylae came to a startling conclusion: the Elders of Tal'el'Dine'h had lied to her.

END OF BOOK 2 of the Shaylae Saga